SEEKING MY DESTINY

SEEKING MY DESTINY

The Doms of Genesis, Book 8

Jenna Jacob

Seeking My Destiny
The Doms of Genesis, Book 8
Jenna Jacob

Published by Jenna Jacob

Copyright © 2017 Dream Words, LLC
Print Edition
Edited by: Blue Otter Editing, LLC
ISBN 978-0-9982284-8-8

This is a work of fiction. Names, places, characters and incidents are the product of the author's imagination and are fictitious. Any resemblance to actual persons, living or dead, events or establishments is solely coincidental.

To
Sean –
The spectacular Master of my pleasure and pain.

CHAPTER ONE

PERCHED ON A stool at the bar inside Club Genesis, I sipped my soda and watched all the *lucky* subs enjoying the things I ached to feel. Their whimpers, moans, and screams scraped over my flesh, like fingernails on a chalkboard. Envy pinched my face and chafed every nerve ending. I wasn't displaying a proper attitude, but I didn't particularly give a shit. I'd been sitting in this same spot for months…waiting for one of the Dominants to grow a pair and put me through my paces. So far, none had found it in their heart to man—or woman—up and paint my ass in red, hot welts.

Wanting pain skeeved most people out. I was one of those people ten years ago but not anymore. Try as I might to pinpoint the reason for my unconventional desires, I'd never found an answer. Nothing bad or traumatic had ever happened to me. I'd grown up in a traditional, non-violent, non-abusive home. After spending years searching for an epiphany as to why I craved pain, I'd realized I was only wasting brain cells. The truth was simple: I found a world of peace beneath a crop, quirt, or whip. That's when I'd finally thrown in the towel and decided to embrace the fact that I was wired differently than most others. I figured some people drank, smoked, or used drugs to cope with stress. Others fed their beast with food, gambling, or shopping sprees. I found my release cuffed or tied while drinking in a Doms pain. Of course, coming to terms with my kinky proclivities didn't help me find a Dom to extinguish my inner fire. They avoided me like I had the plague.

Sliding my gaze to the group of *acceptable* subs all huddled together—laughing, talking, and having a grand old time—I couldn't ignore the stab of jealousy. I'd give my left nipple to be accepted by them…be a part of their clique. Unfortunately, I didn't belong and we all knew it. I wasn't a submissive. I was a masochistic bottom. The only time I dropped to my knees before a Dom was to thank him for sating my needs.

"Ready for a refill, Destiny?" Samantha, the club's bartender—and former Domme, now submissive to Alpha Dom Max—asked with a cheery smile.

I darted a glance at my empty cup and shook my head. "No thanks. I'm going to head home in a few."

"Why are you leaving so soon?"

I scoffed. "You're kidding, right?"

"Aw, honey. It takes time to find the One who'll mesh with your particular needs," Samantha stated as she unconsciously smoothed a hand over her pregnant belly.

"I'll probably die on this barstool waiting for my *One* at the rate I'm going."

"You just might if you don't knock that chip off your shoulder, sunshine." Samantha shot me a grim smile before slightly waddling away.

I need to find a Dom to give you a massive attitude adjustment, girl. The scolding words that Mika LaBrache, owner of Club Genesis, had uttered two days ago echoed in my head. As if conjured by my memory, the man himself climbed onto the barstool beside me.

"How's it going, girl?"

"Oh, you know…same shit, different night," I quipped with a plastic smile. A deliberate smirk crawled across his mouth as he slid a manila folder toward me. "What's this?"

"A contract…an introduction of sorts."

"From who?"

"A new member who'll be arriving in a couple of days."

"Arriving from where?"

"That's confidential. A friend of mine owns a club out of state and has a member who's coming to Chicago for an extended period of time. The traveler's name is Cane. He and I have chatted several times. He's now a member, for as long as he'd like."

"And this means what to me?"

"It's all in there." Mika tapped his finger on the folder. "Read it. If he intrigues you, and you're interested, sign. If not"—he shrugged—"give it back to me."

Hope surged like a tidal wave. The urge to flip the cover open and read its contents crawled up my spine. Instead, I tamped curiosity and optimism down and glanced toward the group of happy subs. Prickles of negativity raked beneath my skin and I lifted my index finger. "Eenie meenie miney mo. Catch a monkey by its—"

"What the hell are you doing?"

I turned and arched a brow at Mika. "I'm laying odds on which sub will sweep Cane off his feet and steal him away from me, like all the others."

Mika frowned. "Read his offer, girl, and ditch your insolent attitude."

"Why?" I countered. "We both know how this is going to end. My track record with Doms is lousy and you know it. I get regularly tossed off like the spunk from a pimply faced teenage boy."

Mika narrowed his amber eyes. "You weren't to blame and neither were any of the other Doms. You damn well know that. You're not an ordinary submissive, Destiny. This guy right here"—Mika slapped his palm flat on the folder—"is no ordinary Dominant. Like you, his tastes run on the dark side. His forte is edge play. I have a feeling that you two might be a match made in heaven. But unless you lose your pissy attitude, it'll be over before it begins."

I bit back the urge to correct him, to point out that I wasn't a submissive. All the times Mika had approached me about scening with a Sadist in the past, he'd never prepped me in this way. Anticipation, like butterfly wings, set sail and fluttered in my belly.

"Listen to me and listen good," he continued. "Don't go losing your heart to this one. He's not offering anything but the relief you need. If you want something more, you're not going to find it with him. Understood?"

I lowered my head and nodded. In other words don't do something stupid like fall in love with this one. The inability to separate my heart from my needs in the past had nearly cost my sanity and my membership to the club.

"Good. I'll leave you to read and make a decision." Mika stood and pressed a gentle kiss to the top of my head. I watched him disappear down the hall that housed the members' private rooms and the set of stairs near the back door that led to his office.

Unable to quell my curiosity, I flipped the file open and began to read.

To my prospective partner, please understand:

I am not looking for a girlfriend or wife. I am seeking a masochist to bask in the glory of pain I wish to deliver.

If you are looking for a boyfriend, Daddy, or husband...stop reading now; you are not who I am seeking.

Sincerely,
Cane

Since you're still reading, I hope the following requirements set forth in this unorthodox agreement will mesh with the desires burning inside you. Be warned. My tastes are specific. My need to inflict pain is unrelenting.

I do not conform to the usual BDSM practice of Safe, Sane, and Consensual (SSC). However, I stay within the parameters of Risk Aware Consensual Kink (RACK).

As long as open, honest communication is extended, I will grant the utmost care to your emotional and physical well-being.

I do not tolerate liars, brats, or drama queens.

Upon acceptance of this mutually exclusive agreement, you will be bound to me in all ways. You may not scene, masturbate, or engage in sex—in or out of the club—unless instructed by me.

A two-week moratorium on all play and sexual intercourse will begin immediately. During this introductory period, you will accompany me to dinner, every other night, to a restaurant of my choice. You will wear the clothing that I deliver to your home or office, behave in a respectful and appropriate manner, and eat what is ordered for you.

Upon our first meeting, you will provide me with:

A detailed list of soft, medium, and hard limits.
A list of all medications prescribed to you.
A recent report verifying you are clean of any STDs.
(A copy of mine will be given to you.)
A list of food allergies or dislikes.

After fourteen days, if both parties amicably agree to pursue our desires together, you will be provided a safe word. You promise to use that word without reservation if or when needed.

Prior to play, our sessions will be negotiated until which time

I deem such discussions are no longer necessary.

Anonymity will be maintained outside the club. Interference with work, family, and social interactions or obligations will not be tolerated.

By signing this agreement, you are willingly placing your mind, body, heart, and soul in my care. If you decide to grant me your un-coerced consent, I will shower you in sadistic pleasures.

Such pleasures include, but are not limited to: restraints, ropes, chains, floggers, canes, crops, quirts, dragon tongues, whips, and other implements I desire, as well as impact play, bruising, blood, knives, needles, piercings, electrical and fire stimulation, acts of humiliation, degradation, and exhibitionism, insertion of toys, fingers, tongue, and cock in any or all orifices of my choosing. Please note, the above can and will be modified in accordance to your list of limits.

In closing, this agreement will be null and void if or when either party rescinds their consent.

I agree to the terms set forth above, and am signing this contract of sound mind and of my own free will.

_____ *Date*_____
Sadist's legal name

_____ *Date*_____
Masochist's legal name

Soaked and trembling, I closed the folder as I took in Cane's words. After swallowing tightly, I sucked in a ragged breath. As with any contract, the corporate side of my brain kicked in with a litany of counter offers. But instinct told me Cane wasn't the kind of beast who liked to negotiate. A suspicion that intrigued and aroused. His proposal had a cold, almost clinical vibe, which was a blessing. I wouldn't be tempted to fall head over heels for the man and make a fool of myself when one of the subs caught his eye and lassoed his heart. Besides, Mika had already warned me that affection wasn't on the table. Thank goodness. My love boat had capsized in the Bermuda Triangle eons ago. But there was something in Cane's offer that contradicted that rule. He'd demanded exclusivity. If he wasn't interested in any emotional attachments, why add such a possessive clause? Maybe he expected me to whore myself out in exchange for a few welts.

An inward chuckle tore loose. *If that's the case, he can suck a fat cock.*

While the idea of going another two weeks without sex didn't particularly thrill me, I could live through it. As it was, my girl parts hadn't partied with anything but my own fingers and vibe for months. I was fairly certain my shitty attitude of late was borne from a lack of sexual release. Sure, I wanted sex…hot, sweaty, blood-pumping sex, but I needed the ability to vent the mounting stress within far more.

Said shitty attitude would have to take a dive in the murky depths along with any pending orgasms if I wanted to accept Cane's agreement. Was it really worth it all?

Hell yes! Sign the damn thing now! the greedy pain-slut inside me urged.

"I can hear the cogs in your brain squeaking from here." Samantha's expression was filled with compassion. "If you need to talk, I'm all ears."

"Thanks. I appreciate your offer, but I have to weigh the pros and cons on my own. I'll see you tomorrow night." I flashed her a genuine smile, plucked the folder off the bar, and headed to my car.

When I arrived home, I changed out of my fetish wear and into my comfy cotton pajamas. Curled on the couch, I sipped a glass of Sauvignon Blanc and read Cane's proposal a second time…and a third. His compelling words spurred images of agony to parade through my head.

My pussy grew wet again.

My nipples drew up tight.

On paper, the man sounded more than capable of granting the relief I craved. Though I couldn't afford to let my pent-up frustrations sway me, the thought of being helpless, bound, and at Cane's mercy twisted me up inside. I had to take the edge off in order to make a sane, rational decision.

Two gulps later, the wine was gone. I tramped upstairs to my bedroom and dragged off my pajama bottoms, pulled back the covers on the bed, and snagged some toys from the nightstand. With clover clamps in one hand and a glass-ribbed dildo in the other, I eased onto the mattress. When I dropped a hand between my legs the moist heat of my pussy enveloped my fingers. I closed my eyes and gently strummed my clit while visions of Tony Delvaggio danced in my head. Though he'd been the first of many Doms who broke my heart, he'd fed my masochistic and sexual appetite with his capable whip and bedroom skills. It was morally wrong for me to fantasize about him, considering he was now married to the beautiful submissive, Leagh. Still, I couldn't erase him from my buzz-bank. He was the only man who'd ever come close to fulfilling all my needs.

Nudging the tip of the icy dildo against my wet folds, I fed the hard, rippled glass inside my wet tunnel. Using slow, deliberate strokes, I dragged the pseudo cock in and out of my clutching core while memories of Tony's thick shaft, burning, stretching, and filling me, danced in my mind.

In a familiar and fiendish rhythm, I worked the dildo deep. Silky pleasure rolled up my spine, yet ecstasy remained just out of reach. Pain was the catalyst I needed to drive me over. Gripping the clover clamps, I captured a taut nipple between the metal teeth. An explosion of searing heat engulfed my flesh, zipped down my spine, and eventually melded with the captivating indulgence between my legs. Submerged in the wicked blend of agony and bliss, I vigorously worked my clit until I surfaced again in a buoyant swell of delight. The other clamp lay attached to the metal chain upon my chest, taunting me with another bite of fire. Pressing my lips together, I prepared the second clamp and hovered it over my naked nipple.

If you decide to grant me your un-coerced consent, I will shower you in sadistic pleasures.

Cane's promise sliced through my fantasies. Gone was the image of Tony. Taking his place was the shadow of a mysterious stranger who promised paradise.

With the snap of my fingers, I set the second clamp in place.

A scream tore from my throat. The brutal pinch arced like lightning through my flesh. Plunging the dildo in and out of my pussy, I tugged and squeezed my clit. My limbs tingled and grew numb while the cacophony of pleasure crested. Arching my hips, I shattered with a piercing cry. My tunnel clutched and quivered around the glass cock while I rode relief to the end. I was pulsating, and twitching with aftershocks, and my breasts throbbed and stung with each ragged breath. I lay boneless and sated, savoring the self-induced tingles until they faded away.

After pulling the dildo from my core I shifted to my side. The chain connected to my nipples sagged, tugging the engorged tips. Sucking in a deep breath, I removed the biting clamps in tandem and barked out a wretched curse. Hissing against the blistering burn, I closed my eyes and gently rubbed the tips, working blood back into the throbbing tissue. I swept the toys aside and drew the covers over my body. Snuggled up with my pillow and the decadent pulse thrumming through my veins, I drifted off to sleep.

In my dream, I was lost in a maze, lured by an intriguing showdown and the sound of a cracking whip. From out of the darkness, a man's erotic voice echoed in my ear.

Take my hand. I'll lead you to the place you seek. Trust me...I will guide you well.

His timbre was unfamiliar but alluringly deep and filled with promise. I hurried through the inky labyrinth only to stop short when the feel of warm, capable fingers stroked my cheek.

Don't be afraid, little one. You're on the right path now. Come. Let me lead you and set you free.

Fear and intrigue sputtered from my head to my toes. As I gathered the courage to peer up at the beguiling stranger, my fucking alarm clock began to chirp. Jerking, I silenced the annoying sound and sat up in bed.

The dream had felt like a premonition. Cane's proposal slammed through my brain like an anvil on a watermelon. While his offer was more than tempting, I couldn't shake the feeling he'd omitted something important. Perhaps he'd penned the document ambiguously on purpose. Maybe he intended to define it more once we'd met and had time to learn about each other. Therein lied the oxymoron. I couldn't know the man unless I signed the damn paper. Clearly, he'd woven the contract as a trap—that realization should have made me über-suspicious. But it didn't. It simply made me more curious.

Two weeks. That's all Cane was asking. I could forego the pleasure of pain and sex for fourteen days. I'd already survived sixty without relief, and though I was a snarky bitch, I was still breathing.

"Okay, I'll sign the damn thing!"

With my decision made, I crawled out of bed, cleaned my toys from last night, and then stepped into the shower. An hour later, I drained the coffee from my mug and smoothed a hand over my hair, now tucked into a tight blonde bun at the back of my head. Checking the clock, I snagged my purse and briefcase and hurried out the door.

While sitting in bumper-to-bumper traffic, I rehearsed the speech I planned to deliver to my board of directors. In the past, the five men had benevolently opened their wallets each time I'd proposed the idea to expand my company. Thankfully, my endeavors had netted them handsome profits in return. Today, I planned to hit them up once more.

Ageless Dreams—an exclusive line of skin care products for men and women—had been a quest of mine since my first pimple. After graduating college, I started the company, and within six months, it had turned a profit.

But sales had recently taken a dive thanks in part to the chokehold on the economy. Unwilling to sit back and do nothing, I threw caution to the wind. I handed over an obscene amount of money and hired Edwards & Pratt—a prestigious advertising firm out of New York. Though I'd only spoken to the man by phone, in a few hours, VP Lawson "Law" Pratt and I were scheduled to unveil the re-branding and no-holds-barred kick-ass marketing campaign he'd created.

I didn't think the board would turn me down, but if traffic didn't start moving soon, there'd be little time for Law and me to rehearse our pitch. With an inward curse, I activated my cell's Bluetooth and called Amber, my administrative assistant.

"Morning, Ms. E. Stop stressing. I have everything under control. Bagels, juice, and coffee were waiting in the small conference room when Pratt arrived ten minutes ago. He's in there now, setting up." Her voice dropped to a whisper. "I, on the other hand, am racking my brain for an excuse to go back and drool over him. Good god, Sasha…he's buckets of gorgeous. I might need to go home at lunch just to change my panties."

I swallowed a soft chuckle. Amber was like me in so many ways it was almost scary. She'd been with me since the start. At first I'd been hesitant to hire my mother's hairdresser's daughter. Not only were we both fresh out of college but I also didn't know a thing about her. I'd left for college in Chicago before she and her family had moved to my small Missouri hometown. Thankfully, bringing Amber on board was the smartest decision I'd ever made.

"Sounds like you need to mop up with some napkins," I teased with a grin. "Look, I'm on my way, but I'm stuck in a bitching snarl of traffic. Is there anything that needs my attention before I meet with Mr. Buckets-Full-of-Gorgeous?"

"Um, maybe one little thing."

Amber's unusually timid tone grabbed my full attention. "Yes?"

"Find out if he's married. Because if he's not, I'll be down on one knee asking for a ring in zero-point-two seconds."

"That impressive, huh?"

"You can't even imagine," she replied on a dreamy sigh. "If this is how they grow them in New York, we need to move the company…now!"

"And what do you plan to do with Ken?" I asked, teasing her about her long-time live-in lover.

"Ken who?" Amber giggled. "I'll leave a stack of napkins on your desk. Trust me, you'll need them when you lay eyes on Pratt."

"Seriously?" The man had a nice voice on the phone. Professional. Courteous. "I'd always envisioned him as middle-aged, gray hair, and maybe a paunchy belly."

"Not even close. Tall. Dark hair. Sexiest blue eyes I've ever seen. The man is built for sin. I'm guessing he's early thirty-something. Young enough to still have the stamina to put a girl into a coma and old enough to have honed the skills necessary to do it. And I'd let him do all kinds of dirty things to me…just sayin'."

Good lord. I was anxious to see the man who incited Amber's hormones to riot in such ways. Would he cause mine to riot as well? The thought of working with to him in the small conference room filled me with unease.

"Do me a favor. Try not to molest him until *after* we meet with the board. All right?" I drawled.

"I'll do my best, but I'm not making any promises."

"Brat," I said with a laugh. "I'll be there as soon as I can."

After ending the call, I caught a break in traffic and pulled into the parking garage a few minutes later. While riding the elevator to the eleventh floor, I squared my shoulders and donned my professional veneer, then hurried to my office. Amber rounded the doorway seconds later with a cup of coffee in one hand and a wad of napkins in the other.

"Just take them. You can thank me later." She grinned, shoving both toward me simultaneously.

"You're a nut." I laughed and accepted only the mug.

With coffee and briefcase in hand, I strode down the hall to meet the infamous and drool-worthy Lawson Pratt.

I hadn't even cleared the portal when the man, standing at the easel, glanced up at me.

Tingles of arousal skittered through me as his pale blue eyes, latched on to mine. His aura of command and confidence drilled me to the core. I bit back a startled gasp. Amber hadn't been kidding. Dark hair, the color of milk chocolate, swept over his brow and kissed the white collar at his nape. He'd discarded his suit jacket over one of the conference chairs and my mouth went dry as I dragged my gaze over his wide shoulders and all the way down to his narrow waist. Law turned and afforded me a full frontal view. My heartbeat sped up and a rush of heat softened my now plumping sex.

Lawson Pratt stood around six foot five. Every sinful inch of him was solid, potent male. His sun-kissed skin and perfectly sculpted features left my fantasies of Tony Delvaggio in the dust. I had a new man to star in my masturbation fantasies, and I was staring right at him.

"Sasha Evans, I presume?" His lazy smile was so decadent and erotic the heat clambering toward my crotch roared into flames. My nipples hardened like granite. As I mutely nodded, he extended his hand and in two powerful strides, ate up the distance between us. "Law Pratt. It's a pleasure to finally meet you in person."

His broad palm engulfed my hand. A strange tingling sensation spread up my arm. My imagination spun out of control. I could all but feel his warm fingers gripping my hips as he shoved his cock inside me.

Oh, yeah. You're really going to last another two weeks…sure you are, my inner voice cackled.

"I am, and the pleasure is all mine." My reply came out in a low, throaty tone. I was mortified, but even more so when a carnal flicker danced across his eyes. My pulse kicked up another notch, and the fantasy of slamming him onto the conference table and mounting him like a deprived sex maniac rolled to the front of my brain. My emotions were like clouds, racing through me so quickly I couldn't help but wonder if a storm was coming. Shoving down the ridiculous images, I placed my briefcase on the conference table and retrieved my notes.

"Shall we begin?"

Law studied me for several long, uncomfortable seconds. The intensity of his gaze made me want to squirm. He then flashed me a knee-knocking smile and nodded. "Ah, right."

As soon as he launched into the speech he'd prepared for the board, my concentration flew out the window. All I could focus on was his deep, sexy voice, pouring over my skin like warm, sticky caramel. I was riveted, not to his words but to the way his mouth moved. I shivered thinking about all the things I wanted him to do to me with those lips, tongue, and teeth. Images of me writhing beneath him warred with flashes of his wide capable hands leaving fiery red imprints all over my ass.

The air in the conference room had risen a thousand degrees, but Law hadn't seemed to notice. He just kept on talking while his piercing blue eyes drilled holes through me like Swiss cheese.

Stop thinking with your pussy and pay attention! The future of your company...your livelihood...your fucking house payment is riding on this proposal.

That little voice in the back of my head, and the wave of panic that accompanied it, sobered me quickly. I worked to shake off my ill-timed fantasies before lifting my chin and forcing myself to concentrate on his spiel.

Two hours later, facing the board, Law was halfway through his presentation. I knew his innovative plan and confident mien had won the members over. I could see them all but chomping at the bit to reach into their pockets and fund the new campaign. It was both thrilling and satisfying. Clearly, I'd hired the right man to do the job.

When the meeting was over, the vote was unanimous. I'd been granted the substantial cash injection needed to re-brand and promote Ageless Dreams on a global level.

When Law and I returned from lunch with the board, we rolled up our sleeves and began implementing phase one. I spent most of the afternoon on the phone with my suppliers. I could feel Law's penetrating gaze raking my flesh. His intense focus was more than unnerving, but I dismissed it and told myself that he was as passionate about executing the changes as I was.

The fluttering in my stomach knew that was a lie.

Hours later, we sat in a quiet corner of the posh restaurant inside his hotel and toasted champagne flutes in celebration.

"To the future growth of Ageless Dreams. May she shed her old skin and profit from her pending face-lift." A sexy grin tugged the corners of Law's lips.

I couldn't help but laugh at his quirky play on words as I raised my glass. "I'll drink to that."

"I'm versed in all aspects of your company and product line, but unfortunately, I don't know much about its beautiful young owner." He was all but purring. My heart leapt and I tried not to squirm. "Who are you, Sasha Evans, besides a striking, brilliant entrepreneur?"

The man was as smooth and well-rehearsed at seduction as he was at giving a presentation. If he'd been anyone but the creative genius I'd hired to increase my bottom line, we'd forego dinner and devour one another upstairs in his room. Oh, how easy it would be to hike up my skirt and let this sexy beast take me to the heavens.

"There's not much to tell," I replied nonchalantly. "I spend most of my time working, either in the office or at home."

Lifting the champagne to my lips, I inwardly reminded myself to go easy on the bubbly. I'd never been much of a drinker. Booze tended to wreak havoc with my judgment, and ignite my hormones. Law was the last man I needed to loose my inhibitions with. Not that I wouldn't enjoy the hell out of getting all hot, sweaty, and horizontal with the man, but that would be professional suicide.

"You have to have some downtime, now and then." Even his frown possessed a brazen, sexy elegance. "What do you like to do?"

Beg men to tie me up and beat me.

I bit back the truth and quickly racked my brain for an appropriate vanilla response.

"Well, I like to visit the museum and aquarium when I have time. I also enjoy discovering new restaurants...like this one. I've driven past this hotel twice a day for years but never stepped inside until tonight. It's quite impressive."

Like you.

"For a temporary home away from home, it's comfortable. Now that we've been given the green light by the board, I plan to find an apartment until our project is finished. Though I must confess, giving up my suite will be hard. I have the most amazing view of Navy Pier. I assume you've been there and ridden the Ferris wheel and carousel?"

When I shook my head, Law gaped at me in disbelief. "I've only been to the pier once but didn't stay to enjoy the rides."

"Why not?"

"I'd just moved here and was spending a few days checking out the city. The pier was amazing, but there was much more to see. Anxious to take in everything I could, I left, planning to go back another day. Unfortunately, I never found the time. I was too busy starting up the company."

"If it wasn't the middle of February, I'd pluck you out of that chair and haul you to the pier to ride the Ferris wheel."

The caveman visual exploding in my head sent a warm, slick rush straight to my panties.

"Sadly, even if it were open, I don't have time. After dinner I need to stop by the office and see what fires need to be put out. I'm sure Amber has left a slew of messages for me that—"

"Can wait until tomorrow," he interrupted. "You need to quit slaving your life away. Take a break now and then. Stop and smell the roses. A few hours away from the stress would be good for you."

True. But if Law knew how I dealt with my stress, he'd freak the fuck out. Of course, the idea of him bending me over a spanking bench and lighting up my flesh before he fucked me into a coma sounded worlds better than riding some stupid Ferris wheel.

As I was about to ask him how he relieved his stress, the waiter appeared, ready to take our order. I'd been so enthralled with Law that I hadn't even glanced at the menu.

"They have incredible steaks here. Do you eat meat?" Law asked.

"Yes, I do."

"Medium rare?"

"Always."

With a smile, Law turned to the waiter. "We'll have two fillets, medium rare, loaded baked potatoes, and the grilled zucchini."

As Law ordered my entire meal, the clause in Cane's contract haunted me.

You will accompany me to dinner, every other night, to a restaurant of my choice. You will wear the clothing that I deliver to your home or office, behave in a respectful and appropriate manner, and eat what is ordered for you.

I blinked up at Law and studied him with a dissecting stare of my own. Wouldn't it be ironic if fate—that cunning little bitch who'd left me high and dry in an empty wasteland for months—suddenly dropped two Dominant men on my path?

Are you already drunk? Law is no more a Dom than you are.

"I overstepped, didn't I?" Law pursed his lips and arched his brows. "Trust me. I wasn't trying to insult your independence. I simply have a bad habit of ordering for my dates."

Date? Oh, shit! I had to set him straight. This was going to be awkward.

"I'm your client, not your date, Law." His eyes narrowed a fraction as if he was miffed at the reminder. He quickly recovered and nodded with a placid smile. "And no...you didn't insult me. I was planning to order exactly what you did. So you see, no harm, no foul."

"Good. I'll stick to a safer topic...*you*. Does the alluring woman behind Ageless Dreams have a husband or boyfriend that she juggles with her busy career?"

The man was definitely fishing, and none too subtly. I couldn't help but wonder what he hoped to snag on the end of his hook. It certainly wasn't going to be me, and that royally sucked.

"No. I'm happily single." *Bullshit.* "What about you? Is there a missus and a Pratt pack of children waiting for you back in New York?"

"No." His answer was so decisive I couldn't help but grin. "I, too, am happily single."

Amber will be thrilled.

A wave of jealousy careened through me. After spending the day with Law and trying to ignore the sexual energy arcing between us, the horny woman inside loathed sharing that information with my assistant. Even now, seated across from him, I felt the pull of some strange, static-charged attraction.

Yeah, he might be hot, but you can't wrinkle the sheets with him, and you damn well know it.

Though logic tried to prevail, my hormones overrode sensibility.

Law wasn't planning to put down roots in Chicago. Once the rebranding, packaging, and expanded distribution phases were complete, he'd hop a flight back to New York.

Spending one night with him wouldn't be catastrophic. But I'd have to wait and jump his bones after our work was done. I couldn't afford any unease between us in the office.

Hello? You'll be working with him for the next three months! Besides, you only have to wait two weeks after you sign Cane's contract...you do remember him, right? You know...the Sadist who promised all your dreams would come true?

I did, and his binding sex clause, as well.

You may not scene, masturbate, or engage in sex—in or out of the club—unless instructed by me.

Dammit! His contract couldn't have come at a worse time.

A sinking feeling settled deep. I hadn't even thought of Cane or his offer all day. I'd been too focused on the call of testosterone Law had been zinging my way. Instead of counting down the days until Cane could beat the tension out of me, I'd been fantasizing about burning it away...in bed, with Law.

Is signing Cane's offer a mistake?

Of course not! Law isn't into kink... Look at him.

As I studied the captivating man sitting across the table, the waiter reappeared with our food. Digging into my steak, I began to try and break down my mystifying attraction to Law.

His commanding demeanor was as potent as his beauty, but try as I might, I couldn't envision him tying me up and flaying my flesh open with a whip. Sadly, he was definitely not a Sadist. While he might be open-minded enough to engage in a little spank and tickle, sex with the man would be as vanilla as ice cream. So why did the idea of turning down a decadent, sweet treat like Law fill me with such sorrow?

Though my mind was crowded, my taste buds reveled in the savory spices and hickory-smoked beef bursting over my tongue.

"You've gone quiet on me, Sasha. What are you thinking?"

I raised my head and met his eyes before chasing down a bite with a drink of champagne. "Nothing really. Simply enjoying this amazing dinner."

He pinned me with a curious gaze. "You're not worried we won't meet the deadlines of the phases we've established, are you?"

"No, not at all. I trust your timeline."

Law's sly smile was accompanied by a mischievous glint in his eyes. He refilled our glasses and raised his flute. "To mutual success." After clinking the crystal together, I brought the rim to my lips and took a healthy gulp. "And open, honest communication."

CHAPTER TWO

*W*HAT. THE. FUCK?
The familiar BDSM phrase rolling off his tongue caused me to choke on my champagne. Coughing wildly, I grabbed my napkin and covered my mouth as all eyes in the restaurant turned my direction.

Panic slid over Law's face as he bolted from his chair and hurried to my side. He vigorously began slapping me on the back. Even in the throes of drowning in bubbly and humiliation, I wanted to lean over the table so I could feel his wide, forceful hands swat my ass.

What is wrong with you?

The list was too long to contemplate at that particular moment.

"I'm good," I managed to croak out.

"Are you sure?"

"Yes." I coughed again. "I'm fine…it just went down the wrong pipe."

I could see in his face he wasn't entirely convinced, but Law returned to his seat. I tried to flash a reassuring smile to the diners who were staring, as my cheeks continued to blaze.

If I hadn't been thinking about Cane and his damn contract, or the wild sex I ached to have with Law, I wouldn't have nearly drowned.

"You're blushing."

"Yes, I know. I don't like making a scene."

"It could have been worse," he said with a playful smile.

"How?"

"You could have gone to the ladies' room and returned with a wad of toilet paper stuck to the bottom of your shoe, like I did once."

"Do I even want to know what *you* were you doing in the ladies' room?"

His smile turned purely devilish. "Do you want the truth?"

"Of course. Open, honest communication, right?"

"Damn. That came back to bite me in the ass, now didn't it? I have a feeling you're going to keep me on my toes, Miss Evans."

"I'm sure going to try. Now, spill it. I want all the dirty details."

"All right. Well, back in college we hosted a frat party. The keg had run dry, but it was still early, so a bunch of us walked, or rather staggered, to a bar down the street. While we continued to drink and raise hell, I was hit with an urgent call of nature.

"When I rushed to the men's room, the door was locked. Being drunk and desperate had made me bold. I tried the knob on the ladies' room, and when it opened, I tossed a fist pump in the air and hurried inside. What I saw on that toilet seat still shocks me to this day. I thought women were above such rude things as wetting the seat. You'd think they pissed flowers with all the hell they give men when we leave the seat up."

Not only was he drop-dead gorgeous but he had a warped sense of humor, like mine. He was winning me over without even trying.

"She must have been *really* drunk, too." I smirked. Finished with my dinner, I pushed the plate away.

"Maybe. Anyway, my guts were cramping like a bitch, so I cleaned up the mess with a wad of toilet paper and dropped it on the floor before sitting down to business. I didn't know it, but when I left the bathroom, that nasty clump was stuck to the bottom of my shoe. As I headed back to join my friends, people were pointing and laughing. I had enough wits about me to check and see if I'd tucked the old bat and balls inside my jeans, and that's when I saw the paper under the sole of my shoe."

Though I tried to keep from it, I couldn't help but giggle.

"Not only was it on my shoe but that damn thing had unraveled. I was dragging a five foot trail of soggy, wet toilet paper behind me." He paused, grinning ear to ear as he watched me laugh. The twinkle in his eyes was all but blinding.

"I'm sorry, I know it had to be embarrassing for you," I apologized, laughing like mad.

"Don't be. It gets even better. For Christmas that year, my frat brothers gave me an industrial-sized box of toilet paper. The damn thing had like a hundred and eighty rolls or some insane amount. Needless to say, we didn't run out of bathroom tissue until a week before graduation."

"That was nice of you to share with them." I smirked.

His carefree smile slowly faded before he held me with a sensual stare.

"I want to share something much nicer…with you." He placed his napkin on the table, stuffed some cash into the check folder the waiter had left, and stood.

I had no idea where he intended to take me, but when he flashed me a devastating smile and gallantly extended his hand, I couldn't refuse.

Law threaded his fingers in mine as we left the restaurant and made our way through the lobby. All the while he thrummed my wrist with a slow, lazy stroke of his thumb. By the time we reached the elevators, heat licked up my body like a fever. He glanced at me as if gauging my reaction when he pressed the up button.

"I'd like to show you something. Will you come upstairs with me?"

His suggestive tone left no doubt the man was asking me to get horizontal with him.

Anticipation pinged while a battle between lust and the virtue of my career warred. This was the stupidest move I could make, professionally. But with Cane's stipulations hanging over my head, it might be the only chance I'd have to taste the tempting man beside me. Obviously the chance of getting laid was incentive enough to blow massive amounts of smoke up my own ass.

Struggling to ease the indecision rising within, I sucked in a calming breath. It didn't do jack as the elevator doors opened and Law led me inside.

"I assume we're going to your room?"

"Yes."

"What is it that you intend to show me?"

Hopefully, you…butt naked, with a cock as big and hard as a sledgehammer.

Law took a step closer. His warm breath fluttered over my lips as he brushed his knuckles down my cheek. The ardent seduction reflecting in his eyes was like a balm that smoothed the prickly edges of my anxiety.

"Something beautiful…though not nearly as stunning as you."

His voice was but a whisper. I held my breath when he leaned in and gently nudged his mouth to mine. Lost in the firm yet supple texture of his lips, I melted against his hard chest. Every cell in my body warned me to pull away, but need held me prisoner to his rugged body.

Law cupped my nape before swiping his tongue over my bottom lip. I opened and welcomed him in. His kiss started out sweet and sensual but quickly morphed into something raw and animalistic. He slid a hand beneath my suit coat and palmed my breast. My nipples pebbled and throbbed while my sex clutched and wept. A muffled whimper escaped my throat as deviant dreams of him laying waste to me ransacked my brain.

"I get the feeling you're trying to seduce me, Law," I murmured, still melded to his mouth.

"Yes. And if you'd like to stay the night, I'd love to have you."

Peeling from his lips, I stared up into his darkened sapphire eyes. "Have me, as in one night…no strings, or promises…nothing more than a wild and sweaty ride?"

"I'm game if you are."

"What if this innocent romp causes friction between us?"

"Oh, there'll be a lot of friction, I promise," he drawled with a rakish chuckle. "But I can separate business from pleasure. Can you?"

Could I? I didn't have a clue.

Though I'd never had a relationship outside Genesis, my track record there sucked donkey balls. Every time I allowed my heart to run away with a Dom, it always ended in a photo finish at the Destiny Derby of Heartbreak. If I didn't keep from setting myself up for another fall, my heart would end up on life support again.

He's not asking for commitment. All he wants is a thrusting, screaming, and stress-relieving fuck…the same as you.

I bravely lifted my chin. "Yes. After all, we're professionals, right?"

A wicked smile lit up his face. "I was hoping you'd say that. It would be pure hell working beside you for the next three months with only the memory of a kiss torturing me."

I sent him a sassy smile. "I hope you're as good in bed as you are at pickup lines."

"I am," he replied, unabashedly.

"Prove it."

He pressed his forehead to mine and smiled. "It will be my pleasure…and yours, I guarantee it."

"I bet you do."

When the elevator doors opened, he wrapped a sturdy arm around me and led me down the hall. Butterflies swooped in my stomach, their wings laced with anticipation. Hopefully Law could keep me planted on a professional path so the hopeless romantic within me didn't get sidetracked.

He stopped at the last door on the left and pulled a key card from his pocket. Pausing, he tugged me against his chest and lightly kissed the corners of my mouth before nipping my lip. Tingles exploded from head to toe, zapping me with tiny implosions as he dragged his tongue below my ear and tugged it between his teeth. A hum of delight and impatience vibrated through me.

"Open the door, Law," I whispered in a tone rife with need.

He stared down at me with a dirty smile. "By the time this night is over, you'll be the one following orders, beautiful."

If his authoritative mien flourished as impressively in the bedroom as it did the boardroom, I'd soon be seeing stars. Still, it was a pity that he wasn't ruthless enough to tame my masochistic soul.

"I wouldn't count on that if I were you. I can be a handful."

He dropped a quick glance to my chest. "I can see that." With an incendiary smile, he swiped the card through the reader and opened the door.

His suite was decorated in bold hues of gray, black, and burgundy. Three walls were comprised of floor-to-ceiling glass panels and revealed a breathtaking view of Lake Michigan. Behind a golden mesh screen, a massive stone fireplace sat across the room. Flames of blue, orange, and red flickered invitingly. Dark leather sofas and chairs artfully grouped near the fire lent a welcoming vibe. The floor as well as the stairs—that I assumed led to the bedroom—were covered in a plush, beige carpet that yielded beneath my feet. To my left I spied a full functioning kitchen. On the right was a gleaming mahogany conference table, surrounded by six high-backed chairs.

"Fancy place you have here."

"You haven't seen the best part yet. Come." He took my hand and led me across the room to the wall of windows. "Check that out."

I peered down and smiled. Bright, colorful lights from Navy Pier lit up the night. Hundreds of people—resembling ants from our vantage point on the fifty-fifth floor—braving the cold, were strolling up and down the wooden pier.

"Wow," I murmured in awe. "You weren't kidding. The view is—"

"Not nearly as captivating as you."

Law pressed his heated body against my back and wrapped his arms around my waist. The muscles in his chest felt like a solid wall, and his thick, hard erection that lay wedged between the cheeks of my ass felt like unadulterated heaven.

"I might have to make a special trip back this summer just to take you for a ride on that Ferris wheel and steal some more of your silky kisses."

"You don't have to wait till summer."

For kisses or a wild ride.

I turned in his arms and lifted to my toes before pressing my lips to his.

Though I had initiated the kiss, Law quickly took control and delved deep with his tongue. The heat of his body and the urgency of his mouth surrounded me in a blanket of warmth. Winding a hand in my hair, he loosened the conservative bun I'd worn all day. In a rush, golden strands spilled over my shoulders.

"You should wear your hair down more often," he murmured.

"I can't. It softens me and defeats my reputation as a Dragon Lady."

Law threw back his head and laughed. "You're not that mean."

"A few of my employees would argue that." I smirked. "Actually, I'm only cruel when I'm forced to be."

"Then I won't force you to do anything that might unleash your inner dragon."

"Wise choice."

"Besides, I'd rather hear you purr and whimper in pleasure than scream and roar in anger."

"You'll soon experience the latter if you don't quit talking and take off your clothes."

He cocked his head and met my challenge with one of his own. "I think I need to put your sassy mouth to work on something."

There were times, like now, that Law definitely sounded like a Dom. I shoved the notion aside. If I waited for him to command me to my knees, we'd be standing here all damn night.

I boldly slid down his body and knelt on the floor. Smiling up at him, I began to unfasten his belt. "I take it you had something like this in mind?"

His thick erection lurched and nudged my wrist as I slowly began to release the zipper. Suddenly, Law reached down and hauled me back to my feet.

"Not yet. I want you naked when I feed every inch of cock into your sexy mouth."

A tremor of anticipation rippled through me.

Of their own volition, my hands brushed away my jacket and began releasing the buttons of my blouse. Freeing the fabric, I peeled the filmy silk off my shoulders. Approval lined Law's face while his gaze skated over the pale, plump flesh spilling from the top of my black bustier.

When I started to unfasten the front clasps, he shook his head. My fingers froze and a quizzical expression wrinkled my brow. Law didn't explain, simply bent and dragged his warm, wet tongue over each swell and valley of my chest, leaving a shock of liquid fire in his wake. My knees began to buckle. I reached up and sank my fingers through his silky hair and gripped his scalp, holding fast to him and my sanity.

The coarse stubble adorning his face prickled my skin when he scraped his teeth over my billowing flesh. Arousal sang through my veins, and I closed my eyes, silently willing him to mark me with his teeth.

He's not a Sadist.

A fact no amount of hopes or prayers would ever change.

There was no pain for me to seize tonight.

No escaping the layers of stress.

Only the bite of a crop, lash of a dragon-tongue, or the slice of a whip could squelch the mountain of chaos within.

Unable to voice my dark needs, I banished my futile longings and focused on the blissful vanilla sensations he granted. Law might not be able to vanquish the pressure inside me, but he could take off the edge with a couple of spine-bending orgasms.

Still singeing my skin with the blade of his tongue, Law released the zipper of my skirt. An instant later, the brushed wool fabric slid off my hips, and landed in a pool at my feet. He eased back and raked a stare down my body, pausing at the garters fixed to the sheer black stockings adorning my legs. A feral smile tugged the corners of his mouth.

"You mean to tell me you've been wearing this under your suit while we worked together all day?"

I softly chuckled and nodded.

"It's probably a good thing I didn't know that. We wouldn't have gotten a damn thing done. Tell me something, Sasha...do you always hide your inner sex kitten beneath conservative suits?"

I flashed him a sly smile. "Yes."

"Fuck me," he whispered. "The perpetual boner I'll be walking around with from now on is going to be a hell of a lot more embarrassing than dragging toilet paper on my shoe."

"You can always pretend I'm wearing granny panties."

"No can do, sweetheart. Not now." He blew out a big breath and dragged a hand through his hair. "I don't get it. No husband, no boyfriend...who do you dress like this for then?"

"For myself." The sword of indignation sliced deep. "Even when I have to be a hard-ass, I enjoy feeling like a woman. It might sound crazy, but it keeps me balanced."

Law's expression softened and he nodded in understanding.

"So, you don't think I'm nuts?"

"Not at all. I get it." He shrugged. "I'm in control when I wear a power suit. Like now."

Law swooped in and seized my lips. Obviously our conversation was over.

With a hungry groan, I stepped out of my skirt and tugged his suit jacket off his wide shoulders. Still locked in a fervent kiss, I felt him busily loosening his tie and unbuttoning his shirt. The heat pouring off his rugged body grew even hotter. I eased back and opened my eyes.

Though I'd stared at his fit frame all day, focused on the solid wall of tanned flesh, stretched over ripped muscles and defined abs, his bare chest was far more tantalizing than I'd ever imagined.

"Mercy," I murmured.

"That's what I thought once you shed that proper suit." Law bent and nipped my neck. "Do you want to go upstairs, or would you rather I shove you up against the glass and give anyone who happens to be watching a naughty show?"

I dragged a glossy red fingernail against his sculpted pecs and down through the happy trail of dark hair, disappearing beneath his trousers. "Upstairs. I'm more a voyeur than an exhibitionist."

He arched his brows. "What other naughty secrets have you been hiding from me, besides this sexy black outfit? I can't wait to hear all the dirty things that turn you on."

I dropped my gaze.

You really don't want to know.

"Don't worry…you won't shock me."

Wanna bet?

Confessing the dirty things that turned me on was not only stupid, it was also dangerous, almost as dangerous as being half-naked in his hotel room. It was time to suck him, fuck him, and say good night, or drag my clothes back on and leave.

Don't you dare think about leaving, my libido wailed.

But I couldn't walk away from him even if I'd wanted to. This was the only chance—in my immediate future—to have sex with the man, and I was taking it.

"Secrets don't matter. Sating this insatiable appetite we seem to have for one another does."

"I intend to take care of that," Law murmured in a raspy growl. "Intend to drive deep inside you, fill and stretch you so tight, you can't take another inch."

I wrapped my hand around his straining erection. The thick slab of heat bucked in my grasp. I sent him a shrewd smirk. "And make me scream?"

Law bent and retrieved my discarded clothing, then stood and smiled. "Until you can't talk or walk for hours…only purr."

My knees began to buckle. He swept me up into his arms, nestled me against his chest, and pressed his lips to mine. My whole world started to spin on its axis as he carried me up the stairs. Our tongues tangled in a lurid dance until gravity pulled me from his flesh when Law placed me on the bed. He raked a wolfish stare up and down my body. With capable hands, he quickly released the garters and glided my nylon stockings down and off, then slid the wet scrap of silk from between my legs away. The scent of my musk hung heavy in the air. His nostrils flared as he drew my thong to his nose, inhaled deeply, and then tossed the fabric to the floor.

"You're so fucking beautiful. I can't keep my lips off you a second longer."

When I issued an eager and consenting moan, Law eased onto the bed and dragged his lips and tongue along each of my legs. Working his way up my body, he inched closer and closer to my dripping core. I felt his hot breath caress my needy folds, soft and ready, I restlessly writhed while I whimpered and moaned.

Instead of diving face first into my aching pussy, like so many others had before him, Law reached down and released the fastenings of my bustier. Peeling the material open, he locked a gaze on my breasts. As he reverently cupped my heavy orbs, flickers of need and approval danced in his eyes.

He made me feel coveted, erotic...desired.

Gently strumming the pads of his thumbs over my nipples, he watched the need and hunger play across my face. His touch was so light...so tender, I couldn't remember any man handling me with such attention or care. His soft reverence was thrilling, but I needed more...needed him to pinch and tug my pebbled peaks so the burn could quench the ache inside.

"Your nipples are so pretty...like hard berries, and your skin...it feels so silky, all the way to your swollen, wet pussy."

"For the love of christ, Law. Stop talking and fuck me," I growled.

Without a word, he climbed off the bed. I opened my mouth to protest, but when he began shedding his trousers, my objections fell silent. He shucked off his boxers and his impressive length sprang free. Jutting toward the ceiling, his cock was long, thick, and hard. My mouth began to water as I watched the bead of liquid slide off the tip and melt down his distended veins.

A whimper seeped from my lips and I reached out to touch him.

"What do you need?"

"You. Your cock."

"Where would you like my cock, gorgeous?"

"My hands...my mouth...and deep inside my pussy."

"In that order?"

"Yes," I hissed impatiently.

"Sit up." His expression was taut and fierce. His voice commanding and strained.

I complied and swung my legs over the side of the bed. Eye level with his glorious weeping cock, I licked my lips. Law wrapped a wide fist around his shaft and slowly stroked up and down as he stepped in close to my mouth. Reaching out, I clasped my hand around his and kept time with his languid rhythm even after he lifted his hand away.

"Wrap those plump lips around me, and suck me down deep."

His forceful order uncoiled a wicked thrill within me. Maybe he was hiding his inner kink like I was mine.

He cupped my chin and sent me an apologetic smile. "I'm sorry. I didn't mean for that to sound like a command. It's just…I'm struggling to take it slow. I don't want to scare you."

Nope. Definitely not a Dom. They don't apologize for giving orders. He was nothing more than a horny man with a gorgeous raging hard-on.

"It's all good," I assured before extending my tongue and wrapping my lips around his wide, slippery crest.

With a long, low hiss, he sank a fist into my hair.

Flicking the tip of my tongue over the sensitive spot beneath the crown, I basked in his feral grunts and groans. Unable to work all of him inside my mouth, I relaxed the muscles of my throat and took as much of him as I could.

"So hot…so wet…so… Fuck," he choked out. "That's it, baby…take me inside… Damn! Your mouth feels like liquid silk."

He gripped my hair tighter. I closed my eyes as luscious prickles of pain slid over my scalp and slithered down my spine. Law began controlling the tempo of each slide and pull. His dark pubic curls tickled my nose, while the ruthless grip and the tug of my hair sent shards of delight skidding over my skull. I poured my heart and soul into bathing him with my tongue while I massaged and squeezed his heavy balls in my palm.

His mumbled curses and hisses of pleasure filled me with pride. It wasn't long before I felt his sac grow tight. Incoherent words spilled from his lips as he tried to pry me from his shaft. I reached around and gripped his ass, the muscles deliciously tight and firm, and kept right on sucking.

"Oh, god, Sasha. Fuck…yes."

Gripping my hair with both hands, Law launched into my mouth, fast, deep, and strong. Suddenly, he stilled. His shaft expanded on my tongue, and he let out an animalistic roar as thick ropes of sweltering slickness slammed the back of my throat. Greedily swallowing his silky treasure, I welcomed every drop.

Law's legs trembled. He rocked back and forth like a giant sequoia being felled. I inched my hands to the backs of his powerful thighs to steady him as I milked him dry. Once finished, I slowly eased from his cock and lifted my chin. His face was covered in a fine sheen of sweat, and his eyes were glassy and unfocused.

"Better?" I asked, unable to mask the amusement in my voice.

"Beyond better." He looked down at me with a hungry smile. "My turn."

He scooped me up and unceremoniously tossed me onto the middle of the mattress. Determination stamped his face as he pulled open the drawer of the nightstand and took out a strand of condoms.

"You plan on using all of those tonight?" I teased.

"Yes, and the other box still inside my suitcase."

"You're awfully sure of yourself."

"Indeed I am."

Prowling onto the bed, Law supported his weight on his hands that were splayed out by my head. As he leaned in low, the ropy muscles of his arms and shoulders flexed and bunched. He traced his tongue over my jaw and down my neck as an enticing trail of heat enveloped me. When he skimmed a tender kiss over my lips, I opened for him and he claimed me fully as he settled in between my legs.

Bending, he circled my nipples with the tip of his tongue. I softly trembled and threaded my fingers through his hair. He opened wide and sucked the tip into his mouth. Hot…so hot I couldn't keep from arching into him, demanding more. He was happy to oblige. Lost in the thrilling sensations, I cried out and dug my fingertips into his scalp.

"That's it, baby. Let me hear how good I make you feel."

Unable to form a coherent sentence, I simply whimpered and squirmed as he scraped his teeth over each throbbing tip. He began migrating up toward my mouth, but I fisted his hair and dragged him back down to my breasts.

"I don't want to make them too sore."

"It's fine. I'm fine. Please…don't stop."

A mischievous smirk played over his lips as he bent and sank his teeth into my pillowy flesh. Sucking deep, he mashed the tip of my nipple to the roof of his mouth and brutally drew on the nub.

Pain, white-hot and euphoric, spread over my chest as my heart and body soared.

"Harder…harder," I begged.

Nipping and tugging at each peak, Law answered my plea. "You like it rough, don't you, baby?"

You haven't a clue. "I won't break, if that's what you're asking."

"It's not, but it'll do." A knowing smile speared his face before he laid waste to my burning nipples once more.

The fissures of pain sent endorphins rushing through me and I began to float away. The subs at Genesis referred to it as subspace, but for me it was a vacation.

A vacation from everything...

The daily compilation of stress.

The never-ending meetings.

The hours and hours of phone calls.

The hiring and firing of employees.

The constant product testing.

The heaping piles of paperwork.

The strangling distribution deadlines...

All of it.

Pain was the only respite I'd ever found that silenced the chaos within and granted me peace of mind, body, and spirit. It fortified me...made me able to cope.

Floating on the cusp of that sweet escape, I issued a heavy sigh.

Law nipped one last time before lifting his mouth. "I have to stop tormenting your nipples before I hurt you."

My soul screamed for him to hurt me so sweetly that I'd fall off the edge of the earth and fly to the heavens.

Stop, or he'll think you're a freak.

I swallowed down the plea poised on the tip of my tongue and locked my desires inside a prison of disappointment. I sent him a tender smile and nodded. "Just make me feel good. That's all I need."

It was a lie, but a necessary one.

"I intend to do a whole lot more than that, Sasha."

Licking a fiery trail down my body, Law paused at the juncture of my legs. His heated breath drifted over my clit. I jolted when he placed the pads of his thumbs on my folds and spread my pussy open. Anticipation rolled up my body, and I held my breath, waiting for him to devour me.

The first swipe of his tongue had my spine tingling.

The second lash, and my eyes rolled to the back of my head.

Moments later Law was doing magical things to me...things that defied logic and gravity.

Each twisting lap had me all but levitating off the bed.

If he was as good with his cock as he was his tongue, I was in for an orgasm-fest.

It didn't take long to realize that going without sex for so many months had left me powerless to deny my release. Poised on the edge too soon, I mentally began reciting the chemical compounds of my best-selling cleanser. But the lash of Law's gifted tongue was inescapable.

Beneath the assault of his fingers and mouth my nerve endings rippled and tightened.

The intensity to implode grew to a frenzy as I writhed and moaned.

Demand coiled like a snake.

The fever between my legs blazed.

I couldn't stave off the inevitable much longer.

Reaching down, I tried to push him away. When that didn't work, I tried to wriggle out from beneath him. But Law wasn't giving up command of my body. Instead, he lashed my clit even harder and sucked the nub between his lips.

An explosion of fire careened down my spine and fused with the flames melting my core.

"Please. Oh, god…please…I need to—"

"Come for me," he commanded in a sharp, Dominant tone. "Come hard. Spill your sweet cream all over my tongue, baby."

Driving his fingers deep inside me, Law suckled on my clit once more.

My orgasm swelled.

Lights exploded behind my eyes.

My muscles strained.

I sucked in a deep breath and bore down.

Fragmenting in a surge of blinding delight, I cried out my ecstasy in a long, loud wail.

Clutching and contracting around his driving digits, I arched my cunt and ground it against his mouth as I rode the waves slamming through me.

Wet and quivering, I lifted my heavy eyelids and peered down at him. Law's face was etched in awe and lust. He slowly pulled his fingers from inside me and replaced them with his tongue. Burrowing deep inside my fluttering tunnel, he lapped ravenously at my spilling cream.

Spearing me deep and slow, he gently strummed my clit with his thumb. I knew then he wasn't going to allow me to fall back to earth—at least, not anytime soon.

My breasts rose and fell as I panted, trying to fill my burning lungs with air, but Law didn't surrender. He cupped the cheeks of my ass, lifted my hips off the bed, and began tongue-fucking me with a vengeance. Any illusions of him steadily building me up to my next orgasm were laid to waste with each relentless stab. I was spiraling toward oblivion again in seconds. Gripping the sheets, I sought an anchor to keep me from flying away, but that was only an illusion. I couldn't hold back…didn't want to…wasn't about to fight the beautiful fury seizing my soul.

"Give it to me, Sasha…all of it. I want it now," he barked.

Either he was psychic or Lawson Pratt had already figured out how to push my buttons.

Dizzy with demand, I clawed for restraint to keep from diving headlong into the abyss. I sucked in a ragged breath and wrenched back the control I'd foolishly handed him. "Fuck me, Law. I need you inside me…need you to fuck me hard."

When he jerked his head up, his mouth and chin glistened with my juices. His eyes speared me like daggers, and I could feel the palpable power and control humming inside him. Holding me with a carnal stare, he swiped his tongue up my folds, sending a tremor to sputter through me. His nostrils flared and a ruthless smiled strained his lips.

"You might take the lead in the boardroom, but in the bedroom, *I'm* in charge. Understood?"

CHAPTER THREE

HIS WORDS WERE wrapped in velvet and steel. Instantly, I cast my gaze downward. The ebb and flow of his command was seriously fucking with my head. Instead of challenging him—like I did the Doms who tried to coerce my submission—I exhaled a shaky breath and nodded.

What was wrong with me? Why hadn't I laid into Law?

Because he's not a Dom. You're here for one night of spine-melting sex so you can sign Cane's contract and live like a nun for the next two weeks without losing your damn mind…or committing mass murder.

But even that truth didn't fill me with warm fuzzies.

The fear that I was already growing too attached too quickly to Law slapped me upside the head like a brick. I needed to rein in my stupid emotions before I made a mess out of an uncomplicated fuck.

"Now that we've got that settled…hand me a condom off the nightstand so I can fill your wet tight pussy nice and full." His voice was smooth, like fine aged whiskey.

He lowered my ass to the bed. As I reached over to snag a wrapper off the table, Law slashed his wicked tongue over my clit. Electricity sizzled and burned.

"You taste sweet, like sugar."

I dropped the condom when he licked my folds. Picking it up a second time, I handed it to him with trembling fingers. A deliberate smile curled the corners of his glistening lips as he tore the cellophane open with his teeth. He rolled the condom on with a hiss. Hearing his desperation filled me with empowerment. He was riding the edge as much as I was.

"You wanted me to make you scream? Well, prepare to do just that," he drawled.

Law raised himself above me. I spread my legs wide and wrapped my arms around his neck as he enveloped me in body heat. Bending his elbows, he pressed his sculpted chest to mine, singeing my flesh before claiming me in a desperate kiss.

My warm, salty essence clung to his lips and tongue as we ate at one another with a gluttonous fervor. Grunts and whimpers melded together in the sexually saturated air.

He slid a hand between our bodies, aligning his crest to the entrance of my pussy. The slick, cold condom warmed instantly before he lifted from my mouth and gazed into my eyes.

"Can you take all of me?" His voice was raspy and desperate.

"Every hard, glorious inch."

With a groan, he slammed his mouth over mine and drove his massive shaft through my passage in one mighty thrust. He swallowed my cries as my narrow walls fluttered and screamed beneath his burning invasion. The conflagration of pleasure and pain rolling through me was nothing short of paradise. I was stretched and filled like never before, and a blinding orgasm careened through me without warning.

I ripped my mouth from Law's and screamed.

"Fuck yes. Suck my cock with your tight little cunt. You feel like silk and lava...soft and hot." Law gripped my thighs and tilted my hips before thrusting in and out of my contracting core.

"Harder," I demanded in a harsh exhale. "Fuck me harder."

A fierce grimace lined his lips and he began pounding deep inside me. I wrapped my legs around his waist, watching determination and delight play across his face. His chiseled muscles strained and sweat broke out over his brow.

"Rough and nasty...is that how you like it?" he taunted in a sinful growl.

"Yes. As hard and dirty as you can give me."

"Mmm. I thought so." Something malevolent flashed in his eyes, then Law reached down and plucked and pinched my tender nipples.

I tossed my head back and hissed, "Yes...yes. Oh, fuck yes."

A salacious symphony of slapping skin melding with Law's grunts and my keening cries echoed in my ears. The exacting glide of his steely shaft battered my G-spot and I climbed the peak in a deluge of sweet, blistering friction.

Oblivion was calling me, and just as I was about to free-fall, Law growled.

"Not yet. Breathe," he panted. "I'm close…we're going to…wait for me."

The combination of his splintered demand and straining muscles was more than I could take. The hum of release droned in my ears while a sting of lust-laced curses tore from his lips.

Seconds later, he brutally pinched my nipples and roared for me to come.

Like a fucking volcano, I erupted.

Clamping down around his shuttling cock, I shattered with an ear-piercing scream.

A ruthless roar blossomed from deep in his chest as Law threw back his head and followed me over. Reveling in his savage grip on my hips, I closed my eyes and mewled as he emptied inside me.

Floating on clouds of rippling aftershocks, I felt as if I'd left my body. Law's cock jerked and twitched inside me as we both slowly hovered back to earth. Covered in a slick sheen of sweat, I felt boneless and more sated than ever before.

Though I wasn't completely sure what Law had done to me, I couldn't shake the fear that he'd ruined me for all other men in my future.

Heaven help me…if he lived in Chicago and knew how to throw a whip, I'd be on my knees that very moment.

What about Cane?

I shoved the unwelcome reminder of the Sadist away. I didn't want the little voice in my head taunting me about a man who aimed to regulate my sex life, at least not while nestled in Law's strong embrace. I wanted to bask in the afterglow and hold tight to the memory of the best orgasms of my life, without guilt or shame. Besides, I hadn't signed my name on the dotted line. Technically, I was free to do whom and what I wanted.

Law raised his head. A crooked smile played over his lips as he pressed his forehead to mine. "Give me a minute and I'll be ready for round two…and three…and four."

Yeah, that wasn't happening. It was time to get up, get dressed, and get out before I did something stupid like spend the whole night riding his spectacular cock.

"That sounds nice, but I can't. I have to run by the office, remember, Mr. Sex Machine?"

Gaping at me, Law's eyes narrowed. A crestfallen frown tugged at his lips. "What happened to burning through all the condoms?"

"That was your idea, not mine."

His brows slashed as his frown deepened. "Hmm. I guess I should have negotiated my terms more clearly."

"I guess you should have."

"Next time, I'll draw up a contract."

I didn't have the heart to tell him there was already one ahead of him. "What happened to one night, no strings or promises, just wild, sweaty sex?"

"That was before I tasted you…" He nibbled playfully at my neck. "I need more. Once wasn't enough."

So sad. Too bad.

I sent him an icy smile. "I'm afraid it'll have to be."

"Why is that?" Pushing himself upward, he hovered over me and studied my face.

"Because I need to leave. One night is all there is…ever."

"I see." He eased his cock from inside me and climbed off the bed.

As he walked away, I admired the angles and planes of his ropy, naked muscles, narrow waist, and tight ass. A strange feeling of emptiness seeped through me. It was as if I was suddenly mourning the fun we'd never get to share.

Depositing the condom in a trash can, he shot me a glance over his shoulder. "Even after such an incredible…what did you call it earlier…oh, yeah, a romp. Why?"

"Because we have to work together. Remember?"

A derisive chuckle rolled off his lips. As he turned, I caught sight of his arrogant smirk, but my attention was glued to the sway of his long, heavy cock slapping against his thigh with each measured step.

You're really going to give all that up for a red ass?

I bit back a moan and tore my eyes from his body before climbing off the mattress. He silently watched as I gathered my clothes and dressed.

"Didn't we work that out *before* we climbed into bed?"

"Yes, but—"

"I'm still an adult and so are you. I don't see a reason why we can't continue to enjoy ourselves over the next few months, unless"—suspicion marred his rugged features—"unless you weren't honest about a lover or a husband."

"I was honest. There is no one else." *Not yet, anyway.*

"Then I guess that means you've changed your mind about acting like an adult?"

His condescending tone, obtuse questions, and the childish way he twisted the rules of our bargain pissed me off. He'd been an amazing lover…fantastic even, but the empty pieces of my soul needed to be filled more than I needed a convenient fuck buddy.

"Mixing business and pleasure was a bad idea."

"That didn't stop you five minutes ago. What changed?"

"You," I snapped, no longer able to control my temper. "Why are you pressuring me for more? Why can't you be happy with what we shared?"

"I already told you. I want more."

"Well, I don't."

A soft chuckle rolled off his lips. "Liar."

When he moved in close, his eyes danced with playful mischief as he cupped my cheek. "Don't stand there and tell me you didn't enjoy yourself. I was here, sweetheart. I watched your eyes roll back in your head…heard your screams, and felt the intensity of every rippling quake that slammed through you *and* your tight little pussy."

A blast of heat spread from between my legs and engulfed my entire body. Even my cheeks caught fire.

Law's expression turned cocky and proud. "Yeah, I didn't think you could deny it."

Smug bastard.

"What motivated you to fall into bed with me in the first place?" Obviously, his interrogation wasn't over. "Was it my dazzling personality or my irresistible charm?"

Priceless. The prick-assed son of a bitch wanted to mock me? Stupid move.

I sent him an icy smile. "I had an itch, so I decided to scratch it."

"Have a lot of itches, do you?"

"That's none of your business."

"You don't seem to think you'll need me to *scratch* that itch again?"

"Positive."

"Why's that?"

I couldn't believe the bastard actually had the nerve to ask.

"Because I have no desire to start some sophomoric, short-term affair. I won't be your *office call girl*." I let the brittle smile fall from my lips. "I don't do nooners."

"So you're going to what…just ignore the connection between us?"

"It's not a connection. It's lust, Law. Pure and simple lust," I lied. The attraction I felt toward him was way more than lust. That was one more reason to nip this in the bud now. "Now that we've fucked it out of our system, it's time to move on and turn our focus to business."

"What you're really trying to say is that you used me, right?"

"I think that intent was mutual, wasn't it?"

A humorless chuckle rolled off his tongue. "What's the matter, gorgeous…wasn't I rough enough for you?"

Prick!

I plastered on another icy smile. "What happened to acting like an adult?"

The sad truth was that we were both behaving like five-year-olds. I had to stop allowing him to push my buttons and quit lashing out at him. One of us needed to take the mature high road.

Law's lips pressed into a tight, angry line. Long gone was the warm, pliant bow he'd pressed against my mouth, nipples, and pussy. He looked pissed enough to snag the belt from his pants and beat my ass.

You wish.

The man was beyond infuriating. So why did I ache to strip off my clothes again, grab him by his big, fat cock, and drag him back to bed?

Do it…do it.

Mentally shoving a ball gag in the mouth of my annoying conscious, I squelched my nymphomaniac urges and searched the far corners of my mind for a rational, working brain cell. I'd wounded Law's fragile male ego and possibly made working alongside him a friction-filled fiasco. *He* was obviously too busy nursing his pride to see the bigger picture.

And men called *us* the weaker sex.

I knew I had to be buckets full of crazy, but I sucked in a deep breath and prepared to smooth his ruffled feathers in a clear, calm, and rational manner.

"I'm sorry, but if you're looking for an emotional attachment, I'm not in a place to give that. I think we should end this now before things between us get any messier."

"Messier for who...you?"

"For both of us."

"All right. I'll walk you to the lobby and wait while the valet brings your car around."

"That won't be necessary. I can do it myself."

"Fine. I'll go hit the shower then. Be sure to close the door on your way out. I'll see you at work in the morning." He flashed me a plastic smile, then turned and walked to the bathroom.

His cold and aloof demeanor, coupled with his blatant dismissal, boiled my blood while it ripped my heart.

Clenching my jaw, I marched down the stairs and out of his hotel room.

"Well, that was a meaningful encounter," I scoffed as I rode the elevator to the lobby, alone.

Since when have you ever wanted meaningful?

Never. At least not outside Club Genesis.

You distance yourself from men who aren't in the lifestyle for a reason.

Yes, I did...because vanilla men couldn't fulfill *all* my needs. Of course, the Dominant men I'd hooked up with hadn't either.

I foolishly wanted the fairy tale...the happy ever after. But then again, what woman didn't?

Waiting outside the hotel for my car, I tugged the collar of my blazer up around my neck. The air was crisp but did nothing to chill out my tumultuous emotions.

Law had been half a Prince Charming who'd sexually blown the doors off my inner safe room. Unfortunately, he'd never do the same with my masochistic needs. At least he didn't seem the type. I didn't know for sure since neither of us had stripped off anything other than our clothes. I didn't have a clue who he really was beneath all that hot flesh.

Confusion and rejection swirled inside me. But most of all I was pissed at myself for breaking my own cardinal rule. What was supposed to be an uncomplicated working relationship was anything but, now. Angry, too, that he'd acknowledged the lusty connection between us. I wanted to deny it but couldn't. I felt the same sizzling bond, and like a drug, I wanted him over and over again. But it was the sadness inundating my soul that surprised me.

His dismissal hurt.

Christ, what is wrong with you? It was a one-night fling. Instead of wasting your time licking your dented pride, maybe you should find out how Lawson Pratt crawled completely under your skin in less than twenty-four hours.

That realization sent panic to slither up my spine.

No. I'd done the right thing. Walking away from him now would save me a world of heartache later.

After tipping the valet, I slid onto the heated seats of my Lexus LC, and drove into the night. Instead of stopping by the office, I headed straight home. I wasn't in the right frame of mind to deal with business. All I wanted was a hot shower, my comfortable pajamas, and to curl up beneath the fluffy down comforter on my bed.

I'd fulfilled those wants when I arrived home, but I couldn't sleep. I tossed and turned and finally drifted off sometime after three.

THE OBNOXIOUS CHIME of my alarm, two and a half hours later, filled me with resentment. To top it off, I knew I was in for a long, stressful day walking on eggshells.

"Oh, joy," I drawled as I rolled over and turned off the alarm.

The movement sent a sublime ache to spark between my legs. Last night's bedroom Olympics with Law—though leaving a residual thrill—had been a fatal mistake. Still, I couldn't erase the memory of how he'd driven into me like a wild animal or the blistering pleasure he'd granted. Even if I could've magically gone back in time and changed everything, I wasn't sure I'd want to. The experience was one I'd always treasure.

"Time to go deal with the fallout," I grumbled, crawling out of bed.

I reached the office before Law and was pawing through a stack of messages when Amber appeared in the doorway holding two mugs of steaming coffee.

"Sorry, I'm running a little—Oh, hell," she gasped.

"What?"

"You're glowing." She smirked. "Oh, you lucky little bitch. You fucked his brains out, didn't you?"

I didn't need this. "What are you—"

"Don't play dumb with me." She hurried to my desk and set my coffee down. "You got laid last night. It's written all over your face. Was Lawson Pratt the one who put that fresh-fucked glow on your cheeks and obliterated the tension you always carry in your shoulders?"

"I've got to get to work."

"Oh, come on," Amber groaned in a tortured whisper. "At least tell me…is he hung? Was he incredible in bed?"

"Like a damn horse, and yes. It was best sex I've ever had…or ever will have again."

I lifted the mug of coffee to my lips and took a sip.

"Like I said…you lucky little bitch." Amber giggled and dropped her ass on the edge of my desk. "Spill, sista. I want details…all of them…every thick, hard inch."

"Go type something." I chuckled softly, waving her away.

"Aw, come on. Ken's been working the night shift for months. I've been burning through batteries like a sex addict. At least give me something new to buzz myself to sleep with. I'm tired of my mafia boss fantasy."

"Mafia boss?"

"I've got this thing for really bad boys," she confessed with a wave of her hands. "You're stalling."

"If you're looking for a new juicy fantasy, I'm afraid you're going to be sadly disappointed. It might be better if you hang on to your Mafia boss and order a whole truckload of batteries."

"Batteries for what?"

Law stood in the doorway, wearing a grin and another dark tailored suit that fit him like a glove. He filled the portal like a linebacker. Of course, all I could see in my mind was the rippling muscles of his naked body and his big, fat cock. My heart sputtered and my cheeks grew hot. Amber cleared her throat and hopped off my desk. Her face was a deep shade of crimson as she scurried out of the room.

"Nothing important," I lied.

Law's brows arched when he stepped aside and watched Amber zip past him. "Ahhh, my bad. I didn't realize I was interrupting girl talk. Were you two comparing notes or something?"

"Not hardly," I drawled, taking too much pleasure in watching the proud smile fall from his face.

I studied him for several seconds trying to get a read on his mood.

If he was still pissed, he didn't show it. The icy attitude he'd presented last night had thawed. It was as if he wanted to pretend nothing had happened between us. Fine by me. I could play that game.

You hope.

"I think we'll move to the large conference room today. We can spread out and give ourselves more room." I stood, gathered my notes and coffee, and then skirted my desk toward him.

Law widened his stance, barring my exit. I drew up short. Teetering on my heels, I looked up and met his sky-blue gaze. Surrounded in the sinful heat of his body and masculine scent, I felt a rush of desire slide through me. Flashing me a carnal smile that sent a wicked thrill simmering between my legs, he winked.

Fuck. Fuck. Fuck.

This was never going to work.

"It's only awkward if we allow it to be, sweetheart," he murmured in the same silky whisper he'd drowned me in last night.

Suddenly, I wasn't concerned about difficult undercurrents between us. I was more worried about not running to the bathroom every five minutes to rub out an orgasm.

Sign Cane's contract…no masturbating. Remember?

"Right."

"Good. Now that we have that settled, I'll get the dry erase board and meet you in the other conference room."

Unwilling to confess that I'd been answering my thoughts, not him, I nodded. Law turned toward the small conference room, while I headed in the other direction.

Amber sat at her desk, eyes wide and a quizzical expression plastered on her face. "Well, that wasn't awkward or anything," she whispered.

"You don't know the half of it," I mumbled as I walked away.

Though it had taken most of the day and numerous silent pep talks, I'd managed to deflect the carnal crosscurrent pinging between us. As long as Law kept his distance, I'd been fine. But the second he breached my personal space, I was mentally back in his bed and my body was on fire. My attraction to him was beyond infuriating.

This day can't end fast enough.

Thankfully it did without me succumbing to my howling hormones.

While Law tucked several spreadsheets into his briefcase, I stood and started for the door.

"Would you care to join me for...dinner again tonight?" His invitation was thick with innuendo.

Freezing in mid-stride, my mouth gaped open as I spun to face him. "You're kidding, right?"

"Actually, I wasn't, but..." He shrugged one shoulder as a look of resignation crawled across his face. "Guess I'll see you in the morning."

Law snatched up his briefcase, and without another word, walked out of the room.

I plopped down in one of the conference chairs, exhaled a massive sigh, and closed my eyes. Massaging my forehead with my fingers, I was stunned he'd asked such a ridiculous question. Did he think me a moron? Had he not spent the last ten hours dodging the same fucking sexual energy that I had?

"What a piece of work," I grumbled. Pushing up off of the chair, I stormed toward my office.

"Need me to grab a bottle of wine and drop by for a while?" Amber offered as she slung the strap of her purse over her shoulder.

"Not tonight. I have plans."

Her eyes grew wide and stilled on me for several long seconds before she turned her head and gazed down the hall. "Again? You and... You're going to—"

"No. I have other things I need to take care of. *He* is definitely not one of them."

The only thing on my list was to sign a contract, or swallow my pride, drop to my knees, and beg a Dom to lay my flesh open. Either way, I had to slam the door on my fascination with Law Pratt.

"Thank goodness," Amber exhaled in a sigh. "You two were throwing off so much estrogen and testosterone today I almost suffocated."

"Ha ha," I drawled. "Go home and burn through some more batteries."

"That does sound better than wine. Thanks for the suggestion." With a clandestine glance, she peered down the hall again. "I know who'll be in the starring role."

"Bitch," I groused as jealousy's teeth tore into my flesh.

Amber blinked. "Oh...whoa. Wait. You and Law... You two aren't done yet?"

"Oh, we're way done...more than done."

"All right!"

"Fantasize away. Knock yourself out."

It took all the willpower I possessed to push those words past my lips. Forcing a placid smile, I waved as Amber headed to the elevators. When she was out of sight, I strolled into my office. Outside a heavy snowstorm was raging. As I made my way to the window, I peered down at the street. Several inches had already accumulated on the ground. Traffic was going to be a bitch.

"Will you be able to make it home safely in all this?"

I jumped as a cry of surprise tore from my throat. "Sorry," I said on a nervous chuckle. "I didn't hear you come in."

"I didn't mean to startle you." Law joined me at the window and held me with a delving stare.

"Yes, I'll be fine. I'm used to driving in snow."

"Good. You'll probably fare better than I will." He darted a glance down at his shoes. "I left my boots at the hotel this morning."

"I can give you a ride if you'd like?" I clenched my jaw as soon as the words hit the air. Fire flickered in his eyes. "I mean...I'll be glad to drop you off at your hotel."

No, you meant give him a ride, all right...all night long, my mind snorted.

The corners of his mouth twitched, but he had enough manners not to smile. "That's...ah, very generous of you. I'll grab my coat."

As we made our way through the parking garage, the silence between us was deafening. When I pulled out onto the white powder of the street, I discovered ice pellets, instead of snow, were raining from the skies. The back of my Lexus fishtailed and Law gripped the dash.

"Whoa." He paled slightly.

"Relax. I'm just getting a feel for the road," I lied. The pavement was as slick as a skating rink.

"Uh-huh," he grunted in disbelief.

I gripped the steering wheel tightly and tensed as cars around me slid, crashing into one another like pinballs.

"How far away do you live?" Law's voice held the same level of strain as my tension-filled muscles.

"I'm only about ten miles north, in Highland Park," I replied as a delivery truck began sliding sideways toward the passenger side of my car. "Look out, you idiot!"

"Maybe we should turn around and crash at the office for the night," Law suggested as the window beside him filled with the image of a giant loaf of bread.

"No. But maybe we should get off the streets and grab some dinner, until the road crews can plow this stuff off and throw down some salt."

"I already invited you to dinner. You turned me down. Remember?"

I briefly jerked my head toward him and scoffed. "Let's be real. You invited me to dinner and dancing in the sheets. Don't try and deny it."

"Okay, I won't."

His truthful answer didn't grant any satisfaction, merely reinforced my sadness. No matter how badly I still wanted the man, the splendor of last night could only be a memory. When I turned off South Michigan Avenue, hoping to find a less congested street, I realized I was headed toward the club. A sliver of guilt wiggled through me. I had to stop pining over Law. An offer to fulfill my desires was dangling right in front of my face. All I had to do was pick up a pen and sign the damn thing.

"This will work." I pulled the car toward the curb and slid into a parking spot in front of Maurizio's. Members of Genesis often met up at the quaint Italian restaurant to have dinner before heading to the club. Thankfully, it was too early for any of them to converge on the restaurant. Besides, with the weather so crappy, the club might not even open. Still, I had no intention of waltzing into Maurizio's with Law by my side. Instead, I opted for the sports bar next door to enjoy a fat, juicy burger and to-die-for fries.

As we stepped out of the car, we were assaulted by the sound of crunching metal. Law quickly stepped onto the curb. Wrapping his arms around my waist, he pulled me up against the building as a beat-to-hell Chevy jumped the curb and veered off into the alley beside the sports bar.

"That was close." My voice quivered with fear.

"Too close. Come on." Law opened the door to the sports bar and all but shoved me inside.

The walls were covered in sports logos and beer insignias. The scent of stale beer hung in the air and loud rock music blared from various speakers around the room. The place was deserted except for the staff. Law led me to a table toward the back, and the harsh music decreased to a barely audible level. I bit back a growl. I'd hoped that the powerful beat of drums and screams from the electric guitars would make personal conversation impossible.

A young kid with blond hair and bad acne hurried to our table. "Uh, sorry about the music, man. We like to rock out when the place is empty."

"Crank it up all you want. That's fine with me."

Law gave me a sideways glance. A slow, knowing smile speared his mouth before he turned and pinned the waiter with an intimidating scowl. "Keep the volume down, please."

"Uh, yeah. Sure." The kid nervously nodded and hastily set our menus on the table. "What can I get you to drink?"

Before Law could take charge the way he had at dinner last night, I ordered a Mexican beer with a wedge of lime. He did the same and smirked at me after the waiter walked away.

"Feel free to order what you'd like, Sasha."

"I intend to." I sent him a tight smile and scanned the menu.

"You're making this more difficult than it needs to be. You know that, right?"

"I think I'll have the Diablo burger. It's spicy and burns in a good way."

Law reached out and snagged my hand. Squeezing it, he frowned. "We need to clear the air."

I dropped my menu, tugged my hand back, and pinned him with a blank stare. "Clear the air? Okay. Fine. We had sex. It's out of our system. We can put it behind us now and forge ahead as platonic business associates."

My sarcasm didn't even faze him. Law simply laughed. I wanted to slap him.

"Oh, Sasha. You're so funny."

"I wasn't trying to be funny. I was being honest." I lifted my chin. "That's what you wanted...open, honest communication, right?"

"You're so transparent yet so reluctant to *be* open and honest."

"I'm open and honest about the work we're doing," I said defensively.

"I'm not talking about work. You enjoyed the hell out of last night. Yet you're now slamming up walls to keep me out. Why?"

"Because we have a job to do. Look, I don't need you playing the role of some armchair psychiatrist, digging into my head, my life, or my body. Got it?"

"Then tell me what you do need."

"For you to forget that last night ever happened. It's water under the bridge. Drop it and let's move on."

"I can't do that." His voice dropped to a seductive whisper. "And neither can you."

"Ha," I scoffed. "I already have."

"Liar."

The waiter returned with our drinks, whipped out his order pad. "Have you decided what you want?"

"I'm suddenly not at all hungry," I stated, pinning Law with a caustic smile, then tipped back my beer and practically drained the bottle. "I'll have a vodka and tonic...make it a double."

"Bring her two." The seductive challenge in Law's eyes sent a shock of arousal straight to my clit. "I'll take the bacon-cheddar burger, well done, please. And an order of fries."

"Coming right up."

When the waiter disappeared, Law's blue eyes filled with compassion. "What are you doing, Sasha?"

Trying to survive the way you dismantle me.

"You're never going to make it through this storm alive if you try driving home drunk."

"I'm a big girl. I can hold my liquor."

Grow up! How many more lies are you going to tell him?

As many as it took to extricate my emotions from the tangled web I'd carelessly woven around me.

Law's lips pressed into a firm line. He held out his hand. "Give me your keys."

"Why?"

"Because if you're going to drink your dinner, I'm certainly not going to let you climb behind the wheel."

"What? You suddenly want to start acting like my father?"

Law leaned in, a wicked spark flaring in his eyes. "If I were your father, I'd turn you over my knee and spank the sass out of you."

A deluge of arousal spilled and saturated my panties.

Heat scorched my entire body.

The air in my lungs froze and my heart hammered against my ribs.

He cocked his head as a lazy smile crept over his lips. "Oh, Sasha…you *are* full of surprises, sweetheart. You'd like that, wouldn't you?"

CHAPTER FOUR

BEFORE I COULD find my voice and attempt to toss back a smart-assed response, or rather another lie, the waiter appeared with my drinks. Without a word, I grabbed the first glass and downed a huge gulp. Savoring the burn that slid down my throat, I ignored Law's knowing smile and piercing stare.

Getting toasted in an ice storm was almost as brilliant as fucking his brains out. But somehow I was able to dodge, duck, dip, and evade his barrage of questions. By the time Law had finished his burger, I was feeling no pain. In fact, I couldn't feel my tongue, lips, or nose. Normally, I would have switched to soda after my first beer, but Law's determination to annihilate my walls and scrutinize every piece of my personal rubble, coupled with my outrageous attraction to him, made the evening anything *but* normal.

I was inside a sports bar, three sheets to the wind while an ice storm of biblical proportions raged outside, sitting with a man who made my girl parts burn like molten lava. If there was ever a good time to get shit-faced, it was now.

Law held me against his rugged frame as he helped me out the door. He plucked the keys from my hand and I blinked up at him with a scowl.

"Do you have an ice scraper?"

"I'm not that much of a cold-hearted bitch," I said with a laugh.

"Not for me, sweetheart...for your car."

I turned my head and saw my vehicle covered in a thick sheet of ice.

"And just when I thought my day couldn't get more fucked up," I groused.

With his strong arms gripping my waist, I focused on staying atop my stilettos as my shoes slid down the sidewalk. Not looking where I was going, I bumped into a wall of solid muscle. When I jerked my head up and offered a slurred apology, I blinked in surprise. Standing before me was Mika, Julianna—pregnant belly all but bursting from her coat—and a tall, broad-shouldered, man with sandy-brown hair and the palest golden-colored eyes I'd ever seen.

"Sasha? Are you all right?" Mika studied me with concern before he studied Law with a suspicious glare. "Do you need some help, girl?"

The spike of tension in the air tried to steal my buzz.

"She tossed back a few too many inside. She'll be fine. I'll take care of her," Law assured.

Mika's chest and chin lifted in tandem. Even the hunk with the stunning gold eyes seemed to bow up like a fighter. "I bet. Who are you, and how do you know Sasha?"

"I'm Lawson Pratt, a business associate. Who are you?" An edge of jealousy sliced through his tone.

"A friend," Mika replied. "A very *good* friend."

Law's body tensed. He flitted a curious glance to Julianna and Mika, then to the stranger who was built hard and lean and looked powerful and unyielding. A sudden burst of heat pooled low in my belly and spread like wildfire through the rest of my body. The club owner's friend was sinfully captivating.

An uncomfortable silence hung in the air. As if sensing it, too, Julianna placed a hand on Mika's forearm. "Hello, Lawson. It's a pleasure to meet you. I'm Julianna. This is my…".

Master, my alcohol-saturated brain supplied. I quickly covered my mouth to muffle a snicker.

"…boyfriend, Mika. And this is our friend"—Julianna held my gaze—"Parker *Cane*."

The air stilled in my lungs.

Cane?

Every warm, blurry trace of alcohol instantly vanished from my system.

Cane?

My eyes grew wide in disbelief.

Oh, fuck…Cane!

Julianna sent me a brittle smile along with a barely perceptible nod.

Every muscle in my body drew taut.

Biting back a curse, I dragged a guilty gaze over the handsome stranger. The weight of his delving stare pressed in all around me. A knowing smirk tugged his lips before he darted a shrewd glance at Law's arm banded around me. Then Cane locked his pale golden eyes on mine once more. The palpable authority emanating off the man was a thousand times more intoxicating than all the alcohol I'd consumed.

"It's a pleasure to meet you all." Law nodded. "Sasha and I have recently started working together. You're the first friends of hers I've had the pleasure to meet."

This was a nightmare…a fucking, nightmare. I wanted to wake up…but I wasn't even asleep.

This was so not happening. Unfortunately, it was.

My knees bowed. A cry of mortification burned the back of my throat.

Law clutched me tighter, keeping me on my feet. "Easy, Sasha. I've got you, gorgeous."

A flicker of jealousy darted over Cane's eyes. I tried to open my mouth and explain the situation, but my brain wouldn't work, let alone my lips or tongue.

"Sasha, I want you to come join us inside Maurizio's. I'll have Scotty brew a fresh pot of coffee and we'll get a few cups in you." Mika made it sound like a suggestion, but I knew the man. That was a fucking command.

I sent him an incredulous glare. Was he insane? I didn't want Law anywhere near my kinky family. And I certainly didn't want Cane's disapproving glare focused on Law's possessive hold of me. The Sadist's jaw was clenched so damn tightly the muscles in his neck were twitching.

"That's an excellent idea, Mas…my love," Julianna stammered and then cringed ever so slightly.

"I agree." Law smiled down at me. "At the very least, we need to get out of this storm. If we can sober you up a bit, all the better."

Oh, hell!

I couldn't miss the silent exchange that passed between Mika and Cane or the censure etched in their faces when they turned their Dominant gazes toward me. Usually, I didn't give a shit what others in the lifestyle thought of me, but Mika's opinion mattered, and his silent reprimand was crushing.

The combination of ice-laden wind biting my face, Mika's displeasure, and Cane's bad-assed demeanor had sobered me up faster and more thoroughly than a gallon of coffee. Hell, I could probably even pass a Breathalyzer.

I dug my heels into the icy sidewalk. "Actually, I don't feel drunk anymore."

"Bullshit." Law chuckled. "You just skipped dinner, downed a beer, and tossed back three vodka and tonics."

Julianna's eyes grew wide and Mika's brows arched in shock. "That's more alcohol than you've consumed in the four years I've known you."

"You can hold your liquor, huh? Coffee. Now." Law scowled and bent in close to my ear. "Spanking your ass is beginning to sound more and more appealing."

Mika chuckled and slapped Law on the back. "I think I'm beginning to like you."

Julianna covered a hand over her mouth to hide a grin.

Cane's nostrils flared as he glared at Law.

Oh, god. Somebody just shoot me now.

Mika clutched Julianna's elbow and led the parade. Law and I were in the middle with Cane bringing up the rear. I could feel his golden eyes boring into the back of my head. I wanted to sink into the slippery sidewalk and disappear.

Nibbling my bottom lip, I darted a glance over my shoulder. Cane's focus was on Law's arm around my waist before he raked a gaze up my back and locked his eyes on mine. An unspoken promise of the painful pleasure he wanted to grant me was etched on his face. A blast of heat tore through me, so blistering that I wanted to strip off my clothes and run naked through the pelting sleet.

All of a sudden, my heel slid out from under me. With a yelp, I flung my arm out seeking something to grab hold of. Cane rushed to my side and gripped my elbow with an overwhelming grasp. My entire body exploded in goose bumps.

Wedged between their rugged, hot bodies, a filthy and arousing fantasy unfurled in my head. My nipples turned to stony pellets. The muscles in my stomach rippled. My pussy clenched while my clit began to throb incessantly. Somehow through the riot of sensations seizing my mind and body, I managed to croak out my thanks. Cane simply grunted and continued to escort me down the sidewalk.

When we stepped into the restaurant, the scent of garlic and oregano caused my stomach to growl loudly. Lifting his hand from my elbow, Cane splayed his palm against the base of my spine. Chills and flames swirled beneath my flesh.

It was then that Law noticed the Sadist's hands on me and nailed Cane with a homicidal glare. Aggression blossomed all around us and the air grew taut and thick. Without an ounce of remorse, Cane simply smiled. I half expected them to unzip their flies, whip out their dicks, and begin marking their territory on me like dogs, until Law began to chuckle.

"You have no idea, man. Not even in your wildest dreams."

"I take it you do?" Cane's voice held an edge like steel.

"Oh, yeah…pure, sweet paradise," Law drawled with a proud grin.

In less than a tenth of a second, I understood the subtext of their exchange.

Affronted and embarrassed, I wiggled from their holds and sent Law a seething glare. "If you gentlemen…or rather, cavemen will excuse me. *Pure, sweet paradise* is going to the ladies' room."

"Need any help?" Cane offered with a suggestive smile.

"No. I've been handling the chore since I was two," I bit out in a haughty tone.

He cocked his head and narrowed his eyes. His scorn nearly singed my skin. I quickly bit my lips together to keep from making this first impression more disastrous than I already had.

"Hold up. I'll join you," Julianna called, shucking off her coat, she stroked a hand over her pregnant belly. "This little gal thinks it's fun to jog on my bladder."

Law's eyes grew wide. "When are you due?"

"In about three more weeks," she preened.

A look of alarm lined over his face while he mutely nodded.

"I take it you don't have kids?" Mika chuckled.

"No," Law replied.

Julianna looped her arm through my elbow and tugged me toward the bathroom. I tensed in surprise. While she'd been one of the more accepting subs at the club, we weren't what you would call besties. Feeling so discombobulated, I was grateful for her compassion and support. After we pushed past the door and stepped inside the sitting room, I flopped down on the red-velvet chaise and exhaled a heavy sigh.

"I know this is a bit awkward for you," Julianna sympathized. "Mika told me about Cane's contract. Though this might not be the way you wanted to meet him, don't freak out. It'll be—"

"Too late. I already am. I don't know what to say or how to act with Law sitting right there. I mean…the man's totally vanilla."

"I figured." She sighed. "As far as Cane goes, and I mean this in the nicest way, watch your mouth. He's, like, über-intense and that look he just sent you…Dayum. His wicked stare had me quaking in my boots. Mika's intimidating at times, but Cane…yikes. He oozes discipline."

"I know…I damn near suffocate every time he looks at me."

"Just keep breathing…you'll be fine. So what's up with you and Law? I didn't know you were dating."

"We're not. It's…it's too convoluted to explain."

"Okay, then how long have you two been doing the horizontal hula?"

"Is it that obvious?"

"Oh, yeah." Julianna grinned.

"Shit!" I dropped my head into my hands and groaned. A dull ache started up behind my eyes. "Just once, but it was *amazing*. I'm trying to kick him to the curb…I have to, it's just…"

"Why ditch him? If he's that good, keep him. I mean…don't repeat this to Mika, but Law is scorching hot."

After I shared the terms of Cane's proposal, Julianna pursed her lips and sighed. Just as she'd started to speak, the door swung open and Mika stormed into the room.

"Are you finished, girl?"

"No, Master. I haven't even peed yet. Sasha and I have been talking."

He arched his brows in warning, like the look Cane had just given me. "Go pee and get your sexy ass back to the table. Our friends are arriving and it's filling up fast."

Friends? Fear, like ice water, filled my veins.

Julianna let out a tiny squeak and hurried into the next room that contained the stalls.

"Who else has joined the group?" I tried to keep the panic out of my voice.

"Drake and Trevor, Nick, Dylan, and Savannah, Ian, James, and Liz, so far. Sam and Cindy are on their way."

"Has anybody, ah...mentioned the club?"

"Yeah." Mika nodded, clearly concerned. "Trevor, *of course*, asked Cane and Law if they were new members."

"Oh, god."

"Relax, girl. No one is going to out you. I told Law we were all members of a dinner club."

I exhaled on a brief sliver of relief. "Is Law sitting with the group?"

"Well, yes. We'd never ostracize one of your friends."

The thought of Law surrounded by fellow kinksters sent anxiety climbing through me once more.

The idea of hiding out in the bathroom held more appeal than it should have. Unfortunately, Julianna reappeared and Mika escorted us both back to the table.

The sight of Law and Cane, leaning over an empty chair, heads bent together in a private conversation, sent the hairs on the back of my neck to stand on end. When they peered up and locked their penetrating gazes on me, separate streaks of want and need careened up my spine. They were as different as night and day, but both held keys to pieces of me I ached to explore. Law's gentle smile was calm, relaxed, and welcoming, while Cane's was wolfish, dark, and primal.

"I saved you a seat," Law announced. "Come on over and sit beside me. Maybe you'll decide to eat something now."

Not likely. While I'd quickly sobered, the vodka felt as if it were burning a hole in my stomach. The idea of adding food to the fire only made the flames leap higher.

As I rounded the table, he and Cane both stood and helped me to my seat.

Being sandwiched between Mr. Sensual and Mr. Sadist, and feeling the decadent heat rolling off their bodies, and breathing in their intoxicating scent had my libido turning cartwheels. Want pooled in my panties, growing steadily worse the longer their eyes bored into the sides of my head. Unwilling to hazard a glance at either man, I kept my focus dead ahead across the table on Ian, James, and Liz. James slid his hand under the table and Liz jolted slightly before a tiny moan slid off her lips. She turned and buried her face against her Master's neck.

Really? You two have to start that shit here...now?

As if reading my thoughts, Ian smirked as he stared at me. "How are you doing tonight, Sasha?"

I wanted to burn him with a caustic reply but simply sent him a tight smile.

The man had balls. He'd barely spoken five words to me since he and James had called a halt to our weekly Dominance training sessions. Okay, so maybe Ian had wanted to help James learn more about being a Master, but in the end, our kinky threesome had been far more educational. What I hadn't realized at the time was that they'd simply been using me as a test dummy for a few weeks, then they'd replaced me with Liz. That insult still stung like a bitch.

"Wonderfully. Thank you. How are things going with your company?"

"Busy, but good. James and I have clients lined up out the door, so it seems."

"What type of business are you in?" Law asked.

"Private investigation," Ian replied proudly.

Liz dragged her mouth from James' neck. "You're not going to start talking shop, are you, M…my love?"

Ian dipped low and nipped the lobe of her ear. "We could always talk about you, darling."

Before she could answer, James cupped her nape and turned her head to claim her with a soulful kiss. When he released her, he smiled. "Yes, you're a wonderful topic of conversation."

Liz blushed brightly. "No. Talking shop is fine."

I was keenly aware of Law studying the trio's open display of affection. Whatever the man was thinking, he masked it well. Without a word, he turned his head and began observing Dylan and Nick, at the other end of the table. The two men were both caressing and kissing their even more pregnant girl, Savannah.

Law eased in close to my ear. The feel of his moist breath on my skin sent a rush of memories from last night to assault my brain. "Your friends are *very* pregnant…is there something in the water?"

Huh? His question caught me off guard. Instead of asking me about the two triads' unconventional relationships, he wanted to know about the babies?

Exhaling a soft chuckle of relief, I shrugged. "I order soda, just in case."

"I take it you don't want children?" Cane asked.

I hadn't realized the man was eavesdropping.

Turning his direction, I was met with a Dominant expression so potent and intense it felt as if he were stripping me to the bone. The fever between my legs grew even hotter.

"I've never given it much thought." Suddenly, I was fighting an inward battle to keep from casting my eyes down.

Dammit!

I'd never wilted away on impulse before. Sure, I showed respect to Doms...once they'd earned it. So far, Cane hadn't. Still, I couldn't shake the urge to yield to him.

Oh, hell!

"That's understandable, as fast as your company has grown," Law stated.

"Ah, that's right." Cane smiled. "You founded a company of skin care products, right out of college."

"A successful line of soon-to-be, *worldwide* skin care products," Law proudly added.

"I see Law's been telling secrets," I nervously replied.

"Not at all." A deliberate smirk lifted one corner of Cane's lips. He leaned in close and whispered, "I've done my homework on you, princess."

How?

He brushed his lips against the shell of my ear. "Sign my contract, and I'll fill your luscious world with all kinds of secrets, surprises, and sin."

I sucked in a shallow breath and shivered.

As Cane sat upright, he straightened the napkin on his lap and dragged his knuckles up the outside of my thigh. Ripples of arousal tore through me like I was having a damn seizure.

"Are you cold?" Law draped his arm over the back of my chair and pulled me against his warm, hard body.

Cane studied the possessive gesture with amusement.

"It's okay. I'm fine."

That was an understatement and a lie. Fine was being home, tearing up my toys, and succumbing to a coma after numerous orgasms. Sitting between these two powerful and intimidating men, determined to fuck with my head, was far from *fine*.

I worried what Cane's *homework* had revealed about me. The man was either a cunning, hard-core Sadist or he was a fucking stalker. One thing for sure, Mika hadn't shared any personal information about me or my company. He was pedantic when it came to protecting the members of his club. There were only two instances where monsters had slipped under Mika's radar. The first asshat had attacked Julianna, and Mika ended up shooting the prick in the head. Chicago PD was still searching for Master Kerr, the other sociopath who'd lost his shit and terrorized several subs.

"You need help taking orders, baby?" Scotty, owner of Maurizio's, called from behind the bar.

"No. I'm good," Carly, his girlfriend and waitress, replied, moving in on the other side of Cane. "What can I get for you?"

"I've been told that your lasagna is amazing. I never pass up amazing." He pinned me with a spine-melting smile. "I'll take an order, and would you please bring another one for Sasha?"

I opened my mouth to protest, but Law reached over and squeezed my hand. "You need to eat, gorgeous."

"We'll both have the house dressing on our salads," Cane continued. "And an order of the cheesy garlic bread I've heard so many rave about."

Still staring at me, Cane closed his menu with a predatory smile.

"It's nice to know I'm not the only one," Law laughed.

I wanted to throat-punch him.

"Private joke?" The curiosity in Cane's voice was thick.

"No, not at all. Sorry. Last night *I* ordered Sasha's dinner for her."

"Ah, a man with class. Well done, Law." Cane raised his water glass in salute.

"Like using the restroom, I'm quite capable of ordering my own food." The words flew out of my mouth before I could stop them.

A sudden hush fell over the table.

All eyes turned my way. Expectant expressions lined all their faces except, of course, Cane's. He simply smirked. I knew then how a bug under a microscope felt. I bit my tongue so hard I tasted blood.

A knowing smirk tugged Mika's lips as he flashed me an encouraging wink.

The tension clinging in the air began to dissipate when James started lobbing questions to Law about marketing. I sucked in a grateful breath. When he asked about Nick's and Dylan's professions, they were happy to tout the pros of owning a construction company and the cons of operating in the cold Chicago winters. The discussion turned to sports when our salads were delivered, and while I merely picked at the lettuce, I was finally able to draw in a deep breath.

"It will be nice when we have the opportunity to talk in private." Cane's savage whisper caressed my ear. "I'm anxious to discuss the questions you have for me, princess."

Fighting the urge to fold myself against his heated frame, I swallowed tightly and shoved the notion down. "I'm sure we'll find time to do that soon."

"Indeed. I am puzzled though. My understanding was that you weren't *involved* with anyone."

"I-I'm not," I whispered.

"Really? In that case, you have forty-eight hours to get rid of the horny boy toy beside you, or I'll rescind my offer."

A millisecond later, Carly set a plate of gooey, steaming lasagna in front of me. My stomach swirled and pitched. For all the wrong reasons, a flood of saliva filled my mouth. Shoving away from the table, I leapt out of my chair and sprinted to the restroom as fast as my stilettos would take me.

Fighting down the urge to hurl, I splashed cold water on my face. After blotting it off with a paper towel, I stared into the mirror.

"I made my decision, and I intend to keep it. No matter how much chemistry there is between Law and me, I have to move on. I can't always have what I want…sometimes I have to just go with what I need."

"And what exactly do you *need* that I can't give you?" Law stood in the doorway, arms crossed over his chest, disappointment lining his face. "Maybe the better question is, *who* can?"

Shit!

"It's personal," I mumbled.

He pushed off the doorframe, and in two long strides, ate up the distance between us. "I've had my tongue and cock deep inside your body, Sasha. I don't know how much more personal you can get than that. What happened to open, honest communication?"

"Law…don't, please."

"Don't what…expect an explanation about why you're trying to talk yourself into rejecting the chemistry between us? I think I have a right to know, considering you don't sound at all convinced that's what you really want to do."

Dammit!

It was only one night.

One night you'd repeat over and over again in a New York minute.

You don't owe him an explanation.

So where was all this guilt coming from?

As if sensing the tumultuous emotions churning inside me, Law wrapped his arms around me and pulled me to his chest. Fire and need leapt to the surface, smoldering my angst.

"I know you're scared because we're moving too fast, but—"

"No. That's not it." I wrenched out of his grasp. The loss of his security and warmth left cold isolation in its wake. "Law…you're a wonderful man, a fantastic lover, and—"

"And you're shutting me out of your life…your personal life anyway."

Though he'd tried to mask it, I still saw the rejection in his provocative blue eyes. Swamped with more guilt than I could manage, I lowered my head and nodded.

He exhaled a long-suffering sigh, pulled me to his chest once more, and rested his chin on the top of my head.

"It's been a long time since I've been dumped. It sucks just as much at thirty-eight as it did at sixteen." He placed his fingers beneath my chin and tilted my face up to his before he brushed a chaste kiss to my lips. "I probably shouldn't tell you this, but what the fuck. Last night is going to be at the top of my spank-bank for a long damn time."

I couldn't tell him that when I had permission to masturbate, he'd be the one filling my fantasies, too. "I'll take that as a compliment," I softly whispered.

"Please do." He sent me a weak smile. "Come on. Your food is getting cold."

Shaking my head, I cringed. "I don't think I can eat tonight."

"Then we'll box it up, and you can take it home." His expression turned somber. "If you ever need a sounding board, a warm body to snuggle, or…whatever, I hope you know you can turn to me."

"Thank you. I appreciate that."

We both fell silent and simply stared at each other for several long seconds. I ached to lift to my toes and kiss him, really kiss him, one last time. But I'd only muddy the already murky waters between us.

Instead, I threaded my fingers through his hand and led him out of the bathroom. It suddenly dawned on me that while the Doms of the club held no compunction about bursting into the ladies' room, Law had taken it upon himself to charge in as well.

In hopes of lightening the mood, I stopped and sent him a quizzical look. "You have a fetish for hanging out in women's restrooms, don't you?"

Law chuckled. "Only when you're the lady in it."

"Thank you," I murmured softly.

"Anytime."

When we rejoined the group, I noticed my food had already been wrapped up and was sitting on the table. I also realized that Cane was gone. I sat down in my chair and darted a glance at the vacant spot beside me before sending Mika a curious look.

"Welcome back, you two." The club owner smiled. "Cane had to leave. He snagged a cab a few minutes ago but asked me to extend his good-byes to each of you."

"That was kind of him," Law replied. "I'm surprised there are any taxis running in this nasty weather."

"They are now," Mika assured. "When I walked Cane out, the plows were clearing the streets and spreading down a ton of salt. It's not as treacherous as it was earlier."

"It's probably safe for us to get moving again then." I glanced up at Law.

He gave me a somber nod and stood. "It was a pleasure meeting all of you. Hopefully we can hang out again before I have to head back to New York."

Watching as Mika and the rest of the Doms smiled and shook Law's hand made me feel like a traitor. By cutting personal ties with the man, I'd all but guaranteed he'd never be *hanging out* with my kinky family again.

"I'll call you later, Sasha," Mika announced as we turned to leave.

I sent him a nervous nod before Law and I stepped out into the bitter night air.

Not surprisingly, he insisted I stay in the car as it warmed while he scraped the ice from the windows. Though it was a stupid, sophomoric thing to do, I couldn't keep from branding the sight of his rugged face to memory.

Stop being so melodramatic. You're going to see him again in the morning.

Yes, but in the morning we'd be nothing but business associates—a gut-wrenching fact that hurt my heart.

Law climbed into the passenger seat. His cheeks and nose were rosy red. He looked adorable. "Are you sure you're sober enough to drive?"

"Positive," I replied, snapping one more image of him to add to the others, I pulled away from the curb.

The street was much easier to navigate thanks to the road crews. Heading toward Law's hotel, I felt the sorrow inside me grow heavier with each passing block.

You have twenty-four hours to get rid of the horny boy toy beside you, or I'll rescind my offer.

I hated ultimatums.

But I hated the fact that I had to give Law up even more.

You don't have *to do anything…you've chosen to.*

Yes, I had. And now that I'd actually met Cane, I knew he'd be capable of assuaging my nagging needs, probably more thoroughly than any Dom before him.

If only Law were wired differently.

My mind quickly wandered down a twisted path. Liz and Savannah both lived with the command and love of two men…why couldn't I?

Do you really think Cane and Law are the types to share?

The taunting voice in my head was right. I quickly shook the delusion away.

"For someone he just met tonight, Cane certainly seemed interested in you…not that I blame him."

Guilt returned with a vengeance. I gripped the steering wheel and forced a nonchalant shrug. "He seemed a bit standoffish to me."

"Only because he isn't as direct as I am when it comes to you."

I forced a laugh. "You're pretty damn direct, that's for sure."

"And it paid off…at least for a little bit."

"Yes. It was fun while it lasted, Law. I honestly mean that."

When I pulled up to his hotel, a wave of panic crawled up my body.

I'd foolishly thought I could have my cake and eat it too. All I'd managed to do was screw myself sideways. I didn't want to end my relationship with Law, but I was out of options.

He reached out and cupped my cheek. Tears stung the backs of my eyes while the thrill of his touch warmed me.

I was a pathetic hot mess.

"I'll see you in the morning, gorgeous," Law whispered before he leaned in and brushed a feather-soft kiss across my lips. "Be careful driving home."

Unable to push words past the lump of emotions lodged in my throat, I mutely nodded. He climbed out of my car and shut the door, sent me a tight smile, then turned and walked away.

A tear slid down my cheek before I'd even pulled out of the hotel's driveway. Angry with myself for being so melancholy, I swiped my face with a snarl. I'd been so enamored with him that I'd let him dig into my psyche and unearth fragile emotions I should have guarded better…especially to one as intuitive as Lawson Pratt.

Normally, I relished the idea of unwinding at home. Not tonight. I was too keyed up to relax. Pulling onto South Michigan Avenue, I drove back to the office.

Minutes later I was sitting at my desk, focused on my computer.

Instead of mourning the loss of Law, I busied my brain poring over spreadsheets of sales stats and projections. Next, I delved into new product testing results until my eyes burned and my head throbbed.

I didn't remember dozing off, but waking up to Law's gentle nudges and unhappy expression certainly left a lasting impression.

"I thought you were going home last night."

His scolding tone made me bristle.

"Not that it's any of your business, but I came back to the office because I wanted to get some more work done."

His lips pressed to a tight line at my haughty response.

He was pissed…definitely pissed. But I was cranky and tired and in no mood to play his games. I needed caffeine.

A slow, devious smirk tugged his lip. "Get your coat."

"Excuse me?"

"I said… Get. Your. Coat."

Like waving a red cape in front of a bull, his mulish command set me off.

CHAPTER FIVE

"YOU ARE *NOT* sending me home like a little schoolgirl. We have work to do."

"Did I ask you to go home?"

"You haven't asked me anything. You've been too busy ordering me around like I'm one of your minions." I jerked my chin in defiance.

"Put your coat on, Sasha. Now!"

"I don't take orders from—" Before I could finish my sentence, Law rounded the desk and plucked me out of my chair. "Let go of me! Have you lost your damn mind?"

"Maybe. But it's you that's making me crazy."

"Me? How?"

"By not taking care of yourself. By working night and day. By not relaxing. By not eating and refueling your body. And by not going home to sleep and rest your stubborn mind."

"Stubborn? I'm not—"

"Oh, yes you are. Like a goddamn mule." Banding one arm around my waist, he leaned over and grabbed my coat off the credenza. "Put this on, and stop arguing with me."

"I will not! Just where the hell are you taking me?"

A brittle sneer split his lips. "It's a surprise."

Law was undoubtedly commanding in the boardroom, but I'd never experienced this unrelenting side of him before. And dammit, he was turning me on in ways I shouldn't enjoy…but I did. Suffused in a puzzling blend of anger and arousal, I let out a low growl.

"That's the same sound you made when you were coming all over my tongue the other night, gorgeous."

"Asshole."

He didn't take offense when I lashed out at him, simply smiled. "One day I'll drive myself deep inside your asshole. Count on it."

"I'm talking about *you*. You're the asshole."

"Would you rather I act like I don't give a shit about the feelings between us, the way you are?"

His truth stung. A part of me wanted to fold like a spineless wimp and beg his forgiveness. But I'd shared enough vulnerabilities with Lawson Pratt. I couldn't cave now.

"You're badgering me so I'll fire you, is that it?"

He drew me tightly against his chest. The decadent heat pouring off him paled next to the flames of desire and wrath that blazed in his eyes.

A humorless chuckle rolled off his tongue. "Sweetheart, you're not going to fire me. You already sank a shit-ton of money into my campaign. Not to mention, the sweet old men on your board of directors have great expectations of you. Are you willing to disappoint them?"

"Congratulations," I hissed. "You've surpassed asshole status and moved all the way up to prick."

"As I recall, you enjoyed the hell out of my prick two nights ago, as well."

His taunting reminder sent a shiver to slam up my spine.

"Stop it," I spat as I tried to pull from his hold. "You're mad because I won't crawl back in bed with you."

"No. I'm pissed because you won't take care of yourself."

"What's it matter to you?"

Sadness filled his eyes, but Law quickly banked it. "My reputation is on the line. What happens if you get sick…end up in the hospital? Your board might be sympathetic, but if you pull this campaign, I'm out a hefty commission."

Though he hadn't used a knife, I felt the pain in my heart just the same. His words knocked the air out of my lungs. He'd never given a shit about me. The connection between us had been nothing but manufactured seduction. All Law cared about was obtaining his precious commission. He was just like the others. Rage, white and hot, enveloped me from the inside out.

"Ah, so that's what this has been about…your fat, juicy commission. You've got some balls, mister." My whisper vibrated with the hurt and fury that was wound deep inside me.

"It's not just about the commission, Sasha," Law snarled. "I know what you're thinking."

A hateful scoff slid out of my throat. "No. It's not about the money…it's about the game. Congratulations. You won. You got your dick wet before the truth came out."

"This isn't a game to me," he snarled.

"Bullshit," I spat. "Get your hands off me, or I'll knee you in the balls."

Law lifted his hands, raised his palms in the air, and took a step back.

"Ah…" Amber stood in the doorway, mug in hand, mouth gaping open, and rapidly glancing between Law and me. "I'll…just come back with your coffee when things—"

"No. Throw it down the drain. I'm leaving. I need some air." Grabbing my coat and purse, I squeezed past my startled assistant.

"Sasha!" Law bellowed as I raced to the elevator.

As I stabbed the down arrow incessantly, his heavy footfalls grew louder. I cursed under my breath and spun on my heel to face him.

"Go away, Law. I need time to think."

"About how I used you?" he taunted with a scowl.

"Among other things, yes."

"And you accuse *me* of having balls. You're sporting a mighty big pair under all that naughty lingerie."

"Fuck off." Spinning away from him, I jabbed the button again, repeatedly.

Law moved in close, suffusing me in his masculine scent and heat. His sweltering breath slid over my neck, and I rolled my shoulder in an attempt to brush him away. He ignored the hint.

"We're equally guilty of using each other, and you know it, gorgeous. But I wasn't the one who got scared, dragged on my clothes, and ran out the door. I feel it too Sasha. You're not alone, but you can't keep ignoring this fire between us."

Yes, I can.

"We need to sit down and come to terms with it…figure out how to make it work, instead of fighting. You can't keep running, Sasha."

I have to.

Finally, the elevator arrived with a ding. Thankfully, the compartment was empty. Law reached around me and gripped the edge of the sensor, holding the portal open. I stepped inside and shot him a beseeching stare.

"Please, I can't do this right now, Law. I need time to sort things out."

"I'll be here when you get back."

That's what worried me the most...the knowledge that I wouldn't be able to escape him for months.

Law stepped back. His blue eyes pierced my heart as the doors closed.

When the elevator started its descent, I exhaled a heavy sigh before sliding on my coat.

"When you fuck up, you *really* fuck up," I mumbled out loud.

It was easy to tell myself that I wasn't responsible for the way he felt about me, but my own baffling attraction to the man was more than physical. I'd only known him for three days. Still, I was infatuated with his sense of humor, his business acumen, and his tender touch. I'd never been with a man who handled me with such a delicate touch.

Of course, in the end, none of this really mattered.

I focused on stepping outside the box and realized that struggling with my bewildering feelings toward Law was futile. Not only would he leave in a few months but neither one of us even wanted a relationship, let alone had the necessary time to devote to one.

I had to get my head screwed on straight and un-fuck the whole craptastic situation.

There was only one way to do that.

Striding to my car with purpose, I sped home and climbed straight into the shower.

As the hot water pelted my skin, I mentally scrubbed Law from both my flesh and soul. Then watched bravely as the what-could-have-beens swirled down the drain.

When I stepped from the steam, my heart felt somewhat lighter but bruised.

After drying off and donning a thick terry-cloth robe, I made my way to the kitchen and brewed a pot of coffee before sitting down at the table with Cane's contract. I read the verbiage over and over again as I pictured the man in my mind.

He was breathtakingly handsome...and his golden eyes were not only penetrating but stunning as well. However, the palpable and intimidating command he exuded seemed to shroud his beauty and lend an air of remoteness.

"This agreement is my saving grace. Cane is perfect. He's handsome, powerful, and emotionally detached…exactly what I need to protect my heart," I reassured myself out loud.

Aligning my pen to the paper, I signed my name and added the date.

Waiting for a sense of relief to smooth the edge of my ragged nerves, I sat back and sipped my coffee. After several long minutes, the tension still hummed low inside me.

Dragging out a sheet of paper, I penned my list of limits. Since I wasn't allergic to any foods, I added a few dislikes and finished up by noting that birth control was my only medication. After printing off a copy of my most recent blood work, I sat back and scowled. A growl rumbled in the back of my throat. I'd just sentenced myself to fourteen more days without relief.

"Unless…" A tiny smirk tugged my lip as a devious plot began taking shape in my brain.

Glancing at the clock, I wrinkled my nose. It would be hours before I could put my plan into motion. I'd find the patience to wait. Then I'd find relief…even if I had to fucking beg.

After tucking the papers into my purse, I climbed the stairs. Seated at my desk in my home office, I sent a text message off to Amber.

> **Sasha:** Sorry about running out on you this morning and leaving you to deal with the angry beast. Have things calmed down there?
>
> **Amber:** That was a quite an argument. And yes, things are nice and calm. Pratt left right after you did…said he needed some air, too.
>
> **Sasha:** Good. Enjoy the quiet. I'll be working from home today. Ping me if you need me.
>
> **Amber:** You got it. I'll see you in the morning.
>
> **Sasha:** Hopefully, without all the fireworks.
>
> **Amber:** Don't sign any peace accords on my account. Pratt's even hotter when he's pissed.
>
> **Sasha:** Oh, for the love of… go file something, will ya?

I grinned and shook my head as I entered the last message.

By one o'clock, I could barely keep my eyes open. After shutting down my computer, I walked across the hall, removed my robe, and climbed into bed. As soon as I closed my lids, blissful blackness dragged me under.

I woke to the sound of my cell phone alerting me that I had a text message. Scrubbing a hand over my face, I sat up and grabbed the device off my nightstand. I noticed it was already dusk and blinked in disbelief at the clock.

Shit. I hadn't planned to sleep the whole day away. It was half past five and the sun was sinking fast.

With a heavy sigh, I checked the message.

Law: *Leaving the office and heading back to my hotel. The Jamison Plastics price quotes came in. Phone if you wish to discuss. If not, we'll go over them in the morning.*

Torn between texting and calling him—to hear the sound of his deep voice—I shook my pathetic pining away and set my phone aside. I might be a masochist, but self-inflicted torture didn't flip my trigger in the slightest. Besides, I wasn't fifteen anymore. I needed to stop believing in knights on white horses. I mean, seriously, I barely knew the man. Yes, the sex was great...*really* great, but it was done...over. I needed to grow a damn spine.

Emotionally distancing myself from Law was the smartest thing I could do, and the only way to accomplish that was signed, sealed, and stashed in my purse. The only thing left to do was hand the contract over to Cane and deliver myself from temptation...after I'd finished one last task.

Didn't you learn your lesson about skirting his rules the first time?

"Oh, shut up," I groused at my conscious. "This is different."

At least I wanted it to be. My tiff with Law this morning had only increased the Mt. Everest-sized pressure bearing down on me. I'd never last another two weeks dealing with the man, day in and day out, without relief.

Besides, Cane expected a well-behaved pain-slut. If I didn't have the rebellion beaten out of me, he'd hand me my walking papers the first week...hell, probably within the first five minutes.

Determined to wipe the slate clean, I climbed out of bed and began to put myself together. Mika and I were going to have a nice long talk tonight. If all went according to plan, by morning I'd be a whole new woman.

After parking in the back lot of Club Genesis, I wrapped my coat around me and proceeded to the front of the building. Though I knew the access code for the back entrance, I'd decided to wait with the other members in the foyer. Mostly I wanted to see if any Dominants were there who were proficient enough with a whip to beat my problems away.

My choices were slim to none.

Master Ink—the sometimes-Sadistic Dom, depending on his mood—was standing beside the long, red-velvet curtain that separated the club entrance from the actual dungeon. His tight black T-shirt, emblazoned with the letters DM, *Dungeon Monitor*, told me he was at the club in a working capacity. I mentally scratched him off my list.

Stepping up to the podium, I sent Master Sam an icy smile. His submissive, Cindy, standing beside him, plastered on one as well. Thankfully, the bitch stayed silent. Ob-gyn Doctor Samuel Brooks was the last Dom who'd handed me my pink slip to pursue Cindy. Since embarrassing myself during that debacle, I strived to stay off their radar. Time hadn't erased his rejection or my humiliation, but at least Cindy had stopped giving me the bitch face. That was a plus.

Was it any wonder I felt like a fucking paper towel around these people? I was the black sheep in an otherwise warm and welcoming family. Still, I wasn't going to let anything deter me. I had as much right to find fulfillment inside these walls as anyone else.

With a nod, Sam handed my license back. "Have a nice time, Destiny."

"Oh, I plan to." My tone dripped with sarcasm.

Sam's disapproving scowl only served to reinforce what I already knew—I needed an attitude adjustment, now. Come hell or high water, I would achieve one tonight.

As I passed through the curtain, I purposely steered clear of any Dom who'd beaten me, fucked me, and left me. If I let my combative mood slip out, Mika would surely banish me from the club. I'd be in a world of hurt then, and not in a consensual way.

I strolled to the bar, set my purse on the glossy surface, and eased onto my usual barstool. How my ass wasn't indelibly imprinted in the damn thing by now was beyond me.

"We missed you the last couple of nights," Samantha stated as she set a club soda down in front of me. "Did you get caught up in that nasty weather yesterday?"

"Sort of… Thanks." I lifted the glass and took a long sip. "Is Mika here?"

"He sure is…upstairs in his office." Samantha lifted her eyes toward the ceiling.

"Would you do me a favor and call him to see if he has a few minutes to talk?"

"I'd be happy to. Hang tight." She turned and picked up the phone behind the bar and punched in a couple of numbers.

I glanced over my shoulder at the sound of a man's scream. Daddy Drake was painting his boy Trevor's lily-white ass with welts using a dragon-tongue.

You lucky little slut, I thought jealously.

Each lash Drake delivered made my pulse quicken and my breath catch. I ached to be in Trevor's place with a pure and primitive longing.

You'll have that chance tonight.

"Mika said to give him twenty minutes, then come on up," Samantha announced before she hurried to the other end of the bar.

"Thanks," I called to her retreating back.

I turned a hopeful eye toward the entrance. Nick, a tall, swarthy Native American, and co-Dom, Dylan, a blue-eyed, blond cutie, came swaggering through the curtain. Their still very pregnant submissive, Savannah, was snuggled between them, laughing at something Nick was whispering in her ear. Behind them, Savannah's equally pregnant sister, Mellie, waddled in with her Master, Joshua. Both sisters' bellies looked like they were ready to burst. The thought had no more popped into my head when Mellie let out a cry, grabbed her stomach, and bent over.

Joshua paled. His eyes grew as big as saucers. A look of sheer terror crawled across his face. He froze for a split second before he gripped Mellie's waist and dipped the other hand into his pants pocket and pulled out his phone.

Nick blanched. He spun around and raced toward the curtain, screaming for Sam to get his ass into the dungeon.

"A Dom giving orders to another Dom is definitely something you don't see everyday." Cane's deep and unmistakable timbre came from beside me.

The air in my lungs froze along with every muscle in my body. Willing my eyes away from the group surrounding Mellie, my gaze locked onto the potent Sadist standing beside me as he continued to watch the uproar unfold.

I quickly realized that last night I'd been either too intimidated or tipsy to fully appreciate the man's sheer beauty. The defined line of his jaw and the gentle slope of his Augustan nose only added to his distinguished allure. The wide expanse of his shoulders and the thick shock of tawny hair framing his face didn't suck either. Even now, when I was stone-cold sober, Cane's aura was as forceful and palpable as the night before. Especially when he turned and locked his golden eyes on mine. Once again, his forceful mien rocked me from my head to my stilettos.

"You think she'll deliver on the dungeon floor?"

I jerked my gaze toward Mellie to find her lying on the ground. Master Sam had one hand on her enormous belly while he focused on the watch at his wrist.

Cane's question, out of left field, stunned me. "Huh?"

He smiled broadly and winked. My heart skipped. "I only wanted to see if you were paying attention to the mommy-to-be or me."

"Both, actually."

"Thank you. Your honesty means a lot, but then you already know that from my contract." Yes. The infamous document promising peace and freedom that lay tucked inside my purse that very minute. "I think it's time to discuss the reason you haven't signed my offer and returned it to Mika."

"Now that we've officially met, why would I give the paper to Mika and not you?"

"Because he graciously extended me the favor of reaching out to you. I would insult his generosity to accept the contract from you. After all, this is his club. I'm simply a guest."

"He told me you were a member now."

"I am, and intend to keep it that way."

Cane's remarks revealed very important facts to me. First, he was eager to begin moving forward with our unorthodox alliance. And second, he respected the hierarchy of the club as well as the dynamics of the lifestyle. He was intimidating in the flesh, detached in his methods to procure a masochist, but wasn't an egotistical prick who thought himself above others.

Following his gaze, I watched Master Sam and Cindy quickly putting on their coats, while Joshua plucked Mellie up into his arms. The foursome hurried toward the entrance, followed by Nick, Dylan, and Savannah.

"Why don't we go somewhere that we can talk in private?" Cane asked, drawing my thoughts from the gruesome images of labor and delivery that were dancing in my head. "I have a room down the hall we can use."

The hairs on the back of my neck prickled. I didn't want to be alone with him yet and risk him finding out I'd already signed the contract.

As if sensing my hesitation, he softly smiled. "If it will set your mind at ease, I'll keep the door propped open."

I couldn't tell him a lack of safety was the crux of my issue. Instead, I nodded and reached for my purse.

Cane wrapped a firm hand around my arm, stilling my movement. "I expect a verbal response to all my questions. Is that clear?"

"Yes."

"Sir will do nicely, princess," he added with a smirk.

I wrinkled my nose at his choice of honorifics—I wasn't in the same solar system as a princess—but I'd broach that issue with him later. Right now, I had more pressing concerns on my mind, like talking to Mika.

"Yes. Sir."

"Very nice."

Cane released my arm. I grabbed my purse and followed him toward the private rooms. He'd barely cleared the archway when he paused and unlocked the first door on the right. At least Mika had assigned him one close to the dungeon. If I let the cat out of the bag and needed backup, I wouldn't have far to run.

Cane stepped inside and went straight to the bathroom, returning seconds later with a towel. As promised, he stuffed the terry cloth under the door, keeping it propped wide open. He then turned and pulled a chair from the wall, spun it around, and straddled it, then nodded for me to sit on the bed.

"Now, then. Ask me what you wish to know."

"Okay." I lifted my chin and steeled my spine. "How set in stone is your two-week moratorium on play?"

"Marble. Why?"

"Because I can't wait two weeks. I need to relieve this pent-up energy…now."

"How long has it been since you've purged this…*pent-up energy*?"

"Months."

"I see." Cane silently pondered my words for several long minutes. "Stand and strip. Kneel on the carpet while we continue exploring this…problem of yours."

My shoulders slumped. I exhaled a disgruntled sigh and rolled my eyes.

Great. Just great!

Not only had another dipshit player slipped under Mika's security net…the asshat thought I was applying for the position of cum-slut. Lacking the time and desire to play games with this clueless bastard, I remained on the bed and pinned him with an acidic smile.

"I suppose you want me to slurp on your cock but not drip any jizz on your expensive designer pants, right? I thought you were supposed to be some big, badassed Sadist, not some horny little pencil-dick looking for a hole to fill. Sorry, but I'm not here for sex. I'm here to have my ass beat. I doubt you know the difference between wielding a crop and taking a crap. Do us both a favor, okay… Fuck off."

I stood and turned on my heel, then started toward the door.

"Destiny!" Cane bellowed. Like thunder, his voice rumbled my bones. "Do not leave this room."

"Give me one good reason why I shouldn't?"

"Because you passed my first test."

"Excuse me? *Your test?*"

"Yes."

The laughter in his voice irked me, but the elated flicker in his eyes pissed me off even more. Cocking my head, I sent him a stare meant to incinerate his happy ass.

"You didn't mention dick about *tests* in your precious little contract. Let's get one thing clear…I'm not a sub. I don't bend over for any man until he's proved himself worthy…not only to give me pain, but to *own* mine. So you can shove your tests right up your ass. I'm done playing your fucking games."

"My, my. You're a fiery little wench." Cane stood and slowly made his way toward me. As he looked down at me, a devilish grin spread across his lips. "Taming you is going to be such fun. I do love a challenge."

I scoffed at his claim. All traces of humor slid from his face as he held me with a daunting stare probably meant to scare me. It only served to turn me the hell on.

Shit!

I couldn't allow him to play me. Sure, he had all the motions and words down pat, but Cane was probably just as ill equipped to *tame* my ass as all the other Doms before him.

He reached down and cupped my cheek. I angrily jerked from his grasp and tried to ignore the comfort his tender caress produced inside me.

"Oh, I aim to put you firmly under my thumb and keep you there. Make no mistake about that, princess."

"Stop calling me princess."

"Why? You don't like the pet name I've given you?"

"In case you haven't figured it out for yourself, I'm more like a bobcat…not a princess."

"True. But I have ways to mold those fierce parts of you and draw out pieces you never knew existed inside you. I am your prince of pain…and you will become my princess…*if* you possess the courage, that is."

His words made my pussy melt, my breasts grow heavy, and my nipples shrink and ache.

"I have a question for you, *princess*."

"Okay."

"When did you and Law begin your…affair? Was it before or after you read my contract?"

I swallowed tightly. Truth, like a noose growing tighter and tighter around my neck, was going to hang me. Forget having my ass beat. If he was ready to bust me on Law, he'd thoroughly nail me to the wall over any kind of scene.

Fuck!

"I fail to see what difference that makes."

"I'm sure you do. Based on the guilt written all over your face, I have my answer." Cane pursed his lips as if something bitter lay on his tongue. He stepped back, folded his hands behind his back, and looked toward the door. "You're dismissed."

Humiliation, rejection, and guilt slammed through me.

Then in the blink of an eye, rage shredded all other emotions.

"Thank you, *Sir*," I sneered.

Gritting my jaw, I lifted my chin, then squared my shoulders and marched straight up to Mika's office. Before I could raise my hand to knock, he jerked the door open and pointed toward the couch.

"Sit," he ordered tersely.

His command intensified my fury.

I wasn't a damn dog.

Things were about to get ugly.

"Thanks, but I'll stand."

"Sasha Genevieve Evans, put your ass on that couch." I wanted to laugh. No one called me by my full name except my mother. I exhaled a heavy sigh and plopped down on the cushion. Mika strolled toward me, massive arms crossed over his buff chest and amber eyes blazing brightly. "Want to tell me what just happened in Cane's room?"

"Since you obviously saw and heard everything, what is there to tell?" I asked, pointing to the wall of brightly lit security monitors across the room.

"Don't try to slap me around with that attitude of yours, girl…I'm two seconds away from pulling you off the couch by your hair, dragging you to the dungeon, and setting your ass on fire."

"Yes! Finally!" I launched to my feet and raised my fists in victory.

Mika slapped a hand to his face and slowly dragged it down over his chin. "I fucking hate trying to punish a pain-slut," he mumbled.

"I don't need punishment…I need relief."

"You expect a reward after you thumbed your nose at Cane like that? It's hell trying to find a Dominant who's experienced enough to throw a whip *and* willing to put up with your shit, Sasha. Why are you making it even more difficult for me with that fucking nasty attitude of yours?"

"Maybe I wouldn't have an attitude if I weren't ready to fucking implode. It's been months, Mika. Months!"

"I know," he softly replied. "But you're making this harder than it has to be, and we both know it."

I couldn't argue with that truth.

"I know you think there's not a man out there capable of handling you, but you're wrong. Until you decide to throw away that mask you keep hiding behind, you'll never find him. Maybe I'm the only one, but I can clearly see through your tough exterior, sweetheart. I know that underneath that don't-fuck-with-me façade lies a broken, scared, and confused young woman."

His balls-on assessment, coupled with the understanding and love suffused in his tone, all but eviscerated me.

My chin began to quiver.

Tears stung the backs of my eyes.

I lowered my head and tried to mentally tie a tourniquet around my hemorrhaging emotions. Mika eased up beside me and pulled me into his beefy arms as if determined to break me wide open.

I was too raw and exposed. I couldn't hold back the tide rising inside me.

My confidence crumbled; my resolve disintegrated.

The accumulation of guilt, stress, fear, and anxiety that had been compounding day after day became too great for me to contain. I could feel the walls inside me begin to bow and give way. Tears poured down my cheeks. As my body shook, mournful wails tore from my throat.

As I came apart at the seams, Mika held me in his arms and murmured softly. He was more than the owner of Genesis—he was the only man I truly trusted. He'd seen me at my best and at my worst—though never breaking down like I was now. I was confident that Mika would guard my weaknesses like he always did my strengths.

Slowly my tears began to wane and gut-churning embarrassment invaded my cells. I leaned back and tried to break free of his hold, but Mika held me in place.

"Easy," he whispered. "Relax. You're safe, Sasha. Go on…let the worry bleed itself out."

"It's not worry." I sniffed. "It's humiliation."

"Whatever you want to call it…let is pass. Give it a minute or two."

"I doubt it," I sighed sadly.

"I've never seen you like this before."

I frowned. "Because it's never been this bad before."

"Why didn't you come to me before this got so out of hand?"

"I thought I could handle it...well, until this morning, anyway."

"What happened this—"

"It's not important. Let's just say my cake is teeming with frosting right now and I need the motherfucker sliced open in ways I can't put into words."

"I'll take care of it."

"Give me a break. There isn't a Dom here tonight who can take me where I need to go."

"I can." A tender smile tugged the edges of his mouth.

"No. I won't put you in that position."

"It's not up to you, girl." Though the warning in his tone had sufficed just fine, Mika arched his brows to drive home his point, anyway.

A sense of foreboding crawled up my back. The man hadn't scened with any sub since he and Julianna hooked up a couple of years ago. If he paraded me through the dungeon and cuffed me to a cross, not only would it crush her, I'd be even more ostracized by the members.

"You can't force me to scene with you, and we both know it."

"I'd never try...we both know that, too."

"Mika. Think about it...Julianna is really pregnant. Her hormones have got to be doing back flips and somersaults. You scene with me, and it'll piss her off so much she'll probably kill me...after she cuts off your dick with a rusty razor blade. I might not show it, but I respect her and the relationship you two share too much to agree to such a thing. Got it?"

With a heavy sigh, Mika released me. He meandered to the wall of windows and stared out to the dungeon below. After several long seconds, he turned his head and studied the monitors across the room. Curious, I looked at the image of Cane. He was sitting on the bed in his private room, talking on the phone. Though the feed was silent, a wide grin lit up his face and his shoulders shook. I could only imagine how his deep, rich voice would sound when he let out a belly laugh. Longing heated my veins.

Don't even think about it. You tried to wriggle between the lines of that contract, and Cane busted you, like the DEA taking down a crack house. There won't be any second chances with that man. You might as well buckup, cupcake, and move along to plan...

Dammit! I didn't have another plan beside the one I was trying to finagle with Mika. But it had backfired on me as well.

He glanced over his shoulder at me and nodded. "Go wait for me at the bar. I'll see if I can find a Dom to work things out of you. Do you consent to whomever I choose?"

"Yes. I trust your judgment. Is there someone you have in mind?"

A part of me wished it would be Cane.

Whoa, damn…you are *a masochist, aren't you? After the way you treated him, that man wouldn't lower himself to swing a paddle anywhere near you…ever. You'd have a better chance asking Masters Sam, Tony, Ian, or James to whip your ass. Hell, even fuck-face Kerr would do it if you could stomach him. Too bad he's banned from the club and running from the law.*

"Possibly Drake," Mika answered. "He's still administering Trevor's after care."

Equal parts exhilaration and gratitude lit up inside me like rays of sunshine. I could barely keep from jumping up and down.

"Thank you, Mika…thank you so much." I hugged him, hard, and kissed his cheek.

"Don't get your hopes up too high, girl. I said *possibly*…that's not a guarantee he'll be willing to help you. He's as fond of your sassy mouth as the rest of the Doms."

"I know, but a *maybe* is light-years more than I had walking into the club."

"Go get something to drink. I'll join you shortly."

"Yes, Sir. Thank you."

I dropped another kiss to his cheek and hurried back down the stairs. As I made my way past Cane's room…or more importantly, his closed door, a stab of regret pierced my stubborn pride.

CHAPTER SIX

I'D BEEN SITTING at the bar less than an hour before Mika pulled out the barstool beside me, and sat down.

"We're going to do this in private."

"Why? Mika, if Drake didn't want—"

"Are you withdrawing your consent?"

"Of course not. I just don't—"

"Good. Then don't say another word until I give you permission to speak."

I begrudgingly stood and followed him out of the dungeon. As we made our way down the hall, I realized that I'd trusted Mika enough to ask for his help, I now had to extend that same trust that him working me wouldn't drive a wedge between him and Julianna. When he stopped at Drake's room and unlocked the door, relief swept through me, but my respite was short-lived. There was no sign of Drake or Trevor.

I opened my mouth to question Mika, but he simply placed his fingers over my lips and shook his head. "I haven't given you permission to speak, girl. Strip and step up to the cross."

With a timid nod, I began to undress while Mika selected several toys from a massive wooden armoire across the room. Naked, I waited at the wooden structure. He moved in behind me and slid a blindfold over my eyes. I was plunged into total darkness. My anticipation spiked. So did my other senses. The glossy varnish on the cross was cool, incongruent with Mika's heated breath that wafted along the side of my neck.

"Empty your mind." His voice was low, firm, and reassuring. "No thinking. No talking. Focus on the sensations, girl. The only word I want to hear you utter is *red*. That is your safe word and I expect you to use it if you need to. Nod if you understand my instructions and consent to this session."

Oh, hell yes!

I nodded and jolted slightly as Mika slid a set of earbuds in place.

"I am going to warm you up fast and set you on fire…hard. Are you ready to begin?"

Vigorously nodding, I jumped slightly as the thump of drums and an erotic melody poured through my ears. The heat of Mika's body warmed my naked flesh as he wrapped my wrists and ankles in heavy fleece-lined cuffs. When he stepped away, the cool air chilled my arms and legs.

The endless months of waiting to banish my chaos were over. I held my breath, eager and expectant for that first burst of pain to ignite my nerve endings. But all I sensed was emptiness around me. The seconds dragged on like hours. Where was Mika and what was taking him so long? Had he changed his mind…had second thoughts?

Tension climbed up my back and crawled across my shoulders while the music's increasing tempo strummed loudly.

Suddenly, Mika gripped a warm, wide hand around my nape. I clung to the lifeline he offered while he massaged my tension away. He then dragged two strong fingers down the length of my spine and I exhaled a sigh of relief. I was safe under his masterful care and melted against the cool, glossy frame.

A thick leather flogger landed with a heavy thud, and the force rocked me onto my toes. I sucked in a startled gasp, arched my ass out—in a silent plea for more—as the concussion reverberated all the way to my bones. Mika obliged and unleashed a volley of sweet, stinging blows. When he slung what felt like a wide paddle across my enflamed flesh, that elusive pain I'd craved burned my skin and started singing to the turmoil swirling within. Exhaling a low hiss, I savored the throbbing heat that spread up my back and down my legs. As Mika had promised, he didn't waste time with a slow buildup. Each brutal slap he delivered sent me free-falling deeper and deeper into the fiery and idyllic agony.

Time ceased to exist…space was nothing more than a concept.

My world narrowed, defined by the cross supporting my body and the intensity of each ruthless blow.

A powerful crack tore a gash in the music oscillating in my ears. Though my thoughts were sluggish, I knew Mika was warming up the whip. An appreciative moan fluttered from my lips. Landing the tip with several gentle strokes, Mika was purposely taunting me with its timid kisses. He knew what I needed, what I wanted, but was clearly determined to force me to wait. Frustration warred with patience, and I bit my lips together to keep from growling out the order for him to hit me harder. I mentally counted the wisps of air that brushed across my throbbing flesh: one….two…three…four, followed by a snap. A tiny pinpoint of pain seared my skin, then another, and another.

By the time Mika began directing the length of the popper across my flesh, leaving blistering welts in its wake, endorphins and dopamine had begun spilling into my brain. A slow, rolling tide of peace descended over me. Each strike severed the web of chaos strung through me. They dissolved like smoke on the wind.

Enveloped in the gray and silent static of my mind's eye, I floated toward a tiny pinpoint of light, far away in the distance. Though Mika's rhythmic blows were still laced with agony, all outward sensation dulled and numbed. I'd never experienced such an all-encompassing state of suspended ecstasy before. The euphoria that consumed me was so staggering I never wanted to leave it.

As I floated in my newfound serenity, fragmented perceptions leapt to the surface, then ebbed away. Flashes of Mika tipping a bottle of water to my lips, draping a blanket around me and hoisting me into his arms registered on some disjointed level of consciousness.

I briefly surged through the delirium to find the blindfold remained in place, and the music, though softer now, still hummed in my ears. Lying on a pillow of softness and cradled against Mika's sweltering chest, I silently nuzzled him in gratitude before floating away to savor the buoyant paradise once again.

The next time I dragged my heavy eyelids open, the blindfold and earbuds had been removed. The room was bathed in a pale yellow hue from the partially closed bathroom door. Mika sat in a chair beside the bed, wearing a tender smile. Lifting the corners of my mouth, I returned his smile as I slowly climbed the lethargy that weighed me down. With a sated sigh, I basked in the throbbing blaze of my ass cheeks and the heated body behind me.

Behind me? But Mika was sitting… Wait. Something was wrong. Very wrong. Confusion sliced through the intoxicating fog filling my brain.

I glanced down at the muscular, sun-kissed arms wrapped around my naked body, expecting to see Drake's colorful tattoos, but they weren't there. What happened to his ink?

That isn't Drake.

Suddenly the familiar masculine scent surrounding me made my liquid muscles tense. Buckets of adrenaline dumped within and poured through me. The intoxicating clouds of rapture turned dark and stormy. The realization that Cane, not Mika, had performed the scene slammed the air from my lungs and I was suffocating on the panic careening through me. My heart hammered against my ribs and my body began to shake uncontrollably. I thrashed for freedom, but instead of releasing me, Cane simply cinched me tighter in his arms.

"Mika?" I choked out in fear.

"Easy, sweetheart. You gave me consent to help you, and that's what I did."

His calm and even timbre was meant to soothe, but it didn't. I still couldn't breathe. Struggling to inhale, I felt as if I were sucking sand. Though a part of my brain grasped the understanding that Cane had been responsible for sailing me higher and harder than any other Dom, confusion and embarrassment continued their urgent stampede. I'd humiliated myself with the man, yet he'd given me exactly what I'd needed. Why?

"You're safe. Breathe. I've been with you the whole time," Mika continued. "I'm not going anywhere until you ride those endorphins back down. I promise."

Endorphins? The shock of finding myself wrapped in Cane's steely grasp had blown any remaining endorphins clean out of my system. My body was still trembling of its own volition as the floodgates opened and a torrent of shame burst free. Had he agreed to beat me in retribution because of my snarky attitude earlier? No. There wasn't a trace of malice in his strokes. Nothing made sense.

Twisting in his arms, I turned my head and peered over my shoulder. "Why?"

"Why what, princess?"

Too confused to cringe at his pet name, I swallowed and worked to align a coherent sentence. "Why did you scene with me after the way I behaved?"

Cane softly chuckled. "Because I heard your cry for help…loud and clear. You needed the release."

Yes, but not the shock that was still quaking through me.

"Lie back and try to relax. We didn't mean to intentionally yank you out of subspace like this," Cane murmured in my ear.

Lowering my head back to the pillow, I savored the sublime burn that throbbed on my ass. It would be so easy to grow addicted to the glorious agony he'd inflicted.

"No. We didn't," Mika reassured. "Let me get you some more water."

With a nod, I tried to calm my riotous emotions as Mika retrieved a bottle of water from the small refrigerator near the bed. As he shut the tiny door, my purse that had been sitting atop the appliance tumbled to the floor. I watched in horror as the contents, most importantly—Cane's contract—spilled out over the carpet.

Mika peeled his focus from the folder and darted a quizzical glance my way. Suffused in guilt, I closed my eyes and exhaled a heavy sigh. Cane quickly released my body, and I felt him sit up beside me on the bed.

"Destiny," Mika prompted. "Look at me."

God, this can't be happening...not now!

But it was.

Lifting my eyelids, I saw Mika had the folder open and was scanning the lists I'd made. Anger, or maybe it was disappointment, lined his face before he turned and pinned me with a look of pity that made me want to crawl into the corner. He had every right to be angry. I'd drawn him into my web of deceit. If I had just sucked it up and suffered two more weeks of hell instead of forcing a scene under false pretenses, none of this would be happening now.

No. The only reason you're in deep shit is because they know you waltzed into the club with a premeditated agenda.

With a shake of his head, Mika closed the folder and handed it to Cane. "I believe this is yours."

Scowling, Cane perused the papers, then turned toward me and arched a brow. "I wasn't expecting this. You're certainly full of surprises, princess," he stated, incredulously. "Mika, would you mind giving us a few minutes alone? I need to talk to this girl."

"You can talk as long as you'd like, my friend. But I'll remain in the room."

A flicker of insult crested over Cane's face before he dragged his stare off me and gave Mika a brittle smile. "I don't intend to hurt her."

"I didn't suspect you would. The reason I'm staying is because I'm responsible for the unclaimed subs, bottoms, and masochists of the club. Besides, I'm curious what Destiny has to say for her actions. Rest assured, if you decide to accept her signature, after this deception, you alone will determine her punishment."

Punishment?

"Wait a minute. I wasn't trying to deceiv—"

"Silence," Cane barked. "You'll have the chance to state your case when I'm done asking questions." A devious smile tugged his lips as he stood and pointed to the floor. "On your knees. And this time, you'll stow your recalcitrant attitude away. Since you manipulated us and got what you wanted, I think you owe Master Mika and me that courtesy, don't you?"

I fucking hated his obnoxious, condescending tone.

"Yes. At the very least, she owes us both that respect and courtesy." Mika glared as he folded his arms over his chest. Nope, he was not a happy camper.

Shit!

I huffed out a sigh and stood. "If you'd let me expl—"

"Ball gags are in the top drawer," Mika said dispassionately as he jerked his head toward the armoire.

Cane chuckled. "Thank you. It might very well come to that."

Great. Now they were tag-teaming me. What happened to the good-Dom/bad-Dom routine?

Pressing my lips together to keep from spouting off something I'd regret, I knelt at his feet. Since I'd been yanked out of my euphoria so quickly: the smoky sweet fog of calmness was gone. Instead of lowering my eyes like a submissive would, I stared straight ahead. Cane bent and cupped my chin. He forced my gaze, a cocky smile playing over his lips.

"Though you've stated you're not a sub, which remains to be seen, you will present yourself to me in a proper submissive pose for the duration of this…interrogation. You do know the correct posture to present a Dominant, don't you, princess?"

I've only been a member of this club for years. Of course, I do, asshole!

As I bit back my caustic reply, Cane squatted in front of me. He held me prisoner with a decisive golden gaze and released my chin.

I thrust my shoulders back, placed my hands, palms up on my thighs, and spread my legs wide. I flashed him a saucy smile that screamed: *voila* and lowered my gaze to the carpet.

The defiant woman inside me howled with rage.

"You're quite a lovely picture in all your submissive glory. Pity the same pride and beauty aren't in your heart," Cane admonished. "If you weren't so busy trying to manipulate me, you could spend time exploring the other needs besides pain that are screaming to be free inside you."

Part of me wanted to argue. I knew exactly who and what I was…a pain-slut. And I wanted to experience the splendor he wielded, again and again.

Right! The only way you'll accomplish that is to start eating crow…fucking feathers and all.

"Let's start at the beginning, shall we?" His arrogant tone raked my flesh like razor blades. "You had sex with Law after you read my contract, is that correct?"

"Yes."

"Oh, princess." He scoffed on a humorless laugh. "You'll answer my questions in the proper manner. Let's try this again. You fucked Law after reading my contract, correct?"

"Yes, Sir," I bit out between clenched teeth.

"I assume that was because you couldn't wait two more weeks to have sex, like you couldn't wait two more weeks to have your ass beat. Correct?"

"Yes, Sir."

"You're either lying to me or yourself. It wasn't because you *couldn't* wait, princess. You simply *chose* not to."

I mulishly pinched my lips together.

"Did you sign my contract before Law shoved his dick inside you?"

"No, Sir."

"You obviously made a conscious decision to accept my proposal. Was it *before* or *after* Law rutted all over you?"

Was he jealous?

"It wasn't like that. I—"

"Yes or no."

"If you'd just let me—"

My words were cut short as Cane gripped my hair and jerked my head back. He leaned in closer, caressing the contours of my face with a penetrating gaze. His lips were but a fraction of an inch from mine, and his hot breath spilled over my mouth, sinful and inviting. I ached to find out if his kiss would be fierce and demanding or soft and toe-curling.

"Answer me, princess." His whisper was so beguiling I wanted to press my lips to his and surrender my very soul. But Cane's redemption wouldn't be found in a kiss, or any other way. The man had backed me into a corner and there was only one way out.

The truth shall set you free.

Not this time, I thought with an internal scoff. I was fucked.

"After," I mumbled. "I needed to scratch an—"

Cane cut off my words with a raw and feral kiss. He didn't wait for me to open my mouth and welcome him, but thrust his tongue past the seam and delved deep.

Claiming.

Owning.

Demanding.

The silky heat of his tongue melted through me. The passion and strength rolling off him made my head spin. Every cell in my body sang with need. Helplessly falling into an unfamiliar chasm, I gripped his wide shoulders, seeking an anchor to keep me from sliding away. The minute my hands touched his body, Cane pulled away from the kiss.

"I could have scratched that itch for you, beautiful. In fact, we could have shared incredible sex," he taunted in a deep, raspy tone.

If his kiss was any indication of his bedroom skills, incredible sex was a gross understatement. My lips were still tingling, my thoughts jumbled and fuzzy when Cane released my hair, and stood. I closed my eyes and hung my head as a mournful whimper seeped out.

Regret thrummed through my veins.

Again, it was time to pick myself up, dust off the dirt—like I'd done with every Dom who'd tossed me away. It mattered little that I was the one who'd fucked up this time. I had a right to be selfish, dammit! I'd *needed* to get laid and beaten.

Cane cleared his throat. "Let's carry on."

Why? What was the point of prolonging the inevitable?

Because, he's a Sadist and probably enjoys watching you squirm.

No doubt.

"The picture is becoming increasingly clearer by the second. Though you'd signed my contract, you came to the club with the intent to skirt my rules, like you did with Law, because you *couldn't* wait to have your ass laid open. But in order to get what you wanted, you had to drag Mika into your little scheme."

I swallowed tightly. Cane made it all sound so…evil.

Um…it was?

"I know this looks…"

"Bad?" Mika offered with an angry expression. "Yes, and then some."

"How did you plan to hide the welts if I hadn't been the one to paint them on your sexy little ass?" Cane asked.

"I knew they'd heal during your two-week moratorium, Sir."

"Though I had no intention to scene or fuck you, I planned to keep you naked as much as I could."

And do what…simply stare at me? Instead of asking, I let the question simmer on the tip of my tongue.

"Explain something to me, Destiny. *Why* did you sign my contract when you knew I didn't tolerate liars, brats, or drama queens?"

"I needed what you were offering, Sir."

"That's blatantly obvious. No doubt you've grown so accustomed to Topping from the bottom that it's become second nature to you. I think deep down you ache to conform to my rules, but you can't get out of your own way. You lack patience and the ability to control your temper, feelings, mouth, and actions. You have no idea how to hand over your power. Instead, you play games and test every Dom to determine if he's strong enough to handle you. While you're beyond desperate for someone to put you in your place, you fear you'll never find him. Trust me. You won't until you stop being so scared shitless to release the death grip you have on your control."

Tears stung the backs of my eyes. Cane had read me like a fucking book, and that was ten times more terrifying than letting go of my control.

"One more question. Was picking a fight with me tonight part of your plan or simply one of your own *tests*?"

"I never intended to argue with you, Sir."

My face burned with shame.

Cane pursed his lips. A contemplative expression lined his face as he intently studied me for long, uncomfortable minutes.

"I don't like my Dominance being questioned, and I especially hate being manipulated." Cane scowled. "While I applaud your honesty, my trust is going to be hard-won. I suspect you've never been trained properly, only sated. Convince me why I should give you a second chance...something other than your need for pain."

A flicker of hope sliced through my despair. I hadn't had to sell myself since I'd applied for my first small business loan. Based on the weight of Cane's stare, I knew I'd have to do a lot more than pass out a ton of spreadsheets and flutter my eyelashes.

I licked my lips, inhaled a deep breath, and squirmed slightly. "A lot of what you've said is true. I haven't been formally trained, but that's because I have no desire to be a sub. I'm strong-willed, and it rubs me the wrong way to kneel before any man."

"Yet here you are," Cane stated with a knowing smirk.

"Yes. Out of respect to you, Sir."

"Respect? What made you decide to show me respect now?"

"Because you helped me achieve the peace I needed."

At least until now.

"You've been a member of this club for years...but you still haven't figured it out yet, have you?" Cane shook his head. "Go on."

"I know my reputation here is...awful, but that's because I don't put on airs and try to conform to what others think I should be."

"So you're naturally rebellious, is that what you're saying?"

"No. I'm saying I don't fit the normal mold around here, nor do I want to."

"Why not?"

"Because I've worked too long and too hard establishing myself as a business leader. I don't want anything or anyone diminishing what I've achieved."

"Your company does not define you. Your strong will and perseverance are the reason you've achieved your professional goals, but every successful entrepreneur has to learn how to balance their needs and wants, or crumble."

"I balance those pressures here at the club."

"No. You're not balancing anything. You're simply using Doms and pain as a coping mechanism to escape."

Well, that wasn't breaking news. Every Dom I'd ever scened with knew it was how I purged my stress. I shrugged my shoulders in a silent *no duh*.

"The power exchange isn't a thing to be played with or taken lightly. If you want to experience the level of freedom you seek, you have to open your mind, heart, and soul. And above all, you have to stop manipulating those who try to help you. Topping from the bottom will get you nothing...at least not from me."

His words rolled around in my head while I tried to control my anger. I'd repeatedly explained to the man that I wasn't a sub, yet Cane seemed to expect me to become one. Did he truly want to me to start at ground zero? To achieve the status of submissive—one I didn't even want—instead of simply whipping my stress away?

Stop kidding yourself. You've always wanted to be a part of the submissive clique. Not belonging is what has pissed you off so badly. You won't even try because you're too scared they'll reject you even more.

And they would. That gut-wrenching truth sent a chill through me.

Cane laid the folder on my open palms. "I'll give you a second chance, princess. But if you attempt to manipulate me or my rules again, I'll rip that contract to shreds. Do I make myself clear?"

"Yes, Sir," I murmured.

Understanding the depth of Cane's expectations made the flimsy document on my lap feel as if it weighed a ton.

I'd foolishly assumed the cost to reap his pain would be sex. But Cane wanted far more than my body...he wanted my soul. Suddenly, I questioned whether or not I could obey his demands. No Dom had ever placed such stringent restrictions on me before.

What if I allowed him to peel away my walls, and he didn't like what he found...what if *I* didn't like who I saw? What if the self-assurance I projected was nothing more than a lie? I'd have no thread of identity left. What then?

A tsunami of panic rose up inside me. The urge to race from the room rode me hard, but in the back of my mind...I knew I'd only be running from myself. There was no easy escape this time.

A tear spilled free. Cane leaned in and sipped the salty drop from my cheek.

"Why are you crying, Destiny?" His warm and inviting question felt like the summer sun...the total opposite of his usual daunting command.

"I'm scared." The confession was but a whisper.

"I know you are. But will you cower to your fears or conquer them?" He bent in close to my ear. "Every day, headstrong and successful women fall to their knees and serve without sacrificing their principles. You're doing that right now. Do you feel any less capable than you did two hours ago?"

"No, Sir."

But I wasn't giving him my power, simply enduring his interrogation and lecture. It was an altogether different and dangerous matter to kneel and surrender to Cane.

"For all you *think* you know, princess…school is just starting." Cane glanced down at the folder and smiled. "You have sixteen hours left to decide what you're going to do with that. Examine your heart, Sasha, and choose wisely."

Without another word, he jerked a nod at Mika and walked out the door.

I dropped my head and stared at the folder, weighing the implications of its contents far more diligently than the first time. Though the rebellious parts of me wanted to deny it, Cane's perceptions of me were balls-on accurate.

The toes of Mika's shoes appeared in my peripheral vision. I closed my eyes and drew in a deep breath before lifting my head and meeting his stormy expression.

"I'm sorry."

"I am, too. I trusted you, girl. I've watched you manipulate and Top from the bottom with Doms over and over again. I never expected you to pull the same maneuver on me. All these years, I adopted a lenient approach with you in hopes that one day you'd finally come around. I guess I was wrong."

Each bitter word Mika uttered drove the blade of my betrayal deeper, twisting and carving a massive hole in my soul. I'd been so focused on my own selfish needs that I hadn't considered the ramifications of my actions. At least not the potential damage I could do to Mika and our friendship.

I felt like the most self-serving bitch on the planet. I probably was.

"You weren't wrong, Mika. I was. Instead of gratefully accepting Cane's contract and drowning you in gratitude, I let my greed take over." My voice cracked, but I swallowed down my heartache. "All that accomplished was to ruin our friendship. I really *am* sorry."

Mika knelt down in front of me and cupped my face. Tilting my head back, he wore a grim expression as he placed his hand on the folder. "Then fix it, but most of all, fix you."

"He wants to turn me into a sub."

"You're already a sub…a colossally bratty one, but you *are* a fucking sub."

My jaw dropped open in shock.

"Don't look so surprised, girl. You know it's true. It's time you stop lying to yourself and decide if you're going to continue to stick your head in the sand or work through your fears and accept who and what you are."

"I thought I'd already done that."

"You haven't even started to unearth the real you yet."

Nor did I want to. That was one of my biggest fears…discovering the *real* me.

"Cane will help you far more than me or any of the Doms here. The second chance he's giving you is one hell of a gift. Don't take his offer lightly," Mika warned. "I guess the million-dollar question is…will you let him?"

"I don't know yet."

Mika scoffed. "I find it hard to believe that a smart, successful woman like you would turn down an offer to fulfill all your desires."

"It's not all about fulfilling my desires, it's about the toll it might take on my psyche. There's no guarantee that I'll ever find the place that I belong."

"No, but you'll never find your place if you refuse to try." He sent me a sad smile. "What do you truly have to lose?"

"My identity."

"Ah," Mika nodded. "Once upon a time, Julianna was scared of that very thing. Since becoming my slave, she's more confident and headstrong than ever before."

"But…doesn't that create more friction between you two?"

A slow smile tugged his lips. "Why…because she's feisty, mouthy, and from time to time, a redheaded ball of fury? Trust me, girl. I wouldn't want her any other way."

"Can I ask you something?"

"Of course."

"Why did you set me up like that with Cane?"

"I didn't *set you up*. I found a Dom who could give you exactly what you needed, with your full consent. I even asked if you wanted to rescind your permission."

He had, but it still felt as if he'd pulled a fast one.

"Like Cane said, you needed it," Mika added with a knowing smirk.

Yes, and it had been the most glorious experience of my life, until…

"Now I need to decide what I'm going to do, and I only have sixteen more hours to make up my mind." I briefly lowered my eyes. The contract all but singed my palms.

A thoughtful expression tugged his brows. "Maurizio's tomorrow…noon. Julianna will meet you there. Talk to her… Let her explain how her fears were put to rest."

I nodded. "I'll be there."

"Sir."

"I'll be there, Sir."

His smile widened as he leaned in and kissed my forehead. "Put your clothes on. Then go home and get some sleep. You're probably going to be blindsided with major sub-drop. Prepare yourself for it, girl, and I expect you to call me if you can't handle it. Understood?"

"Yes, Sir."

"Let me know when you've reached a decision. I'll apprise Cane of whatever choice you make."

"Thank you, Mika."

He nodded once and then left the room.

Clutching the folder, I closed my eyes and exhaled a worried sigh. The burning ache on my backside beckoned me to ride the clouds as they filtered through me once more. Instead, I stood and began to dress. The fire blazed and screamed through my tissue when I began dragging on my pencil skirt. Lowering the garment, I crossed the room and entered the bathroom. Turning, I admired the aftermath of Cane's lashes in the mirror.

"What the fuck?" I gasped in disbelief.

It was no surprise that Cane had marked me…marked me in beautiful, angry red stripes. My shock was born from the skill he possessed to etch the word M-I-N-E into my flesh.

Mine.

Reaching behind me, I gently traced my fingertips over each welted letter. Was his message an invitation, a hope, or did he already think of me as his? Equal parts optimism and terror clawed up my spine.

Every day, headstrong and successful women fall to their knees and serve without sacrificing their principles. His words echoed in my mind. Mika's followed closely behind. *You'll never find your place if you refuse to try.*

Though I couldn't afford to be tired and confront Law in the morning, I knew Cane and Mika's phrases would haunt me all night as I wrangled with my decision. If I had any hope of finding sleep, I needed to leave.

When I finished putting on my clothes, I tucked the contract back in my purse and stepped out of Drake's private room. The hallway was empty except for the soothing sounds of play coming from the dungeon. I could be cuffed to a cross or bound to a spanking bench every night instead of sitting at the bar pouting if I had the guts.

Sucking in a deep breath, I squared my shoulders and headed out the back door. The winter wind nearly stole my breath as I raced to my car. As the engine idled, the defrosters worked at melting the faint glaze covering the windshield. I closed my eyes and let my head loll against the headrest as my mind raced.

The cacophony of breaking glass caused me to jolt upright. A car alarm began to bleat. In tandem, taillights lit up the night in a red ominous strobe from a car a few rows in front of me. Instinctively, I gripped the steering wheel as a shadowy figure, hunched over and dressed in black, darted away from the vehicle. Unfortunately I couldn't see the person's face, only their retreating form. I grabbed my purse and whipped out my cell phone. With shaking fingers, I selected Mika's number and waited.

"Mika."

"It's me, Sasha. I'm in the parking lot and I think someone just tried to steal one of the members' cars. I heard glass breaking and now an—"

"Get inside your car and lock the doors. I'm on my way."

Before I could tell him I already was, Mika hung up.

CHAPTER SEVEN

SECONDS LATER, THE back door swung open. Mika and three black-T-shirt-clad DMs came running down the steps. Right on their heels were several Doms. My heart leapt when Cane raced out into the bitter night as well. My gaze was locked on the man until I heard Mika shout for someone to go back inside and find Sir Justice.

A sick feeling rolled in the pit of my stomach. Rumor had it that Symoné, Sir Justice's new sub, had endured physical and mental abuse at the hands of banned club member Kerr.

I didn't know if he was the figure I'd seen running away or not. Hell, I couldn't tell if it was a man or a woman. The one lone streetlight on the other side of the parking lot didn't give off enough illumination for me to glimpse the person's face. Surely Kerr wouldn't be stupid enough to return to the club. Not while Chicago PD had a warrant out for the prick's arrest. And especially not after Mika had pulled a gun on Kerr when he'd tried to kidnap Symoné from in front of the club a few months ago.

Filled with worry, I threw open my door and stepped out of the car.

"He ran that way." I pointed toward the inky darkness.

"Get inside and lock your doors," Mika barked.

"You're welcome," I mumbled under my breath before I eased to the seat and followed his orders.

I knew he was trying to keep me safe, but he didn't have to bite my head off. On the other hand, I was lucky he was even talking to me after the stunt I'd pulled earlier. Tendrils of guilt swept through my veins. When Cane made his way toward my car, that same shame became a bubbling brook, tumbling over jagged rocks. As he approached the opposite side of my car, he bent and nodded at the empty passenger seat.

The smartass inside me wanted to crack the window and tell him Mika had ordered me to keep the doors locked. But I'd provoked Cane's wrath enough for one night. I pressed the button and disengaged the locks. The gorgeous, intimidating climbed into the seat beside me. As soon as he closed the passenger-side door, he engaged the locks again.

"Did you walk to your car alone?"

"Yes. I always do."

"Next time, please ask someone to escort you."

Though he'd included the word *please*, his tone made it clear it wasn't a request but rather a demand. Hackles raised, knee jerking and jaw opening, I quickly snapped my teeth together and pushed my irritation down.

"Yes, Sir."

A soft smile bloomed on his lips. Even in the darkness, his gold eyes sparkled. "What did you see?"

"Just a dark-clad figure, hunched over, running away."

Peeling my gaze from him, I peered out the windshield. Justice was looking over his shoulder as he bound down the metal stairs. When he reached the bottom, he gestured for his sub, Symoné, to go back inside. She defiantly shook her head, but the look of panic was visible to all. Standing at the top of the stairs, she wrapped her arms around her waist as if to hold in her fears. DM Master Ink stood beside her. He puffed out his chest, clenched his fists, and wore a glower that promised instant death to anyone who tried to attack Symoné.

Justice gave the man a silent nod of thanks before racing toward Mika and the others gathered around the car. Justice reached into his pocket and pulled out a fob that silenced the screaming horn and flashing lights.

"Is the club always this…active?" Cane asked. "Subs nearly going into labor and vandal's breaking out car windows, and—"

"And a pain-in-the-ass, greedy masochist so selfish that she screwed up big-time?" My semi-confession was teemed in apology. "No. It's usually quiet, well, except for the screaming subs."

He chuckled softly. "I like this humble side of you, princess."

He reached out and gently brushed the hair from my cheek. It was all I could do to keep from nuzzling against his fingers. I liked the warmer, less intimidating side of him as well.

"This is my mea culpa mood. It oozes out when I really screw up."

He softly chuckled, then sobered and studied the contours of my face. "I'm giving you the chance to redeem yourself."

"Yes, and I failed to thank you for that, Sir."

"Appreciation accepted." He reached down and threaded his fingers through mine. Heat enveloped my entire arm. "I won't apologize for being brutally honest with you earlier. I expect the same level of communication to flow both ways if you decide to accept my offer."

"You don't apologize for much, do you?" I smirked.

"No. And I'm not about to apologize for this."

He snaked his hand around my nape and pulled me against his lips. Unlike the previous kiss, this one was a benevolent caress that told me there was a whole lot more to this man than an intimidating Sadist. Cane took his time exploring my mouth, nibbling at the corners before laving his tongue over my lips. The man was a paradox, complicated and confusing. One minute he was as venomous as a snake, threatening to strike without warning. Then the next, he was warm and erotically charming, like now. His touch was so tender a hunger swelled inside me like a living, breathing entity all its own. My folds softened. My nipples grew tight, and my clit throbbed in need. Lost in the ache to indulge the sexual call he stirred inside me, I was powerless to stop myself from moaning and melting against his lips. He tasted like danger and sin, and I wanted nothing more than to gorge on him.

As he trailed fervent kisses along my jaw and down my neck, laving and nipping a trail of decadence, I desperately wished we were back in Drake's bed, where I could surrender to Cane's every desire.

A light tap on my window caused me to jerk away from his mouth. Before I could turn to see who was at my car, Cane hauled me back with a growl. He claimed my lips with a feral, chastising kiss. When he released me, his eyes were hooded and glowing with desire, a look that made him all the more sexy and alluring.

"Now you may find out what Mika wants." His voice was raspy and hoarse.

Mika? Oh, right...he must be the one outside my car. I tried to power the window down but was so discombobulated that I hit the lock button instead. Without me touching the handle, the door swung open. Mika bent down and peered into the car. A knowing smirk tugged his lips before he sobered and scowled.

"Were you able to get a look at the fuck-nut who broke the window of Justice's car?"

"No. I couldn't see his face. He was hunched over and running away."

"Fuck!" Mika scrubbed a hand through his hair. "I'll call upstairs and see if Bent-Lee can see anything on the video feed from the parking lot."

"Do you think Kerr's come back?"

"Yes," Mika spat. "That chicken shit son of a bitch has crawled back out of his hole and is taunting us again."

An icy chill slid down my spine. Though I had always been leery of the man, I'd made the fatal mistake of accepting Kerr's invitation to play in the dungeon one night. Since he wasn't proficient in throwing a whip, he'd used every other implement of pain he could get his hands on. While he'd succeeded in giving me pain, I hadn't found an ounce of escape. The way he'd landed the blows felt as if my body was nothing more than a bulls-eye...a target he could vent his anger on.

"I need to get back. The cops are on their way. Be careful driving home, girl. Make sure no one is following you."

"I will. Sorry I couldn't be more help."

"You did fine." Mika directed his next comment to Cane. "I'll be in touch with you soon."

"The sooner the better," he replied. I closed my door as Mika left. Cane squeezed my hand. "You will be followed home tonight, princess."

"Huh?"

"Not Kerr. Me. I'm going to follow you home."

"You don't—"

"It wasn't an offer."

No. It was a damn order. I could fight him, like a spoiled brat, or graciously accept. Okay, maybe not graciously, but I could suck it up and not give him a reason to rip the contract up here and now.

"I want to make sure you arrive safely, Sasha."

"Yes, Sir."

He dragged a knuckle down my cheek and smiled. "What's your address?"

"I thought you'd done your homework on me?" I teased.

"I have, but I didn't dig so far as to violate *all* segments of your anonymity."

I rattled off my address before Cane opened the door and stepped from the car.

My lips were still tingling as I pulled out of the parking space. A dark-colored BMW sports car eased in behind me. Gripping the steering wheel, I sucked in a deep breath and headed for home. Though I had no intention of trying to lose him, I knew any attempt would be futile. Cane stuck like glue to the back of my bumper. When I turned into my subdivision, I grew anxious. Was he expecting me to invite him in for a drink, or would he think such an offer manipulation? I was in unfamiliar territory and wasn't sure how to proceed. The last thing I wanted to do was overstep my boundaries.

You don't have any boundaries. You signed the damn contract.

But I hadn't given it to him.

Twisting semantics had gotten me into my current mess. My signature *was* etched on the paper, and even though my intentions were as clear as mud to me at the moment, I had to walk a fine line or risk having my final decision taken away from me.

A nervous energy hummed through me as I pushed the garage door opener and eased inside. Cane pulled in behind me and stopped. I glanced up at my rearview mirror and watched as he climbed out of his car. Grabbing my purse, I met him in the garage. He briefly darted a glance around the sparse, uncluttered space. A few gardening tools clung to nails driven into the wall. I hadn't realized until now, my shears, trowel, and miniature hoe were hung up in the same fashion as the toys at the club. The knowing gleam in Cane's eyes told me the similarity hadn't gone unnoticed.

"Would you like to—"

"Go inside, change your clothes, and climb into bed, princess," he interrupted as he placed his hand on the roof of my car. The motion brought him inches from my face. The air around me was charged with his tempting masculine scent. "If you were mine, I'd remind you to keep your hands above the covers tonight, but…"

Mine.

"The message you left on my ass implies you already think I *am*."

A huge smile speared his lips and he started to laugh. His deep, rich, and inveigling timbre echoed off the walls of the garage and poured over me like sunshine and honey. Goose bumps erupted over my flesh, and I swallowed the moan bubbling up from the back of my throat.

"You saw that, did you? Good. I want you, Sasha...want you as mine." Cane leaned in and kissed me softly, but just as quickly he pulled away. As he walked to his car, he stopped and peered back at me. "I hope to hear from you soon."

He climbed back into his car and motioned for me to close the garage door. It was then that I realized I hadn't moved. I'd simply stood where he'd left me, frozen in place. Shaking away the sublime sensation of his mouth, I hurried toward the door leading to the kitchen and pushed the button, sending the garage door down.

As I set my purse on the kitchen table, a sense of rightness settled over me. The more time I spent with Cane, the more I realized he wasn't such a badass after all. He was much warmer and more caring than I'd first thought after reading his contract. He loved to wear a coat of intimidation that made butterflies swoop and dip in my belly, but maybe that wasn't such a bad thing. Hooking up with him would be an experience, that's for sure.

Kicking off my stilettos, I was making my way from the kitchen and into the family room when the doorbell rang. Frowning, I couldn't imagine what Cane might have forgotten or wanted to tell me. I flipped on the outside light and pulled the door open.

"Did you have a nice *date*?" Law was standing on my front porch.

A cry of surprise slid off my lips as an explosion of shock rent through me.

"What are you doing at my house?" I shrieked.

He held up a key and shook his head. "You really should hide this a bit better, Sasha. Everyone looks under the mat. If I weren't such a gentleman, I would have waltzed right in."

His patronizing tone had me ripping the locks off the cage holding my inner bitch.

"If you expect me to thank you for not invading my privacy, you're in for a long wait. *What* are you doing here?" I gritted out as I ripped the key from his fingers.

A brittle smile tugged his lips as he casually inched closer. His eyes were no longer sky blue, but a darkened, fiery indigo. "I was worried about you and wanted to come by and make sure you were safe. I guess you don't find Cane as *standoffish* as you protested, huh?"

"He's… That's none of your business."

"Did he show you a nice view of Navy Pier before he seduced you?"

Jealous much?

"As a matter of fact, he didn't."

"Didn't what? Try to seduce you?"

"No. Didn't show me a view of the pier. I think it would be best if you left now."

"I'm afraid I can't do that."

The hair on the back of my neck stood on end and a tremor of fear sputtered through me. Was Law like Kerr…a dangerous predator? Had he tracked me down to rape and kill me? Ice chugged through my veins. I wanted to slam the door in his face, but he was too close. All Law had to do was put a hand up and he'd block the move, then he'd be on me, like a lion taking down a gazelle. As my imagination spiraled out of control, panic enveloped me, and I wrapped my arms around my middle.

"Why not?" My voice trembled as fear pummeled me.

I obviously lacked a good poker face, because Law's smug demeanor vanished. His brows slashed before a look of shock stole over his face. "Give me a break, Sasha. I didn't come here to hurt you. You think I'm some kind of monster?"

Yes. No. Maybe.

While his assurance relived some of my anxiety, it didn't absolve him from showing up at my house, or interrogating me about Cane.

"I can't leave until I call another cab," he said with a shiver. "Do you mind if I come in?"

It suddenly dawned on me that he didn't have a car. "How long have you… Yes, of course. I'm sorry. Come in."

I stepped aside and pulled him into the house by the sleeve of his coat. His lips were purple. I inwardly cursed myself for failing to notice he'd turned into a meat Popsicle. I ushered him to the fireplace, lit the gas starter, and tossed on several logs.

"How long have you been standing outside?"

"Long enough that I can't feel my fingers," he replied with a crooked smile.

"*Why?*"

"I told you. I was worried about you." He shrugged off his coat and bent in close to the fire.

"Bullshit. You're trying to micromanage my life."

"No, but I am curious. You dumped me to be with Cane, didn't you?"

Only because I had to.

I lifted my chin. "I am *not* having this conversation with you, Law."

"Answer the question, Sasha."

"I don't owe you a damn thing, much less an explanation of what I do or who I do it with." I slapped my hands on my hips.

"So you *did* have sex with him."

"No!" I screeched before poking a finger to his wide chest. "Despite your sleazy opinion of me, I don't go hopping into bed with every man I meet. But even *if* I did, that's none of *your* business. *You* don't own me."

"Does Cane?"

Not yet, but he will soon.

Law didn't need to know that…ever. "*No one* owns me."

My claim seemed to punch the jealousy from his system.

He exhaled a heavy sigh and scrubbed a hand over his face. "Look, I'm sorry. I didn't mean to go crazy on you."

"Then why did you?"

"Because I think Cane's an over-possessive prick."

Look who's talking about over-possessive!

"Last night, every time I touched you, he looked at me like he wanted to kill me. I'd rather you not spend time with him. I'm worried about your safety."

"You don't get to make that choice, Law. I do."

He raised his palms in surrender. "I know… I know. You're a big girl, and you can make your own choices. It's just…I don't trust that fucker as far as I can throw him. If you plan to keep seeing him, be careful. I don't want to see you get hurt. All right?"

"First of all, Cane is not some crazed sociopath, and secondly, you're right…I am a big girl. I can take care of myself."

Law hesitated, then wrapped his icy hand around my wrist and lifted my finger from his chest to his lips. He brushed a soft kiss over the pad of my finger, sending heat to blossom between my legs.

"I know you think you're tough, but I know all about the soft, sweet side of you. You're the perfect blend of warrior and woman. I like that…like everything about you."

It was sweet that he wanted to worm his way back into my heart.

Heart nothing. He wants to lure you back into bed.

Staring into his baby blues wasn't helping dissuade me from that idea in the least. But I couldn't go down that rabbit hole, or we'd wind up destroying each other.

I needed to be tactful but honest…well, as honest as I could be.

"I like you, too, Law, but I'm still not going to bed with you again. It was a mistake."

"You might think it was a mistake, but you'll never convince me of that, sweetheart." I jerked my chin and opened my mouth to debate him, but Law simply placed a chilly finger over my lips. "I had the time of my life with you, Sasha. Let's just leave it at that, okay?"

As I stood drinking in the sight of his handsome face and rugged body, memories of how we'd been lost in passion…drowning in the upsurge of need and desire, and the spine-bending climaxes, unfurled in my head.

I nodded and bit back the urge to tell him I did, too.

It was unnerving to be attracted to two such potent, yet polar opposite men. They each captivated me for entirely different reasons. Fate hadn't dropped two *Dominant* men on my path but she was making it damn difficult to decide which one to choose.

Determined to take Cane up on his second chance, I savored the feel of Law's strong arms around me for the last time. I'd find a way to make peace with my decision…eventually. I tried to embrace the sadness settling in my soul and flashed him a sympathetic smile.

His gaze stilled on my lips. "I guess I need to call to the cab company," he murmured. "Oh, I almost forgot."

I watched as he picked up his coat and pulled out a manila folder and thrust it in my hand.

A feeling of déjà vu assailed me.

"I brought you the quotes from Jamison Plastics on the off chance you wanted to look them over before our conference call in the morning."

"Th-Thanks," I stammered. "I'll scope them over before I go to sleep."

"Great." An awkward silence slid between us. "I guess I'll go ahead and get out of your hair."

"Thank you for coming over to check on me, but next time…call first."

A crooked smile tugged a corner of his mouth. "I will, but find a better place to hide your key, or I won't wait patiently on your porch, but rather in your bed."

I quickly shoved away the images of his naked body and thick erection from my mind and swallowed tightly. While Law phoned a cab, I skimmed over the figures in the file. Waiting for his ride, I kept our discussion focused on business and not the ache throbbing inside me that urged me to invite him upstairs to my bedroom.

Don't be dumb. If Cane catches you in any more lies, he'll wipe his hands of you.

Law brushed a featherlight kiss across my lips when the cab arrived. As I watched him jog away, I bit back a forlorn cry.

You made your choice. Now live with it.

Oh, I'd be living with it, all right…every damn brutal day, right beside Law.

I groaned and inwardly told my well-meaning conscious to, *get fucked.*

THE NEXT MORNING when I arrived at the office, the sight of Law leaning over Amber's desk—sharing a flirtatious laugh—filled me with jealousy and anger. I inhaled a calming breath and struggled to align my chi, but the pink hue staining my assistant's cheeks made that almost impossible. Gripping my green-eyed monster in a chokehold, I tried to wrangle my irrational emotions.

"Are you ready to go over the Jamison quotes now, or do you need a few more minutes to seduce my assistant?" I regretted not only my choice of words but also my sharp tone of voice long before the question finished rolling off my tongue.

Amber gasped and her eyes grew wide.

The smirk that crawled over Law's lips screamed *gotcha.* It was all I could do not to bite his arrogant head off. He slid a tender smile back to Amber and winked. "We'll chat more at lunch if you're not too busy."

Prick.

Amber stammered something inaudible as her face turned bright red. She launched to her feet and hurried down the hall toward the break room.

"Retract your claws, Sasha. We were simply getting to know one another is all."

"Amber is in a relationship, a *serious* one, in case you weren't aware."

God, why couldn't I shut up?

A wide grin followed the knowing flicker in his eyes. "Thanks for the heads-up, but she already told me all about Ken."

"Good. Shall we get to work?"

As the morning bled closer to noon, Law hung up after coordinating the delivery of the new branding art to the plastics company. He stared at me for several long seconds before flashing me a hungry smile.

"I have to know. What color of sexy lingerie is under that power suit today?"

I glanced up at the clock. Julianna would soon be arriving at Maurizio's. I sent Law an arctic smile. "I have a lunch engagement. Be back in an hour."

"With Cane?" he asked flatly.

"No, a girlfriend of mine, not that it's any of your business." I stood and straightened my suit jacket. I wanted to tell him to try and keep his dick in his pants around Amber, but instead, I simply strolled out of the conference room.

As I drove toward the restaurant, I scoped out the numerous taxicabs around me. If given a chance, Law wouldn't be above following me. Though I believed him when he said he'd never hurt me, he was persistent enough to track me down for the way I'd dismissed him.

After finding an empty parking space, I grabbed my purse. The weight of Cane's contract felt like a ton of bricks, but I knew the heaviness would abate soon. When I stepped inside, I looked around but didn't see Julianna. Choosing a table near the rear of the restaurant, I'd no sooner sat down than the couple arrived.

Mika escorted Julianna to my table and helped her into the chair beside me. My hands trembled as I reached inside my bag and plucked out the folder. I sucked in a deep breath and handed the contract to Mika.

"Thank you, girl. Cane will be pleased."

Julianna flashed a huge smile.

"I'll leave you two to talk." Mika bent and kissed his girl, strode to the bar, and sat down.

"Are you okay? You're as white as a ghost," Julianna stated.

"Handing that contract over makes me feel like I've just seen one."

"It'll be fine. Master told me what happened last night. Just so you know, he's forgiven you. He knows how hard all this is for you, because he explained some of it to me. I hope you're not upset with him for doing that."

"Not at all. He's an amazing man, and I can't thank you enough for agreeing to talk to me. I've never told you, but I'm glad you two found each other."

"Thank you, Sasha. That means worlds to me." The smile that lit up her face settled me a bit. "I'll do all I can to try and help ease your fears. Believe it or not, I've been in your shoes. When I first met Mika, I was a hot mess. But taking a chance with him was the best decision I ever made. Maybe it will be for you, too."

"Not everyone is gifted the kind of relationship you and Mika share. Besides, Cane's not looking for happy ever after. He's only here for a short time. All I can hope for is some fulfillment and much needed peace."

"You never know…the short time you spend with him might be life-altering."

"Maybe. I'm just worried about…hell, I'm worried about a lot of things."

Julianna grinned. "Then toss them out. We'll sort through them and see if we can whip them into shape before they drive you crazy."

Apprehension fluttered in my belly. I only had one real friend, Amber. But I'd never shared my masochistic alter ego with her. I didn't want her thinking me a freak, or god forbid, saying something that would get back to my family.

We ordered lunch and sipped our drinks. Julianna stroked her massive belly and I suddenly remembered the hoopla at the club last night.

"Did Mellie have her baby?"

"No," Julianna sighed sadly. "It was false labor. They sent her home."

"Oh, that's too bad." I frowned.

"I called her this morning. Poor thing was so disappointed she was in tears, but then all of us who are pregnant right now are crying at the drop of a hat. Stupid hormones."

There was an awkward silence. I gathered up my nerve and sucked in a deep breath.

"I can't believe you'd offer to help me. I mean, my reputation and attitude haven't been…"

Julianna shook her head and started to laugh. "You didn't corner the market on attitude. Trust me. I wasn't a poster child for submission a few years ago, either."

"You?"

"Oh, yeah."

Waiting for our food, she told me how Mistress Sammie—before she'd switched to the submissive side—had physically dragged Julianna out of her house and hauled her to the club. She'd waited outside Mika's door for days, wearing a pissy attitude on her sleeve. It wasn't until a dream forced her to open her eyes and accept who she was that she finally attained her storybook ending.

Though I'd only had one short dream about Cane, it wasn't anything like the epiphany Julianna had experienced.

"Trust me. It was rough sailing at first," Julianna continued as she speared a piece of veal Parmesan. "I had this hang-up about the word *slave*. I was all right with being a submissive, but the whole connotation of the word *slave* scared the living crap out of me."

"Why?"

"Because I'd convinced myself that once I became a slave, I'd be giving up my whole identity. That I wouldn't be me anymore but an extension of Mika…the Master I served."

"I feel that way about submission," I confessed sheepishly.

"Really?" She blinked, clearly taken aback. "I've seen you kneel at the club."

"Yes, but I only do that to thank the Doms willing to work me."

"Hrmm." She considered my statement with pursed lips for several long seconds. "So what prompted you to say yes when Ian was looking for a submissive to help teach James about Dominance?"

I shrugged. "I suppose having sex with them and hoping that eventually Ian would use me to teach James how to throw a whip had a whole lot to do with it."

"So…basically, greed." Her laugh was so infectious I couldn't help but join her.

"Well, I mean, come on." I grinned. "Those two are beyond *hawt*, and Ian knows how to wield a mean whip. I'd be a fool to turn that offer down."

"Oh, I hear you. But they were asking specifically for *submissives* to volunteer…and yet you did." Her aha expression had me pausing to analyze myself a bit harder.

"You don't actually think I'm a sub, do you?"

"I do!" She grinned. "A really bratty one, but that's only because you're trying to fight the label. Sorry, sister, but if the shoe fits…" Julianna raised her water glass in a mock toast.

"No." I shook my head. "Just because I want to get laid and beaten doesn't mean I'm a sub."

"Okay. When Kerr, that miserable piece of shit, got shot…who was gathering up clean towels and giving them to Master Sam, Cindy, and Liz so they could try and stop the bleeding?"

"I *thought* Sam and I were in a relationship."

"But what drove you to make sure he had what he needed to help Kerr?" Her upper lip curled in disdain at the mention of the asshat's name.

"I saw that he needed help. I wanted to be the one to do it for him."

"Semantics, Sasha." Julianna sucked in a deep breath. "I spent years looking for my *One*. The minute Mika came along, I knew I'd found him. But he didn't want a sub. He wanted a *slave*. The last thing I thought I'd ever do was give *any* man that much power over me. But with his patience and understanding, he taught me how to bend to his will…though not always cheerfully, and that I'm still me, even when I'm obeying him. I never lost *me* in the process. I submit to Mika because"—she paused and smiled—"well for a lot of reasons, but mostly because I crave to fulfill him, the way he does me."

Julianna let me absorb her words.

"Let me ask you something," she continued. "When you're up on that cross, or bound to a spanking bench, what are you after, besides pain?"

I'd never taken the time to think of it in those terms. "That the Dom who works me gets something out of it, as well…to make him proud and... Oh, shit." The words tumbling off my tongue slapped me square in the face.

Julianna smirked, dusted off her hands, and sat back preening. "I rest my case."

I shook my head in denial. "Just because I decide not to be a greedy wench one hundred percent of the time doesn't make me a sub."

"Don't." She held up her palm. "I had to stop lying to myself before I could hand Mika my control. It's time for you to do the same with Cane."

Maybe, but I didn't know where to start. I was safe hiding behind my walls. The thought of breaking them down to stand naked before him, was beyond terrifying.

But the intuitive prick already knew that.

"What's the use? Even if I did, no one in the club is ever going to accept me as a sub, and we both know it."

"Nice try, but that's a cop-out." Julianna refuted dryly. "You've never put forth an effort to learn about submission. They don't judge you because you try and fail, they shun you because you won't bother trying at all. It's a two-way street, Sasha." Julianna reached over and clasped my hand. "I'm not trying to be mean, but you reap what you sow, sweetie. Whether you're aware of it or not, you walk around the club sending a palpable *fuck off* vibe toward everyone."

Though she was only speaking the truth, it still stung. I hung my head feeling seven shades of guilty. "I know. They all think I'm a bitch."

"You're the only one who can change that." Julianna peered over at Mika and smiled. "If you'd like, I'll talk to Master and see if Cane will give you permission to come to the Saturday morning submissive classes. Would you be interested in doing that?"

"I need to start somewhere. If the other subs laugh me out of the club, it'll be on your head."

She giggled. "They won't. You'll see."

My phone chimed and I looked down at the message.

Amber: *Your conference call with Law's traffic manager starts in twenty.*

I quickly typed out a reply: *Heading your way now.*

"I need to get back to the office. Thank you so much for this,

Julianna. Though I'm a lot more freaked out than I was when I got here, you've definitely given me a lot to think about."

"Yay!" She raised her fists and laughed. "You'll be fine. I'm here if you need me. Don't ever hesitate to ask for my help. All right?"

"I won't. Thank you."

I stood and tossed a twenty on the table, then turned and practically slammed into Mika. "I've talked with Cane. He has your cell number now and will be reaching out to you soon."

I nervously nodded. "Thank you, Sir...I think."

Mika chuckled as I hurried out the door.

I hadn't even made it back to the office when my cell phone rang. A number I didn't recognize appeared on the dashboard display. My gut told me it was Cane and I drew in a shaky breath and connected the call.

"Hello."

"Good afternoon, princess." My heart sped up as Cane's whiskey-smooth voice spilled from the speakers. "First, I'd like to thank you for accepting my offer. You've made me a very happy man. Secondly, a package will be arriving at your office shortly. You know what to do. One last thing, I'm sending a car to pick you up outside your building. You'll meet the limo at six thirty sharp. Any questions?"

Only a million, but I held my tongue. "No, Sir."

"Excellent. I look forward to seeing you, princess," he said and hung up.

Butterflies took flight in an anxiety-induced free-for-all as I pulled into the parking garage.

CHAPTER EIGHT

THE CONFERENCE CALL seemed to last for hours. My thoughts were so focused on the conversation I'd had with Julianna and my pending date with Cane, I could barely focus on business. When we finally wrapped up the call with New York, Law mouth slashed in a frown.

"Do you mind explaining to me what happened to you at lunch?"

"Nothing," I lied. "I just have a lot on my mind."

"Yes. I can tell. And none of it's business." He leaned his elbows onto the table and held me with a penetrating stare. "What's on your mind that has you so unfocused?"

"It's personal."

"Ah, pulling out the old *personal* card on me again? Fine." He stood and gathered his notes. "I need your input on this process at all times, Sasha."

His chastising tone irked. "And you have it."

"Good." He stood in the doorway, studying me once again before he turned and walked down the hall.

Come on, girl. Get your shit together.

I gave myself a resolute nod and headed back to my office.

"Hey," Amber called out. "You know I wasn't hitting on Law earlier, right?"

"I know. I'm sorry I was so..."

"Jealous?" Amber grinned. "I would never mac on your man, current or past."

"Thanks." I sighed in shame.

"Oh, by the way. There's a package on your desk. It's from Nordstrom's. What did you get?"

Not a damn clue.

"Just a little something I've been eyeing for a while."

"Ohhh, I can't wait to see it." She rushed out from behind her desk.

Neither can I.

As I entered my office, Amber followed closely behind me. Lifting the lid of the dress box, my hands shook. When I caught a glimpse of what was inside, I nearly choked on my saliva. The silky fabric of the dress, a champagne-colored number with a plunging V-neck sheath, peekaboo lace at the waist, and embellishments enhancing the bust, all but melted beneath my fingers. Tiny spaghetti straps were the only support for my breasts. I knew wearing a bra was completely out of the question.

"Oh, wow. That's sexy as sin…what little there is of it, anyway," Amber said with a soft chuckle. "You even got matching shoes and a purse. Sweet."

Hiding my shock, I lifted a pair of sparkling stilettos and a beaded clutch from the box. Cane had attended to every detail for our date.

"It's beautiful, but where on earth do you plan to wear something like that?"

"I don't know." At least *that* was the truth. "It was just so sexy I had to have it."

"I bet Law would love to see you in it, and out of it," she whispered, still grinning.

"Not happening again. Okay, fashion show is over. Back to work…both of us."

I quickly closed the lid over the box. After seeing the revealing dress Cane had sent, I knew the likelihood of me doing anything but pacing my office the rest of the afternoon was slim to none.

My body hummed with nervous energy as the hours dragged on like days. I tried to convince myself that once I laid eyes on Cane, I'd find my calm. The biggest problem was surviving until then without stroking out. Eventually, I lost myself in spreadsheets. Law tapped on my door and I jerked with a start.

"I'm heading out. Want me to walk you to your car?"

"Oh." I glanced at the clock, totally unaware it was already past five. "No. I'm going to finish up here. I won't be far behind you."

"All right. See you in the morning."

"Have a nice night, Law."

"You too." He paused, flashing a seductive smile. When I didn't take the bait, he slowly walked away.

A few minutes later, Amber waved from the doorway. "Night, Ms. E. Do you need anything before I go?"

"Nope. I'll see you tomorrow."

Amber stepped out of sight. I heard the ding of the elevator and bolted from my chair. I closed and locked my office door. It was then that I noticed my knees were shaking.

"Relax. He's only taking you to dinner." I mumbled, aiming to calm my prickly nerves.

The executive restroom, adjoining my office, consisted of a toilet and sink, and I quickly stripped down and washed up. Turning, I admired the marks still red and welted over my ass, especially the message Cane left for me. Tingles slid up my spine. I was already hungry for more.

After touching up my makeup and brushing out my hair, I slid into the skimpy dress. Staring at myself in the mirror, my eyes grew wide. My boobs were nearly spilling out from the delicate lace cradling them, while the lower half of the dress hugged my curves like a glove.

As I stepped into the shoes, a nervous chuckle vibrated my throat. "If he's taking me to dinner at a strip club, I'll fit right in. If not, I'm going to stand out like a hooker in church."

After spritzing on a little perfume, I strode out of my office, toward the break room, to grab a bottle of water. When I opened the refrigerator the scent of garlic overwhelmed. Spying the container of lasagna I'd failed to eat the other night, I plucked the Styrofoam box out of the fridge and tossed it into the trash. Bending over, I reached for the water.

"That's almost too much temptation to resist, gorgeous," Law growled from behind me.

I let out a yelp and bolted upright. "Stop scaring the crap out of me all the time!" I barked. "What are you still doing here? I thought you left."

He didn't answer, simply stared at me, eyes wide, mouth gaping open.

"Oh, for crying out loud. Put your tongue back in your mouth, you perv," I scolded. "You've already seen what's under this dress."

"Yes, I have." His voice was low and gravelly as he continued to strip me bare with his eyes. "But that's an awfully sexy package you've wrapped yourself in, Sasha. What's the occasion? You obviously have a special night planned."

"I-I..." *Have a date?* Yeah, that was so not the answer Law needed to hear now. "Have plans, yes."

"Cane's a lucky man."

"I never said I was going out with Cane," I huffed.

"Tell me you're not."

I couldn't. I didn't want to lie to the man. "Go home, Law."

A devious smirk played over his lips as he ate up the distance between us. He crowded close into my personal space. His eyelids were hooded, but I could see the raw, primal need that dilating his pupils. "I plan to. And when I get there, I'm going to strip off my suit and climb into bed. Then I'm going to wrap a tight fist around my cock, stroke fast and hard, and fantasize that it's your snug little cunt milking me. Damn. I'd love to be the one peeling you out of that sexy outfit...with my teeth."

He dragged his fingertips down my arms, then leaned in and skimmed the tip of his tongue over my collarbone. A ripple quivered low in my core. Goose bumps freckled my body.

"You look simply edible," he murmured in a buttery-soft voice against my flesh. "Tasting your skin again makes me ride the razor's edge of control, sweetheart."

The quiver turned into a full-blown tremble and I melted against his rugged chest. Wrapping an arm around me, he held me tight to his hot body. His alluring scent lit up my hormones like a Christmas tree. Law tucked two fingers under my chin and deliberately tilted my head back, forcing my gaze to crash into his.

I was lost.

A powerful rush of need and desire slammed through me. He slanted his lips over mine and claimed me with a luscious, soulful kiss. A hungry whimper blossomed in the back of my throat. Without thinking, I opened and invited him in. He growled and swept his silky tongue inside my mouth. Every cell in my body ached for him to strip me naked, slam me up against the wall, and drive his glorious cock inside me...fuck my ever-loving brains out, right there in the break room.

I doubt Cane would appreciate you doing that, my conscious snidely chided.

Cane! Oh, shit!

Panicked, I tensed and pried my mouth from Law's sizzling kiss. Stumbling back on wobbly knees, I pressed a palm to my racing heart while trying to clear the carnal fog from my brain.

"I'm sorry, Law. I-I need to go."

Like a scared rabbit, I raced back to the security of my office. Law stood in the doorway watching me as I donned my coat and snagged up the tiny purse.

"Have fun, but not *too* much." A slow, incendiary smile spread over his succulent mouth.

Slickness slid between my folds, and for a brief moment I remembered the feel of how perfectly he'd devoured me. I mutely nodded and squeezed past him, practically running toward the elevator.

When I stepped outside, the bitter wind did nothing to decrease the flaming hunger Law ignited with his provocative seduction. I desperately needed to tell him to back the fuck off but lacked the willpower to shut down the attraction I felt toward him. It was crazy. No man had ever tempted me the way he did. Somehow, someway, I had to stand strong against the animal magnetism. God help me, I didn't have a clue how to dissuade him more than I already had.

My body was still vibrating with need as a black stretch limo pulled to the curb. An older man in a tailored suit and black hat emerged and hurried around the vehicle.

"Miss Evans?" he asked in a crisp, professional voice.

"Yes."

He opened the door, sent me a friendly smile, and invited me inside with a sweep of his hand. "Mr. Cane is waiting for you to join him."

"Ah, thank you very much." I exhaled and climbed into the limo.

The driver leaned in and plucked a bottle of champagne that was chilling and popped the cork. He efficiently filled a flute with bubbly. Before I could refuse, he pressed the drink in my hand.

"Mr. Cane would like for you to sit back and relax."

I sent the driver a tight smile and raised the glass. When he closed the door, I issued a long-suffering sigh. Evidently, Mr. Cane got what he wanted from most everyone.

Including you.

Dismissing the mild annoyance, I brought the glass to my lips and took a sip as the driver pulled from the curb. I wasn't paying attention to where he was taking me until the limo exited the highway and I recognized the familiar surroundings. We were heading toward my suburb of Highland Park. Knots twisted in my stomach. I set the empty glass aside and peered out the window.

After several anxious minutes, the limo turned east toward Lake Michigan. A short time later, he pulled into the driveway of a beautiful and massive mansion.

This was no restaurant. It had to be Cane's home. But it couldn't be, could it? No. There had to be some kind of mistake. He was only in Chicago for a few months. Surely he wouldn't buy, or even rent, a four-plus million-dollar mansion, would he? Anxiety crawled up my back as more questions spooled through my brain. A frown settled on my face. Something wasn't adding up.

When the driver opened the door, I almost demanded that he take me back to the office. Instead, I stepped from the limo and squared my shoulders.

"Would you like me to escort you to the house, miss?" the driver asked.

"No. I'm fine. Thank you."

He nodded and returned to the vehicle. Before I made it to the front door, the car pulled out of the driveway. As I reached for the bell, the portal opened and Mika met me with a wide grin.

"What's going on?" I asked, unable to mask the confusion and fear in my voice.

"Relax, girl. Cane thought it would be nice for the four of us to sit and visit before you two head out to dinner."

"This is *your* house?"

Julianna slid in beside him, wearing an equally wide grin. "Let her in, Master…it's cold out there."

Mika took my hand and led me inside as he scowled at Julianna. "Watch yourself, little one. I have no qualms with asking our guests to wait while I drag your insolent ass to the dungeon and remind you who you're speaking to."

"Sorry, Master. It's just…so cold."

"Cane is *here*?" I asked, working to process what the hell was happening.

"Yes." Julianna nodded. Her long, red curls bobbed wildly. "He's playing with Tristan in the family room."

"Cane is playing with your son?"

"Yes, silly." Julianna giggled. She turned, bumping Mika with her pregnant belly.

As we rounded the corner, I saw Cane sitting on the ground beside the toddler, playing cars. The big, bad Sadist was making engine noises with his lips. The air whooshed from my lungs. As man and boy rammed their metal cars together, Tristan's light laughter tinkled in the air.

When Cane looked up and saw me, he grinned and scrubbed a hand over the toddler's hair. "Thanks for letting me play cars with you. Next time, we'll play longer."

"Okay," Tristan replied with an infectious smile.

"Let me take your coat, girl," Mika announced from behind me.

I shucked the heavy wool off my shoulders and handed it to him. When I spun back around, Cane was standing. He dragged an approving, hungry gaze up and down my body as he strode toward me.

"You look ravishing, princess." He lifted my hand to his lips and placed a gentle kiss on my palm.

"Thank you. It's a beautiful dress."

"Not nearly as beautiful as you." Cane winked. "I hope you don't mind us spending a bit of time with Mika and Julianna before dinner."

"No. Not at all... I-I'm just a bit surprised."

He leaned in and brushed a whisper-soft kiss beneath my ear. His warm breath skittered over my flesh. My sex clutched. "Good. I have plenty more surprises in store."

"Grab some cocktails, and make yourselves at home," Mika instructed as he bent and lifted Tristan into his arms. "Julianna and I are going to take our little man upstairs so the nanny can get him ready for bed. We'll be down shortly."

"Take your time." Cane nodded. "I need to speak with Sasha for a bit."

"Breathe," Julianna mouthed to me before turning to follow her Master and son.

"I'm going to have a hard time keeping my hands off you tonight in that dress, princess." Cane smirked.

"Ah-ah-ah. It was your idea to put that pesky two-week clause in our contract," I teased with a sassy grin.

"That's what I want to talk to you about. Come." He clasped his warm hand around my elbow and led me to a chocolate-brown leather couch, then gestured for me to sit. "Would you like another drink?"

"No thank you. I'm fine."

"Very well." He sat down beside me, twisting slightly to face me. "Since you have already felt the bite of pain and the accompanying pleasure at my hands, I feel it's a moot point to maintain the two-week moratorium in our original agreement. I'd like to strike it from the contract, but your opinion on the matter will determine if that's doable or not."

He wanted to remove that clause from the contract? *Hell yes!*

"Yes. Yes. Take it away."

Cane chuckled. "I had a feeling you might say that."

He reached across the coffee table and retrieved a leather folio. Pulling the contract from inside, he drew out a pen and handed them both to me.

"Draw an X through that portion and initial it, please," he instructed with a wolfish grin.

With a sweep of the pen, I obliged as excitement sang through me. When I was finished, I watched Cane scrawl his initials next to mine before he tucked the items away and moved in closer to me.

He nuzzled his lips against my neck and nipped the lobe of my ear. "I'm glad we could come to an agreement. Being unable to touch you the way I want for two damn weeks would have strained my patience."

Cane extinguished the sultry chuckle spilling off my tongue as he cupped my cheeks and pressed his hungry mouth to mine. Ruthlessly, he plunged past my lips, and like lightning, his powerful force surged, crushing me beneath an onslaught of passion and possession. Fissures of heat blistered my veins. My nipples grew hard. My skin felt tight. Need drummed a wild rhythm between my legs.

He tasted like danger, desire, and untold carnal imaginings.

He melded his mouth to mine and branded me with his forceful demons and angelic compassion. The synapses in my brain sputtered. Thoughts fragmented into shards, swirling aimlessly, as he took possession of me with one single kiss.

When he grudgingly pulled back, stippling my lips with tiny kisses, he pressed his forehead to mine. I felt dazed and spellbound. The hunger in his iridescent gold eyes made my pulse skitter. Tingles ignited, like kindling, and spread through me in a flashfire.

"I can't wait to get you naked and beneath me."

"Now would be fine," I said breathlessly.

Cane chuckled and shook his head. "You really are a greedy minx."

"And that's a bad thing how?"

"I think we'll forego drinks—"

"*And* dinner, so we can move into the fun stuff?" I asked with a saucy smirk.

Thunderclouds rolled across his face. Lightning flashed in his eyes. My quirky grin fell from my lips. "Do *not* ever attempt to Top me from the bottom, princess. You won't enjoy an ounce of pleasure with my punishment."

"I-I…" My throat closed up before I could tell him I was only kidding.

Sliding my gaze to the floor, I hid my embarrassment. When I saw his thick erection jerk beneath his trousers, I nearly swallowed my tongue. Obviously the kiss had excited him as much as it had me. I longed to reach out and stroke the impressive bulge, but I kept my hands to myself.

"Yes? You were saying?" His taunting tone scraped deep.

I raised my head and met his smug smile. His *no brat* tenet might very well be the death of me. I'd have to choose my battles and my words wisely with this man. Cane was cunning, calculating, and sly. He wasn't above leading me into a trap.

Slamming a lid on my pride, I shook my head. "Yes, Sir. I understand…no Topping from the bottom."

He brushed his lips over my cheek. When he pulled back, I saw a look of triumph glowing on his face and in his eyes. "Hopefully all the lessons I intend to teach you will be received as easily."

Don't hold your breath.

The man wasn't stupid, but then neither was I. In comparison to what he had in store for me, this was but the tip of the iceberg. Of course, I had to be willing to accept his tutelage. Parts of me were open to discovering what he'd uncover within, but the premonition that he'd fashion me into some kind of Stepford sub filled me with hesitation. Twenty-four hours ago, the idea of opening myself up to the man would have sent me sprinting away. But after my lunch with Julianna, I had to open my heart, or continue to bury my head in the sand.

I wanted something new. Something different. Cane promised me those things. I'd only short-change myself if I gave up and walked away.

Besides, I didn't want to.

Much like Law, Cane drew me with the same perplexing force. It didn't matter the men were as opposite as geographical poles. The fiber of allure connecting me to both of them was real and as indestructible as titanium. I could only hope that the fire Law bred inside me would soon snuff itself out. Unfortunately, after our little interlude in the break room, I knew those odds were the same as me sprouting wings and learning to fly.

Cane inched back slightly when Mika entered the room.

"I'm sorry that took so long. Tristan is insisting that Julianna tuck him in." He looked at the empty glasses and bottle of wine sitting untouched on the coffee table. "Nothing to drink?"

"No. Thanks, man. Next time."

"What? You need to leave now? Dammit. I was hoping we could talk a bit about"—Mika stopped and turned a mischievous smile on me—"submission."

I rolled my eyes and bit my tongue.

"We'll dive into that later. Sasha *will* be at the sub meeting Saturday morning," Cane assured.

"I will?"

"Indeed you will." Cane nodded. He stood and pulled his phone from his pocket.

I opened my mouth to argue, but quickly snapped it shut.

Cane wasn't the one who'd be subjected to ridicule. That was all on me. I'd have to pay the price for hiding my fears behind a veil of attitude, not him. Attending the sub meeting was galaxies outside my comfort zone, but if I wanted to embrace the idea of submission, I had to step outside myself and face my fears head-on.

Of course, if it got too ugly, I could always slap on my bitch face and retreat behind my walls again.

"I'm looking forward to it." I nearly choked on the words.

Cane drew back his hand and landed a hard slap on my ass. I yelped and shivered as the tender welts came alive beneath a fiery burn.

"Don't *ever* lie to me," he scolded.

I pressed my lips into a mutinous line.

Mika chuckled. "Good luck to you, brother. You're going to need it."

He wasn't the only one. It was going to take more than luck for me to hold my tongue.

Maybe you shouldn't try to push him.

The thought slid through my brain as Julianna hurried down the stairs. When we said our good-byes, she wrapped me in a tight hug.

"You can do this." Her whispered encouragement helped soothe my unsteady nerves.

With the folio tucked under his arm, Cane led me to the limo now parked in the driveway while he stroked soothing circles along the base of my spine. Once inside the vehicle, he refilled my champagne flute and poured himself a glass.

"To new beginnings." He smiled as he clinked the crystal rim to mine.

I wanted to chug the bubbly liquid to calm my fluttering stomach, but instead simply took a small sip. If I got shit-faced again, the man would think me an alcoholic. Besides, being alone with Cane put me in a whole new realm of *whoa, damn*. I had to keep my wits about me.

A serious expression settled over his face when he pulled out the contract.

"Let's discuss limits."

He moved in closer and surrounded me in his intoxicating warmth. We spent the next twenty minutes talking about the lists I'd compiled. Though short, Cane's questions were centered around my medium limits.

"Why tattoos?" he asked with a tiny smile.

"I love to be marked, just not permanently."

"What about piercing? You've not noted that anywhere, princess."

"I've thought about having my nipples done, but…"

"But what?"

I knew he'd laugh, but he wanted honesty. "I'm not comfortable whipping out my boobs for some guy in a tattoo parlor."

Cane dragged his knuckles down my chest to the swell of my cleavage. A tingle sped beneath my skin.

"You have beautiful breasts, Sasha. Full. Pert. Luscious." His voice was thick. "I didn't think you were so shy."

"I am. Except at the club. I mean…pretty much everyone's naked in the dungeon. It's no big deal."

"Are you shy around your lovers?"

I shook my head.

Cane wiggled his fingers beneath the lace and pinched the tip of one hard nipple. I inhaled a sharp gasp as my pussy clenched.

"Respond the correct way. Are you shy around your lovers?"

"No, Sir." My voice quivered.

"Good. I hoped I wouldn't have to try and seduce a nun."

Cane strummed his thumb over my pebbled peak. Arousal bloomed between my legs. I closed my eyes and softly sighed at the cultivating ache.

The limo stopped and I lifted my heavy eyelids. Cane positioned himself in the seat so he could watch me. A smoldering lust blazed in his eyes. I darted a quick glance over his shoulder and discovered we were back in the city.

"I can't wait to devour you," he murmured before slanting his mouth over mine.

His kiss wasn't soft like before. No, he claimed my lips with feral and unrelenting demand. Cane was all power and strength…a force to be reckoned with. I knew if I let his potent spell drag me under, I'd be courting disaster. I could easily lose my heart, but even more daunting was the fear that I might lose myself.

He tugged my nipple. "Tell me what's rolling through your mind."

"Just imagining all the fun we're going to have, Sir."

"Mmm."

The sound vibrated from low in his throat as he bent his mouth to my breast. When he dragged the lace-covered cup down, my nipple peeked out. Without warning, Cane sank his teeth into my pillowy flesh and bit down hard. I let out a loud scream while pain streaked from the point of contact, around my chest, and up my neck. He gave a sharp tug and released the burning tissue.

"I warned you about lying to me, girl." A harsh scowl lay on his face and in his tone.

My body trembled and I sucked in deep breaths, trying to ride the stinging waves rippling through me. Glancing down, I saw the angry, red imprint of teeth covered in his glistening saliva. Ordinarily, I'd welcome the blaze consuming my flesh, but the pain he'd inflicted wasn't a reward. It was punishment. Remorse and defiance clashed like mortal enemies. My emotions were all over the map.

"What were you thinking?" Cane demanded impatiently.

"Of ways to protect myself, Sir."

"Protect yourself from what?"

"From you."

He jerked his head up, brows slashed in confusion. A knowing smile slowly lifted the corners of his mouth before he bent in close. "There is no protection from me, princess. I'll be the one who protects you, because I own you. You're mine. If you ever doubt that, just check your ass in the mirror."

Cane dragged his tongue over the shell of my ear. A shaky breath slid from my lips. "Yes, Sir."

"I'd rather drown you in painful pleasure, but one way or another, you *will* obey my rules."

Tracing his fingertips over the imprint of his teeth, Cane dipped his head and gently laved his tongue over the throbbing flesh. Each soothing stroke eased the anguish inside and out.

It was blatantly obvious that all the tactics I'd used on the Doms at the club were useless. Cane had drawn clear and concise lines. There'd be no stepping outside them. No pushing and very little playing. I had to walk the straight and narrow.

I waited for the burst of defiance to consume me, but it never surfaced. Instead, a sense of security enveloped me…pressing in all around, like a blanket I'd never known I'd been missing.

Tears stung the backs of my eyes. "You're going to destroy me, aren't you?"

Cane cupped my cheeks. A benevolent smile softened his rugged features. "Oh, yes. I intend to annihilate you before rebuilding you with all the things you've kept buried deep inside. I *will* bring you a sense of peace and balance that you've never known exists."

A foreboding chill skittered over my flesh.

"Relax, Sasha. You've willingly put your trust in my hands. I give you my vow. I'll guard and keep you safe." He glanced up when the limo pulled to a stop. "Remember that, especially now."

When I looked out the window, the familiar hotel lobby sent panic charging through me.

No fucking way! This is not happening!

Of all the restaurants in the city, Cane had chosen the *one* in the hotel Law was staying at.

What if he was in there now having dinner?

My heart leapt against my ribs like a wild animal, trapped in a cage.

As I stared at the entrance, images of the night I shared with Law came rushing back in pussy-clenching detail.

I couldn't step foot inside that hotel again, at least not with Cane. I had to do something...now.

"I don't mean to dash your plans, Sir, but this restaurant has a nasty reputation. I've heard they have terrible food and lousy service."

If Cane realized I was lying again, he'd probably bite my whole boob off.

"I don't know who told you that, but they're full of shit. I eat breakfast and dinner here nearly every day. The food is fantastic and the service is impeccable."

"W-why do you eat here so much?" I sputtered, trying to figure another way out of this pending fiasco.

"This is where I'm staying, princess. I have a suite upstairs."

Un-fucking-believable!

"Here?" I gaped. "You're staying *here*?"

It was a blessing that the driver opened the door at that exact moment. The cold air swirling around me kept me from passing the hell out. Cane ignored the other man and pinned me with an unhappy expression.

"What's *really* bothering you, princess?"

Shit!

"Law is also staying here," I blurted out. My cheeks grew hot.

Cane flashed me a wicked smile, then stepped out of the car. When he extended his hand, I placed my trembling fingers in his palm. Still wearing a cocky grin, he led me inside the hotel.

"I assume you and Law...entertained one another here, in his room?"

"Yes, Sir," I murmured.

"I see. I guess we'll have to make some new memories for you, princess."

The smile I sent him was as tight as the pressure in my lungs.

As Cane led me through the lobby, I nervously skimmed a gaze over the tables searching for Law's wide shoulders and chocolate-brown hair. A wall suddenly blocked my view and I realized that Cane wasn't heading toward the restaurant, but instead, the elevators.

Questions zipped through my head like a cyclone.

"I've arranged for us to share dinner tonight in my room. I suspect you'll now enjoy the privacy."

A soothing, wave of relief rolled through me. "I will. Thank you. It sounds wonderful, Sir."

When we stepped off the elevator, on the same fucking floor as Law's room, an overwhelming sense of déjà vu slammed me. A flicker of gratitude eased my fears when Cane ushered me toward the opposite direction of Law's suite. Maybe I'd make it through this ironic crapfest unseen and unscathed.

Pausing at one of the doors, Cane was pulling the key card from his pants pocket when the portal opened. Several white-coated employees filed out with smiles.

"Your dinner is on the table, Sir," the last server stated.

"Thank you. I appreciate you arriving and setting it up so promptly." Cane placed a tip in the man's hand before he pushed the door open.

The layout of Cane's suite was exactly like Law's, and I struggled to force the haunting memories away.

"Give me your coat, princess, then we'll sit down and have a nice dinner."

Sliding the warm wool from my body, I turned and started to drape it over Cane's hand, when Law strolled out from the kitchen, wearing a wolfish smile. The coat slid off my fingers and landed on the floor.

"Thank goodness you two finally made it. I was beginning to think I'd have to eat alone."

My body trembled.

My knees began to buckle.

Splotches of black blurred my vision.

CHAPTER NINE

"GRAB HER, MAN. She's going to faint," Law barked as he rushed toward me.

"Easy, princess," Cane whispered.

The next thing I knew, far-off voices were calling my name. I opened my eyes to find myself cuddled up on Cane's lap, wrapped in his arms.

"There you are." He smiled and lifted a glass to my lips. "Drink some water for us."

Us?

I took a quick sip and swiveled my head to find Law crouched down beside us.

"Sorry, gorgeous. We didn't mean to startle you quite that bad." The apology in his words and on his face was genuine.

"W-what's going on? Why are you here?"

"Looks like it's time to come clean, man." Law grinned up at Cane.

Every muscle in my body tensed like the strings on a bow. "Come clean? What the hell are you—"

"No cursing, princess," Cane admonished.

Defiance and confusion roared in me. Wiggling out of his grasp, I shoved my hand against his chest and launched to my feet.

"Easy, gorgeous," Law cooed as he rose and reached out to steady me.

"Get your hands off me," I barked. "What the hell is going on here?"

Cane stood and both men started advancing toward me. "If you'll calm down, we'll explain."

"*Explain?* Start talking, right now!"

"Take her upstairs," Cane instructed. "I'll join you two in a minute."

"With pleasure." Law chuckled.

"I'm not going any—" Before I could launch into a tirade, he'd cut my words short and hoisted me over one wide shoulder before striding toward the stairs. "Put me down, Lawson Pratt. Put me down this instant!"

Instead of ceding to my demands, he landed a solid slap on my ass. I let out an indignant scream and began kicking wildly to escape his hold.

"You'd better settle down, sweetheart, or you won't like what happens next."

"Shove your threats up your ass! Let me down."

He buffeted two more brutal spanks across my backside before unceremoniously dropping me onto the bed. Before I'd even stopped bouncing, Law pounced on top of me, caging me beneath his steely body. He gripped my wrists and shoved my arms up over my head as he repositioned his legs around my hips and pressed his heated crotch to mine.

Fear, bitter and caustic, along with an unwelcome surge of arousal clashed through my system.

"You must enjoy making things harder on yourself."

"Fuck you," I spat.

"If you'd play nice, we might be able to arrange that."

"That wasn't an invitation you cocksucker." I bucked, trying to shove him off me.

"For such a gorgeous girl you certainly have a dirty mouth," Law tsked. His lips thinned to a tight line as he gripped my wrists more firmly. "Settle down. And we'll explain."

"Get off me and I might," I growled.

"You're spitting so much fire right now, I'm liable to lose my balls if I let you up."

"Damn right you will. I don't know what game you two are playing, but you're not playing it with me!"

"We'll see about that." Law smirked before glancing over his shoulder. "You might want to step it up, man. It's going to take both of us to tame this tiger."

A condescending scoff rolled off my tongue.

Cane appeared in the doorway wearing a scowl. Clenched in his fist were several bundles of rope. My heart slammed against my ribs and I fought even harder to free myself from Law's steely grip.

"Damn. If you two were naked, I'd be enjoying the hell out of this sight."

Law chuckled. "I don't see that happening anytime soon. Not until our little hellcat calms way down."

Cane lifted his shoulders with a nonchalant shrug. "Guess we'll just have to tie her down and force her to listen."

"You will not!"

Fire flickered in his golden eyes as he leaned over Law's shoulder. "Watch me."

"I will not lie here and let you tie me up." My chest heaved as I panted and writhed.

"Oh, yes you will." A wicked smile speared Cane's lips. "We have a contract. Remember?"

"Yes...with *you*. Not *him*!"

"Surely you remember this part… You may not scene, masturbate, or engage in sexual intercourse—in or out of the club—unless instructed by *me*." Cane's words landed like a deluge of ice water. "Now, take some deep breaths and relax."

Pinning him with a scathing glare, I managed to bite back the caustic demand for him to kiss my ass. He softly shook his head and stood before unwinding the smooth cotton rope.

"Sasha," Law whispered, drawing my gaze. "It doesn't have to be like this."

"Yes it does," Cane scoffed. "She likes to Top from the bottom. That little game stops here and now."

"Why? Do you have a better one in mind?" I spat.

I tried to diffuse my anger, but the wick was too hot.

"Grab that ball gag out of the nightstand," Law instructed.

Cane opened the drawer and pulled out a fat, red rubber gag. Panic pumped like lava in my veins.

"Please. No. I'll shut up."

"Ah, that's right. You don't like gags. They were on your list of medium limits, weren't they?" A knowing smirk played on his lips as Cane set the bothersome toy on the bed and quickly sobered. "Your safe word is *attitude*. I suggest you change yours now, princess."

"I thought we were supposed to negotiate all scenes."

"This isn't a scene. *This* is only a friendly Q&A. I simply assigned you a safe word early," he replied with a sardonic smile.

Q&A my ass. It was another interrogation.

"We're simply having an *adult* conversation," Law taunted as Cane bound my ankles to the bed frame.

"How long have you two been playing this game?" I bit out between clenched teeth.

"Oh, it's not a game," Law assured.

"Definitely not a game. We've been friends for close to twenty years," Cane stated, securing my other ankle.

Twenty years? I was stunned.

They must have shared dozens, if not hundreds, of women in that time frame. Had they conned other women using this same elaborate scheme? My twinge of jealousy was short-lived. Rage ran roughshod over my green-eyed monster. The bastards had played me…played me like a fucking fiddle.

I felt foolish and used.

What did they hope to gain by springing the news of their twenty-year friendship?

And what the hell were they after? If they wanted to fuck me together, why didn't they just say so?

Questions and rage swirled within, like a hurricane.

I was overwhelmed by the onslaught, and tears stung the backs of my eyes, but I quickly blinked them away. No. I would *not* lose my shit in front of them. They'd done nothing to earn my tears.

"Why all the lies?" I asked, trying to mask the quiver in my voice.

"We had to be sure, sweetheart," Law tenderly replied.

"Sure about what?"

"That we could help you find your way."

Was I really so lost they had to resort to subterfuge in order to save me?

Yes. You've been wandering alone, searching for answers for far too long.

Was it still nothing but a pipedream, or could these two men actually hold the keys to unlock the elusive peace I madly sought?

Some unknown but complex emotion stirred beneath the surface of Cane's calm demeanor.

"Release her wrists," he instructed Law. The pressure lifted, and blood flowed into my fingers. "I gave you a vow, Sasha. We'll explain everything, but you have to listen. Give me your arm."

I could have refused him and walked out the door. Or I could swallow my pride and fears and listen to what they had to say.

The thought of tossing away my armor was daunting. Sure, it had served me, protected me from pain, but it was a cold and lonely friend. If I didn't stop allowing my stubborn pride to rule my world, I might be throwing away the last chance to fulfill my dreams.

With slow resignation, I extended my arm toward him. Cane pressed a tender kiss to my palm in silent reward.

"Good girl." Law's praise spilled over me like warm honey and coated my remaining tendrils of doubt.

While Cane secured my arms, Law peppered the corners of my mouth with feathery kisses. Instead of delving inside, he nipped my bottom lip between his teeth and gave it a gentle tug before pulling away.

"It's time to talk, then we'll..." He shrugged his shoulders.

"Talking would be nice. I feel like a mushroom...kept in the dark and fed nothing but bullshit." Okay, so thinking about holding my tongue and actually doing so was going to take a lot more control.

Cane tickled my flesh as he trailed his fingertips down the inside of my shackled arm. "Throw away your doubts, your pride, and the anger you're clinging to. You don't need them for protection anymore. That's our job now." He kissed me softly.

"What do you mean *our* job?" I felt it was a fair question considering the lies they'd been spinning.

"We're going to enlighten you *together*. Starting now," Cane explained.

The two men moved to the end of the bed. Shoulders squared, legs slightly parted, and hands tucked behind their backs, they looked forceful, imposing, and way too edible.

"We plan to work you together; therefore, you will address us both as *Sir*. Understood?" Cane asked.

"Yes, Sir," I replied automatically as the puzzle pieces began falling into place. When Law had ordered my food, verbally commanded me to come, and used the phrase: *open, honest, communication,* they had all been clues. I'd chosen to ignore or dismiss.

The man's a fucking Dom!

As if reading my mind, a guilty smirk kicked his lips up. "It wasn't easy to play a vanilla role. Yes, sweetheart, I've been a Dom for a long, long time."

His confession wasn't an easy pill to swallow, but I choked it down because I needed more answers.

"Why did you tell me not to trust Cane?" Without giving Law time to answer, I struck Cane with a seething glare. "And why tell me to kick my boy toy to the curb?"

"It was a test," Cane replied.

"Oh, of course. Another *test*," I scoffed. "Do you two get off pitting yourselves against unsuspecting women?" Unwilling to be another pawn in their childish game, I fought the ropes. "Untie me! I might have signed your contract, but I sure as shit didn't *sign up* to be tossed around like a damn football."

"Quit fighting and let us explain!" Law growled. "We had to evaluate your needs and your connection to us."

"Why?"

"We'll explain shortly." The way Cane sidestepped my question didn't fill me with warm fuzzies. In fact, it only served to convince me that their game was in full swing.

"When you hired Edwards & Pratt, I started researching you and your company...thoroughly," Cane stated.

"When he discovered your profile on FetishWorld.com, we were pleasantly surprised." Law's soft voice was laced in awe.

"But I-I'm on the site as Destiny, not Sasha."

"Image tracing app," Cane revealed smugly. "Like I said...I'm *thorough*."

His tactics leaned more along the lines of stalking. I almost dreaded discovering what other secrets the pair were keeping from me. Despite my reservations, I had to know. I looked up at Law. "Does Mika know *you're* a Dom, too?"

"Yes," Cane answered. "Though he wasn't particularly thrilled with our plan at first..." *Why didn't Mika warned me?* Another blow pounded my self-confidence—one far more damaging. Mika was my friend. Why would he play a part in this humiliating farce? "But after I explained the motive behind approaching you separately, he understood."

"*Motive?* What could possibly be so important he threw a *friend* under the bus?"

The quick glance passing between the men held an edge of unease.

Cane pursed his lips. "Watch your tone, princess," he scolded. "We can easily leave you here until you harness your temper while we enjoy the lovely dinner waiting for us downstairs."

"Fuck my temper, and fuck you! You two can choke on the food for all I care. Tell me why Mika used me as much as you two did."

Cane met my mulish scowl and sighed.

"He didn't throw you under the bus," Law assured. "Mika worked with us in order to help you."

"Right," I drawled while rolling my eyes.

"I am right," Law bit out. "He loves you and has been concerned about you for a long time, but none of us are convinced you'll abide by the rules."

"I've already proven I'm quite capable of that. I'm not the one who *lied*."

"No, but you certainly like to manipulate," Cane jabbed. "That ends now. We approached you separately for a reason."

"What reason is that?"

"We had an issue with our last sub, one we don't wish to repeat." My temper ebbed at the sorrow in Cane's tone. "After the first year, our girl, Ruby, wanted the contract amended."

"What part?"

"The part about wanting a boyfriend, a Daddy, and a husband, princess. She fell in love with Law's Dominance. She no longer craved the pain I desired to inflict." Cane's tone was laced with rejection.

"Oh," I murmured.

Guilty of the same crime, I felt a rush of shame clamber through me. Mika had nearly stripped my membership to Genesis before I opened my eyes. I thought I was in love with nearly every Dom who'd scened with me. In reality, I'd been in love with the illusion of finding a soul mate who could consistently quiet my riot within. Sadly, the heartache I'd endured each time a Dom dumped me for a *proper* sub had been wholly self-inflicted. Still, I hadn't found the courage to knock the chip off my shoulder. Pride was a badge but also a bitch. I might not wear them proudly, but misery had taught me how to wear them well.

"When she realized I didn't have the those kinds of feelings for her, Ruby asked to be released. She's now married and expecting her first child."

Unlike Cane, Law's tone lacked any hint of bitterness.

"Mika explained how difficult it has been for you to separate your heart while having your needs met." I was relieved that Law's tone held no accusation. "His insight, combined with Ruby's infatuation, has heightened our awareness. We'll proceed cautiously, but we are determined to try and help enlighten you."

"I don't need *enlightening*, I need pain," I beseeched.

"You need far more than pain, princess," Cane admonished. "You're blind to the fact that you're screaming for Dominance." As I opened my mouth to argue, Cane held up his hand. "You've convinced yourself that you're not a sub. But trust me. Once you discover the world of submission, you'll see life in a whole new light."

"Even knowing I might screw up and fall in love with one of you, or even both, you're still willing to work with me?"

"Yes."

They were taking a huge risk, but then so was I. Could I do this? Could I lock my heart inside a lead vault to learn whatever it was they wanted to teach me?

"I still don't understand why you tried to pit me against each other."

"To see if you would choose one over the other." Law's tone was matter-of-fact. "Though you'd chosen Cane, you still struggled with your attraction to me."

I darted a quizzical look at Cane. "Doesn't the fact that I can't fight my attraction to Law worry you?"

"Of course it does, but helping you outweighs the risk of my ego taking back-to-back blows."

Though annoyance still hummed within, I couldn't help but chuckle. "I think your ego can take a couple of punches and still remain bigger than Texas."

Cane flashed me a toe-curling smile. "Clever and defiant. We're going to have a lot of fun with you."

"Doing what…breaking my will?"

"No," Law whispered. "Discovering ways to mold all that sizzling fire you possess into something astounding, that you can be proud of."

"You have to learn to walk before you can run," Cane stated poetically.

I wanted to fight him...fight them both, but their words held such hope my anger fragmented and wafted away. The ridged contours of their bodies and crushing Dominance weren't helping me cling to my rage, either.

But what touched my heart the most was the fact that they were offering me the world I'd always dreamed of. A lump of emotion clogged my throat. "What if I fail you?"

"Now we're getting somewhere," Cane whispered with relief. "You will, but we'll be there to pick you up, dust you off, and set you back on the path. We aren't seeking perfection, but we do expect a willingness to learn, to bend, and to grow."

"Will you give us that?" Law studied me closely.

This was the moment of truth. No matter how intimidating my fears, they wouldn't let me hide behind my walls. Cane and Law were like wrecking balls, ready to turn my safe haven into dust and rubble. I felt more naked and exposed than if Cane had stripped me bare before he bound me to the bed.

A tremor rocked me.

"We can see you weighing your decision, sweetheart," Law stated. "It's written all over your face and dancing in your pretty blue eyes. You might think you want to run, but your heart is telling you that's not the right choice. You know it, and we know it, or we wouldn't be here."

Damn. And I thought Cane could read me like a book. Law just proved he was equally gifted as well. A niggle of warning kept me from throwing caution to the wind and saying yes.

"Exactly what is it that you plan to do to me?"

"Open your eyes," Law promised.

"Yes, you've said that, but...how?"

Cane rounded the bed and sat down beside me. There wasn't a hint of displeasure lining his face, only determination. Reaching out, he deliberately lifted my chin, forcing my gaze. "There is no blueprint for success. Like the lifestyle itself, ours isn't a one-size-fits-all proposition. You'll simply have to trust that we know your needs and how to fulfill them."

"Trust? After this stunt?" I arched my brows.

"We're willing to trust you, even after you blatantly and selfishly disregarded the rules of my contract to get what *you* wanted," Cane reminded.

Yes, that knife cut both ways.

"But we barely know one other," I countered without defiance.

Law eased onto the other side of the bed next to me. A familiar low, sexual vibration hummed in the air around us. It was almost impossible to swallow the punch of hunger constricting my throat. "We have to start somewhere."

Cane's capable fingers slid away. "Kiss her," he instructed. "She's starving for your touch again."

I darted a look of surprise his way, but Law simply cupped my cheeks and slowly eased my focus back to him. "Is that true?"

The lust sparkling in his eyes and the rich timbre of his silky voice made it impossible for me to lie, even if I'd wanted to. Excitement was rising inside me like a tidal wave.

"Yes," I whispered breathlessly.

Law slanted his mouth over mine, claiming my lips in a fierce, blazing kiss. A low moan bubbled in the back of my throat as I opened for him. He accepted my invitation and plunged his tongue deep. I opened wider. He took his time exploring and reacquainting himself with every nook and cranny.

Like lightning, memories of the one spectacular night we shared lit up my brain. The need to feel his hot flesh again rolled through me, and I tugged at the ropes. Neither man made a move to release me. Helplessly, I surrendered to Law as he stole my power and my mind with his ardent, primal kiss.

Dizzy with desire, I writhed restlessly as flames danced and licked my core.

Nipping and tugging my lips, he slowly released me.

When Cane cupped my nape and gently turned my head, his mouth hovered so close we shared the same breath. A feral spark flared in his eyes before he crushed his lips to mine, plundering my mouth as well.

I knew then we were done talking.

At least I hoped so.

As I basked beneath Cane's equally raw and passionate kiss, my thoughts scattered. The fire sluicing under my skin churned into a steady flow of lava. Dragging his tongue over my jaw and down my throat, he nipped and laved a singeing tail of liquid silk. Pausing, he flattened his tongue against my thundering pulse point before scraping his teeth over the tender flesh there.

Lost in the intensity of their passion, I whimpered. The ache to feel him crawl on top of me, press me deep into the mattress, and put out this raging fire sang through every cell.

As he trailed lower still, I felt Law slide the lacy cups of my dress away, exposing my breasts. Cane issued a grunt of approval before he lifted from my flesh, opened his mouth wide, and sank his teeth into the same spot he'd marked in the limo. A jolt of pain clamored through me while a slash of fire zipped up my spine. The pleasure centers in my brain ignited and sent currents of electricity careening to my clit.

Law sucked my other nipple into his hot mouth. He laved his tongue over the stony peak. I arched my breasts in offering, moaning in delight, as a provoking throb settled between my legs. Lost in the liquid fever of gliding tongues and the sharp sting of nipping teeth, I tumbled down a landslide of pleasure.

Quakes of demand shook me.

The conflagration billowed out of control, leaving me in a smoky fog of desperation.

I needed them…needed them both to claim me, stretch me with their thick cocks, and fill all the empty places inside me.

Instead, of granting my reprieve they both pulled away, leaving a cold void assaulting me. Panic at the thought they might leave me here…wet, aching, and delirious, clawed up my spine.

A mournful wail tore from my throat.

"Easy, princess," Cane murmured, admiring the marks he'd left on my breast.

"Pretty," Law murmured in awe as he traced the tip of his finger over the imprints burning my flesh.

"If you think that's pretty, wait until you see the lovely lines I painted on her ass last night."

Law's brows arched. "Oh, really? I bet they're stunning."

"And then some," Cane growled as he pulled a knife from his pocket.

The slash of terror roared within, like a lion.

"Wait…please. I-I need you to warm me up before you cut me." I dragged a pleading gaze from Cane to the blade in his hand.

"You beg so sweetly, gorgeous," Law cooed.

"We're not engaging in knife play. This isn't a scene. Remember?

But I'll warn you now, be careful what you ask for. I have a reputation." Cane slightly grinned.

"A reputation for what?"

"For granting no mercy."

The wolfish grin crawling across his mouth sent a tremor rolling through me. When he sliced through the rope, my arm flopped to the bed. He quickly passed the knife to Law, who freed my other limbs. They slid the rope from my flesh and gently massaged the blood back into my fingers. I closed my eyes and sighed, and basked in their benevolence. Cane quickly brushed the rope from my ankles before rubbing my feet as well.

Law stood and extended his hand. When I slid my fingers into his palm, he helped me off the bed and tucked my breasts back beneath my dress. They'd stoked a fire inside me and were obviously leaving it unattended to burn itself out.

Hollow hunger and disappointment sang through me. "Is that it? Are we done?"

Cane's sharp gaze zeroed in on me. "That depends."

"On what?"

"On you," they replied in unison.

"Will you accept our offer to help teach you?" Law asked.

Studying them both, I felt as if I were seeing them through a new set of eyes.

Law was all tender compassion…enticing.

Cane was all power and command…addicting. I realized then I was fucked…fucked in ways I couldn't yet fathom.

If I was going to go down, it might as well be in flames.

"Yes, Sirs. I do."

The relief and happiness erupting over their faces took my breath away. My knees quivered and my pulse raced.

"Good. Let's go downstairs and enjoy dinner." Cane smiled.

"Surely the food's cold by now."

Law chuckled as he led me toward Cane. "You seriously lack faith in our abilities, sweetheart. Don't worry, we'll fix that soon enough as well."

I shot him a look of challenge.

Cane landed a sturdy slap across my ass. "Lose the defiance, brat."

I sent him a mock pout. "And just when I was finally coming to terms with princess, you go and change it. Brat? Really, Sir?"

"If the shoe fits." Cane smirked.

"Humph." My mock frown splintered into a grin.

Law let out a hearty laugh and squeezed me against his side. "You're more than a brat, but we can handle you."

"One thing's for sure. There won't be a dull moment with our little hellion." Cane chuckled, sliding his arm around my waist beneath Law's.

The lighthearted banter continued as we made our way downstairs. I was surprised that Cane had traded in his stoic reserve. He actually seemed to be enjoying the playful ribbing. Law eased his arm away and grabbed a pillow from the couch before joining us at the now empty table.

"Where's the food?" I asked.

"Staying warm in the oven," Cane stated. "I'll be right back."

Law tossed the large, fluffy pillow on the floor next to the table. "Kneel, sweetheart."

I blinked up at him. "Excuse me?"

"Excuse me, *Sir*," he corrected. "I said kneel. Don't make me repeat myself again, pet."

"Pet?" I cringed.

"We might need to have her hearing checked," he called out to Cane.

A wicked laugh rumbled from the kitchen. "I'll bring a wooden spoon out with me. That'll fix her hearing right up."

"I really don't like it when you tag-team me," I huffed.

"Then do as you're told, sweetheart." Law pointed to the pillow.

"Am I eating dinner from a dog bowl or something?"

"Not yet, but that could be arranged if you'd like." He chuckled.

I sent him a scowl and flopped down on the damn pillow.

"Bring two spoons, we're going to need them," Law yelled with a grin.

When Cane rounded the corner of the kitchen, he carried two plates heaped with food in his hands and a pair of wooden spoons tucked under his chin. After placing the dishes on the table, he handed one spoon to Law and tapped the other to my lips. "Open."

I stared up at him indignantly. "Why?"

Taking advantage of my open mouth, Cane slid the smooth

wooden handle between my lips. "Because I said so. I'm also hungry, and don't want to run back upstairs for the ball gag."

His threat did nothing to curb the humiliation coursing through me. I felt like a damn dog. If they wanted to keep their balls, they'd better not rip the spoon from my mouth, toss it across the room, and tell me to go fetch.

"You'll remain calm, quiet, and respectful while we prepare your plate." Law stared pointedly at me. "You might not like us tag-teaming you, sweetheart, but until you learn to temper that mouth of yours…you'd better grow accustomed to it."

I wrinkled my nose. With a throaty noise, part scoff and part growl, I lowered my head to hide from his censuring gaze.

Holding the spoon between my lips made my skin crawl.

Oh, get over yourself, my conscious jeered. *These two aren't going to let you make the rules anymore. Either deal with it or walk out the door.*

I'd be lying if I said a part of me didn't want to spit out the spoon and storm away. But the memory of their kisses still tingled my lips, and branded my brain. I couldn't find the strength to turn and walk away from the possibility of more, even if I'd wanted to.

Law reached down and lifted the spoon away. He then lowered a fork with a chunk of crispy chicken cordon bleu speared in its tines. When I reached for the utensil, he quickly pulled it away.

"I will feed you tonight, and every other meal the three of us share in private."

While I was relieved he didn't intend to perform the ritual during business luncheons or out in public, it chafed to know that any time we were alone he intended to feed me like a toddler.

Chewing, I swallowed the warm, gooey goodness. When I opened my mouth to tell him I was capable of using a knife and fork, he shoved another bite between my lips. Our stares collided. The daggers I was shooting at him melted beneath the serenity dancing in his sparkling blue eyes.

What could Law possibly gain from my humiliation? A need for superiority? A stroke to his ego? Or was he simply achieving some twisted caveman thrill?

Cane threaded his fingers through my hair and gently massaged my scalp. When I glanced up at him, he simply smiled and lowered a glass of wine to my lips.

Great! Now he's getting in on the act.

As I swallowed the tart, fruity liquid, confusion and fury warred.

"Your body is tense. Relax, Sasha," Cane soothed. "We realize this is new and different, but we're going to expose you to a lot of new and different things. Some will be uncomfortable, but just because it's foreign doesn't mean it's bad. Over time, you'll learn to study the sensations that are emerging inside you."

"You'll be able to chart your growth, just as we will," Law added in a voice swimming with compassion.

"I've never envisioned plotting my feelings out on a spreadsheet. I'm a person, not a flowchart," I murmured, feeling less human by the minute.

Law tsked, then leveled a spoon to my lips. The scent of rich, creamy chocolate made my mouth water. *Bastard!* Tempting me with mousse was underhanded and cruel.

"You're purposely missing the point. Don't worry, Cane and I will keep a close eye on you…gage your progress, and make adjustments when necessary."

Unease sank deep until he placed the spoon on my tongue. I let out a satisfied moan as the sugary sweetness exploded over my taste buds. Law smirked as he took a bite himself.

Dropping the spoon on his plate with a clatter, he bent and pressed his lips to mine. He slid his cold tongue over the seam of my lips before easing into my mouth. Our tongues swirled and tangled as we chased the whipped dessert between us. I longed to strip him down, spread the creamy treat all over his body, and slowly lick it off him. After several delicious minutes he lifted from my mouth. Wearing a purely carnal smile, he licked his lips.

"It's not so bad having Law pamper you, now, is it?" Cane taunted.

No, but it would suck a whole lot less if I didn't have to kneel at his feet. It annoyed me as always. I didn't understand how Law gained satisfaction treating me like a toddler, or worse… an obedient dog.

Without warning, Cane gripped my hair and yanked my head back with a brutal tug. A startled gasp exploded from my lips. "When I ask you a question, princess, I expect a prompt and courteous answer."

Delightful prickles of pain skittered over my scalp. "Yes, Sir," I exhaled on a dreamy sigh.

"I think you need to thank him for wanting to center you, offering his compassion and safety, while nourishing your body and soul."

A strange rush of warmth spread from inside me.

"As soon as you learn to tamp down your pride, you'll be able to seek out your feelings, sweetheart."

Law didn't know it, but I'd already started trying to sort out my emotions. The realization that he wanted to take care of me, nurture and protect me…that he gained his reward from my surrender, was like a giant wind, blowing my preconceived notions and ideals to the four corners of the earth.

It had been a long time since anyone actually cared about me or my feelings. The woman I thought I'd known my whole life shifted. Like the sands beneath a massive earthquake, I could physically feel myself morphing. Into what? I hadn't a clue. But a transition was taking place all the same.

I lifted a bewildered glance toward Law. "Thank you, Sir."

He leaned forward and held me prisoner with his blue-velvet eyes…shimmering in understanding. Gratitude for what he longed to give me slammed into me, swelling like a mighty ocean tide.

I was on the verge of tears when Cane cinched his fist tighter, lifting my head back ever farther. Staring at the ceiling, I savored the delicious shards of pain sizzling down my spine. Leaning over me, he aligned his face with mine. An evil sparkle flickered in his golden eyes.

"Drink in my pain, girl," he rasped before crushing his mouth to mine.

Cane's wild and primal claim was nothing like the tender coax of Law's command.

Opposites in every way…like day and night, yet when combined, their provocative darkness and intriguing light permeated the dark and desolate places in my soul.

I felt alive…truly alive, for the first time in my life.

The realization was overwhelming and exhilarating.

But reality roared through me with a terrifying reminder.

They're not here forever.

Whatever this was, whatever connection we shared…whatever light they'd breathed into me was only a temporary reprieve.

Sorrow curled the edges of my soul, but I quickly shoved it away.

I wasn't going to allow anything to rob me of the feelings they evoked.

No, the three of us didn't have forever. All we had was here and now.

But as the clock continued to tick inside my brain, certainty stared me in the face:

I had to slay my fears, tear down my walls, banish my pride, and welcome them fully into my soul. Only then would I still hold them, feel them, and touch them when they were gone.

My reservations melted away.

Wrapping my tongue around Cane's, I suffused him in the passion and hunger, trust and hope, and pure yielding energy I'd kept chained inside me.

The air grew thick and heavy.

Law slid a hand beneath my dress, plucking and teasing my tightly drawn nipples. Liquid heat spilled from my folds. Restlessly rolling my hips, I tried to ease the need engulfing my system.

Cane pulled from my mouth with a mighty roar. He narrowed his eyes, and a fierce expression lined his face. "Dinner is over. Upstairs. Now!"

As if also at a loss for patience, Law pushed back from the table.

Cane gripped my shoulders and hauled me to my feet. My knees wobbled still reeling from his kiss. I reached out and grabbed Law's arm. A devilish smile tugged his lips as he plucked me off the ground and into his arms. Melding his mouth to mine, Law carried me up the stairs. Their heavy footfalls thudded against the carpet, keeping time with the impatience pounding inside me.

Holding my lips in a prison of passion, he eased me onto my feet when we reached the bedroom. With nimble fingers, he slid the straps off my shoulders before brushing the dress down over my hips. Cool air wafted over my sweltering flesh, causing my nipples to pebble and crinkle even tighter. My mind and body screamed for more of his bewitching touches. Thankfully, I didn't have to wait long. Law cupped my breasts with a hungry moan. Lifting the heavy orbs, he strummed the pads of his thumbs back and forth over my distended peaks. The slickness spilling from within me scented the air around us in my feminine musk. Tearing his mouth from mine, he slid a stare down my body that felt like a tender caress. Glancing over his shoulder, he softly chuckled.

Cane was plucking several wicked toys out of a large black duffel bag on the corner of the tufted bed bench. A fierce expression lined his face.

"What did you do to provoke his beast?" Law whispered as he turned back toward me and nipped my earlobe.

The sliver of pain he bestowed was but a tease. "I surrendered."

CHAPTER TEN

LAW LIFTED STUDIED me. Suspicion wrinkled his forehead. "Without a fight?"

"We don't have enough time for me to let my fears rule me or for me to hide behind my walls."

"True." He slid a hand to the small of my back and pulled my hips to align with his. The feel of his thick erection prodding my stomach and his crisp cotton shirt teasing my bare nipples was like a double shock to my system. "Just how did his kiss lead you to that conclusion?"

"Yes, I'm curious about that myself," Cane stated.

Leaving the toy bag, he moved in alongside us and wrapped his strong hands around my hips. Their breath combined sending heated ribbons to cascade over my flesh. Law lifted one hand away and Cane immediately took possession of my breast, pinching and plucking the aching tip. I didn't want to talk anymore. I wanted them to strip off their clothes and meld me between them.

"Answer the question, Sasha." The edgy tone of Cane's voice pulled me back from my eager fantasy.

"There isn't time to work up my courage. I have to dive in headfirst and hope…"

"Hope what?" Law prodded.

"That I can keep a tight grip on my emotions."

"Explain that statement," Cane directed.

"I've naïvely spent years searching for my *One*," I blurted out. Law's muscles tensed. Cane's expression grew dark. "Wait…I'm not assuming or clinging to any illusions of grandeur that you're him, I'm simply saying I need to guard my heart with what you're offering."

"Does that include what I'm offering as well?" Law arched his brows in disbelief.

"Yes." I nodded. "I don't know if I can embrace submission as deeply as you'd like me to, but I want to try. It's just that…"

"Go on," Cane prompted as I struggled for a way to put my feelings into words.

"I convinced myself I only need pain to feel whole, but when Cane explained what feeding me did for you…it unlocked something inside me. I'm not sure I'd label it submission—because I really hate that term—but I feel like I have…purpose. Maybe that's wrong, because when I say it out loud, it sounds really selfish. I-I don't know how else to explain it."

Cane chuckled softly. "That you've opened up enough to *try* is a huge step."

"That's why it's called a power exchange, Sasha. If it were only one-sided, it'd be abuse, in a bad way."

"I only want to abuse your flesh and your mind in treasured, consensual ways," Cane growled as a mischievous flicker lit up his eyes.

"Where does the line for that start? I'd like to be first."

"Not tonight, my greedy girl." He shook his head. "I tore your backside up enough last night. While I might tease you a bit, we will wait for your welts to heal before I paint your pretty canvas again."

"Can you spell *ours* with the whip next time?" I taunted with a cheeky grin.

Cane laughed and shook his head. Law's expression was lined with confusion.

"I'll sure try. Turn around. Show him the marks I gave you."

"Yes, Sir."

They released me and when I spun around and presented my backside to them, Law let out a long whistle. "Mine. Nicely done."

"Thanks. I had fun," Cane replied.

"So did she by the looks of it."

When Law clutched my hips, I peered over my shoulder and watched him crouch down on the carpet. He pressed feather-soft kisses and laved his tongue over each mark, as if he was branding his own compassionate imprint to my flesh.

Cane cupped my cheeks and claimed my mouth in a torrid kiss, swallowing my sigh of delight.

"Spread your legs," Law coaxed, gliding his tongue along the ridge of my butt crack.

My legs trembled as I inched them apart. He slid his fingers over my swollen, wet slit, gathering up the moisture. Cane released my lips, and as Law began painting the slickness over my puckered rim, I tensed for a split second before letting out a dreamy sigh.

Cane's lips slashed in a primitive smile as he took a step back. Law continued to tease and toy with my backdoor. It was all I could do not to close my eyes and float away in the sublime sensation. But the sight of Cane shucking off his clothes had my gaze riveted on his chiseled body. My mouth watered at all that tan skin stretched over defined edges and hard valleys. When he slid off his trousers, a thick shaft of weeping flesh jutted from between his legs. I wanted nothing more than to fall to my knees and open my mouth. As he stepped in close to me, I placed my palms flat against his flesh and floated my fingers over his marbled skin. Power and heat tingled past my hands and up my arms.

Cane fisted his cock and began slowly stroking from stem to tip. The glistening bead on his swollen crest swelled and dribbled down over his knuckles. The sexual tension in the room soared.

"Rub your clit, princess," he instructed. His voice was primitive, raspy, and strained.

"I'm afraid to, Sir."

"Why?" The tiny smirk on his lips told me he already knew the answer.

"Because I'm afraid I'll come, Sir."

"Oh, you *will* come… *when* we give you permission."

He stepped in close. The heat of his body surrounded me in a dizzying blanket of safety.

Law squeezed the tip of a finger through my tightly gathered ring. Shards of lightning-laced delight ignited through me.

Cane guided his slick length against my equally slick folds. Tingles ricocheted down my spine and pooled beneath my clit. Lust and need etched his face. "I enjoy inflicting agony on your mind as much as I do your body."

"You're stalling and not following Cane's directions, sweetheart," Law warned before scraping his teeth over the sensitive marks on my ass.

Pain burst beneath the welted flesh and a cry tore from my throat. He worked to extinguish the fire by laving his tongue over my blistered flesh.

"Such pretty, pretty sounds," Cane murmured.

His praise was like sunshine, bright and warming.

When he guided my hand between my legs, I stared into his eyes. I saw promise, compassion, and hunger. Sliding my finger between my slick folds, I strummed my clit and rode the jagged peaks of pain until they smoothed and softened. He gripped my nape and slammed his lips to mine. Feeding. Claiming. Owning. Cane didn't relent, and I didn't want him to. I only wanted to drown in the feel of his firm and silky mouth.

My lips burned when he abandoned my mouth and bent, latching on to a nipple. With brutal suction, he pulled the flesh deep. Blood surged to the stony peak. Cane flicked his tongue back and forth, keeping time with the sinful sawing rhythm of Law's fiendish finger.

The friction from their busy hands, fingers, and mouths consumed me.

Pulses of pleasure coiled and collided, carrying me away. I ached to dissolve in an explosion of ecstasy.

Chasing the roaring oblivion, a burst of panic fused itself to my frenzy.

"Wait," I cried. Panting and gasping for breath, I jerked my hand from my pussy. "I need to stop."

"That's not your safe word." Law wiggled his finger in deeper.

Lights exploded behind my eyes.

A groan of desperation laced with frustration peeled off my lips. "I-I know…but… Oh, god…I'm going to come if you don't stop."

Cane answered my plea with a sharp bite to my nipple.

Liquid lava burst through my veins.

Instead of taming the burn with the lave of his tongue, as Law had done, Cane lifted from my breast and scowled. "We haven't given you permission yet."

"I know," I helplessly panted. "But I can't hold back."

"You can…and you will," he warned in a soft whisper.

"Who controls you?" Law taunted.

"Both of you," I mewled, both loving and hating the brutal pact I'd made.

"Yes. And the fact that you stopped us before you came screams that you don't want to fail us…that you long to please."

Law hadn't said the word, but his claim shrieked, submission. A chill slid beneath my skin and I wanted to defy him but couldn't. He was right. I didn't want to fail or disappoint them. My heart ached to make them proud.

"You can do this." Cane's tone was edged in a haunting mixture of caution and conviction. He swirled the tip of his tongue over my throbbing peak. "It's safe for you to surrender…to trust us. We won't let you fall."

Maybe not today…but when they left Chicago, I'd be squashed beneath a cement block of emptiness. Mentally shaking my head, I shoved thoughts of my dismal future away and focused on the present.

As if sensing my disconnect, Cane wrapped his hand around my wrist and brought my fingers to his lips. With a hungry gleam in his eyes, he licked the glistening essence that clung to my fingers.

"Sweet and spicy, just like I'd dreamed," he murmured.

The jerk of his cock sent my stare to settle on his heavy and hard thickness. My palm itched and my mouth watered. Instinctively, I reached toward his shaft and raised my lashes. "May I touch you, Sir?"

Law slowly eased his finger from my backside before striding to the bathroom. The sound of water carried into the bedroom as Cane's gaze roamed the contours of my face.

"On your knees, princess," he instructed.

Resentment roared within. Instead of allowing the negative knee-jerk reaction to rule me, I reminded myself that I wasn't in charge. When I knelt onto the carpet, Cane placed his fingers beneath my chin and tipped my head back. The heartwarming smile of approval that glowed on his face silenced my lingering rebellion.

"You look absolutely stunning."

So did he.

Pride, warm and soothing, enveloped me.

"Beyond stunning."

Law's praise startled me.

I hadn't noticed the water had stopped running, but I was hyper aware of the noise of fabric rustling behind me. Seconds later he moved into view. Naked and erect, Law fisted his cock as he stood alongside Cane. I skimmed my gaze over their glorious naked bodies, locking my gaze on their beautiful, weeping shafts. Swallowing the saliva flooding my mouth, I struggled to temper my impatience.

"During your time with Ian and James, did you have sex with them together?"

Cane's question knocked the air from my lungs. How did he know that I'd...

Mika!

Anger flared like a rocket. The club owner had violated my privacy and fed Cane information about me. I clenched my jaw and pinched my lips together.

"Wipe that angry look off your face, girl, and answer the question," Law warned.

"I have every right to be angry with Mika," I spat.

"No. You don't," Cane remarked coldly. Both men released their cocks and shifted into their imperious and infuriating Dominant stances. "Early on, I paid a visit to Genesis. While I was in Mika's office, I watched you with the two men."

"But...that was last summer," I gasped.

"Yes, two weeks after you'd hired Edwards & Pratt." Cane nodded.

"You two began concocting this...this scheme *last summer*?" Shock pinged through me even more violently.

Cane nodded once. "When I watched you basking beneath Ian's single tail, I knew, somehow, someway, we had to have you."

His confession sliced through me like a blade. Part of me was thrilled that I'd enamored him to such a degree, while the other felt as if I'd been targeted by an obsessed stalker. An ominous chill slid up my spine.

"I didn't tell you that to scare you, Sasha. I simply wanted to eliminate all secrets between the three of us. I expect an answer...did you have sex with Ian and James?"

"Yes...a couple of times."

"Double penetration?" Cane pressed.

"Yes." I had no idea why, but embarrassment warmed my cheeks.

"Yes, what?"

"Yes, Sir."

"Then you already know what to expect." Law's words were brimmed in relief.

"I do, Sir."

"Enough talking," Cane bit out. "Open your mouth, princess. Slay my cock with that wicked tongue of yours."

A naughty thrill shot through me. I flashed him a saucy grin, then quickly sobered. Dropping my jaw, I extended my tongue. Law issued a muffled curse as he started stroking his shaft once again. With his other hand, Law threaded his fingers through my hair. Gathering up a handful to lock me in place, he held my head in place while Cane inched in close. The scent of his masculine musk called to me on a purely primitive level. My body hummed as Cane lowered his cock onto my tongue.

His salty, warm essence burst over my taste buds. My blood boiled and I pulled him deep inside my mouth. Swirling my tongue around his throbbing column, I explored each pulsating vein as he issued a savage hiss. Cupping his balls, I lifted my lashes and peered up. His gaze was locked on my mouth as I glided up and down his heavy length. Pleasure rolled over his features, sending slivers of exhilaration speeding through me.

"She feels amazing, doesn't she?" Law murmured.

"So hot…so slick…so unfucking-believable." Cane exhaled a moan.

"That's it. Worship his cock," Law coaxed. "Take him all the way to the back of your throat. Let him feel your silky softness."

Drawing a deep breath through my nose, I wiggled Cane's fat crest deeper and then swallowed. A string of delightful curses rolled off his tongue as he, too, clutched my hair. His breathing grew labored; his grunts turned harsh and raspy. The muscles in his legs trembled. Brimming with empowerment, I gave him my all. Bathing his cock with each swirl of my tongue, I increased the friction and squeezed my lips tightly around him. His animalistic growl only steeled my determination to milk him dry…and if he ended up walking with a limp tomorrow…all the better.

"Son of a bitch," Cane snarled, pulling free of my mouth. "I need… Fuck," he panted. "I need a minute to get myself under control."

A satisfied grin tugged my lips. I'd brought the big, badass Sadist to the edge.

He narrowed his eyes but couldn't keep the mock censure locked in place. With a discerning smirk stamped on his lips, he shook his head. "Your mouth is impressive and skilled. But I suppose you already know that, don't you?"

"I've never had any complaints."

"I bet not," he murmured and took a step back.

Law leaned toward me and skimmed a knuckle down my cheek, drawing my focus. The benevolence reflecting in his blue eyes softened every muscle in my body.

They complemented one another perfectly.

I suddenly grasped the reasons I was so attracted to them.

Cane was hard-edged and unyielding, a taskmaster who challenged my unconventional spirit. Law was his counterpart in every way—kind and compassionate: a lover who nurtured the femininity I kept hidden from view.

I needed more than just their bodies. I needed Cane to guide me through my inky fears and Law to brighten the path so I wouldn't lose my way. They *were* darkness and light. Two opposing forces that not only lightened the emptiness inside me, but held the power to make me whole.

Here, on my knees and at their feet, awareness seeped through me.

For the first time, I'd found peace. Not from a whip or with pain, but beneath their commanding insight and masterful hands.

The fact that they knew me better than I did myself sent a ripple of fear sailing through me.

"How deep are you planning to slice me open?" My voice hitched.

"All the way, sweetheart," Law murmured.

Holding me with a stare teemed in promise and safety, he gripped my hair and dragged his slippery crest over my lips, painting them with his glistening essence.

Jagged shards of lightning sizzled beneath my skin.

Opening, I welcomed him into my mouth and savored the refuge I found in his familiar taste. Reaching up, I wrapped my hands around his strong thighs and held on. Law groaned as he thrust past my lips and over my tongue with long, exacting strokes. Sucking him deep, I trembled at the feel of his pulsing veins cradled inside my mouth.

Cane crouched down beside me. Enveloped in the heat of his body, I cast him a sideways glance. Once again, his gaze was locked on my mouth, watching as Law's cock disappeared and reappeared from between my lips. Cane lifted my hand from Law's thigh and guided my fingers to his own shaft. Fisting him tightly, I stroked his hot, velvet column while working my tongue all over Law's.

"I'm going to drive my fat cock inside your hot little ass while Law squeezes his into your sweet pussy." Cane's tawdry pledge was wrapped in buttery softness. He slid his warm hand up my stomach and circled my nipples with the tip of his finger. My pussy clutched and my clit thundered. "We're going to stretch you…fill you full with every hard, hungry inch."

I issued a muffled whimper. Cane squeezed my nipple and then gave it a vicious tug. A mournful cry leapt from my throat. Law hissed out a curse as Cane danced his fingers to my other nipple, and bestowed the same sublime torture.

Demand throbbed through me like a drum as I greedily slurped Law's cock.

Without warning, he released my hair, cupped my jaw, and pried himself from my mouth. "Bed. Now!" he barked impatiently.

Before I could push myself off the floor, both men plucked me up and led me to the edge of the bed. Law stripped off the comforter and tossed it to the floor. Splaying his hand over the middle of my back, he pressed my chest to the mattress before slowly dragging his fingers down my spine.

"I want to have a little fun before we move into more serious matters."

My ass was poised in the air. Tiny quakes of anticipation rippled through me.

"I knew you'd want to." Though I couldn't see his face, I could hear the laughter in Law's voice. "I'll gather what we'll need for when you're ready to get *serious*."

Things had already surpassed serious and were quickly sailing toward critical, but I decided to keep that observation to myself.

"What is your safe word, princess?" Cane traced the tip of his finger over the welted claim, *Mine,* he'd branded in my flesh last night.

I shivered and swallowed tightly. "Attitude, Sir."

"Good girl."

"Do you have any questions or need to negotiate what we plan to do to you?"

"No, Sir."

"Very well." Cane landed the first strike with such surprising softness that I jolted. He'd chosen a heavy flogger instead of a paddle or crop or some other toy that left a biting burn in its wake. Using the same light stroke, Cane drew the thick falls over my ass. A gentle warmth spread over my flesh; impatience warred. I needed to feel the sting of something far harsher than a inept flogger. After several more delicate lashes, I couldn't take it anymore.

"Please, Sir," I moaned.

"Please what?" Cane wielded another slap, then leaned in close to my face.

"I need more...I need pain."

"No. You need to hand over your control and learn to accept what I give you."

"But...it's not enough."

"And it's not going to be, at least not tonight." An agitated sound crawled from the back of my throat. "I told you earlier, your ass is too raw for play. I also said I might tease you. That's exactly what I intend to do. If the thuddy flogger distresses you so much, use your safe word."

"I'm not in distress, I'm just frustrated."

"Ah." A cocky expression lined his face. "Then use your safe word and end the frustration or...find ways to cope. The choice is yours, and always will be."

Asshole! I didn't want a psychology lesson. I wanted him to light my flesh on fire.

"Or...better yet, surrender your masochistic side as you did your submissive side. Until you're willing to part with all the pieces of your soul, you'll never find completeness, only fragments."

Cane's words sent a chill careening through me.

He pressed a brutal kiss to my lips before standing and lightly dragging the flogger over my ass once again.

The faint, silky strokes felt foreign and internally scraped my psyche, inflicting more agony than if he'd chosen razor blades. I didn't know how to process such subtle sensations. They made me want to crawl out of my skin. My knees buckled. I cried out in misery as I tried to shrink away from the tickling falls.

Cane slapped my ass with his open hand, then dragged his fingernails over my already marred flesh. Ripples of pain curled through me and I moaned in relief. He tossed the flogger aside. The burning ribbons quickly dissolved and melted away.

Squeezing my eyes shut, I bit back the urge to beg and plead for more. Swallowing down a howl of defeat, I buried my face in the bed.

The mattress dipped on both sides of me. Law began to stroke my back. I recognized his tender touch. "It's all right, sweetheart. We'll work those frustrations out of you. By the time we're through, you'll be as sated as a newborn kitten, I promise."

He trailed his strong fingers up my neck and into my scalp before gripping my hair and tugging my head back. I met his carnal stare and drew in a quivering breath. "Would you like us to take the edge off?"

A tiny smirk tugged my lips. "Is that a trick question, Sir?"

Law pinned me with a hungry stare and pulled me onto his naked lap. After searing my lips with a fiery kiss, he glided his teasing mouth down my neck before settling on the ticklish spot below my ear. The heat of his body, his pulsating erection pressed against my stomach, and his moist breath streaming over my flesh swamped my senses.

"I've been dying to be with you again," he murmured.

He wasn't the only one. Working beside him every day, taunted by his alluring scent, seductive stares, and the compelling connection between us, played hell with my hormones.

Law skimmed his tongue over the shell of my ear. Tingles sputtered over my body. My legs trembled. My thighs strained. I couldn't keep from writhing on his lap. He latched on to my mouth with a passionate kiss, then grabbed my calves and pulled them behind him. The movement caused my clit to rub against his shaft. Groaning, I locked my ankles at the small of his back and ground my pussy against him.

"So sensual…so responsive." Cane's voice held a world of awe as he moved in behind me.

I felt drugged by the heat of their bodies and the intoxicating scent of testosterone filling the air. With an unexpected and reverent touch, Cane brushed the hair off my shoulder before dragging his teeth over the racing pulse point at the base of my throat. He slid a warm palm down my back. Gliding lower, he dipped his fingers into my dripping pussy, then painted the slippery liquid over my puckered opening. Law swallowed my desperate whimper as I pressed my hips down until Cane's finger breached the rim. An evil chuckle rolled off his lips as he landed a wicked slap to my ass.

"Who's in control?" he taunted.

When Law released my mouth, I noticed his lips were slightly swollen and glistening. Ignoring Cane's question, I leaned in for another kiss, but Law jerked his head back and narrowed his eyes. He reached up and softly rolled the tip of my nipple between his finger and thumb. I placed my fingers around his and pinched the turgid nub, sighing as fire swelled and spread through my tissue. Law shook his head in warning, then dropped his hand between my legs before teasing and toying with my clit.

"Answer him, now," Law rumbled.

"You are, Sir...I-I mean, you both are."

"Are we?" Law taunted, still slowly strumming my swollen nub. "I think you're still trying to orchestrate things, sweetheart."

"I agree," Cane stated dryly. "We might have to wait to glove up and claim our girl until another time."

Until another time? Oh, hell!

Cane's threat to leave me wet and suspended in need as punishment sent a blast of fear charging through me. So did the fact that I'd irrevocably placed myself in their hands and at their mercy.

Do you really want to fail them?

No. I didn't. A realization that struck me like a gong.

"I'm sorry, Sirs. It's just...I need... I want—"

"We know exactly what you need and what you want, princess," Cane barked. Laving his tongue along my collarbone, he nipped the thin, sensitive flesh there. "If you'll stop Topping from the bottom, we'll satisfy more than your needs and wants...much, much more"

Peering up at him, I nodded. "I will...I promise, Sir."

"Good." Cane shifted his attention toward Law. "It's time to tame our wild minx."

"Past time," Law growled.

Cane lifted me from Law's lap. The sudden loss of his body heat left me bereft. I didn't have to mourn for very long. Cane set me on my feet facing him, plowed his mouth to mine, and wrapped me in his arms.

"Nice," Law murmured as I listened to him walk away.

The crinkle of the condom wrapper was like music to my ears. Hope soared and I mentally reminded myself that if I wanted even a morsel of relief, I had to go with the flow.

"Before we start, there's something I need to do," Cane declared.

"Wha—"

My question was cut off with a squeal as he flipped me to the mattress on my back.

"Spread your legs," he demanded in a hoarse tone.

Without hesitation, I parted my thighs. His stare fixed on my throbbing center for half a heartbeat before he plunged his mouth over my sex. Driving his tongue deep inside, he scraped his teeth over my clit. Crying out, I gripped the sheet as sparks of lightning detonated behind my eyes. Bucking beneath his assault, I moaned as he ate at me like a man possessed.

Law climbed onto the bed, condom in hand, and flashed me a carnal smile. "Turn your head and open your mouth."

Yes. Yes. Oh, god...yes! They weren't going to make me suffer...or maybe they were...in all the right ways.

Law thrust his cock past my lips while Cane continued tongue-fucking me with a vengeance. Hisses, grunts, and moans swelled in a symphony of sexual splendor. I greedily inhaled the primal fragrance of arousal inundating the air. Cane's cunning tongue was driving me to the edge of no return. Tingles of need numbed my fingers and toes. I poured my soul into worshiping Law's cock to keep from exploding all over Cane's unrelenting tongue.

Sucking Law deep to the back of my throat, I swallowed his crest in a tight hug. A primitive growl rumbled from deep inside his chest, followed by a hissing curse. I loved hearing Law vocalize the pleasure charging through him. It thrilled me to know that he derived that depth of pleasure from me.

In tandem, Law pulled from my throat as Cane lifted from my cunt. Blinking through the lustful haze fogging my brain, I could see his lips and chin were glazed in my juices. But it was the fervent fire in his eyes that captured all my attention. Cane crawled onto the bed like a wolf. Never leaving my gaze, he slid his fingers through mine and dragged my arms up over my head. As he pressed his weight against me, his face was etched in lust...his eyes filled with compassion. Everything about him unraveled me.

"We'll go slow and let you adjust to us both," he quietly explained. "But by the time we're through, you'll know exactly what it feels like to be claimed...owned. Every time you breathe, move, or speak, you'll remember the brand we're leaving on your heart, mind, body, and soul." The conviction woven in his quiet words made anxiety and ecstasy shudder through me.

I was still trembling when he lifted away.

With a grunt, Law rolled the condom down his angry cock before cinching his strong hands around my waist. He pulled me to his chest, then pivoted and flopped to the bed on his back, taking me with him. I let out a yelp of surprise followed by a nervous laugh. A knowing smirk tugged his lips as he arched his hips. His cock skated between my slippery folds, and I let out a needy moan when his crest nudged my clit. As he rocked against me, I closed my eyes and savored his torment. It took all the strength I had not to grab the base of his shaft and stuff every delicious inch deep inside me. Lost in his cock's languid glide between my folds, I jolted when Cane skimmed a warm palm down my back.

"Relax," he murmured. In a louder voice, he asked Law, "Are you ready, man?"

"Beyond ready. My cock's going to split open if I don't get inside her."

Thank god!

Cane grunted and gripped my hips. Digging his fingers deep into my flesh, he lifted me while Law aligned his fat crest to my entrance. I sucked in several deep breaths and struggled to relax as he wedged each hard inch into my clutching core. Stretching me…filling me, he wore a look of awe as I stared down at his gorgeous face.

"Christ, you feel good. You're as tight and silky-hot as the first time, sweetheart."

Gripping my hair, he pulled me to his mouth and claimed me in a harsh, punishing kiss. When he was fully seated inside, Law began rocking his hips. As he dragged his swollen crest over the tingling cluster of nerve endings buried deep, my heart pounded and my breaths grew shallow.

The scruff adorning Cane's face rasped over my skin as he dragged his tongue from one butt cheek to the next. Pulses of pleasure thrummed through me. Law drank in my purrs and my muffled yelp of surprise when Cane spread my butt cheeks apart and swirled his tongue over my crinkled flesh.

Wracked with tremors, electricity and rapture sizzled beneath my skin.

The longing to come strained through me, but I chained my release down.

I refused to fail them.

Cane speared his tongue through my rim, withdrew, and unexpectedly abandoned his torment. I issued a quivering whimper. Law massaged my scalp to help ease my frustration.

"Don't worry, princess. I'm just getting started," Cane growled.

Replacing his tongue with a cold, lube-covered finger, he gently coated my tiny opening while rubbing his hand over the small of my back. He prepared me with such tenderness it brought tears to my eyes and twisted my heart.

Law's hips stilled. He kissed me again and reached between us and strummed my clit while Cane worked his slippery fingers in and out of my ass. Stretching and thinning my tightly gathered rim, he surged deep, sending rippling streaks of fire ricocheting outward.

Eager for Cane to fill me, I whimpered and arched my back…thrusting my hips toward him. I'd expected him to chastise me, but he didn't. Instead, he squeezed his thick crown beside his fingers and slowly pressed forward.

Colorful lights flashed behind my eyes.

Law gripped my hair and lifted my head back. Abandoning my lips, he peered up at me from beneath heavy lids. "Breathe as he works himself inside you, girl."

I nodded nervously and filled my lungs as Cane slowly fed his steely cock into my dark passage.

Law tensed and clenched his jaw. Sweat dotted his brow.

My nerve endings screamed and burned.

Stretched.

Filled.

Pressure built like a summer storm.

Neither man moved. Like a vice, they held me with their rigid sabers.

The sensation was excruciating, mesmerizing, and glorious.

"Are you all right?" Concern knitted Law's brows.

"Yes," I hissed before sucking in a gasp. "Move…please. I need someone to move."

A flicker of lust dashed across his face as he lowered his hips into the mattress. The pressure retreated, only to amp back up when he thrust inside me again. Cane then slightly withdrew and glided his slick cock back inside my ass. My eyes rolled to the back of my head as a salacious moan rushed off my lips.

Alternating thrusts, they quickly found their rhythm. Time and space were confined to the slick, hot friction of their driving shafts, the electricity from their stroking fingers, and the strained sounds of pleasure rolling off their tongues.

I felt as if I'd been set free.

Relentlessly, they slammed into me, claiming and owning my soul with wild and devastating command. The sound of slapping flesh melded with their animalistic grunts and my keening cries.

Drowning in pleasure, I surrendered.

The demand to shatter clawed me.

Swelling.

Surging.

Threatening to annihilate me.

Salvation from their sublime torment was just *one* word away.

I needed that word now.

"Help me!" I screamed.

Freezing in mid-thrust, Law's fingers stilled on my clit. A look of warning strained across his face.

Cane slammed balls deep before clutching my ass and holding me immobile. "Hold it back, girl."

CHAPTER ELEVEN

THE HITCH IN Cane's voice and the quivering muscles of his legs, pressed against my thighs, along with the savage expression contorting Law's face, confirmed that we were all fighting the same losing battle.

"I can't," I pitifully wailed. "It's too much. Please!"

Law moved his hand from my hair and cupped my cheek. "Suffer, gorgeous. Suffer sweetly."

He thumbed a tear from my cheek, one I didn't know I'd shed, and then arched deeper inside me. I bore down around them, squeezing with such force they shouted out curses in tandem.

"Please. Oh, god, please," I begged unabashedly.

Want had decimated my pride.

Tears streaked down my face as I continued to plead.

Cane's warm breath caressed my ear. "Just a little longer."

Sinking his teeth into the top of my shoulder, he bit down hard. Law strummed my clit once more as they hammered in and out of me. The eruption of pain and pleasure rolled me under in a wave of ecstasy. Shadows of darkness blurred my vision as the hum singing inside me swelled to a deafening cacophony.

"Please!" I wailed.

Mentally flailing, I tried to find a lifeline to keep me from toppling over the edge, but I was too far gone. Law tensed and stilled. Cane gripped my hips in a brutal hold as his cock jerked and swelled deep inside me. A rumbling roar leapt from Law's chest. They both began shuttling manically. The burning friction sent me up in flames, scorching my resolve. Sailing headlong into oblivion, like a freight train, I yelled out in mournful defeat.

The waves of release sucked me under just as they barked out my salvation in unison. "Come!"

Plummeted beneath the force of their slamming bodies, I threw back my head and screamed as the spine-bending orgasm ripped through me. Clamping down hard, I convulsed around their driving shafts. Our cries of rapture melded together and thundered off the walls, vibrating me to the bone, as they spilled deep inside me.

Melded together, our ragged breathing slowly calmed. My body continued to spasm and quake while their rigid shafts pulsed and twitched inside me. The muscles in my arms gave way, and I sank toward Law's chest. He cupped my face and drew me to his lips. The passion and adoration in his kiss overwhelmed. Emotions rushed to the surface and I couldn't stem the flow as I sobbed helplessly against his mouth.

After carefully easing from my ass, Cane covered his hot, rugged body over my back. "Shhh, princess. We've got you. It's all right."

Though his words were meant to soothe and reassure, they only served to split me open even wider. The walls I'd foolishly built around me came crashing down in an earthquake of clarity.

I had surrendered to them…surrendered my soul. A feeling of vindication warmed me as I lay surrounded by their sweat-soaked bodies. Law continued to bathe me in lush, soothing kisses, while Cane nuzzled his lips against my neck. I exhaled a sigh of contentment.

I was lost in their affection, and my thoughts scattered. Sated and at peace, I felt small and incredibly fragile, but safer and more secure than I could comprehend.

With my head resting on Law's chest, listening to the reassuring beat of his heart, we lay meshed as one for several long minutes. It was Cane who finally broke the spell and slowly lifted from my back.

"Stay right there. I won't be but a minute."

Simply purring in compliance, I couldn't muster the energy to open my eyes. Water began running in the bathroom while Law's fingertips traced indiscriminate patterns along my back.

"Are you all right, sweetheart?"

"Mmm." My sated hum tickled the back of my throat.

Law's chest shook in a silent chuckle. "I'm going to like keeping you all soft and satisfied."

"Me, too," I murmured with a tiny smile.

Law moaned as he eased from inside me as Cane returned with a warm washcloth. With the same bewildering tenderness he'd displayed earlier, he cleaned me up.

"Get some sleep. You've earned it," he murmured before pressing his lips to mine in a kiss teeming with devotion.

You can't fall in love with him...with either of them, I inwardly reminded.

A fact I needed to keep in the forefront of my mind. I might not be able to fall in love with them, but I could enjoy what little time we had together. There were no rules prohibiting that.

Cane climbed onto the mattress and lifted me to the middle of the bed. Wedged between their heated bodies, I laid my head down on the pillow and closed my eyes.

Immediately, they flashed open again. "Wait. I can't stay," I blurted out as I sat up. "Tomorrow is Friday. I have to be at work."

"*We* have to be at work, sweetheart." Law sat up beside me. Placing his hands on my shoulders, he eased me back down to the mattress. "I've set the alarm on my phone. You'll be up in plenty of time for us to drive you home so you can get ready."

"We'll stay here again tomorrow night so we can take you to the submissive meeting on Saturday morning," Cane added matter-of-factly.

I felt my hackles rising inside me.

My lethargic muscles grew tense.

It was true what they said about old habits dying hard. Mine were rising to the surface faster than I could herd them in another direction. Both men leveled me with harsh, quizzical expressions, as if daring me to fight them.

You didn't just surrender your all to leave claw marks in your pride by snagging it back. Decide what you want, because you sure as shit can't have it both ways.

A part of me felt as if I were rolling over...exposing my underbelly to their Dominant talons, but I couldn't allow myself to retreat. While this new, unchartered path felt foreign and intimidating, I had to trust they'd stay true to their words and not let me fall.

I swallowed tightly and nodded. "Thank you, Sirs. I appreciate what you're both doing for me."

Slow smiles curled their lips as the two men shared a silent glance.

"Good night, gorgeous," Law murmured as he leaned in and brushed a kiss over my lips.

Cane swept the hair from my face and pressed his lips to mine as well before they both settled down beside me. Law slung a strong arm around my waist and tugged my back against his chest. Cane curled onto his side and pressed his tight ass against my stomach. Once we were lined up like spoons in a drawer, he reached up and turned off the bedside lamp.

Enveloped in their heated bodies and the raw maleness of them, I simply closed my eyes and melted away.

WHAT SEEMED ONLY minutes later, I was stirred awake by the feel of roaming hands and hungry mouths careening over my flesh. Writhing beneath their sweet assault, my body throbbed with a delicious ache. Through the hazy fog enveloping my brain, images of last night and the pleasure they'd bestowed unspooled like a motion picture. My nipples grew taut and moisture gathered between my legs.

"It's time to wake up, sleepyhead," Law whispered before slanting his lips over one pert nipple and sucking it deep inside his hot, slippery mouth.

"Mmm," I moaned. "Five more minutes…please?"

Cane chuckled and slid his fingers between my folds. "Wet. Ready." He growled as he teased my clit. My pussy tightened and my stomach muscles rippled. "Pity, five minutes isn't enough time to do the things we'd like to do to you."

"I don't mind being late." I rolled to my back and spread my legs.

"Greedy little girl." Law cupped a breast and stroked my nipples. Hunger sluiced through my system like quicksilver leaving a delicious throbbing trail in its wake. "We have a conference call in two hours."

The petulant moan rolling off my tongue quickly turned to a gasp when Cane landed a biting slap to my mound. "Get up and put on your dress. I'll have the car ready in ten minutes."

"You don't need to go to all that trouble. I'll grab a cab back to the office, pick up my car, and drive myself home." Cane frowned. Obviously, he didn't like my suggestion. "Or I can get out of bed now and—"

"Can you handle the call alone?" he asked Law.

"Absolutely." A wicked grin kicked up the corners of his mouth.

"Looks like you're going to be late for work after all, sweetheart."

Before I could even process what was happening, Law lifted me off the bed and set me on my feet. He caught the condom Cane tossed his way, and they both quickly sheathed their twin erections.

"I predict you're going to have a long, frustrating day, princess." The evil laugh that tore from Cane's lips sent a shiver all the way to my toes.

"Frustrating? I don't think so," I purred. "Waking up this way is far better than coffee."

"I wouldn't bet on that," Law chuckled as he grabbed the bottle of lube off the nightstand and coated the latex hugging his cock.

They moved in close and pressed me between their hot bodies. I closed my eyes and drank in the sinful sensation.

"Hands behind your head, Sasha." Law's hard and demanding tone brooked no argument. I quickly complied. "Good, girl. Leave them there. Understood?"

"Yes, Sir."

Dragged under by the shock of their busy fingers and tongues, I was thrust into sensory overload beneath their all-out assault. The slow, enticing seduction from last night was gone, replaced by a calculated, unrelenting, and well-choreographed ambush. I had no doubt they'd practiced this same carnal punishment a million times.

Drowning in a flurry of fingers and mouths, I didn't know who was touching me where. I only knew that Cane was facing me and Law was at my back while they inundated me beneath a relentless barrage of strokes, pinches, kisses, and tugs. I abandoned the effort to decipher their individual touch, and surrendered with a whimper, to bask in the ecstasy they granted.

Law nipped the slope of my shoulder as he wiggled two slippery fingers over the rim of my ass. Bursts of tiny explosions detonated as he pressed first one finger, then another past my gathered ring.

"Oh, god," I whimpered.

"You can't wait for me to squeeze my fat cock inside this sweet, tight hole, can you, sweetheart?"

"No," I wailed. "Please…"

"I love hearing the desperation when you beg so sweetly," he taunted, wiggling his fingers.

I whimpered mournfully.

"Yes…suffer hard for us, gorgeous."

Cane's strong, muscular thighs nudged my legs apart. His fingers strummed my clit, stoking the inferno blazing there until I feared I'd spontaneously combust. The conflagration grew even hotter when Cane unmercifully slammed his cock into my pussy. I exhaled on a grunt and squeezed my fingers to keep from gripping his shoulders, wrapping my legs around his slim waist and riding him like a wild beast.

Lost in the beautiful oblivion of his golden eyes, I clutched at Cane's cock and rocked my hips, meeting his fervent strokes. His nimble fingers teased and tugged my clit as I sailed toward the heavens.

Cold, slick lube trickled over my backside. Anticipation melted up my spine as Law diligently coated my opening. Seconds later, he removed his fingers, replacing them with the bulbous head of his cock. Panting and groaning, I writhed as he stretched inch after agonizing inch through my tiny rim.

Bolts of lightning zapped me. I was stretched and filled to the point of pain, and the pressure enveloped me in a decadent burn. I cried out and rolled my hips in an effort to quell the wicked blaze.

"Easy, baby," Law murmured. "We'll make it better."

Once again, they found their rhythm. Chained beneath their powerful thrusts, friction scraped…burned…tingled. Cane's busy fingers dancing over my clit only served to fuel the white-hot inferno clawing within me.

Blinded by the flames, I clamped down around them. Keening cries spilled off my tongue.

Shuttling in and out of my pussy, Cane held me with a fierce stare.

"I warned you…" he panted. "I…grant no…mercy." Gripping my hips tighter, his muscles trembled. His nostrils flared and his chest expanded. He slammed deep inside me and paused. "You…don't have…permission," he bit out in a snarl.

With a feral roar, he erupted inside me.

Law plundered my ass, cursing and grunting.

My whole body sizzled.

His bellicose growl thundered through me as he exploded as well.

My mind screamed for release as their cocks jerked and pulsed.

"Please!" I screamed.

"No!" they barked in tandem.

It was then I realized they had no intention of letting me come.

Tears of frustration spilled down my cheeks.

Fucking bastards!

Anger, bitter and far hotter than the useless orgasm raging within, expanded.

I saw red.

Their chests heaved against me in labored breaths. I lowered my hands and sucked in a ragged breath of my own. Tensing, I clenched my teeth. Cane, still pulsing inside my cunt, gripped my cheeks and pinned me with a glare. Daggers of fire shot from his eyes.

"Don't do this, girl. You earned the punishment. Accept it, or we can give you more if you let your anger to take over. Understand?"

"No. I don't understand," I bit out as I tried to wiggle away from their embedded cocks.

"Sasha," Law warned, digging his fingers in my hips and firmly holding me in place.

"Don't Sasha, me," I snapped over my shoulder. "How does offering to drive myself home deserve a punishment?"

When they silently pulled from inside me, I felt hollowed out…empty and alone.

"You rescinded your surrender…took back your control, over something as petty as a fucking ride home." The sharp, bitter edge in Cane's voice sliced deep.

He stormed away, following Law into the bathroom.

Guilt bled through my veins, annihilating every drop of my self-righteous anger.

Though I hadn't meant to, I'd failed them…failed miserably.

Swallowing back the lump of emotion lodged in my throat, I blinked away my tears as they returned.

"So that's it?" Though my question was laced with bravery, I felt lost and insecure. "I suppose you're going to toss me to the curb like all the others, now?"

A tear slid down my cheek and I angrily swiped it away.

Law's expression grew dark—Cane's turned even harsher.

Like a panther, Law stalked toward me. His lips curled in a nasty smile. Gripping my hair in a tight fist, he yanked my head back and stared into my eyes. Fury rolled off him in potent and sizzling waves. "Don't compare us to what you've experienced in the past. We're not those Doms," he ground out as he tore his hand from my hair.

I'd never seen this aggressive side of Law before. He was every bit as intimidating as Cane.

A shiver slid down my spine.

Ironically, Cane was the one dispensing compassion and trailed a tender knuckle down my cheek. "No one is tossing you to the curb, princess. You've paid the price for your transgression. We'll put it behind us now and move forward."

His forgiveness didn't erase the bitter taste of defeat that lay on my tongue.

"Yes, Sir." I darted a wary glance Law's way.

The bewildering need to try and soothe his savage beast consumed me. Though I felt as if I were dodging landmines, I wrapped my arms around Law's waist and laid my head on his chest. The thundering beat of his heart reverberated in my ear while I gently stroked his back.

"I'm sorry I upset you, Sir."

He gripped my jaw and claimed my mouth beneath an angry kiss. Remorse tumbled through me.

"Don't let it happen again, girl," he growled.

"I-I'll try not to." *But I always seem to fall down.*

Cane eased in behind me and draped my dress over my shoulder. "We need to get our clothes on."

"Yes, Sir." I slid my arms from Law's body and peered up at him. "Are we okay?"

A shadow of a smile fluttered over his lips. "We're fine, sweetheart. Take your time getting ready at home. I'll handle the call with Brent about the packaging."

I nodded and bit my tongue, fighting the urge to remind him that my sales rep was an asshole—a fact Law knew well already.

"Thank you, Sir."

As I moved to get dressed, he snaked an arm around my waist and pulled me against his hard body. "If the prick gives me any shit, I'll line up another packaging company. I don't like you subjecting yourself to Brent's misogynistic bullshit."

A wide smile spread across my lips as he pressed a kiss to my forehead. "Thank you. I appreciate that."

Minutes later we were dressed and out the door. Law hurried down the hall to his suite as Cane and I stepped into the elevator. "Are you coming home with me?"

"I hadn't planned on it, but I can if you'd like."

Suddenly, I didn't know how to answer. I didn't want to dig myself back into a world of trouble. As if sensing my hesitation, he flashed me a toe-curling grin.

"Go home and get ready for work. The car will wait and bring you back to the city. I have some things I need to take care of."

The doors opened and he escorted me through the lobby. Glancing down, I cringed and wrapped my coat tightly around me. Though I didn't take the walk of shame often, I loathed it all the same. As we reached the front door, Cane pulled me in for a slow, sultry kiss.

"Go ahead and pack a bag so you can stay with us this weekend."

Excitement and apprehension fluttered through me. "Okay."

Cane flashed me a disapproving scowl.

I took quick inventory to make sure no one was within earshot before I whispered an amended, "Yes, Sir."

"We'll work on honorifics." He smirked before landing a discreet swat to my ass.

Outside, he settled me into the car, pressed a soft kiss to my lips, and pinned me with a sober stare. "No masturbating, princess."

I couldn't lie. The thought had crossed my mind more than once thanks to my slick folds still throbbing with a vengeance. The disappointment that lined their faces when I failed them earlier clung to my flesh like sand on sunscreen. My body might want to rush home and rub out an orgasm, but my heart wasn't in it.

"I won't, Sir."

Cane flashed me a mischievous grin and closed the car door.

An hour and a half later, I stepped into my office to find Law pacing like a caged tiger.

"What's wrong?"

"Brent," he spat, over-enunciating the *t*.

"What happened?" I asked, tossing my coat on the credenza before snagging the cup of coffee from his hand. As I took a long, greedy sip, his brows arched in warning.

"At work, we're equals. You can't whip out your *D* card at the office. Interference with work, family, or social interactions and obligations will not be tolerated. Remember?" I quoted Cane's contract with a sassy smile.

A devilish grin crawled across his lips as he moved in close to my ear. "I know, but you might want to remember that, after hours, your ass belongs to me."

I flashed him a sultry smile and lowered my voice. "How could I forget, *Sir?*"

Amber hurried into my office clutching a stack of messages in one hand and a steaming cup of coffee in the other.

"Bless you," I exhaled on a grateful sigh.

"Did you tell her about butthead Brent?" Amber asked Law as she handed the cup and memos to me.

"I was just about to."

"Oh, good." She rubbed her hands together with an evil smile and lowered her backside on the edge of my desk. "Law had the little weasel on speakerphone. You're going to blow a gasket."

I took another gulp of coffee to steel myself. "Okay. I'm ready."

Law shot an irritated glance Amber's way as his lips flattened. "I was going to tone it down a bit, but…"

"You don't have to candy-coat it for Ms. E," my assistant assured.

"I hadn't planned to candy-coat any—"

"Enough!" I barked at their banter. "Tell me!"

A promise of retribution flashed in Law's eyes, and a wave of heat rushed through me. When he began revealing the details of the conversation, nothing about Brent's comments surprised me, until the end.

"Even with all his sleazy remarks about your tits and ass, I didn't completely lose my shit until he confessed that he's always wanted to fuck you. He knew he'd never have that chance, so he offered me ten dollars if I could get you into bed and videotape us having sex. After I called him every four-letter word I'd ever learned and threatened to rip his heart out with my bare hands if he called or tried to contact you again, I fired him."

The air in my lungs froze while the rest of my body erupted in volcanic rage.

Amber plucked up the phone and punched in some numbers while I paced in absolute fury.

"Good afternoon, Cardness Distribution, Sasha Evans' assistant here. Ms. Evans would like to speak with Herbert Cardness immediately." Amber paused. Her lips curled in a malicious smile. "*Indeed* this is an emergency. Thank you."

I stormed toward my desk as Amber handed me the phone.

"And that's my cue to leave," she giggled as she hurried toward the hall.

"Ditto. I hate hearing a grown man cry." Law chuckled as he strolled from my office, closing the door behind him.

Forty-five minutes later, Herbert Cardness had promised to fire Brent Fuckwad Morris and offered to distribute my products for the next six months at no cost. I rescinded my threat to file a sexual harassment lawsuit.

Riding high after the call, I sought to give Law the good news. I found him in the main conference room with his cell phone pressed to his ear. Eyes closed, he scrubbed a hand through his hair. His face was etched in hard lines and irritation rolled off him in waves.

Pausing, I stood in the doorway fearing there was a glitch in the ad campaign.

He exhaled a heavy sigh and pinched the bridge of his nose. "Don't cry. I'm sorry for what happened, but there's nothing I can do, Ruby."

Ruby? The former sub he and Cane had shared…the one who'd fallen in love with him?

A blast of jealousy thundered through me and I had to fight the urge to race into the room, rip the phone from his hand, and tell Ruby to go fuck herself. Blindsided by my visceral and possessive reaction, I reared back and swallowed the panic rising within.

Was I already losing my heart to him…to him *and* Cane?

No. Oh, god…no! I inwardly mewled. Immediately, I began slapping bricks and mortar around my heart. I'd agreed from the start that I wouldn't let my emotions get tangled up in such ways. I'd just started this new journey, dammit! I couldn't let them banish me the way they had Ruby. I was stronger than her…more determined. Still, the time had come to divide my heart and body, and I needed to do it now.

"I know you're scared, but I can't save you." Law opened his eyes and caught sight of me in the doorway. He motioned me to the chair beside him. I shook my head and took another step back, ashamed for being caught eavesdropping. A scowl lined his face as he insistently pointed to the empty chair beside him. With a frown, I eased into the chair while my insecurities uncoiled like snakes.

"We've been over this before. Begging will accomplish nothing. My feelings aren't going to change." Law pinched the bridge of his nose and shook his head. "Absolutely not! You are not moving in with me. I suggest you take your sister's offer and stay with her. I have to go into a meeting. I'll try to check in with you later."

Without saying good-bye, he hung up. He pressed his lips together in a tight, grim line.

"Is she okay?" I asked, easing into the chair.

"No. Her husband wiped out their checking account and left her…left her penniless and pregnant."

"You were rather hard on her, don't you think?"

"I'm not a heartless bastard, Sasha. If it had been anyone but Ruby, I would have been far more sympathetic and helped. But she constantly calls and tries to manipulate me to ride in on a white horse and save her. I'm trying to be tactful and firm." Law's expression grew even darker.

His explanation eased my jealousy and my fears. "She's not over you…and simply wants you back."

"No. Ruby has other issues…private ones I won't share with anyone."

The staunch vow to protect her privacy intensified the respect I held for him. The man possessed far more integrity than I'd given him credit for. I felt myself shifting as warmth and admiration rolled through me. If I didn't bind my heart in steel and barbed wire, I'd easily lose it to him and Cane, exactly like I had with all the others. Unwilling to tempt that level of pain again, I mentally slapped another layer around my heart.

"I didn't mean to intrude on your conversation."

"You didn't. I invited you…remember? I won't hide anything from you, Sasha. I believe in open, honest—"

"Communication," I cut him off with an angst-laced chuckle.

"Exactly." The sexy smile curling on his lips wiped away my unease and stirred the embers low in my belly. Before my brain fixated on the orgasm still simmering inside me, he steered my focus toward work. "How did your talk with Herbert go?"

After filling him in and sharing the good news, we returned to my office and concentrated on Ageless Dream. Three hours later, Amber tapped on my door and announced she was going to lunch, but promised to bring us back a pizza. A few minutes later, my cell phone rang. I checked the screen and answered Cane's call with a happy smile.

"Hello, princess. I trust you and Law are keeping busy?"

"Yes, we are."

"Good. But it's time for you to take a break now."

"I-I don't understand." I looked at Law in confusion. A slow, lazy smile crawled across his mouth as he simply shrugged.

"Open your office door," Cane instructed.

"Yes, Sir."

Rising, I pulled the door open to find him standing in front of me. I stumbled back in surprise as he pocketed his phone and strolled in. After kissing me soundly, he closed and locked the door behind him.

He and Law sat down on the couch, both wearing expectant expressions. It was blatantly obvious they'd plotted something nefarious. Curiosity, excitement, and a hint of fear hummed in my body while a million questions tangled in my mind.

"What have you two schemed up now?"

"I hear you wear naughty lingerie under your conservative suits. Show us what you have on today, princess."

I felt the blood drain from my face. "Excuse me?"

"Strip," Cane ordered.

"But…but…this is my office. I've employees who might… Your contract states that—"

"I'm well aware of *every* word, girl," He growled. "Thanks to Law's texts, I also know that your assistant is at lunch. We're completely alone. Now *strip*."

Like a snarling beast, defiance roared to the surface. Biting back the order for him to go fuck himself that lay poised on my tongue, I pressed my lips together, silently seething.

"Take it down a couple notches," Law warned.

Kiss my ass, you texting traitor!

"As we suspected, this is a particularly difficult challenge for you. Why?" Cane asked.

"Because you're asking me to strip in my *office*. This isn't a dungeon or a bedroom," I bit out, singeing them both with a fiery glare.

"The door is locked," he replied nonchalantly.

A low growl slid from the back of my throat.

Law's expression was grim determination. "This is your turf, your fortress. You're queen of the hill here. There's no one above you. *You* control it all."

Damn right I did, and I was good at it, too. Why did they want to rip away my confidence?

"Stripping off your clothes is a metaphor, girl. You're smart enough to understand that. It's time to remove the final layer separating us from *all* of you."

"You mean abandon my identity," I spat.

"Watch your tone," Law warned. "We have no desire to steal your identity. We simply want you to place all the beautifully bold and fragile pieces of yourself in our hands."

"Why? So you can inspect and dissect them, too?"

"Yes. We've handled your heart with kid gloves while we laid claim to your luscious body. And we intent to continue guarding it. But it's time you surrender your soul, Sasha." Cane's voice was gentle, yet each syllable felt like razor blades, shredding the flesh from my bones.

"We're not going to allow you to stay tucked inside your comfort zone forever," Law stated sympathetically. "That would be a great disservice to you, and us, as well. It's time to let us in…all the way in."

I didn't know if I possessed the strength to hand them both my sexual power and my professional power. It meant I'd literally have to tear myself in two. They were asking the impossible.

I found a wealth of comfort and security being Sasha Evans, Owner and CEO of Ageless Dreams Skin Care. Why were they bent on stripping that away?

As if a light exploded in my brain, I realized their demand had nothing to do with my identity, but everything to do with my stubborn pride.

Casting my eyes to the floor, I choked down the anxiety and fear roaring inside me.

Sucking in a deep breath, I raised my trembling hands and slid off my suit coat.

"That's our brave and strong girl." Law's warm encouragement did little to tame the turbulence raging within.

When I inched the zipper of my skirt free, the garment slid over my hips and pooled at my feet. A tremor of indecision shook me. Tentatively fingering the collar of my blouse, I dug deep and released the buttons before tossing the silky fabric to the floor.

Standing before them wearing a pink corset, matching lace thong, stockings, and stilettos, I felt more vulnerable and exposed than when

I'd been naked in bed with them.

The fear of Amber cutting her lunch short and attempting to stroll into my office with a fucking pizza invaded every corner of my brain. She was neither stupid nor naïve. There wasn't any logical reason for me to have the door locked, alone with two gorgeous men in my office, that wasn't steeped in sexual innuendo. Knowing she'd have to knock didn't buy me any comfort. I'd never be able to throw my clothes on fast enough without arousing her suspicions. Adding to my angst, I had no idea what Cane and Law planned to do next. Did they intend to bend me over the couch and fuck my brains out? Dear lord, how was I supposed to mask the scent of sex in the air?

Humiliation crawled up my body from the tips of my toes to the roots of my hair.

This was not the time, and definitely not the place, to play fucking head games. They might have annihilated my walls, sexually, like a hot knife through butter—and thankfully the fallout had been minimal—but expecting me to toss off my armor in the one environment I felt most secure and successful was asking entirely too much.

Icy panic sluiced through my veins. The minute I raised my chin, I'd expose every flaw, failure, and insecurity that I'd painstakingly hidden from view. Like rabid dogs, they'd both be on me, biting, snarling, and ripping out my jugular.

Slammed sideways beneath a tempest of humiliation, I bit back a scream.

I couldn't let that happen. Contract or not, I wouldn't surrender to them. Not here. Not now. This was my office, for shit's sake! I had a company to run…a reputation to protect. It was time to put my clothes back on and end this charade.

Ah, so you're willing to fail them…willing to give up the life-altering fulfillment they ache to give you, just to keep your pathetic pride intact? Brilliant!

I wanted to bitch-slap the little voice in my head. Still, I couldn't turn a blind eye. Holding my pride in a death grip would be the same as inviting the jaws of failure to open wide and swallow me whole.

My whole body shuddered.

"Sasha…it's all right," Law assured.

Sending up a silent prayer they wouldn't fall off the couch laughing, I mentally ripped the cloak of confidence from me. Slowly lifting my head, I lowered to my knees.

"Wow," Law murmured. "There she is…in all her elegant glory."

"And more stunning than ever before." Cane's voice was teemed with awe.

CHAPTER TWELVE

STANDING, THEY RUSHED to me and knelt by my side. They wrapped me in their arms as I trembled and cried. Law and Cane whispered words of praise and encouragement while they caressed my arms and back. I couldn't find words to convey the depth of gratitude as their unconditional approval spilled through me, so I simply nuzzled my head on Cane's chest first, then Law's.

"Thank you, princess. Your surrender is blindingly beautiful." Cane tilted my chin back and kissed me with more passion than I'd ever felt in my life. When he begrudgingly pulled away, a wicked smile kicked up a corner of his mouth. "I can't wait to peel that sexy outfit off your hot body tonight."

"*We* can't wait," Law growled before claiming my mouth in an equally toe-curling kiss.

Closing my eyes, I inwardly sighed in relief.

Instead of tumbling to my death when I'd cast off my pride, I'd found myself surrounded in their safety net of compassion—just like they'd promised from the start. Law nipped at my bottom lip and slowly released me.

Both of them lifted me to my feet. I wanted to weep at the loss of their delicious affection.

Though it had been touch and go for several uncertain minutes, and while the ground beneath me was far from stable, I'd been able to complete their task. A sense of rightness filled me.

"You may put your clothes back on, sweetheart." Law gently stroked my cheek.

That's it? They weren't going to send me back down on my knees for a blow job, or wedge themselves inside me for a quickie?

As if reading my thoughts, Law grinned. "You don't do nooners. Remember?" I felt my cheeks burn as he turned toward Cane. "Do you have time to join us for lunch, man? Amber is bringing back pizza."

Cane glanced at his watch and smiled. "I'll *make* time for pizza."

Drying my eyes, I picked up my clothes and began putting them on.

Dread wiggled inside my brain. I hadn't a clue what to tell Amber, or how to even introduce her to Cane. While I didn't *owe* my assistant an explanation of any kind, we *were* friends, and I didn't want to lie or drive a wedge between us. She was the only other female on the planet that I'd ever truly bonded with.

My pensive expression captured Law's attention. He cocked his head and arched a brow. "Problem?"

"Yes," I replied, dragging on my suit coat and pressing my palms over the fabric. "I don't know what to say to Amber about Cane."

"Tell her the truth," the man in question barked.

I blanched. "I can't! She and I share a lot, but she has no idea I'm involved in the lifestyle. I'd like to keep it that way if you don't mind."

"We're not saying confess your kink," Law drawled. "Tell her that he's my new business partner."

"Your what?"

"That's right," Cane preened.

"You work for Edwards & Pratt, too?"

"No."

"Ageless Dreams is the last job I'm contracted to complete in order to fulfill my obligations to Edwards," Law began. "I gave my notice while designing your campaign. I always finish what I start."

"So...you two are what...partnering up and starting a new company?"

"That's the plan." Law opened my office door and peered toward Amber's desk. "Let's continue this conversation in the break room. It will look less conspicuous that way."

I mutely nodded. I tried to absorb the bombshell about their new company as the three of us strolled down the hall.

"So what exactly is it that you do?" I asked Cane as I set paper plates, napkins, and waters around the table.

"I was a marketing manager at a different agency."

"In New York?"

"Yes." Cane nodded.

"So is that how you two met?"

"No." Law grinned. "We were roommates in college."

"So who introduced whom to the lifestyle?"

"Penelope Aston," Cane said with a wistful, over-dramatic sigh.

His unexpected theatrics made me giggle. "I take it she wasn't as prim and proper as her name implied?"

"Not even close. She was a nasty, horny little vixen who taught us volumes about kink," Law laughed.

"And craved pain like bears do honey," Cane added.

"I can't wait to hear this." I sank down in the chair between them, propped my elbows on the table, and dropped my chin to my palms.

"You won't get jealous, will you?" Law teased.

"Pfft," I scoffed. "The seamless style you two possess, I'd have to be jealous of half the subbies in New York. I'm good, trust me."

"All right." Cane chuckled. "We were starting our freshman year at Columbia. Penelope was in her last year of graduate studies and happened to be our floor advisor. Law and I both had been selected to intern at a decent ad firm, so while the other kids went back home to celebrate Thanksgiving with their families, we stayed and worked."

"Aw, that must have been a rough holiday for you two."

"Not really," Law said with a smirk.

"Penelope didn't want us spending Thanksgiving alone, and since she didn't have any family, she invited us to dinner. We hit a hamburger joint in Times Square and then headed back to school. She asked if we wanted a drink, so we followed her back to her room. She gave us some nasty alcohol that tasted like prison-brewed formaldehyde." Cane wrinkled his nose and shuddered from the memory.

"After a couple of shots, our clothes pretty much fell off. She pulled a big suitcase out of her closet, and that's when our education began...in earnest," Law added with a grin.

"Aw, hell. You skipped the best part, man."

"No. We're not going to talk about that." Law adamantly shook his head.

"Oh, no. Open, honest communication. Remember?" I challenged with a laugh.

"Shit," Law groused. "Fine. I let her use a paddle on my ass...once. But I didn't like it."

"You liked it when I hit your ass with it." Cane pinned his pal with a look of gotcha.

"Fuck you," Law barked, then shot me a look of innocence. "I didn't like it."

Barely able to bite back a howl, I tried to sober. "You let him spank you?"

"Just once, but like I said...I didn't like it, especially when Cane wouldn't let me return the favor and whack the shit out of him."

"Hell no. I was smarter than that," Cane boasted.

Picturing them drunk on their asses and wielding toys they had no idea how to use, I laughed until I cried.

"Thankfully, Penelope taught us about safe, sane, and consensual that night or we'd have probably ended up doing something dangerously stupid."

"I started out doing dangerous and stupid things until I learned more about the lifestyle."

"Who introduced you?" Law asked.

"Billy McNabb. He was a senior and I was a junior. One night he parked his Chevy van behind the Food-Mart and pulled out a silk scarf and a paint stirrer. We spent a spanking-good summer together until he left for college."

"Did you grow up here in Chicago?" Cane asked.

"No. I'm from a tiny little town in the Ozarks of Missouri."

"A country girl, huh?"

I nodded to Law and smiled. "Are you both originally from New York?"

"Nope," Cane replied. "I was an army brat. We moved a lot."

"Did you live in exotic places?" I asked, envious of him traveling.

"No. We didn't leave the mainland except for a couple of years in Honolulu."

"I was born and raised in Butler Beach, Florida," Law offered. "It's a little peninsula on the Atlantic side not far from St. Augustine."

"I love the beach," I said wistfully. "I bet it was fun growing up there."

"Lunch is here," Amber called as she strolled into the break room. "Oh!" She jolted in surprise and nearly dropped the pizza box as she stared at Cane. "Sorry, Ms. E. I thought you and...Mr. Pratt were still hunkered down in your office."

I wanted to giggle as she drank in Cane sitting beside me.

"I-I would have bought an extra if I'd known you had...um,

company," Amber stuttered. She set the box on the table, then grabbed a stack of napkins and handed them to me with a knowing smirk.

Both men stood before Law made introductions. "Amber, this is my partner, Parker Cane. Parker, I'd like you to meet Miss Evans' assistant, Amber."

Cane bowed and lifted her hand and touched his lips to her skin. A bright crimson blush rushed to her cheeks. "Would you like to join us, dear?"

"Ah...ah. No...I mean... Yes," she stammered. "I would love to, but I've already eaten, and...I, ah...I have work to do. Enjoy lunch." She jerked her hand back and raced out of the room.

"Always playing the big bad wolf," Law chuckled to his friend.

"She's darling." Cane smirked, then glanced at me. "You sure she's not in the lifestyle?"

"No. She's...she's... No."

"She's what?" he pressed.

"Shy."

"Most of them are, princess." Cane chuckled.

Seconds later, my phone chimed, alerting me that I had a message.

Amber: *Dear God...there aren't enough batteries on the planet! I'm not sure who it's going to be, but one of those hotties will play the starring role in my fantasy tonight. Maybe I'll get down and dirty and pretend I'm with both of them. Fuck! How the hell am I supposed to get any work done now?*

I wanted to throw my head back and laugh. Instead, I dropped my phone into my pocket and reached for a slice of pizza.

We talked about our families, our dreams, and the roads we'd traveled that had ultimately led us to where we were today. They derived gratification from the power exchange differently—Cane achieved his by inflicting pain, while Law triumphed via nurturing and coaxing control. Yet the end result of fulfilling the sub's needs was the same.

As they opened up to me, I felt a stronger connection...more confidence and trust in them than I'd experienced with any Dom or Doms before. I found offering up pieces of myself that I'd kept locked inside liberating, freeing, and cathartic. Simply being with them was like a breath of fresh air.

Don't forget how to breathe in the smog. They won't be around forever, I inwardly cautioned.

A wave of melancholy settled deep, but I dismissed it. The day would come when I'd be forced to mourn the loss of these two amazing men, but it wasn't today.

"I'm standing there on second base, watching Cane hauling ass in from center field." Law's blue eyes danced in delight as he regaled me with stories of their glory days on the softball field. "He raised his glove to catch the fly ball, screaming, 'I got it! I got it!' Then out of nowhere, Tank Tucker slammed into him and knocked Cane out cold. The big bastard was so stunned that he'd taken my man down, he forgot all about the damn ball that landed beside him with a thud."

"When I came to," Cane seamlessly took up where Law left off, "the big oaf was kneeling over me. I was so pissed that I slammed my fist in his face and broke his damn jaw."

"Needless to say, we weren't invited to join the team," Law howled.

"You two play rough." I laughed.

"Exactly how you like it, princess," Cane growled in my ear.

"I do. And I'm all right with that now."

"So are we." He gripped my hair and dragged my lips to his in a poignant and passionate kiss.

Law bathed my lips and tongue in an equally spine-melting kiss that stirred my hormones to the surface. They tasted like pepperoni and sin. I wanted to gorge on their thick salamis and scream to the heavens since I'd been denied earlier. The only thing that kept me from offering myself up for dessert was the fact that we could be too easily discovered. Trying to ignore the incessant throb between my legs, I quickly cleaned up the remains of our lunch.

As we walked to the elevator, sadness settled deep inside me. I didn't want Cane to leave. He glanced up and down the hallway before stealing a kiss and landing a light swat on my ass.

"I'll meet you two outside at six thirty. Don't keep me waiting, girl. Law and I have plans for you tonight."

Anticipation soared, causing the needy throb to multiply.

"I'll make sure she wraps up work on time," Law assured.

"I'm sure you will." Cane flashed his cohort an evil grin as the elevator door closed and he disappeared.

A quiver clutched my needy sex.

I had no idea what they had designed for me but I suspected, like all the other lessons they'd imparted, I'd discover a deeper sense of peace beneath their masterful hands.

"I need to make some calls. I'll join you in a few," Law stated.

"Sounds good. I need to do the same."

When I sat down at my desk, my mind refused to focus on work. Instead, I found myself studying the strange and intriguing path they had placed me on. Unsure of the why of it all, I couldn't ignore that it was a totally different journey than any I'd taken before.

Why is being with them so much different?

The question floated in my mind like a balloon lost in the clouds.

I'd thought I'd found the right path with Tony and had fallen hard for the man. Hands down, he'd given me all the pain and pleasure I'd sought, yet there'd been something missing. I'd desperately wanted him to be the answer to all my desires, but we'd never really clicked on anything but a physical level.

How am I just realizing that now? I wondered.

Digging deeper, I began to analyze the relationship I'd shared with Ian and James. While I'd volunteered to help Ian mentor James, I'd once more projected the hope that the two would be my salvation. Like with Tony, the connection outside of sex had been missing.

My time with Sam had been altogether different. He'd stepped up and assumed the duty to Top me but hadn't tried to tame me. His demeanor had been considerate…too considerate. The man always gave a pass to my bratty behavior—at least until the end. Still, as with all the rest, my judgment had been colored with the fantasy that I'd found *him*…found the missing piece of my soul. Of course, by the time I realized I'd merely set myself up for another brutal fall with Sam, I'd made a complete fool of myself in front of him and the entire club.

That's when Mika had stepped in and put me in my place.

The memory sent shame and embarrassment to singe my veins, only to be swallowed up with the fear that I was repeating a familiar but cruel pattern.

Or was I?

The time spent with Cane and Law felt totally different from all the other relationships. Though it had only been a few days, the connection we shared was real and growing stronger. Not only that, but I wasn't pining for them to rescue me and deliver my dreams on a silver platter I wanted to work for it. Still, I couldn't shake the worry that I was painting my world with the same hopeful brushstrokes I had with Tony, Ian, James, and Sam.

"Oh, no," I wailed softly and dropped my head in my hands. "I will not do this to myself again…I can't."

Pushing back from my desk, I stood and paced as I tried to compartmentalize my churning feelings. No matter which way I dissected the time I'd spent with Cane and Law, the truth refused to be ignored.

They *weren't* like the other Doms.

They'd anticipated my unruly reaction when they'd finally approached me together and tied my angry ass to the bed. They'd allowed me to vent my rage and taken my surly attitude in stride, but didn't absolve me for my behavior. And they didn't allow me to try and Top from the bottom or take back my control when I came undone from one of their lessons. No, they'd reacted with patience while providing me a safety net, to keep me from crashing to the ground and shattering into a million of pieces. They wouldn't allow me to tear apart my hopes and dreams and shove them under a blanket of disillusionment, but made me face each fear, conquer it, and bask in victory.

They filled my emotional void like none before them. But that wasn't incentive enough for me to go tumbling off the deep end and toss my heart at their feet. Not only was the idea foolish to ponder, it was pointless. I'd already agreed *not* to fall in love with them, either of them. Keeping that line drawn in the sand would save me. It had to. Pausing, I closed my eyes and sent up a silent prayer.

When Law returned to my office, my mind was clear, my emotions were in check, and the rest of the afternoon went by smoothly.

At six thirty, Law and Cane swept me into the limo, after securing my overnight bag in the trunk. I was pressed between their glorious hot bodies, my mind shifted from work to play. I wanted to strip off my clothes and beg them to give me the orgasm they'd denied me that morning.

Patience. You need to trust that they'll give you what you need and what you've earned, a little voice inside my head soothed.

I couldn't argue such truth.

"We'll have dinner first, then move on to *other* things." Law skimmed his hand up the inside of my thigh, stroking his fingers along the top of my stocking.

Tiny zaps of electricity arced through me and I lifted my hips ever so slightly, encouraging him to reach up higher.

"Watch yourself, minx, unless you'd like to suffer through a repeat performance of this morning," Cane warned.

With a tiny squeak, I shook my head. "No thank you, Sir. Not that I wouldn't enjoy a repeat performance, but only if it has a happier ending."

"You still think you make the rules?" Law asked with a chuckle.

"Absolutely not. I was simply being open and honest…communicating my needs." The line spilled off my tongue and I couldn't keep from laughing with them.

"Sassy wench," Cane growled.

"You wouldn't want me any other way," I quipped with a cheesy grin.

"Oh, there are hundreds of ways I want you, princess. Make no mistake about that."

"Thousands," Law added with a sparkle in his eyes.

A naughty thrill slithered up my spine. "I look forward to fulfilling all your wants, Sirs."

A low growl rumbled from deep in Law's chest. "If we weren't so close to the restaurant, I'd put that sinful mouth of yours to work."

"There's always dessert, Sir."

"Or a main course of you, spread on top of the table." Cane arched a brow.

I blinked up at him, my mouth opening and closing several times. "I-I'm good, Sir. I mean…*dammit*… whatever you desire?"

"Now you're beginning to grasp the rules." He smirked.

"I don't know." Laughter hugged Law's words. "An all-you-can-eat, Sasha smorgasbord sounds damn appetizing to me."

"And what exactly would you put on a Sasha smorgasbord?" I asked.

"My tongue," they replied in unison.

The carefree banter we shared was refreshing and fun. I'd never let my guard down and enjoyed this type of exchange with any of the other Doms. I was still giggling as the limo pulled up to their hotel.

The swelling thrum between my legs and the softening of my wet folds amplified my anticipation. My wait was almost over, as long as I didn't do something stupid during dinner and end in orgasm-denial hell.

We were seated side by side in a large, secluded booth away from the other diners. Cane picked up my menu and casually tucked it behind his. I didn't say a word, simply took a sip of water and reminded myself to behave.

Law's arm lay across his menu on the table while his other hand nudged the hem of my skirt up my thigh. Dancing his fingertips in tiny swirls over the tops of my stockings, he studied my reaction with an intense stare.

Well aware of his partner's teasing fingers, Cane's lips twitched, but he held back a smile and studied the menu. "I take it you already know what you want?"

"Oh, yeah. I know exactly what I want. It's not on the menu," Law answered in a ragged tone.

"I meant *for dinner*," Cane drawled sardonically. "We both know what we're having for dessert."

My breath hitched and my pulse raced. The suggestion to forego dinner and head straight upstairs singed the tip of my tongue. I extinguished its flame with another sip of water.

"Steak or seafood?" Cane asked.

"Steak. I'm ready to sink my teeth into something hot and juicy." Law smirked as the waiter strolled up.

Straightening, I leaned forward, attempting to shield Law's roaming fingers. My appetite had increased to an insatiable level that had nothing to do with food. As if sensing my distress, Cane dropped a hand beneath the table and joined in his own form of torment. Trailing light pinches on the insides of my thighs, he soothed the sting with soft caresses. I clenched my teeth and tried like hell not to yelp while my brain aligned the velvet strokes with the biting tweaks assailing me.

Cane's voice was nothing but a low rumble as he placed our dinner order. I was so focused on the growing need they conjured I didn't have a clue what entrée would eventually be placed in front of me.

As soon as the waiter walked away, I sucked in a shaky breath and rolled my hips.

"Problem?" Cane taunted.

"Yes," I hissed helplessly.

"What is it?" Law goaded.

"If you two are trying to kill me, it's working. I'm dying here."

"We're simply warming you up," Cane stated proudly. I wanted to groan. This might be the longest, most sexually frustrating dinner of my life. "We want you wet, aching, and hungry for us when dinner is through."

"I already am, Sir."

"Yes. We can smell your arousal, sweetheart," Law confirmed. "Simmer harder for us."

"I'm past simmer, Sir. I'm in pressure cooker mode. I'm just praying the lid doesn't go flying off and I make a mess here on the seat."

They dragged their fingers higher and slid them beneath my thong. Cane teased my clit, while Law drove two fingers deep inside my dripping tunnel. I instantly squeezed around his embedded fingers and closed my eyes, letting the electrifying sensations consume me.

"Come if you'd like," Law enticed on a dark whisper. "Though I'd wager you'll hold it back. The desire to please us burns brighter and hotter than the orgasm you crave."

His invitation was tempting. I could shatter so quietly the other patrons wouldn't even know. But Law's intuition fueled an epiphany. This unorthodox power exchange we were discovering wasn't all about *my* needs, but theirs as well. Each test, each lesson was deliberately designed to not only open my eyes, but also to forge a stronger, more secure *us*.

"You're right, Sir. I want to make you both proud."

The matching smiles beaming over their faces as they eased their hands from beneath my skirt made my heart melt and filled me with triumph.

"You do, girl." Cane solemnly nodded. "And we couldn't be prouder."

His praise warmed me all through dinner and well after the slice of cheesecake we shared for dessert. When we left the restaurant, my nerves were jumping. I wanted to race to the elevator and fall into bed with them. But when they directed me toward the front of the hotel, I darted a look of confusion between them.

"We're going to drop by the club for a bit," Cane stated.

Glancing down at my clothing, I frowned. Perhaps they'd let me strip off my business wear in the coatroom. No one would bat an eye at the sight of me in pink lingerie, but every head in the club would turn if I paraded in wearing a suit.

"Is this another test?" I asked when we were settled into the backseat of the limo once again.

"Yes and no," Cane replied. "Think of it as blurring the lines."

"Blurring the lines? What does that mean?"

"The lesson in your office earlier today was only the first part of a two-fold exercise," Law explained. "Your choice of clothing—the conservative power suit on the outside masking such feminine lace beneath—screams volumes."

"You've spent a great deal of effort projecting your independence as a masochist and distancing yourself from the other subs. You've taught your subconscious to only see yourself as black or white." Cane reached down and squeezed my hand. "We're about to introduce you to the kaleidoscope of colors that you truly are…the ones you refuse to see. Blur the lines."

"How?" My voice trembled.

"Do you trust us?" Law arched his brows.

"Yes."

"Then it shouldn't matter." He pressed a kiss, teeming with reassurance, to my lips.

Cane's moist breath caressed my neck as he leaned in close. "We'll keep you safe and secure in the palm of our hands…right where you belong."

The angst within me melted but didn't completely evaporate. Unable to wear my usual flippant attitude as armor, I dreaded walking into the club with two new Doms by my side. I anticipated an icy reception, which filled my veins with shame. They'd done nothing to deserve the scorn I knew would be tossed their way, but *I* had. I'd done plenty over the years.

As the limo pulled to the curb outside Club Genesis, a rush of panic filled me.

"I-I need to apologize to you both before we go inside."

"Apologize?" Cane asked.

"What for?" Law pressed.

"I've never behaved properly here before. My reputation is…well, to put it bluntly, it sucks."

"We know." Law smiled softly.

"That's why we're here. Not only to change the perception you have of yourself, but of those inside who truly have an open mind."

I wanted to scoff and tell him not to waste his time trying to change the minds of those who'd seen me at my worst. But I kept that sarcastic response to myself since it had earned my less-than-stellar reputation from the start.

I sucked in a fortifying breath as we entered the foyer. All heads turned our way. I quickly cast my eyes to the floor to avoid their patronizing stares. I realized my action had been purely submissive when a low buzz of murmurs filled the air. I clenched my jaw and resisted the urge to flash them all an incendiary stare.

"Let them talk and stew," Law whispered in my ear. "They'll be stunned when we're done resurrecting your honor."

I couldn't help but grin, and admire the snide evil streak hiding behind his compassionate sheep's clothing.

I kept my eyes locked on the carpet, and tried to ignore the cynical hum increasing as we slowly made our way to the podium.

"Good evening, Destiny." Drake's deep and commanding voice rolled over me. A flicker of dread followed in its wake as I lifted my head.

"Good evening, Sir." My lips softly trembled.

Surprise flickered in his gray eyes. As he darted a glance between Cane and Law, a slow smile speared Drake's face. His boy, Trevor, frowned as he took in my conservative and abnormal attire.

"Are you going to chur—"

"Not another fucking word," Drake thundered in warning.

Trevor sent me an apologetic cringe. "Sorry," he mouthed.

"Good to see you again, Law." Drake smiled. Cane, a pleasure as always." He thrust out his hand in greeting. "Mika said you three might be joining us soon. He might still be sitting at the bar if you want to say hello."

"We'll do that." Cane nodded as he released Daddy Drake's massive paw.

Trevor hurried to the red curtain that led to the dungeon and parted it for us. As I passed him, he darted a clandestine glance toward Drake—who was busy checking in the next member. "Double your pleasure—double your fun, sister. You go, girl!" he giggled and gave me the thumbs-up.

I flashed him a crooked grin as Cane and Law each clasped a hand to my elbow and ushered me into the dungeon. The familiar scent of leather and sex, along with slaps and submissive cries, settled over me like a comfortable blanket.

"Nice place," Law stated as he took in the spacious room and numerous play stations. I could feel the members' stares. Shutting them out completely, I focused on him and Cane. "I can't wait to cuff you to the cross, sweetheart."

"What would you do once you had me there?"

"Warm you up for me." Cane sent me an evil smirk.

I quickly searched the dungeon and pointed. "There's an open cross over there."

"You're far too eager," Law growled.

"Is there really such a thing as too eager to please, Sir?" I couldn't help but giggle.

"I think it's time to rein in our girl."

Law nodded in agreement with Cane's observation before they led me toward the bar. Samantha's eyes widened along with her smile as she welcomed us and took our drink order. I tugged at my skirt and started to claim my usual spot at the bar.

Cane cinched his hand around my elbow tightly. "What do you think you're doing?"

"Sitting down where I normally do."

"Did either of us give you permission to take a seat?" Cane's voice and expression were like steel—hard and unforgiving.

"No, Sir."

"Just because you're in familiar surroundings doesn't give you permission to erase everything we've taught you."

I could feel my anger bubbling to the surface. "You haven't *taught* me how I'm supposed to behave in the dungeon."

"We shouldn't have to. Not unless you've been blowing smoke up our butts. Is that what you've been doing, Destiny?" Law bit out.

"No. I—"

"You're not Destiny the pain-slut anymore. You're ours," Cane said, cutting me off. "Look around, princess. Where are the subs?"

Following his directive, I saw they were where they'd always been. "Some are sitting at the tables over there, some are busy playing at the stations, and some are sitting on the floor beside their Owners."

"Are any sitting at the bar?" Law asked.

Images of me high on the barstool, with a regal and exalted chip on my shoulder, filled me with shame. I'd never taken the time to notice how other subs and bottoms displayed their compliance, until Law pointed it out.

"Oh, my god," I whispered.

"You may go sit at a table alone." Cane held me with a feral stare. "Or you can hike up your skirt and kneel beside us here at the bar."

I glanced at an empty table before dropping my eyes to the floor at my feet. The thought of kneeling at the bar brought back bitter memories.

After discovering that Sam had his sights set on Cindy, I'd thrown a jealous fit, embarrassing him and myself. Adding insult to injury, he'd punished me by forcing me to hold a dime to the face of the bar with my nose. Both sitting alone and isolated at the table and kneeling at the bar and choking on the acrid memories held zero appeal.

Smoothing my hands over the pockets of my suit coat, I opened my mouth to propose a counter offer. Then it struck me. I wasn't at work. The contract I'd signed was nonnegotiable. I'd willingly surrendered my power to both Cane and Law. Did I honestly want to take it back because I didn't like the choices they'd given me?

No. Hell no!

I quickly snapped my mouth shut, tugged up my skirt, and lowered to my knees.

A not-so-quiet feminine gasp came from behind me.

"Would you look at that? Holy… I don't believe it," said a somewhat familiar, catty female voice that I couldn't quite place. "Who are those guys and how'd they manage to brainwash Destiny?"

Tears of humiliation and remorse slid down my cheeks.

Though I wanted to succumb to the warm, enticing veil of self-pity, wrap it around me, and ignore my culpability for her hateful words, I couldn't. I had no one to blame but myself for the members' loathsome opinion of me. I'd wielded my pride like a sword and shield and only ended up eviscerating myself.

Biting back a sob of guilt, I watched in horror as Cane and Law stood and faced the hateful woman maligning me. Guarding me between their powerful legs, they faced the woman. Shame coalesced with my guilt. If I hadn't been such a bitch to everyone in the club, there'd be no need for either man to try and defend my honor.

CHAPTER THIRTEEN

"WHERE IS YOUR Master, girl?" Cane thundered. "I assume you have one…you're wearing a collar, or is that just for show?"

"Huh?" The woman's tone of disbelief chafed my skin.

"Per protocol, we need to speak with your Master about your rude and insolent behavior. Where is he?" When the woman began to stammer, Law's tone took on a shockingly sharp edge. "Christ, girl. Do you even know what protocol is?"

"Of course I do," she huffed indignantly. "I've been a sub longer than *her*. Why are you sticking up for *Destiny*? Everyone knows what a total bitch she—"

"Piccolo!" Mika roared.

I should have known it had been *that* cow. The know-all, be-all, self-proclaimed perfect sub hated my guts.

"I'm sure your Master would agree to let you help the cleaning crew scrub the toilets in the private rooms this evening." Mika's voice dripped in disdain.

"Sir, I—"

"Or you can apologize for your recalcitrant behavior and every ugly insult that just spewed out of your hateful mouth."

"I-I'm sorry, Master Mika," Piccolo stammered.

"Not to *me*," he growled impatiently. "Apologize to Masters Cane and Law, *and* Destiny."

"You want me to apologize to *her*?" Piccolo screeched.

"Cuff Master," Mika called out, loudly. "I need a word with you."

"I'm sorry, Sirs…and to you, Destiny. I'm really, really sorry. I won't say any more mean or cruel things ever again. I swear." Piccolo babbled her apology in a rush of panic. "I'm sorry, Master Mika. Please don't tell my Master. I swear it'll never happen again."

"Why shouldn't I tell your Master, girl?" Mika growled.

"He'll refuse to scene with me tonight and I've been waiting a solid week."

Try going without for months, you whiny little bitch. The retort lay on the tip of my tongue, but I swallowed it down.

"Is there a problem here?" Cuff's arrival shut Piccolo's complaints down like a Pittsburg steel mill.

"I think it's better to take this discussion up to my office," Mika suggested.

As Piccolo's mournful wail retreated, both Cane and Law crouched down beside me.

"Are you all right, girl?" Cane scowled.

I quickly nodded. "Yes, Sir. I'm sorry I've brought so much disgrace to myself…and to you both."

"We aren't here to judge your past. You'll only answer to us for present, and future actions." Cane softly smiled.

"We know how difficult that was, but you held your tongue. We're very proud of you, girl," Law praised. Brushing the tears from my cheeks with the pads of his thumbs, he pressed a kiss to my lips.

"I want you to rise, go to the ladies' room, and remove your suit."

By the twinkle in Cane's eyes, I knew he wasn't only giving me a command but a reward as well. Warmed by the ascending thrill, I gave them both a watery smile and stood. "Thank you, Sirs."

Inside the restroom, as I removed my clothes, I felt as if I were peeling off my own skin. The sensation was foreign, and I couldn't put my finger on the reason. I'd dreaded coming to the club in my business suit purely because this wasn't the usual armor I wore. The outfit lying on the vanity signified success, self-confidence, and all I'd achieved in life thus far. The woman now staring back at me in the mirror, wearing silky lace, and nylon, hadn't accomplished shit. She was guarded, combative, and a miserable failure. She didn't fit in and would probably never find a Master to fill the empty shadows inside her soul when Cane and Law left.

The door swung open and Julianna waddled in.

"Haven't you popped that baby out yet?" I teased.

Redirecting attention from myself was a tactic I often used at the club, usually with a ton of scathing sarcasm. I shielded the self-depreciating insecurities within me like I was hiding them from Julianna now.

"Ugh. Don't remind me. I still have three weeks to go, and that's *if* she decides to make her grand entrance on my due date." She smiled, then quickly sobered. "Are you all right? I heard Piccolo insulted you."

"Sticks and stones," I said with a dismissive wave of my hand. "She has no tolerance for those who don't conform to her idea of submission."

"Tell me about it." Julianna rolled her eyes. "She came to one of the sub meetings once and started running everyone into the ground for not submitting the *proper way*. I shut her down by reminding her the lifestyle is an individual choice. She never came back…thank goodness. Speaking of which…I hear you're coming to the meeting tomorrow morning, right?"

"Yes. At least I don't think Cane and Law have changed their minds."

"Good. I'm anxious for you to join us."

I scoffed. "I'm glad one of us is."

"Don't belittle or berate yourself. We expand our level of understanding in our *own* time."

"I'm not sure what I'm seeking, or if I even *want* to understand it all."

"Sure you do, or you would have already found a way to weasel out of attending."

I pursed my lips, pondering her statement as she gave me a quick hug and hurried into one of the stalls.

Gathering up my clothes, I headed back to the bar. When I didn't see either Cane or Law sitting where I'd left them, I scanned the dungeon. They were standing beside an empty cross at one of the stations.

Law beckoned me to join them with a crook of his finger. My heart did a little somersault, and I swallowed the dryness in my mouth. I could feel hundreds of eyes on me as I made my way across the dungeon on trembling legs. It wasn't the apprehension of pain that held my terror like a vise, but rather that I'd do or say something to disgrace my two Doms.

Law took my clothes and set them down, then took my hand and led me to the cross.

"What do you want me to do, Sir…kneel, or…?"

"I want you to stand there, exactly as you are, my pet."

My pet. I'd always loathed that endearment. It sounded so debasing and insulting to hear Doms addressed their subs…as if they were dogs or something. Funny, I didn't have the same knee-jerk reaction when Law uttered the phrase. It rolled off his tongue with warmth and admiration and felt more like a soothing caress.

While he began to unfasten my corset, I watched Cane pick up a single tail. He swung the whip over his head with a natural grace that made my heart race. With a slight flick of his wrist, the sailing tail cut the wind with a brutal crack. Goose bumps rippled over my skin and a shiver of hunger mixed with anticipation sluiced through my veins.

Law dropped his hands to my garters. When he released the clasps, my corset fell to the floor. Sliding my stockings down my legs, he lifted one foot, then the other to remove my shoes before brushing the nylons off my toes.

All the while, Cane cracked the whip, sending the wicked sound to dance over my flesh and pirouette in my mind. I wanted to clamber to the cross and offer myself up as a human target.

Law caressed his fingers over my face. Peace, confidence, and protection sparkled in his light azure eyes.

Lost in his gaze, I blocked out everything and everyone else around me. I mentally wrapped us in our own private bubble where others' opinions couldn't hurt me. Though I wasn't the same woman I used to be, I still didn't know where I belonged…how I fit into the club. While the learning curve was sometimes scary and unfamiliar, I wasn't going to give up until Cane and Law were finished helping me discover the *real* me.

Sliding a warm hand to the small of my back, Law pulled me in tightly. Slanting his mouth over mine, he cupped my nape. His slow, sensual kiss belied the clawing urgency to break free and position myself on the cross.

You're not in control anymore, whispered a little voice within me.

No. I wasn't, and for the first time, that awareness didn't pummel me with anxiety but instead brought an unexpected sense of serenity.

Law continued exploring my mouth with his tongue, leisurely consuming not only my lips but also the swell of my impatience. Exhaling a kitten-soft sigh, I melted against his chest.

Having drained all the tension from me, he pulled back and smiled. "Stay relaxed, sweetheart. I'm going to warm you up before Cane takes you where you need to go. Any questions?"

"No. Thank you, Sirs," I whispered in reply.

Darting a glance over my shoulder, I wanted to be sure both men heard the gratitude in my voice.

Cane flashed me a wink before he and Law pressed their palms at the base of my spine and eased me against the cross. When they both stepped away without cuffing my wrists or ankles, I turned my confusion toward them.

"You're bound to us, not the wood." Law's tone was slathered in conviction.

"Are you ready to prove that theory to us and yourself?" A hint of challenge lay in Cane's words.

"You bet, Sirs."

I spread my legs, aligning them with the angle of the slats at the bottom, then raised my arms and placed my palms flat against the glossy wood. Inwardly reminding myself not to move, I inhaled a deep breath and closed my eyes.

Placing his wide hands on my shoulders, Law began massaging my muscles. Taking his time, he kneaded the knots at my neck as he slowly worked his way to my shoulder blades. By the time he started on my lower back, my bones already felt like liquid. Kneading the cheeks of my ass, he raked his fingernails over the sweet marks still adorning my flesh.

Dragging a finger over the word Cane had etched into my flesh, Law chuckled. "Make that say *ours* when you're done, man."

"I'll do that," Cane replied as he, too, skimmed his fingers over the words. "You heal quickly, princess...almost too quickly. I enjoy seeing my work for days and weeks after a scene."

"You'll have to mark me deeper then, Sir."

He gripped a fist in my hair and tugged my head back. His scowl was fierce. And he leaned in so close his lips touched mine. "Are you challenging me, girl?"

"No, Sir," I adamantly replied. "I was simply offering a suggestion so you could admire your marks longer."

"Hrmm." He smirked, obviously not buying the excuse. "I'm glad you weren't trying to Top from the bottom or anything."

"No, Sir. Not me. Never." I quickly bit my lips together to keep from grinning.

Cane chortled, tugged my head to the side, and sank his teeth into my throat. A ripple of pleasure rolled up my spine as a wistful sigh fluttered off my lips.

"I think it's time to warm her up, Law. The mouthy minx is making me lose my patience," he growled, then leaned in close to my ear. "Just remember, princess…your ass is ours, but it's going to be all mine very soon."

"And can I just say…I can't wait, Sir."

His deep, rich laughter spilled over me like syrup. Striding behind the cross, Cane stood in front of me. "I want to watch your reactions as Law drives you to the clouds. Then I'm going to send you past the stars."

Since discovering their penchant for working subs together, I'd secretly wondered what Law's role had been. I was about to find out.

The first slap of his hand that met my ass wiped away my misconceptions of the man. While I never thought him weak, Law's demeanor seemed more geared to dispensing aftercare, not inflicting the rolling fire spreading across my flesh.

"You look surprised." Cane smirked. "Did you let his easygoing manner fool you?"

"Yes, Sir. I certainly did."

"I'm full of surprises, my pet," Law taunted.

"Show her," Cane prodded.

The next blow wasn't from Law's hand but a wide wooden paddle and set me onto the tips of my toes.

"Oh, yes," I moaned in delight.

With each sharp slap, lightning ignited. The burn sank deep into my tissue as Law pushed me hard and fast. I spiraled into the sublime and blistering paradise, while Cane plucked and tugged my nipples, then slid his other fingers between my folds. Gathering the silky liquid spilling from my core, he painted the slickness over my clit as Law continued to brand me in spine-sizzling pain.

Using the perfect amount of pressure and friction, Cane burnished my distended nub until I was keening and clutching the cross in desperation. I'd never been assaulted beneath an avalanche of conflicting sensations in this way before. I was floundering. I didn't know how to process the anomaly of paradise and agony, not when both had me gripped in their teeth at the same time.

Sexual satisfaction dominated the flames.

My legs grew numb.

Darkness shrouded my vision.

I began spiraling into oblivion.

"Don't do it, girl," Cane growled.

Even the understanding that I was going to fail him didn't stop the freight train of release thundering through me.

It was the raw and primal slap of Law's paddle that yanked me back from the abyss.

Seizing the lifeline he'd granted, I abandoned my quest for orgasm and chased his pain. Wrapping it around me, I held it close...grounded in a cloak of protection.

"Good girl," Cane murmured against my lips.

Expecting a longer, harder kiss, I moaned and leaned forward when he pulled away. Long minutes passed before I dragged my heavy eyelids open. Cane was gone. In his place stood Law. Lust and command were etched on the sharp features of his face.

"It's Cane's turn now, little one," he whispered.

My heart clutched and softened.

"Thank you for warming me up, Sir. It was heavenly." My voice was hoarse, my words slurred.

The lines on his face relaxed as he threaded his fingers through my hair. Tingles skittered over my scalp and I purred as he bent in close. "I look forward to warming you up again and again, sweetheart."

A strap of leather collided with my ass and I sucked in a startled gasp. There was no rolling fire, like Law had granted, but a white-hot flash of blistering pain echoing through my flesh. Clenching my teeth, I bit back a howl and squeezed my eyes shut. I clambered on top of the agony by weaving the explosion with the endorphins flooding my system, coalescing both pain and pleasure into a familiar bright light.

Law stroked my pussy and teased my clit. Working his fingers with slow exacting finesse, he kissed my lips and laved my nipples, soared me to the cusp...before gently gliding me back down.

I was lost in the splendor raining down on me as they peeled away every layer of protection I'd swaddled around me. Their combined forces, Law's field of sunshine and Cane's dark forest of night, melded and encased me in their beautiful, brutal affection.

I was helpless to do anything but cede to their conflicting demands.

Each stinging slap Cane landed heightened my indulgence.

The world disappeared beneath the surging thunder careening through me…everything but the unrelenting and glorious connection binding me to the two amazing men.

The single tail cracked in the air.

My heart soared.

The first strike blinded me beneath a searing flash of pain.

Cane landed the popper with unrelenting force and precision. Slashes sizzled and coiled while streaks of liquid lightning flashed behind my eyes.

As Law's tongue delved deep into my mouth, I instinctively reached up to sink my fingers into his soft hair, but squeezed my hand into a fist. Understanding dawned like a breathless sunrise. My arms were free, my legs unsecured, yet I was bound to them…chained in the inescapable demand to please them.

The chaos within me grew quiet, and my thought process slowed. It was as if my mind was too fractured to fully absorb the clashing sensations bombarding me. A fleeting thought skipped through my brain—I'd never lost control of my mind during a scene…until now.

White, shimmering clouds descended in my mind's eye. Reaching out, I clung to them and sailed off into the welcoming silence of serenity. Surrounded in peaceful tranquility, I floated aimlessly in buoyant surrender.

A volley of spine-sizzling blows yanked me from my pacifying haven. I pinched my lips together and swallowed back a cry. My legs quaked and my knees knocked against the wood. I sucked in deep, long breaths as I struggled to process the blistering pain and rise above it.

Silent tears spilled down my cheeks.

Cane pressed his sweat-soaked body against my back as he bent close to my ear. "Use your safe word if you need it."

"I'm good," I softly sobbed as Law sipped at my tears.

"You're better than good, princess…you're fucking perfect," Cane growled before sinking his teeth into my shoulder.

He stepped away and snapped the whip across my ass. Over and over the popper tore into my flesh.

"Scream for me, princess," Cane demanded.

A blast of panic pierced the agony and froze the air in my lungs. Unable to speak, I shook my head.

"Destiny!" Law growled. He cupped my cheeks and locked his blue eyes on mine.

Cane's hot body enveloped mine once more.

"Focus on my voice," Law instructed. "I want you to relax and breathe."

Struggling to comply, I sucked in quivering gasps.

"Talk to us. What hidden trigger did I just hit?" Cane's voice dripped with concern.

"I-I can't scream here. I...hold it inside," I stuttered as I tried to explain the reason for refusing his edict.

"Why?" Cane pressed in the same apprehensive tone.

"So they can't...use my weakness against me," I sobbed softly.

He gripped my hair, and pulled my head back until we were face-to-face. "You're not weak. And you're not giving your power to the people in this club. You're giving it to us. Do you think we'd ever try and use the beautiful gift you're giving us against you?"

"No, Sir." I sniffed.

"No. Never." Cane captured my lips with a kiss so primal and scorching I couldn't keep from sobbing harder. Releasing me, he pinned me with a feral stare. "Now, scream for me, princess."

He pressed my body against the cross again, and stepped back.

Law kissed me with the same visceral passion that Cane had, then slowly smiled. "Let him hear the sounds of the sweet agony he's wielding over you, gorgeous. Let us both drink in your ecstasy."

Fighting the demons of my insecurities, I clenched my jaw as Cane began landing the whip once again.

"Hand your power over to us, Destiny. It doesn't belong to you anymore. It belongs to us...*you* belong to us," Law murmured.

Pain, pleasure, and hope flooded my system...consumed me beneath the pressure of promise so sublime I threw my head back and screamed.

Shouting and crying, I shared the freedom they'd granted me...shared the rebirth that was taking place inside me. Not only did I share it with Cane and Law but with the whole damn universe, too.

My throat was raw when they both eased me from the cross. Cane wrapped a soft cotton blanket around me before Law hoisted me into his arms. Closing my eyes, I burrowed in against the safety of his wide chest and sobbed as we left the dungeon.

Cane strummed his hot hands over my face, keeping pace with Law's long strides. The members' murmurs ricocheted off me, but faded with the other sounds of the scenes.

Inside Cane's private room, Law placed me in the center of the bed. Snuggling against the cool sheets, I closed my eyes and savored the burning throb that enveloped my backside.

Together they climbed onto the bed and wrapped me between their now naked bodies. Cane lay on his side, facing me and sipping the tears falling from my eyes. Law stroked my arm and murmured low, sweet praises in my ear.

Cocooned in their arms and suffused beneath their affection, I couldn't contain the soul-quaking sobs that tore from my throat.

I felt treasured…

Whole…

Complete.

"We've got you, sweet one. Let it out. You're safe," Law cooed.

"And that's exactly how we intend to keep you…safe," Cane comforted.

Their words of reassurance spooled through my head. I slowly stopped crying and latched onto the clouds once again, then set sail to ride out the billowing endorphins.

When I lifted my heavy eyelids, I found Cane propped up on his elbow, head resting in his palm, watching me with a lazy smile.

"Did you enjoy your vacation?"

"Mmm," I purred. "It was the best I've ever had."

"You were absolutely stunning, sweetheart," Law preened as he leaned over to stare down at me.

I didn't have words to describe the incredible peace within me. Thanking them with words was altogether too paltry compared to the awakening saturating my soul.

They'd granted me a respite from the chaos, provided me a means to escape. But even more, these two incredible men had freed me from my self-imposed prison and taught me how to conquer my own worst enemy…myself.

"I love you…love you, both," I murmured.

"Sasha." Cane's tone was soft but laced in warning.

"Wait." I shook my head. "I don't mean that I've fallen *in* love with you, either of you." *Though it would be so fucking easy to do.* "I love you for opening my eyes…my mind. For helping me discover there's more to this lifestyle than simply escaping."

"What exactly is it that you've discovered?" Law's piercing stare was riddled with suspicion and doubt.

I understood his guarded demeanor. No doubt he still struggled with guilt that Ruby had fallen in love with him but not Cane. I didn't know how it was possible for her to separate her feelings in such a way. To me, they were two halves that, without the other, would never be whole.

"That instead of going with the flow, I've been fighting the current. I sit at the bar here, night after night, wearing a suit of armor to hide nearly every ugly emotion you can think of."

"Kind of like the suit you wore when you walked in the door?" A knowing smirk curled Cane's lips as he arched a brow.

"Yes. And the reason I loathed wearing it inside the club was because it represents my achievements. Wearing it inside the club was a powerful reminder of how miserably I've failed here."

"You didn't fail tonight," Law reminded. The suspicion had left his face.

"No. But that was all thanks to you two."

"I disagree. If you hadn't been willing to strip off your *armor*, we wouldn't have had the chance to scene with you," Law continued. "You risked your pride and chose to trust us. I wouldn't call that failing."

"And that's *why* I love you both. You taught me some very important lessons and have given me hope. When you two are gone"—I swallowed the grim reality of them walking away from me soon—"I might find a Dom who'll *want* to own me, instead of scening with me out of pity or rejecting me for being a rebellious brat."

The two men shared a somber glance.

"Leaving doesn't necessarily mean forever, girl," Cane replied cryptically.

My brows wrinkled in confusion.

"It's time to tell her," Law somberly stated.

"Tell me what?" I glanced over my shoulder and found Cane wearing a furtive expression.

He dragged his knuckles over my cheek and nodded in agreement. "She's earned it."

"Yes. And if she continues to respond like she did tonight, I foresee a long and fulfilling future in store for us all." Law smiled.

"Oh, come on! Stop playing games. The suspense is killing me. What evil little plan have you two cooked up *this* time?"

Pinching the tip of my nipple, Cane scowled and twisted before releasing with a brutal tug. Arching my shoulders back against Law's chest, I let out a cry.

Pain raced down my spine and exploded through my body. I wanted to weep. Not because of the pain, but his fierce command that kept me from reverting back to the woman I needed to outgrow.

"She's not ready yet." Though his reply was directed to Law, Cane's eyes were locked on mine as if searching or waiting for me to respond in anger.

"I'm sorry, Sirs. I meant no disrespect." Cane blinked at my contrite reply. Yeah, he hadn't been expecting *that* to come out of my mouth. I figured if I was going to blow him away, I might as well do it up proper. "When you feel I've earned an answer, I know...no, I trust you'll tell me."

"You manipulative little minx." The corners of his lips twitched as he tried to fight back a grin but failed miserably and issued a laugh. "Law, my friend...you and I have our work cut out for us, brother. She's a handful."

"I knew that the second she snatched up her clothes and tore out of my hotel room," Law drawled. "We'll keep her in line, man. I have faith...*and* an evil mind."

"And I have a wicked whip that I can set on a shelf, making sure she won't feel an ounce of pain until she behaves."

My eyes flashed open wide and I gasped. "That's cruel and unusual punishment, Sirs."

"Then I guess you'd better walk the straight and narrow." Cane grinned.

"Not too straight and narrow," Law amended. "We like taming your inner tigress...in moderation. If you get too out of hand, we can always tie you to the bed again."

"Being totally honest, Sirs...next time you tie me to the bed, can we have a lot more *activity* than the last time?"

"Trust me," Law growled. "We can definitely arrange that."

A wistful sigh fluttered from my lips.

I found comfort in the fact that they weren't planning to transform me into some kind of submissive robot. I was free to be me—the good, the bad, and the ugly.

We lay in bed for several hours, talking, laughing, and bolstering the captivating connection that bound us. All in all, it was the perfect end to a day fraught with landmines and quicksand. Thankfully, with their encouragement and understanding, I'd made it through each lesson unscathed. Well, all except for my ass. The still-throbbing tissue was an idyllic reminder of the success I'd achieved with them…for them… and for myself.

"It's getting late," Cane began. "Let's head back to the hotel, call room service for some ice cream, and climb into bed."

"Chocolate chip cookie dough?" I asked, my eyes growing wide with excitement.

"Fudge ripple, girl," he replied sternly.

"Pralines and cream," Law voted.

"Why not all three?" I giggled.

"All three it is. Now get your clothes on. I left them over there." Cane nodded toward the tall walnut-stained dresser across the room.

When I crawled out of bed, Law let out a long, low whistle. "You've got some lovely marks, sweetheart."

Excitement bubbled up inside me. I turned and lifted onto my toes and stared in the mirror at the wicked red welts covering my ass. There, right above the crack of my ass, he'd left a new word: O-U-R-S. Tears of joy stung the backs of my eyes. Locking my gaze with Cane's reflection, I sent him a trembling smile.

"Thank you, Sir. Thank both of you for a spectacular night."

It truly had been spectacular…the single most amazing time I'd ever experienced in my life.

If only they didn't have to…

I slammed the lid on the thought and blocked it from my mind. They were here now, and each day I could spend basking in their command was a precious gift that I would hold in my heart for all time.

Dressed, we stepped into the hall, Law on my right and Cane on my left. They each clutched my elbow as we made our way to the dungeon. Though it was late, it was a Friday night. Members would stay and scene until the wee hours of the morning.

Mika swiveled on his stool at the bar and stood. He quickly ate up the distance between us and paused. "Law…Cane, do you two have time for a quick chat?"

"Of course," they answered in unison.

"Since Julianna is upstairs resting on the couch in my office, let's head toward the back. There's a private room that's not being rented at the moment."

"Sounds good." Law nodded. "You my sit *at* the bar this time. We won't be long."

"Thank you, Sir."

Mika's eyes widened slightly before an insightful look swept his face.

As the three men walked away, I gently eased onto my familiar barstool with a hiss. Immediately, I noticed something was different.

"Would you like the usual?" Samantha asked with her usual sunny smile.

"No thanks. I'm good."

With a nod she strode away to the other end of the bar. Her Master, Max, stood behind the bar as well. Leaning up against the wall, his arms were crossed over his buff chest, and his eyes never left Samantha. The look of love etched on his face was mixed with pride.

With a grin of happiness for the couple, I turned and looked out over the dungeon. In the center of the room, Mika's inner circle, his closest Dominant and submissive friends, were clustered around a group of tables they'd shoved together.

Drake and Trevor, Tony and Leah, Justice and Symoné, Sam and Cindy, and Ian and James were laughing at whatever Liz was saying.

A tiny smile tugged the corners of my lips as I watched. Stunned by my reaction, I blinked. The contempt I'd once felt for the clique had all but disappeared. In the few days I'd spent with Cane and Law, everything had changed...especially *me*.

I was no longer wallowing in self-pity and pissed at the world.

Though I had plenty of bad habits left to break, Cane and Law were teaching me how to sever the ties that bound me to frustration and disappointment. Ironically, I welcomed the changes. I was transitioning and it felt...right.

Suddenly, sitting there at the bar, in my usual spot, started to make my skin crawl.

I no longer wanted to be mired in anger or wrapped up in a pity party. Didn't want to listen to the old tapes of negativity and inadequacy playing in my head anymore. I couldn't stomach the thought of being labeled the club brat any longer, or the bleak and empty cocoon I'd trapped myself inside.

I wanted to spread my wings and fly.

Jumping from the barstool, I raced down the hall to share the epiphany with my two Doms and thank them for setting me on a bright, shiny new path.

As I reached the end of the hallway, I stopped by the back door and chuckled. In all my excitement, it hadn't dawned on me that I didn't know which room Mika had taken them to. Deciding to wait, I suddenly sensed movement behind me. I turned as Julianna stepped out of the stairwell that led to Mika's office.

"You okay?" she asked.

"Yes. Mika is talking to Cane and Law in one of the rooms. I just don't know which one. I'm sure they'll be out soon."

Nodding, she tugged me out of the way as Joe, the bar-back, came toward us lugging a large plastic bag of trash.

"Excuse me, ladies." Joe smiled.

"Here, let me help." A blast of cold air hit me as I shoved the metal door open.

He paused and sent me a genuine smile. "Thanks, Destiny."

Joe hurried down the steps, and just as the door began to close, I heard him let out a loud grunt.

I snapped my neck toward Julianna. "Did you hear that?"

"Yes. I hope he didn't hit a patch of ice and fall."

Brushing past me, she pushed the door open. We both stepped onto the landing at the top of the stairs. Peering toward the dumpster, I saw Joe lying motionless on the ground.

"Oh no. He's hurt," I cried as I vaulted down the stairs. Aware of Julianna right behind me, I called over my shoulder. "Get help!"

Rushing toward the downed man, I saw a dark blur from the corner of my eye. A split second later, I was slammed to the ground. Knees pinned my shoulders to the cold pavement, as a heavy weight lay heavy on my chest.

"Sasha!" Julianna screamed.

"Why don't you come over here and join us, you fat, pregnant cow? We'll have us some real fun." The voice of the pervert on top of me sounded familiar, but I was too busy struggling and bucking like a maniac trying break free to bother looking at the man. When he sneered down at me, fear gripped every cell in my body and squeezed.

Kerr.

The crazy, abusive asshole who'd been terrorizing subs for months had returned.

There was no way I was going to let the cocksucker get his hands on Julianna. The man hated Mika. God only knew what horrors Kerr would unleash on the club owner's girl and their unborn child if given the chance.

"Run, Julianna. Get help!" I yelled.

"Shut your fucking mouth, whore!" Kerr spat.

The sound of Julianna's feet clanging up the metal stairs filled me with hope.

Kerr looked down at me. His face was contorted in maniacal glee, but it was the promise of death reflecting in his lifeless eyes that made my stomach bottom out.

No matter what...he planned to kill me.

"Let her go!" Julianna sobbed from the top of the stairs.

While Kerr held me pinned to the ground, I could hear her frantically punching numbers into the keypad on the lock.

"Run along now, bitch...run to your *Master*," he taunted Julianna. "Tell that spineless, dickless prick I'll trade him. I'll give him back the club bitch if he brings me Symoné. I know she's in there. I've been watching the club for hours...I saw her and the judge go in. I want her. Now!"

"Neither Mika nor Justice will hand Symoné over to you, especially not for me!" I spat in a tone of defiance I didn't feel. "You picked the wrong woman to negotiate with, you crazy douchebag."

"Then I guess you're going to die!" When Kerr dragged his tongue up the side of my face, I wanted to vomit.

"Oh, come on," Julianna moaned and kicked the door before punching the number pad once more.

"But not before you and I have a little fun. I might take you and Symoné with me. It'll be a fun little torture party. I'll carve you both up like Thanksgiving turkeys and take turns fucking you while you scream. Then when I've had my fill of you nasty cunts, I'll slice your fucking throats."

The cold ground beneath me was sweltering compared to the icy horror squeezing in around me. The man wasn't only delusional, he was demented, too.

Julianna's scream for help was cut short by the slam of the metal door.

Alone with the madman, I shoved down the waves of panic drowning me and forced my muscles to relax. If I could lure Kerr into a false sense of security, make him think that he'd won, I might be able to toss him off me and run.

My plan worked, partially. I was able to jerk one arm free, but when I pulled back my fist, my elbow slammed against the concrete. A jarring jolt of pain shot up my arm as I punched him in the throat and bucked my hips up hard.

My ineffectual hit didn't faze him at all. The fucker didn't even blink or cough, he simply pinned me with a horrible smile.

I knew I was dead.

I saw the hit coming…saw him draw back his fist. Though I tried to turn away from the impact, there wasn't anywhere for me to go.

Kerr landed the blow to my jaw.

Lights and pain exploded as my head bounced against the pavement. I tasted blood on my tongue as inky darkness dragged me down into a silent abyss.

CHAPTER FOURTEEN

"SASHA!" LAW'S ANGUISHED cry lured me to the surface.

"I've got her. She's coming around," some strange woman assured as I felt myself being passed off to unknown arms. "Please, Sir, go help take care of that…*thing*…for all of us."

Dizzy and disoriented, I sat and watched as a parade of men…big men, with wide shoulders and long legs, streaked past me. Their thunderous footsteps vibrated the frozen ground beneath me. Their enraged screams and curses echoed in my ears, amplifying the explosion of pain hammering away in my brain and jaw.

"Wrap those blankets around her. We need to cover her up and move her inside, before she goes into shock. Somebody take Joe inside, now that he's conscious."

The same woman who'd spoken earlier was giving out orders. The men ignored her. They were too busy surrounding a guy in the middle of the parking lot and yelling threats and obscenities. The rage pouring off the mob was palpable…deadly.

Heavy cloths were draped over me, and people were trying to help me stand. I pushed them away and sat, struggling to make sense of the violence unfolding before me.

What the hell was going on?

"Kill him! Kill the son of a bitch!" a woman sobbed from behind me.

Dragging my attention off the mob, I glanced up to find myself surrounded by a group of women. They were subs from the club…subs who despised me.

The sobbing woman was Symoné.

"Down on your knees, Kerr," Mika bellowed.

Thank god. They'd caught the son of a bitch and had him surrounded.

"Suck my dick, LaBrache," Kerr spat. "I'm not kneeling for you or anyone else. Fuck off, and get back."

"Come on, Destiny. We need to get you inside, get you warm, and check you out."

Without looking up at the woman who'd been helping me, I held up my hand. "Shhh. I want to watch this."

"It's over, you pathetic little bitch," Justice, Symoné's Master, growled.

Kerr lunged toward Justice. The other men sprang forward.

"Back off, this piece of shit is mine!" Justice bellowed.

"We get what's left," Mika sneered.

"All that's left of him," Cane growled.

Justice laughed and briefly broke eye contact with Kerr. The weaselly bastard threw a sucker punch and clipped Justice in the jaw. The Dom's head snapped back, but unlike me, he didn't lose consciousness. He simply spat out a wad of blood and doubled his fingers tightly.

"Master!" Symoné screamed from behind me.

"Is that all you got? Bring it, fuck-face, or do you only like hitting girls, you miserable piece of shit?" Justice taunted.

Kerr's eyes blazed with rage. He jabbed with his right hand but missed. In a blur, Justice threw a succession of punches that knocked the bastard flat on his back. Unsatisfied, Justice reached down and pulled the man to his feet before unleashing another violent torrent. Seconds later, Kerr was back on the ground.

"Damn," Ian exclaimed. "Who the fuck trained you…Ali?"

"Idaho state boxing champ, two years in a row," Justice preened.

"Fuck me," Mika murmured in stunned surprise.

Justice shrugged before scowling down at Kerr. "Come on. Get up and fight, you worthless cocksucker."

With an audible groan of pain, Kerr rolled to his side.

"That's what I thought, you fucking pussy," Justice scoffed angrily.

When Kerr rolled back over, the gun in his hand shimmered in the dimness of the single streetlight, illuminating the parking lot. Several women behind me gasped. My heart hammered against my ribs as fear spiked.

"All of you…hands above your heads. Nobody move," Kerr screamed. He stood slowly, pinning Justice with a hateful glare. "Who's the pussy now, Judge?"

"Put the gun down, or we'll make you regret it," Mika warned.

"I don't think so, boss man." Kerr let out a demented laugh.

Kerr narrowed his eyes as he kept them locked on Justice. "Call your little slut over here, Judge." When Justice refused, Kerr aimed the gun on Mika. "Now, or the big, bad boss man dies."

"Don't shoot him! Please don't shoot him," Julianna wailed.

"Aw, isn't that touching?" Kerr patronized. "The baby-breeding whore doesn't want me to shoot him. Bring me your bitch…now, Judge, or little momma over there will be giving birth to an orphan."

The veins in Justice's arms pulsed; his muscles flexed and bunched. His lips thinned to an angry line. Everyone could see it was sheer willpower keeping him from pulverizing the bastard to a bloody pulp with his bare hands.

"Symoné," Justice called without breaking eye contact with Kerr.

"No! I will not go to him," she screamed in between sobs. "You can't make me."

The fear in her voice sent goose bumps erupting all over my skin.

"Come to me, girl," Justice ordered, his voice low and patient.

"I-I can't," she wailed.

"Get her and bring her to me," Kerr demanded impatiently. "You do anything stupid, she dies, you die, and boss man dies. Got it?"

Fear held me in a stranglehold. Disbelief was a close second. Was Justice actually considering handing his sub over to the madman to save Mika's life?

My eyes fell to the 9mm in Kerr's hand before I began counting the number of men and women in the parking lot. The idiot didn't have enough bullets to kill us all, but I couldn't wrap my head around someone dying before we could take the bastard down.

Symoné was screaming hysterically as Justice slowly walked toward her.

I stared at both Cane and Law. The unadulterated rage lining their faces was identical as they stared at Kerr. I sent up a silent prayer that they didn't do anything foolish that would get them killed. As Justice and Symoné made their way past me, the big Dom pulled her close to his side.

"When we get up there, love, pretend to faint. Fall to the ground, and I'll take care of the rest."

"Oh, god," she sobbed. "Please don't do this, Master...please."

My heart clutched. I wanted to somehow warn my two Doms to get ready, but when I locked eyes on Law, he simply winked. They knew Justice wasn't playing into Kerr's hands. I should have known as well...known that he wouldn't ever give up his most prized possession without one hell of a fight.

I sucked in a shallow breath and waited for the grand finale to play out.

When Justice and Symoné faced Kerr, the whole world grew quiet. You could have heard a pin drop.

A brittle smile of triumph spread over Kerr's lips. With a sick and demented lick of his lips, he undressed her with a revolting gaze up and down her body. Justice tensed even more.

As if Symoné were a puppet whose strings had been snipped, she crumpled to the ground. Justice immediately bent down beside her. I watched in stunned silence as he lifted his pant leg and plucked out a gun while playing the role of worried Master.

"Pick her up and carry her over to me," Kerr bellowed furiously.

"Do it yourself, you fucking coward!" Justice growled as he stood and leveled the gun between Kerr's eyes.

Suddenly time slowed to a crawl. Symoné remained at Justice's feet while the other Doms dropped to the pavement.

Blue and red lights swirled to life all around us, bouncing off the brick buildings in a blinding strobe. Three police cruisers plowed into the parking lot, spraying gravel and dust as they lurched to a stop. The car doors opened and uniformed officers poured out, each drawing their weapons and pointing them at Kerr and Justice still poised in a standoff.

"Drop your weapons and put your hands on your heads." One of the cops ordered in a fierce and unrelenting roar.

"I am Judge Kellan Graham," Justice announced. "I am not dropping my weapon until you have this fugitive, Davis Walker, cuffed and in custody."

"I'll be a son of a bitch," the officer mumbled.

Kerr's eyes darted wildly, finally settling on Symoné. Longing swept over his face but was quickly replaced with rage when the commanding officer ordered him to drop his weapon a second time.

Kerr dragged in a deep breath and unleashed a bone-chilling battle cry as he spun toward the cops. At the same time, Justice dropped to his knees and flattened his body over Symoné's. Her scream of fear became muffled as Justice dragged her beneath him, protecting her like a human shield.

The other Doms from the club followed his lead and folded like cards to the ground.

Kerr aimed his gun at the officers. "Fuck you!"

The silence was severed as the cops opened fire, unleashing a torrent of thundering explosions.

Bullets tore into Kerr's flesh.

Blood spurted and rained out in the frigid air.

His body jerked.

Gravel scuffed beneath his stumbling feet.

Then he slumped to the ground, twitching slightly before he fell limp.

The reality of what was happening was too surreal for me to process. As if watching a movie, I felt removed from the nightmare unfolding before me.

Everyone remained frozen in place as the officers, with guns drawn, advanced toward the still body. The cop who'd ordered Kerr to drop his gun squatted down beside the lifeless form and pressed his fingers to Kerr's neck.

With a grim expression, he stood and faced his men. "Start taping the scene off. I'll call the chief and the coroner. Looks like we'll be filling out paperwork tonight, boys."

Mika was the first to move. He stood and locked eyes on Julianna before striding straight to her and wrapping her tightly in his arms. She broke down, sobbing.

Symoné was as well, as she clutched tightly to Justice's shoulders as he cradled her in his arms.

"Call for an ambulance, too. Sasha's hurt," yelled the woman—the same one who'd been giving orders beside me earlier.

Peeling my eyes off Cane and Law, who launched off the ground and started rushing toward me, I turned my head to see who the mystery woman was. I blinked in disbelief, and my mouth gaped open. The shadow of a fragile smile briefly tugged Cindy's lips.

"Thank you." My voice cracked and I swallowed the lump of emotion lodged in my throat.

She simply nodded. "I'll have one of the girls run inside and get Sam. He's helping the DMs move the other members to safety."

Before I could respond, Cane and Law were kneeling beside me.

"Oh, god," Law groaned.

They tucked the blankets closer to my body, then held me in their steely arms. Both men were trembling as badly as I was. Steering clear of my split lip and already swollen jaw, they bathed me in feather-soft kisses.

Cane pulled back slightly and studied my face. "We're going to take you inside and wait for the EMTs."

"I don't need an ambulance…just something to make this wicked headache go away."

"It wasn't rhetorical, girl." His harsh tone matched his dark scowl.

"I didn't plan for this to happen, you know!" I spat, and pressed my hand to my throbbing head.

Law squeezed me tighter and whispered words meant to soothe, but this time they weren't working. I was angry, scared, and my head pounded like a drum line. I'd just watched a man get killed and my emotions were swirling like a tornado. I certainly hadn't asked for the fucking lunatic to try and kidnap me or punch me in the face and knock me out. The last thing I wanted was to listen to Cane's orders or see his disapproval. All I wanted…no, *needed* was to snuggle back into his safe, warm arms until the terror bled from my veins.

"Easy, sweet girl," Cane murmured as he gently combed his hand over my head. "I know that. All I want is to get you someplace warm." His voice cracked. Tears shimmered in his golden eyes. "I don't want you out of my sight. And I sure as fuck don't ever want to feel the terror I did when we found you lying on the ground unconscious."

A tear slid down his cheek and I crumbled.

Burying my face in his chest, I sobbed.

"It's all right, now, love," Law murmured.

I knew by the sound of his voice that he was on the same shaky emotional ground as Cane…as me. I shrugged off the blanket and wrapped an arm around his trembling body.

Sirens screamed in the distance and grew louder as more police cars whipped into the parking lot.

"Where's Sasha?" Sam's familiar voice drew me from Cane's chest. When Sam spotted me, he hurried and knelt down beside me, too.

"Let's go inside so I can take a look at you, all right?"

The Dominant doctor's question wasn't directed to me, but rather Cane and Law. Following protocol, he sought my Masters' permission.

With the same tenderness he'd afford a newborn kitten, Law eased me off the ground and held me to his chest before heading toward the stairs.

"We're taking Destiny inside," Cane informed Mika as we passed him and Julianna still locked in an embrace.

"Use the room we were in earlier. It'll be closer for the EMTs." Mika reached into his pocket and handed Cane a set of keys. "The red one is the master key."

"Thanks, man."

The horde of members who'd gathered outside when the shooting stopped parted like the Red Sea as Law carried me into the club. Cane unlocked the door to the private room, while Law followed behind him and gently placed me on the bed.

Sam and Cindy each took a place beside me. Their Dominant and submissive demeanors vanished as their professional veneers fell into place. Cindy took my pulse, while Sam gently palpated my jaw and checked my pupils.

"Any idea how long she was out?" Sam asked, raising his question to my two Doms.

"Not sure. Maybe a minute or two," Cane offered.

Sam's serious expression didn't change. He simply nodded. "Are you nauseous, Sasha?"

"No. My head's all that hurts. It feels like my skull is splitting in two."

"Pulse is eighty-three and steady," Cindy announced.

Again, Sam nodded. "You'll need a CT scan to check out your jaw and head. You might have a concussion. I'm sorry, but I can't give you anything for the pain until we get you to the ER." Sam patted my hand. "They've got stronger stuff than I have on me. A healthy shot of morphine will help with the pain."

"Thank you, Master Sam."

His lips twitched and his expression softened. "You haven't addressed me as Master Sam in months, girl." Glancing up at Cane and Law, he smiled. "I think you've finally found what you've been searching for."

I glanced at both of my Doms and exhaled a contented sigh. "Yes. I have."

At least for a little while.

"We'll bring the EMTs to you when they get here. For now, rest if you can."

"I will. Thank you…" I turned my focus on Cindy. "Thank you both."

As soon as the couple left, Cane and Law crawled in beside me. Wedged between them, I closed my eyes. Instead of focusing on the security they offered, my mind was stuck…consumed by the horrific events with Kerr, in a never-ending spool. Tremors rippled through me.

"Try to erase it from your mind," Law softly coaxed.

"I can't."

"Maybe we should give you something else to concentrate on." Cane's voice held a hint of mystery.

That worked. He'd roused my curiosity. "Like what?"

"Like the fact that Law and I won't be going back to New York once your campaign is wrapped up."

My eyes flashed open and I started to sit up, but the sharp blade that sliced through my head made me sink back to the pillow and slam my lids closed. But even the pain didn't distract the ridiculous rush of hope sailing through me.

Careful. Don't invite disappointment, a little voice warned.

A million questions plowed through my aching brain, but I plucked out the most important one first. "Where are you going?"

"A spacious, restored building off North Lakeshore Drive and Superior. We signed the lease last month, It was finalized, yesterday."

This time I did sit up, though slowly, and gaped at them. "You two are messing with me. You're kidding, right?"

"Nope." Law chuckled.

A blast of shock and happiness left me stunned and speechless.

"Pratt & Cane Advertising will open its doors in the spring." The pride in Law's voice made it all the more real. "Possibly earlier, thanks to Cane. He's been soliciting companies here and has amassed an impressive list of potential clients."

It was all I could do to contain the burst of excitement blossoming inside. "If you need any testimonials, I'll happily tout your qualifications."

"Endorsing our business skills or our *other* skills?" Cane flashed me a devilish smirk.

"Business, Sir. I'm not breathing a word about your other skills. You two wouldn't be able to manage the list *that* would generate."

"There's only one name we want on that list, sweetheart…yours." Law brushed a fragile kiss over my lips.

"So, I guess there'll be an extension on our contract?" I arched a brow at Cane.

"You failed to notice that I never put an end date on it, princess?" He chuckled.

I furrowed my brow as I sifted through each clause of the document that I had branded to my memory. He was right…there was nothing about a time frame, only rescinding the contract if mutually agreed upon.

"You're right. I can't believe I missed that."

"You didn't ask," Cane stated.

Maybe it was time to determine when the proverbial rug was going to be pulled out from under me so I could prepare for the inevitable. "Do you have an end date in mind?"

"No," they answered in tandem.

Before I could delve deeper and ask more questions, the door opened, and Sam escorted two EMTs into the room. My head was still spinning and throbbing. The onslaught of poking and prodding and the litany of questions weren't doing anything but irritating me.

When they wanted to haul me off to the hospital, I let them know—in a testy tone—that I didn't want to go and that I'd be fine.

"You are going to be checked out, and that's final," Cane handed down in that glorious Dominant tone.

"There's the little hellcat we all know and love," Sam said with a chuckle.

I let loose a string of inward curses as they loaded me onto the stupid gurney. Law shook his head and smiled. "Yes, but we'll be sure not to tame all the sass out of her. It's one of the many things we love."

"Loving me is against the rules," I muttered.

"For you it is, princess. Not for us," Cane stated in challenge.

They might not have been messing with me about opening up a business in Chicago, but all the talk about love was simply to rattle my cage. The two men thrived on keeping the ground beneath me rumbling and rolling. I dismissed their comments and bit my tongue as the EMTs wheeled me back out into the cold night air.

Portable floodlights had been set up in the parking lot, now surrounded in yellow crime-scene tape and crawling with police and plain-clothed detectives. A man with a camera was taking pictures of Kerr's body that still lay exactly as he had fallen on the cold ground.

A ripple of revulsion rolled through me. I could still feel him sitting on top of me, pinning me to the concrete. Still see the demented look of murder in his eyes. Still hear his promise to slit my throat.

"Sirs!" A wave of panic gripped me hard. I reached out for them, even though I couldn't see either man.

"I'm right here." Law hurried alongside me and took my hand. "I'm not leaving your side, Sasha. But since only one of us can ride with you, Cane is going to meet us at the hospital. Sam and Cindy are headed that way now."

Relief sped through my veins. Whispering my thanks, I closed my eyes to block out the sight of Kerr's dead body as the EMTs loaded me into the ambulance.

True to his word, Law sat beside me and held my hand as we raced toward the ER. He stroked my tattered nerves with soothing words and his gentle nature.

Thanks to Sam, a neurologist and another doctor were waiting when I arrived.

Cane was pacing the small examination room when they wheeled me in. Hurrying to me, his face was fraught with worry. I reached out to try and alleviate his fears. He gripped my hand and held on tight while I was transferred onto yet another bed.

The staff moved with purpose. I was whisked away to the CT lab and, just as quickly, returned to my Doms. The only thing better than seeing their handsome faces was the injection of pain medicine I received a short time later.

My attitude improved as the pounding in my head and the ache in my jaw all but evaporated. Thankfully, there was no sign of concussion and no broken bones. Along with a prescription for pain pills, I was ordered to rest. Both Cane and Law assured they'd see to that, and I was finally released. After thanking Sam and Cindy, my Doms helped me into the limo.

I was surprised to see the sky beginning to grow lighter toward the east.

"What time is it?"

"Close to five in the morning." Law yawned.

"Let's go get breakfast!" I giggled.

"I have a better idea," Cane said, sliding onto the leather seat beside me. "Let's take you back to the hotel, climb into bed, and order room service when we wake up."

"Hey! I never did get ice cream," I pouted.

"We'll order some with room service. Bacon, eggs, juice, and ice cream…yum."

I laughed at the cringe that wrinkled Law's face. "Chocolate chip cookie dough ice cream."

"Anything you want, princess." Cane chuckled.

He snuggled in close beside me. I placed my hand on his thigh as I rested my head on Law's chest and closed my eyes.

"All I want is you two," I mumbled.

Lured by the hum of the tires and the sway of the limo, I drifted into the darkness.

WHEN I WOKE up, I was naked and in bed. As if the feel of our tangled limbs hadn't been enough, my body hummed, aware of both men's presence. Lying still, I breathed in their masculine scent, felt the heat of their delicious bodies, and smiled.

I was thrilled they were staying in Chicago.

I couldn't imagine having to say good-bye to them or going back to the empty existence I'd been living. They'd stormed in like a hurricane and taught me how to trust, how to knock down my walls and allow them inside. Shining their light into the darkest recesses of my soul made me feel not only whole but also treasured…loved.

I knew the rules and the subsequent punishment if I didn't guard my heart.

Problem was…I might have already fucked up and fallen in love with them.

Icy fingers of dread marched up my spine.

No. It wasn't love. People didn't instantly fall in love overnight.

This was just some stupid sophomoric crush or puppy love or…or I was simply reverting back to my old familiar pattern.

But to find…what?

Comfort?

Or was false hope ruling my better judgment…again?

Been there. Done that. Have way too many T-shirts in the closet already.

So why does this time feel so much different than the others?

Trying to put a label on the powerful current arcing between us was useless. It didn't matter if it was infatuation, hero worship, or puppy love. My feelings would pass…in time. They had to. Falling in love with them would ruin everything. I still had so much more to learn.

Law's warm lips on my shoulder wiped away all the thoughts swirling in my brain.

"Morning, gorgeous," he said in a sleepy whisper. "How are you feeling?"

"Sore, but I slept like a rock between you two." Not wanting to wake Cane, my reply matched Law's whisper.

"I'm glad. My night sucked."

Carefully turning to face him, I frowned. "Why?"

"Too many nightmares." He kissed my forehead. "We were running and running down the parking lot, but we couldn't get to you before that maniac tossed you into his car and drove away."

His body trembled.

It was my turn to comfort him. "Shhh. Kerr could never hurt me. He never stood a chance, not when you two rode in on your white horses to rescue me."

I brushed a soft kiss to his lips as I threaded my fingers through his hair.

When I pulled back, Law's face hardened in fury. "We didn't even get a chance to lay a finger on him, much less beat him to death for hurting you."

I cupped his face and smiled. "Kerr hurt Symoné in far worse ways than he did me. Justice deserved to punish him for her pain."

"Yes, but it doesn't change the fact that we weren't able to punish him for yours," Law growled. "*Nobody* messes with the woman we love."

My body tensed, and I snapped my hand back, while my heart

hammered against my ribs. My brain instantly rejected his claim, but the urge to run wasn't so easily dissuaded.

"I need to use the restroom. I'll be right back," I whispered and started inching toward the foot of the bed.

Cane opened his eyes and tossed an arm around my waist, pinning me in place as he shot a glance toward Law. "Way to go, ace."

Law chuckled. "It just…slipped out, brother."

Anxiety spiked. I rolled over and wiggled free of Cane's arm, then knelt on the bed, daring a nervous glance between them.

"You go and drop the *L* word, and now she's all freaked out." Cane sighed. He sat up and skimmed a gentle hand over my jaw. "How are you feeling this morning, princess?"

Wait just a damn minute!

Did he honestly think I was going to sit there and let him change the subject…roll over me like a damn bulldozer?

"I'm fine, and Law wasn't professing his love. He was simply emphasizing the point that no one has permission to touch me without your say-so."

"It's true. No one has our permission to touch you, but that's not what he was saying."

Cane's dissecting stare studied me closely. I couldn't mask the wave of terror cresting. Though I tried to put on a brave face, my body was shaking like a leaf.

"I know it sounds crazy. Hell, we're as stunned as you are," he continued. Both he and Law moved in beside me before caressing their hands up and down my arms. "We knew last night when we saw you on the ground, bleeding and unconscious."

"When they took you down for the CT scan, we talked about how quickly you'd captured our hearts." Law smiled tenderly.

Confusion, anxiety, and dread swirled.

Claws of denial shredded my soul.

They were going to release me…not because I'd fallen in love with them but because they'd fallen in love with me.

A howl of anger and pain shrieked within me. Instead of succumbing to the blinding rage and disappointment uncoiling in my heart, I quickly gathered every thread of dignity I could and lifted my chin.

"I understand. I'll get my clothes on. If you would be so kind as to call a cab, I'd appreciate it." My tone was cold and distant.

Before I could climb off the bed, Law gripped a fist in my hair. Obviously afraid of hurting me, he gently pulled my head back, exposing my throat. Cane swooped in and nipped at my neck as he pinched my nipples.

"Pride isn't going to push us away or save you anymore," Law thundered.

As he claimed my mouth with a feral and brutal kiss, Cane distracted me from the pain sliding over my jaw by suckling my breasts and toying with my clit.

Consumed by sensation, I mentally raised a white flag.

I was exhausted from fighting the battle between logic and emotion.

Tired of searching for balance and a place where I belonged.

Weary of believing I didn't deserve this gift I'd craved for so long.

I wrapped my hands in their hair and let go of all the worn-out emotions that had bound me in grief.

Like quicksilver, the awakening shot through me in a ball of shimmering light.

I knew why my relationship with Cane and Law had felt so different from all the others.

Trust.

Cane's and Law's dogged faith in me gave me the strength to show them all my ugly emotions.

They didn't walk away, didn't toss me to the curb. They suffused me in the one thing I'd convinced myself I'd never have...their unconditional love.

Yes, it was fast.

Yes, I was scared.

Terrified it could all blow up in my face.

But I had to put my faith in them, as completely as they'd placed theirs in me.

Life didn't come with promises—only risks, rewards, and failures.

I was through failing.

When they released me, the room was spinning, my mind was finally clear, and my body was on fire.

"We need to stop," Cane rasped out. His voice was hoarse and saturated in desire.

"Yes." Law's tone was equally strained. "You have to rest. Doctor's orders."

"What if I don't want to rest?" I asked in a full-on sex-kitten whisper.

On the nightstand, Cane's cell phone began to ring.

"We'll lace your ice cream with pain pills and knock your sexy ass out." Law chuckled.

"Then tie you to the bed." Cane grinned, rolled over, and reached for his phone.

I smiled up at Law. "I'll wake up eventually."

"Hey, Mika," Cane greeted. "Yes. She's doing fine. Slept through the night without any problems." He paused, turned to look at me, and smiled. "No. No concussion. She's sore and has a knot on the back of her head. And I'll lay odds that she's got a suit in her closet that will complement the colors already coming to the surface on her jaw."

My eyes flashed open wide and I lifted a hand to my face. It was swollen and indeed sore, and I scurried off the bed and hurried to the bathroom. Flipping on the light, I peered into the mirror and groaned. I looked like I'd been in a prizefight…and lost.

"We'll be there. Thanks for letting us know. See you soon."

Be where…for what? I leaned back from the sink and watched as Cane set his phone back down. I sent him a quizzical look.

"Mika called to see how you were doing and to let us know that they've pushed back the sub meeting to four o'clock this afternoon. I guess the police were there all night. They just now finished their investigation and took down all the crime tape."

"Do you feel up to going still?" Law climbed out of bed and strode toward me.

Funny, a few days ago I was dreading the thought of sitting around with a group of perfect subs. But today? I was ready, anxious even, to learn all that I'd been missing.

"Yes. I'm looking forward to it."

Cane joined us in the bathroom, rubbed a hand over my welted ass, and sent me a proud smile. Without a word, he walked to the shower and turned on the water. The carnal flicker in his eyes filled me with hope…hope that he'd changed his damn mind, and all three of us would have a screaming good time.

CHAPTER FIFTEEN

I CLOSED MY eyes and sighed as I stood beneath the hot water spilling from the showerhead. The water running over my raw welts made my ass burn, but I was too focused on Cane's soap-slick hands gliding up and down my body, and with Law's tender fingers gently massaging my scalp as he washed my hair. The sweet man was being so careful not to touch the goose egg on the back of my head.

"You two are spoiling me," I murmured. "I've never been this pampered before."

"Get used to it, my love," Law drawled. "We're going to pamper you in ways you can't imagine."

I grinned. "Be careful. I have a pretty twisted imagination."

"Oh? Tell us," Cane prompted.

"I'd much rather show you, Sir."

"Minx," he growled. I jumped and began to purr when Cane slapped a wet hand to my pussy. "Start talking."

When I confessed a few of my fantasies, their rigid cocks eagerly nudged my hip and thigh. Both took turns plucking my nipples and skimming their fingers down my belly to tease and toy with my clit. Writhing between them, I stopped telling them my naughty secrets to keep from shattering without permission.

"The club has a medical station. When you're well and all healed up we'll have to make your dirty doctor fantasy a reality," Law promised.

"I'm feeling one hundred percent fine right now, Sir."

Cane landed a hard slap on my ass. "You know better than to lie to us, girl."

"I wasn't…" I swallowed down my need to argue and not spit out another lie. "Yes, Sir. I'm sorry…and horny."

They both started to laugh.

"Think of it as doctor-induced orgasm denial, love," Law teased.

"Yes, and just think how primed you'll be when we decide to lift that ban," Cane chimed in.

I groaned. "I might have to drown my frustration in ice cream...*nightly* ice cream."

"I see no problem with that. We'll be happy to lick it off your body, won't we, Cane?" Law teased.

Blinking through the cascade of water, I sent the man an over-dramatic pout. "Why not let me lick it off *your* bodies, Sir?"

"Because your jaw needs to heal first." Cane scowled, then immediately smirked. "Don't worry. We'll have all the time in the world to keep your sassy mouth busy once you're well."

"Let's get you dried off and back into bed so we order room service," Cane said, turning off the water. "I want you to rest for a few hours before we head over to the club."

They each grabbed a towel and began drying me off together. While they wiped the water off their own enticing bodies, I stood at the mirror, finger combing my hair and staring at the ugly bruise decorating my jaw.

Memories of Kerr's bloody, bullet-riddled body lying slumped on the gravel made my stomach pitch. I wondered how long it would take before that visual stopped invading my brain.

Needing to wipe the image away, I let my mind wander. I wanted to ask the two men behind me what happened next. How was our relationship going to work? Were we going to date, per se, or simply hook up at the club a few nights a week and have sex...whenever they decided?

I didn't know what to expect, or what *they* expected.

Talk to them. Open. Honest. Communication. Remember?

Cane and Law sidled up beside me.

They stole all my worries away when they dragged their lips and tongues up my shoulders, over my neck, and settled in behind my ears. Tingles pinged through me. My nipples pebbled. My pussy wept, and a mournful moan seeped from my lips.

"You're going to torture me every waking minute, aren't you?"

"Pretty much." Cane grinned.

"Ugh!"

"Think of it as practice," Law taunted.

"Practice for what?"

"On focusing, sweetheart."

"Trust me, Sir. I'm focused. I'm focused on nothing but"—I reached down and gently dragged my fingertips up and down their erections—"these and making you both feel good."

In unison, they reached down, wrapped their hands around my wrists and dragged my fingers off them.

"I'll get the rope," Law stated pointedly to Cane.

"I'll order room service. Ghost peppers, raw ginger, and ice should do nicely to begin with." He beamed evilly.

"Sounds fun! I'll call Sam and see if he'll give me the all-clear to play." I flashed them both a sassy smile. If they were willing to dish it out, I was more than willing to toss it right back.

"We're going to need a lot more rope…and ball gags. Lots of ball gags." Cane's tone was pure exasperation.

Delighting in the playful banter, I kissed them one after the other.

Being myself with them was easy, loving them…effortless.

"I think it's time to modify our contract, don't you, princess?"

I stared at Cane's reflection in the mirror. The love in his eyes was all but blinding, but then so was mine. "Yes, Sir. I think that's a wonderful idea."

"I think this calls for a champagne breakfast," Law announced. As we settled back in the big bed, I glanced at the clock on the nightstand.

"It's almost two in the afternoon."

"Champagne brunch then." He shrugged.

"I'll handle everything," Cane preened, perusing the menu.

I didn't doubt him for a second. The man would take care of all of us, exactly the way he'd been doing for days. Snuggled in Law's arms, I listened as Cane sat beside me, phone to his ear, ordering brunch.

"And a bowl of chocolate chip cookie dough ice cream," Cane growled.

I squealed as he hung up the phone and kissed him hard. "Thank you, Sir."

He just laughed and shook his head. "Soft boiled eggs, oatmeal, champagne, and ice cream. God help us if you ever get pregnant."

"Pregnant?" Law blanched.

"Easy, Sir." I patted his leg. "I have no room for diapers and midnight feedings in my life."

"Someday?" Cane cocked his head.

"Maybe. But not today."

"Thank god." Law's exhale was so loud Cane and I laughed.

I WAS A bundle of nerves when we arrived at the club. While I no longer scoffed at the idea of submission and was ready to open my mind and learn, my insecurities had resurfaced with a vengeance. I was terrified to find out what kind of reception I'd receive.

Even though I was safely tucked between both Cane and Law, a tiny tremor slid up my spine when we entered the dungeon. Every sub sitting in a circle on the floor turned their head our way.

Symoné leapt to her feet and rushed toward me. Cringing as she stared at my jaw, she turned toward Cane and Law. "Permission to speak to your girl, please, Sirs?"

"Granted." Cane smiled.

"Of course, pet," Law approved.

"Oh, my god, Destiny," she groaned. "I'm so sorry for what Kerr did to you."

Justice stepped up behind her and sent a look of sympathy my way as he shook hands with Cane and Law.

"It wasn't your fault, Symoné." I smiled. "He was a crazy asshat who needed to be put down. Thankfully, the cops did that. His reign of terror over you is done."

She sucked in a ragged breath, nodded, and wiped her eyes.

Julianna joined us wearing a smile that could have lit up all of Las Vegas. "I'm so glad you're here. Come…sit with us."

For a long second, my feet refused to move. I was frozen in place.

Symoné leaned in close to my ear. "If anyone gives you any attitude, I'll be happy to bitch-slap them for you. Deal?"

All the tension inside me and rushed out in a strangled laugh. "You're on."

"Language, angel," Justice warned.

"Oops. Sorry, Sir."

I swiveled a beseeching glance at Cane and Law.

"Go on, sweetheart."

"We'll wait for you at the bar with the other Doms," Cane instructed. "Enjoy your meeting."

Flanked by Julianna and Symoné, I sucked in a deep breath and strode to the circle. Joining them, I averted my eyes and waited for the ugly comments to begin.

"Looking at what he did to you makes me wish they could kill him all over again."

I jerked my head up at the pain in the other woman's voice. Mellie was sitting across from me on a pillow, gently stroking her pregnant belly with one hand and wiping the tears from her cheeks with the other.

"I was collared to him once," she confessed.

I nodded. It was no secret that the woman had been Owned by Kerr.

"Back then, he was just a cocky asshole, not an abusive stalker and kidnapper. I don't know what happened to him…what made him snap."

None of us did. Kerr had always been full of himself, but his irrational and ominous behavior had come out of the blue.

I bravely slid a glance around the circle. Some of the other subs were crying, some stared off blankly, while others openly showed their sympathy.

"And we never will," Julianna announced firmly. "It's no one's fault but his. Dry your eyes, Mellie. Stress and worry aren't good for your baby."

I couldn't help but smile a little. No doubt the redheaded spitfire beside me gave Mika a run for his money…constantly. I thought back to our luncheon and realized her fear of losing her identity had been as real as my own fear of letting anyone in. There was a lot I could learn from this one woman, but as I glanced around at the others again, I figured I could learn a lot from all of them, too.

"Can I say something?" I asked nervously.

"Of course." Julianna smiled.

"I just want to apologize to all of you for the way I've acted in the past." The look of shock that lined their faces was like a kick to the gut. I paused and stared pointedly at Cindy, then Leah, and finally Liz. "I was wrong…about…well, about pretty much everything. I'd like to try and make it up to you all…somehow. I'll understand if you're not willing to give me another chance." My voiced faded, and I blinked away the tears stinging the backs of my eyes.

"We've all been in your shoes before, Destiny," Cindy softy stated. "I'm proud to have you here, and I hope…I hope we'll grow to be good friends."

Slapping a hand to my mouth, I held back a sob and nodded. Tears blurred my vision. I swallowed the ball of emotion blocking my throat before I swiped the tears from my cheeks. "Thank you."

A collective welcome sang though the group.

None of the women I'd snubbed or condemned shunned or judged me. Instead, they welcomed me with open hearts.

I lowered my head and wrapped my arms around myself to keep the guilt and embarrassment from ripping me apart. All I wanted to do was lie down on the floor, curl into a ball, and howl.

Suddenly, Cindy wrapped me in her arms and simply rocked me for several long minutes as we both sobbed.

"I didn't treat you any better," she confessed, choking on her words. "None of us did. I'm sorry."

"What the hell is going on here?" Mika thundered, wearing a menacing and intimidating expression "There's no crying at sub meetings." He then smiled. "Save your tears for when your Master lights up your ass."

"Oh, Master, quit. Please," Julianna sniffed. "We're trying to heal old wounds, clean the air, and bond. It's messy emotional work."

"Evidently," he drawled and gave me a wink. "Good to see you've knocked that chip off your shoulder, girl. Bet the load's a lot lighter not hauling that heavy-assed thing around, isn't it?"

"Much, Sir," I sniffed with a watery smile.

"I'm proud of you…damn fucking proud." Mika glanced around the group and nodded in approval. "Damn proud of all of you."

Trevor slid to the floor, out of breath but wearing a huge grin. "Are you proud of me, too?" he asked Mika.

"No. You're late, boy!" Mika growled playfully.

"It's Daddy's faul—err, I mean, yes, I am. Please forgive me, Sir."

"Not a great save, but it'll do." Mika laughed. "Okay, I'll leave you to your meeting, little ones. But remember…no more crying." He cupped his hand to his mouth in a conspiratorial whisper. "All the wailing and sobbing is scaring your Masters, but you didn't hear that from me."

"No. Never, Sir." We chided in unison, then laughed.

Mika walked away, shaking his head, while Cindy hugged me one last time and hurried back to her spot in the circle.

Trevor cringed when he saw my jaw, then a huge grin lit up his face. "There's only one good thing about that bruise, sister. You can honestly say…you should see the other guy."

Our tears turned to laughter.

"I know your Master hates me, but god, I love you, Trev." I laughed.

"Daddy doesn't hate you…he just wants to beat the sass out you. Of course, you and I know, that's not how you punish a masochist." Trevor snapped his fingers and wiggled his hips.

"How do you punish a masochist?" Symoné asked.

"You ignore us," I replied.

"Or make us sit and watch," Trevor whined. "And let me tell you, sitting by your Master, wishing you were up on that cross or tied to that bondage table is pure *hell*. It's the worst torture on the planet. Worse than waterboarding or bamboo shoots under the fingernails. Uh-huh!"

Several subs paled at his words before Julianna called the meeting to order.

The topic for the day was the purpose of serving a Master. I found the discussion totally captivating. I learned more about the meaning of the power exchange in one meeting than I had in all the years I'd sat observing the subs. The lessons had been in front of me all that time, but I'd never understood, until now.

Not only had I knocked the chip off my shoulder, as Mika observed, but I'd duly knocked myself off my own high horse, as well. None of the submissives in that meeting were meek or mild. They were like me…strong-willed, successful, and even a little mouthy. Except for Trevor—he was a whole lot mouthier. Not in a disrespectful way but in a funny, no-filter-whatsoever way.

As the meeting winded down, some of the subs stood and took a seat at the empty tables in the center of the room, I assumed to wait for their Doms.

"Hey, we're all going to Maurizio's after this," Tiffany, a perky brunette revealed. "Do you think you and your Masters can join us for dinner?"

"I-I, don't know. Maybe," I answered. Turning toward the bar, I watched Cane and Law talking and laughing with the other Doms.

"Oh, I'm such a ditz." Tiffany slapped herself on the forehead. "It's probably really hard for you to eat, isn't it?"

"No, not really. I did fine with brunch." I understood then why Cane had ordered such a bizarre combination of scrambled eggs, oatmeal, mashed potatoes, and of course, ice cream for me. He'd chosen all soft foods. His benevolence sent tingles dancing over my arms and legs. "I think I can manage lasagna or ravioli."

"Sweet!" She grinned as she looked up at her Dom, Master Brax. "Hopefully we'll see you there. It was great finally getting to know you, Destiny."

"You, too." I smiled.

My soul was much lighter as the meeting ended and I watched the couple walk away.

"Are you ready to go, our brave and mighty girl?" Law asked. Cane stood by his side wearing an expectant expression.

"Yes, Sirs. Thank you for bring me to the meeting and coming to fetch me." I grinned.

"Look at you." Cane glowed with admiration.

"Thank you, Sir."

"Wow!" Law exclaimed. "We like the confidence you found, sweetheart."

"I'd hope so. You're the ones who've instilled it in me," I replied with a saucy wink. "I've just learned how to polish it up a bit."

"Then you can continue to polish it every Saturday from here on out without fail. Understood?"

"I'd like that. Thank you, Sir."

"Grab your coat. We're going to join the other members for dinner at—"

"Maurizio's?"

"Yes, and don't interrupt me again, you sassy little wench," Cane admonished with a grin.

"Sorry, Sir. I'm still learning how to polish."

He and Law gathered me up in their arms and hugged me. "You're doing a phenomenal job, sweet girl," Law praised. "We couldn't be prouder."

Their approval spread a soothing fire inside me and warmed the deepest recesses of my soul.

After an amazing dinner of wonderful food, newfound friendships, and laughter, Cane insisted we bid our good-byes and head back to the hotel so I could rest.

I wanted to beg them to take me to the club, but realized he and Law were simply doing their Dominant duty and putting my health above my wants. Still, the day had been filled with so many thrilling revelations, I didn't want the magic to end.

"You're awfully quiet," Cane observed. "Are you hurting?"

"No. Not really. I'm just thinking."

"Out loud with it, love," Law prodded.

"I wanted to go to the club." The words fell out of my mouth. I cringed, knowing I sounded like a petulant child.

"So did we." Law shrugged.

"Then why aren't we going?"

"Because we care about your physical health and mental health equally," Cane replied.

"But…Kerr's dead. Nothing is going to happen to me. I swear I won't go outside again without either of you by my side."

Cane softly snorted. "Damn right you won't. But this has nothing to do with protecting you against lunatics, though I'm sure there are plenty more wandering around the city."

"You used to sit at the bar and watch the others scene around you, correct?"

"Yes. You know that, Sir." I nodded to Law's question.

"How did that make you feel?" he continued.

"Worthless."

"Exactly." Cane stroked my leg. "How would you feel if we went to the club and made you sit and watch the others scene tonight? Knowing full well we wouldn't lead you to a station and use you hard?"

Sitting by your Master, wishing you were up on that cross or tied to that bondage table is pure hell. It's the worst torture on the planet. Worse than waterboarding or bamboo shoots under the fingernails.

Trevor's words came roaring back to me.

I lost my heart to both the men beside me even more.

"You're taking me back to the hotel because you don't want to punish me."

Law choked and blinked down at me.

"Damn! What the fuck? Did they teach you all our Dominant

secrets at that class?" Cane gaped.

"Pretty much." I smirked shyly.

"That's exactly why we're not going to the club, my love." Law grinned. "Instead of torturing you, we're taking you home for ice cream, Netflix, and pain pills. Then we're going to tuck you into bed."

"Tuck me in properly?"

"No!" they both barked.

"Damn," I mumbled.

WE SPENT THE next day snuggling in bed, gorging on room service, watching movies, and driving each other crazy with teasing touches and passionate kisses. Time could have stood still, with us cocooned in that bubble of perfection, and I'd have been perfectly content for life.

Sunday morning, as we woke in a tangle, Law smiled and brushed the hair from my face. "After breakfast, we need to talk and get some things settled."

"What things?"

"Expectations, living arrangements, that sort of thing."

"While room and maid service are nice, we can't live in this hotel forever," Cane added. "Now that I've secured the building for our business, I have extra time I can devote to helping launch your campaign."

"You mean, work with us?" I asked, unable to hide my glee.

"Yes. I'll be able to keep an eye on you all day long."

And no doubt order me to strip for your hungry stares in my office again. Unlike a few days ago, the notion didn't fill me with panic, but a wicked thrill instead.

"I'll be doubly hard-pressed to focus on work."

"We can come up with some creative ways to help you concentrate if you'd like," Law offered. The evil gleam in his eyes told me I'd best discover my own ways, yet, I was intrigued.

"Like what?"

"Wearing a butt plug while you work, or maybe a pair of nipple clamps…ben wa balls. Nothing overt, just a subtle reminder to help keep you centered." Cane chuckled.

"You're evil. I won't be able to think about work wearing any of those things."

"You will if we ask you to. Won't you, sweetheart?" Law plucked my nipple.

Pressing my shoulders into the mattress, I lifted my breasts in offering. "Yes, Sir."

Cane slid his fingers down my stomach and spread my folds.

"How much longer before you decide I'm well enough to play, Sirs?"

"What's the rush, princess?" Cane taunted.

"I'm horny…still."

"Well, we can't have that now, can we?"

"Oh, thank you, Sir!" I squealed. "Now? Can we play now?"

They both chuckled.

"Breakfast first, discussions second, then play." Law arched his brow as if expecting me to argue.

"Wonderful, Sir. I'm in serious need of coffee."

With a look of awe, he shook his head. "The change in you is inspiring, my love."

"I have you two to thank for opening my eyes."

"That's our job…well, part of it, anyway." The wolfish smile Cane sent me caused my pulse to double.

"And you both do amazing work."

"This isn't our first rodeo." Law grinned as he rolled over and picked up the hotel phone.

No, it wasn't, but I could always hope it would be their last.

"Everyone good with bacon, eggs, hashbrowns, pancakes, juice, croissants, and coffee?" Law asked.

"Good grief. Hungry, Sir?" I giggled.

"Oh, I plan to work off all the calories, them and a whole lot more." He wagged his eyebrows and licked his lips suggestively.

And they had the nerve to call *me* a brat?

Cane chuckled. "Sounds good to me. Hey, ask them to set it up for us downstairs. We'll be *busy* in the shower."

Turning an expectant glance Cane's way, I nibbled my bottom lip. Yesterday morning in the shower, things had gotten quite heated—and I didn't mean water temperature, either—until both men called a halt to our mutual exploration. I hoped this morning I'd be allowed to feel more than my soapy hands sliding over their hard flesh.

Cane rolled his eyes at my hopeful expression. "You're not trying to manipulate us again, are you, my conniving little vixen?"

"No way, Sir. I'm simply wishing."

"Wish and simmer, princess." He pulled me in against his chest and tapped a long finger to my lips. "We don't want any attitude if you don't get what you want, understood?"

"I already have everything I want, Sir." I kissed his finger before sucking it inside my mouth and swirling my tongue all around it. His strangled moan filled me with the right kind of pride.

With a growl, Cane swatted me on the ass. "Go start the shower, girl. We'll join you in a minute."

I was rinsing the shampoo out of my hair when they stepped inside. As I drank in the sight of their beautiful naked bodies and stiffening cocks, desire spiked and sizzled.

"Our turn to take over." Law grabbed the body wash with one hand and cupped my breast with the other. Thumbing my nipple, he slanted his lips over mine and swallowed my needy moans.

"Do we really have to talk first?" I choked out on a heaving breath.

"Yes, you impatient little minx," Cane growled before slamming his lips to mine. He left no doubt who was in charge. My body answered the call of his power with a deep, pulsating throb.

"We're only warming you up for later." Law nipped and laved my neck.

Warming me up was a massive understatement. Inundating me beneath an onslaught of their slippery, toying, and tormenting fingers and hungry lips, teeth, and tongues, they aimed to not only set me on fire but also drive me out of my mind.

Void of the fear of punishment, I boldly stroked their cocks and massaged their heavy sacs, giving back every bit as good as they gave. My hungry whimpers fused with their hisses, groans, and guttural curses, until Law expelled an animalistic roar and shut off the water.

"I'm beginning to question who's submitting to who right now." With a snarl, he pressed me up against the travertine wall and laid siege to my mouth with his.

He swallowed my keening whimpers as I opened myself up to him in every way and wrapped my legs around his waist. As he gripped the cheeks of my ass, his wide crest lay throbbing at my entrance. Desperate to impale myself on his hardness, I rocked my hips, but Law simply held me in place.

Cane drove his fingers into my quivering core, plunging in and out, as sexual energy throbbed around us, like strobes.

"Enough!" Cane snarled. "Our breakfast is getting cold."

"Fuck breakfast," Law groaned.

"No. Fuck *me*!"

Law grinned against my lips, kissed me hard one last time, and lowered me onto my feet. "Still giving orders?"

"Never, Sir. I'm just stating my needs…openly and honestly," I gasped, working to steady my breathing.

"Let's dry off and talk so we can take care of *all* our needs." Cane dropped a bleak glance at his swollen erection.

I couldn't snag the bath towels fast enough.

A short time later, when we were dressed and downstairs, the aroma of hickory smoked bacon, maple syrup, and rich, strong coffee filled my senses. Kneeling on my pillow beside the table, I no longer felt like a humiliated dog but a privileged and pampered princess.

"Have you ever thought about selling your house, Sasha?"

Cane's random question caused me to nearly choke on the piece of pancake Law had placed on my tongue. Glancing up at Cane, I shook my head. "No, Sir. I-I love my house."

A thoughtful expression lined his face. I waited for him to say more but he merely picked up his coffee, took a sip, and continued eating.

Neither of them mentioned the subject again while we ate. Instead, they discussed the upcoming Valentine's Day party at the club.

"You'll wear something sinful and red, girl," Cane instructed. "If you don't have anything, I'd like you to go shopping."

"Shopping?" My eyes lit up and a wide grin stretched across my lips.

They both laughed.

After we'd finished our meal, the three of us climbed the stairs to the bedroom.

I didn't assume that our *talk* was over, but as my eyes landed on the bed, I hoped it wouldn't take long. My fantasies were crushed, and a sense of anxiety rushed in when Cane plucked out the contract and a pen.

"As you know, this document can only be rescinded by mutual agreement," he began. "I'd like to void our contract, Sasha."

His words plowed into me like a wrecking ball.

My knees threatened to give out. I grabbed the dresser to keep from sinking to the floor.

Questions chased the fear flooding my system.

Darting a panicked glace between the men, I felt as if the walls were closing in all around me.

"Ha-have I done something wrong?" Both my voice and chin quivered.

"No. God no!" Cane dropped the pen and paper. He pulled me to his chest and held me as I trembled and then kissed my forehead.

"Oh, Sasha. You've done everything right." Law banded me in his arms as well.

"We don't want our relationship defined by the clauses in these pages anymore. We want to live and love each other freely," Cane explained.

The wave of relief that slammed through me held as much force as the swell of terror that had assaulted me seconds before.

Stunned, I worked to process the ramifications of what he was suggesting.

Tears filled my eyes.

Hope took flight on golden wings, soaring higher and further than I'd ever felt before.

"Will you agree to terminate our contract, Sasha? To live and love us without the confines outlined in this piece of paper?"

I nodded because I couldn't find my voice.

This time, Cane didn't bother reprimanding me for my nonverbal answer. He simply smiled and sipped the tears that tumbled down my cheeks. "Void it, princess. Void it for all of us."

Pressing the pen in my fingers, Cane smoothed the paper out on the dresser.

My hands trembled and tears stained the print as I stared at the document.

It seemed like a lifetime ago that I couldn't decide if I even wanted to sign the page. In many ways, it *had* been a lifetime. The angry, selfish, and isolated person I'd been: didn't exist anymore.

Cane and Law had resurrected a new me...a happy, caring, brave new woman.

More self-aware.

More self-assured.

And hopelessly in love with the two men who'd changed her whole world.

Bursting with gratitude, joy, and hope, I didn't hesitate to scrawl the glorious word V-O-I-D over the page.

A strangled sob of redemption tore from my lips, followed by a watery laugh of absolution.

I was lost in their soulful kisses. My head swam. My heart soared.

Law eased back and thumbed the tears from my cheeks. "Thank you, little one. Let me be the first to say, I do not want us commuting between separate houses. And I do not want to live out of a suitcase anymore. I want us all under one roof…living together."

"I couldn't agree more," Cane seconded and cupped my chin. "How do you feel about having roommates, girl?"

"You mean…you want to move in with me?"

"If you'll have us. After all, it is *your* house, love." Law chuckled.

"Oh, my god. Yes! It's way big enough for all of us, unless…"

"Unless what?" Cane prompted.

"Unless you want to live in something bigger, like Mika's house."

"No. I don't want a mansion." Cane frowned. "Your house is as close to a mansion as I'll ever want."

"Which begs the question…why such a big house for just you?" Law asked.

"For the mortgage interest, Sir. My accountant suggested I buy something big." I shrugged. "So I did."

"It's perfect, love, just like you." Cane smiled. "Are you sure you want us moving in with you though? There've been a lot of changes in your life in a short amount of time."

"Are you kidding?" My heart nearly burst out of my chest. "I can't think of anything more wonderful than waking up in both of your arms in the morning and falling asleep in them every night."

"I can't, either," Law murmured, low and enticingly.

"When were you thinking of moving in, Sirs?" Shaking with excitement, I wanted to pinch myself to make sure I wasn't dreaming.

"Is tomorrow too soon?" Cane's grin was panty-melting.

"No, Sir!" I squealed.

"I figured this room's paid for." He shrugged. "We might as well tear up the sheets another night here before we christen yours."

Sinking his fingers deep into my hair, he meshed his lips to mine in a slow, spine-tingling kiss. I was glad they were holding on to me, or I'd have melted into a puddle at their feet.

When he released me, Law cupped my cheek and turned my head, then pressed his warm lips to mine with the same soul-stealing passion.

Cane eased away while I tangled my tongue with Law's in a searing carnal dance.

"This bed is getting mighty cold," Cane called out.

Law abandoned my mouth with a soft laugh. Turning, I saw Cane lying on one side of the bed. He stole my breath. All naked, hard, and ready, he'd never looked so inviting.

As I raced to join him, he held up his hand.

"Not yet." His voice was edged in that same toe-curling Dominance that always took my breath away. "Strip. Then stand at the foot of the bed."

I had no idea what had prompted his bizarre request, but I certainly wasn't going to ask any questions.

Well, that's a first, the little voice in my head laughed.

Ignoring the comment from my inner peanut gallery, I watched Law quickly strip down and claim the opposite side of the bed. My two Doms lay deliciously naked and—based on their proud erections that were weeping and twitching on their hard stomachs—eager for me to join them.

Not half as eager as I was.

"Take off your clothes, my love," Law instructed.

I wasted no time peeling them off as their hungry gazes torched my flesh. Naked, I stood at the end of the bed and awaited their next commands.

"You know by now that we're in love with you, Sasha." Cane's golden eyes glowed with the emotion.

"Fallen fast and hard," Law added. "We hadn't planned for it to happen, but then no one can explain the ways of love…it just *is*."

My heart fluttered.

My body trembled.

Every fiber of my being wanted to scream the words back to them, but…

You voided the contract. What's holding you back this time?

My eyes grew wide as realization sped through me.

"We need to hear you say it, princess."

"Say it loud and strong," Law coaxed.

They were granting me permission to love them!

My throat closed up.

I swallowed tightly, forcing down the ball of emotions gathered there.

Their images blurred as tears of joy filled my eyes.

I blinked them away so I wouldn't miss the looks on their faces when the words I'd kept trapped inside could finally be set free.

"I love you…love you both."

Matching, big and glorious grins spread across their mouths.

They opened their arms wide…inviting me into their hearts, lives, and souls.

I dove into bed between them and was immediately enveloped in their strong, rugged arms.

There, wrapped in love, safety, and passion, I'd found all the missing pieces…found bliss…found my dreams.

As I drown in their kisses, my mind skipped to the first night they'd claimed me. I'd marveled at the sheer magnitude of light they'd brought to my cold and desolate existence. They'd changed me in ways I'd never imagined possible.

They truly held the keys that had unlocked a whole new life for me, and taught me how to seek a brand-new destiny.

ABOUT THE AUTHOR

USA Today Bestselling author **Jenna Jacob** paints a canvas of passion, romance, and humor as her alpha men and the feisty women who love them unravel their souls, heal their scars, and find a happy-ever-after kind of love. Heart-tugging, captivating, and steamy, Jenna's books will surely leave you breathless and craving more.

A mom of four grown children, Jenna and her alpha-hunk husband live in Kansas. She loves reading, getting away from the city on the back of a Harley, music, camping, and cooking.

Meet her wild and wicked fictional family in Jenna's sultry series: ***The Doms of Genesis.*** Become spellbound by searing triple love connections in her continuing saga: ***The Doms of Her Life*** (co-written with the amazing Shayla Black and Isabella La Pearl). Journey with couples struggling to resolve their pasts and heal their scars to discover unbridled love and devotion in her contemporary series: ***Passionate Hearts.*** Or laugh along as Jenna lets her zany sense of humor and lack of filter run free in the romantic comedy series: ***Hotties of Haven.***

Connect with Jenna Online
Website: www.jennajacob.com
Email: jenna@jennajacob.com
Facebook Fan Page: facebook.com/authorjennajacob
Twitter: @jennajacob3
Instagram: instagram.com/jenna_jacob_author
Amazon Author Page: http://amzn.to/1GvwNnn
Newsletter: http://bit.ly/1Cj4ZyY

OTHER TITLES BY JENNA JACOB

The Doms of Genesis Series
Embracing My Submission
Masters of My Desire
Master of My Mind
Saving My Submission
Seduced By My Doms
Lured By My Master
Sin City Submission
Bound To Surrender
Resisting My Submission
Craving His Command

The Doms of Her Life – Raine Falling Series
(Co-authored with Shayla Black and Isabella LaPearl)
One Dom To Love
The Young and The Submissive
The Bold and The Dominant
The Edge Of Dominance

Hotties Of Haven Series
Sin On A Stick
Wet Dream
Revenge On The Rocks

The Passionate Hearts Series
Sky Of Dreams
Winds Of Desire (Coming Soon)

Made in the USA
San Bernardino, CA
12 January 2018